M
HYLAND   SLM
   TOP BLOODY SECRET

WITHDRAWN FROM THE
SAN MARINO PUBLIC LIBRARY

San Marino Public Library
San Marino, California
282-8484

10-69

TOP BLOODY SECRET

TOP BLOODY SECRET

by

STANLEY HYLAND

THE BOBBS-MERRILL COMPANY
Indianapolis and New York

THE BOBBS-MERRILL COMPANY, INC.
A SUBSIDIARY OF HOWARD W. SAMS & CO., INC.
PUBLISHERS / INDIANAPOLIS • KANSAS CITY • NEW YORK

COPYRIGHT ©1969 BY STANLEY HYLAND
ALL RIGHTS RESERVED
LIBRARY OF CONGRESS CATALOG CARD NUMBER 77-81285
PRINTED IN THE UNITED STATES OF AMERICA
FIRST PRINTING

To Biddy
With Love

NOE DIVLIST KALDEC ADMIN ARMEN

Author's Note

WHEN A MAN'S body was found in Big Ben's Clock Tower (it was revealed by an old friend of mine called Fred Armytage who was working on the rebuilding; it was on the 10th May 1956) a group of Members of Parliament formed themselves into an unofficial committee to investigate the man's death and the reasons for it. They caused themselves a lot of hard work and, in the end, quite a lot of embarrassment; enough of both, one would have thought, to discourage them from pushing their necks out again. Several of them have retired from politics. One of them, Oliver Passmore, Q.C., believe it or not, took a judgeship in the Aden Protectorate. He became known there as the Non-Hanging Judge, and not without reason. A couple of them have died but three of them are still in the House. And here they are again.

Kathleen Kimmis is very busy indeed over-lording it among the Social Services with a special interest in what she insists on calling "adequate financial provision for divorced mothers with dependent children". It is said that her trip to the Lebanon in 1956 changed her life. And not only hers.

Two other members of the Committee of Investigation in 1956 are still in the House. They have both got, as the phrase goes, cast-iron seats; and both have got on in the world as I think one would have expected. Then, they were pretty new and raw back-benchers; then, as now, they sat on opposite sides of the Chamber; but now, they have moved up front and glare at each other across the Table and the two Despatch Boxes. One of them, Hubert Bligh (now the Rt. Hon. Sir Hubert Bligh, Kt.) is a member of the Shadow Cabinet, though not yet its leader. He still represents the Brockley Division of Lambeth in South-east-London. The other, the Rt. Hon. Alex C. Beasley, is Prime Minister and First Lord of the Treasury. He still represents East Liverpool as he did some twenty years ago. It was once said of him (and it is probably true) that he started life as an undertaker's assistant. He is, fairly certainly, the only undertaker's assistant who has managed to become Prime Minister and good luck to him.

There is of course only one Prime Minister at any one time—in this country anyway; only one Mr Speaker; only one Clerk of the House; only one Serjeant-at-Arms in the House of Commons. (There is another one in the House of Lords and there are others, lesser ones, dotted about all over the place.) There is only one Lord Chancellor. The list of holders of unique Government and Parliamentary offices would fill a book twice this size. Just think of Whitaker's Almanack.

This is the difficulty which faces any author who writes a book like this one. He must make it quite clear (as I am doing) that the characters in his book (even though they hold those actual and unique offices) are wholly imaginary. I ask readers of my book to project the time-scale forward far enough to put me and my story in the clear.

All references to *Erskine May* (if any) are to the twentieth edition. I imagine that will be far enough ahead.

Prologue in Erzurum, Eastern Anatolia

THE RIFLE FIRE was sporadic but getting nearer, and very quickly. A fat man, known from one end of the province to the other as Bashtug—"chief horsetail"—sat sweating with excitement in the cold February air and fidgeting with delight. He was wearing his best black suit of rough woollen cloth and his shirt, collarless and fairly clean, was buttoned up to his bristly throat in honour of the occasion. A burst of automatic gun-fire came from the dome of the Mosque close behind them and all but the Bashtug turned with a gasp of surprise. Two young children began to shriek with fear as the tension grew about them.

The grandstand—a temporary thing of wood held together with rusty nails—swayed and groaned at the joints, and the seven Military Attachés, who, with their aides-de-camp, their wives and their privileged children, made up the whole of the second row back, steeled themselves for the explosion which they knew would come in the next few seconds. They had heard it all before.

But the explosion came ten seconds too late (the firing mechanism had had a slight fault in it which burnt the thumb of the man who pressed the button) and the youngest Military Attaché (the one in a sky-blue cap with gold leaves all round it to show that he came from the United Arab Republic) had by then relaxed his muscles. When it did come, he jumped six inches out of his seat and hurt his bottom. "Drinks all round tonight," said the American Colonel on his right. "Mine's Scotch." His voice changed and dropped to a growling whisper. "Here comes the bloody farce."

Twenty young men on horseback rode into the city square and galloped, shrieking, past the grandstand, their pistols blazing, their ragged clothes streaming like filthy banners in the air behind them. "It's the Leader." The Bashtug was shouting. "He shot thirty-one Russkis," and the crowd round the square screamed with delight. "Thirty-one. Thirty-one." Young boys took it up as a chant (it has a lilting sound in Turkish, *otuz bir, otuz bir*). It has another (and a very indelicate) meaning which made them shout it all the more gleefully, and the crowd reeled in a transport of joy.

After the cavalry, the tough boys of the town, the irregulars play-acting at history, came the modern tanks and the heavy guns, the bands and the marching infantry to celebrate with a demonstration of power (as they do every year) the delivery of their city from the Russians in 1918. The Eastern Command of the Turkish Republic is impressive and big, and the Four Star General who marched at their head as they passed the saluting base and the grandstand was obviously a proud man. He saluted the Governor of Erzurum Province, one of the most important "Valis" in the whole of Turkey, and then stepped aside to see his army stream past, symbolically from west to east, past the low, flat buildings of hard grey volcanic stone, the bee-hive mosques and the squat minarets of the biggest city of the Eastern Anatolian plain.

Then the fly-past began. Sixteen new F113's (modified for the wicked mountainous terrain of the Eastern Caucasus) and a stream of heavy-bellied troop transporters dipping ponderously in salute. And in the rear a single plane, an ordinary S26X vertical take-off military workhorse job, fast, manoeuvrable and not especially beautiful or interesting.

The Military Attachés in their places of honour in the grandstand were bored but scrupulously respectful, nodding with polite enthusiasm at the display of military power, and applauding, within the strict bounds of protocol, the strutting modified goose-step, part European, part Oriental, of the infantry.

Only for one moment was their interest roused, when a gasp of horror and fear was wrenched from the crowd of ten thousand people who lined the military route through the city. As the S26X flying low reached the Vali's saluting base in front of the grandstand, its engines cut out and for a dizzy second or two the plane swooped towards the ground. And then miraculously the engines fired and the plane climbed again to continue its flight towards the mountains in the east.

The American Colonel looked thoughtful (he even forgot to remind the UAR Attaché about his Scotch). The Russian Colonel looked angry and ill at ease, but then the Russian Attaché was always angry and ill at ease (and with reason) after the annual Erzurum display.

"It's like inviting the French Naval Attaché to Trafalgar Square on the 21st October," said the British Attaché's attaché, mainly to show his knowledge of the military calendar. "Stupid buggar," said the Group Captain, and his Attaché flinched. He never knew why his chief had spoken like that because he had not noticed (as the Russian and the American as well as his own chief had noticed) that the S26X—a British plane attached to the Turkish Air Force—had been climbing, and climbing fast, for three seconds *before* the engines fired to take her out of her stall.

I

CONSTABLE P. WILTSHIRE OF the Metropolitan Police counted the arches of Westminster Bridge. All present and correct. He yawned behind one of his thick navy-blue gloves and grunted. His grunt turned into a sneeze as his glove tickled his nostrils. He was bored and very cold. He thought for a moment of going down into the subway beneath the Victoria Embankment and having a quiet smoke. Then he remembered that he hadn't any matches, and, he reflected, if there's one thing a policeman can't do it's ask a passer-by for a match. And in any case there weren't any passers-by. He took a long sweeping look along the river. It was black and cold and was moving sluggishly. He found himself counting the lights which stretched into the distance in a long curve beyond Blackfriars but then gave it up in utter boredom before he reached the Festival Hall. For the tenth time that night he wondered why the hell he'd joined.

He turned to look up at Queen Boadicea. She looked rigid with cold in her décolleté gown, and preoccupied with her pair of rampant stallions. Her attendant maidens, bare from the waist up, looked transfixed. He gave the whole bunch of them an encouraging nod and his eyes travelled up from their cold metal bosoms to the face of Big Ben. "Good Lord," he said, "three o'clock." The night was lasting for ever.

As he spoke Big Ben's chimes began. They were strangely muffled in the misty night air. Wiltshire hummed the tune as he peeled off his glove and fished around inside his tunic for his watch. Like every Londoner, he hoped some day to find the great clock had gone wrong. He glanced up as the first stroke rumbled over the roofs of Westminster, and as he looked up, the lantern light, forty feet above the clock face came on.

"Serves 'em right," he muttered as he put his watch back in his pocket. He knew very well that the lantern light went on whenever the House of Commons was sitting after dark. And then he jumped. The House of Commons was *not* sitting. He walked a few feet on to Westminster Bridge and glanced along the river terrace of the Houses of Parliament. It was deserted and in total darkness.

"What the hell!" he muttered as he looked up at the clock face, and as he spoke, the light went off again. "Queer," he said as he set off walking across the traffic lights at the end of the Victoria Embankment towards Cannon Row Police Station. As he turned the corner past Boots' Chemists he looked up again at Big Ben's tower high in the air above him. The light was on again. "Bloody queer," he said and he quickened his pace.

*   *   *

A tall young man was standing at the window of Room 2513 on the twenty-fifth floor of the Hilton Hotel in Park Lane, a mile north-west of the Houses of Parliament. He saw Big Ben's lantern light quite clearly through powerful field-glasses.

"It's on," he said urgently. "Bang on the dot." He began to count out the seconds. "One - and - two - and - three - and - four - and - five - and - six - and - seven - and - eight - and - nine - and - ten - and - eleven - and - twelve. Out." He waited three more seconds, then turned away from the window. "It's gone off again," he said. "Tell him it was on for twelve seconds at three o'clock precisely."

The older man, sitting on the farther of the two single beds, grinned with relief. "O.K.," he said. He spoke with quiet urgency into the telephone receiver in his hand.

"Sind Sie noch da? Gut. Zwölf Sekunden um Punkt drei."

"Gut." The voice on the telephone had a peculiar muffled quality as though being filtered through a handkerchief. "Gut. Ihr wisst nun was ihr machen müsst."

"Jawohl. O.K."

"Also. Versaut die Sache nicht."

There was a loud click and another voice came on the line through a hum of receding resonances.

"Vous avez fini, monsieur?"

"Ja. Fini." The man on the bed put the receiver down carefully. He sighed as though relieved of a great and unpleasant burden. "The bastard," but he said it cheerfully and without venom. Then he jumped to his feet as the younger man at the window began to wave his arms about. His whisper was piercing, like a strangulated scream.

"Hold him! Hold him! Get him back!" He turned back to the window and stared out across St James's Park at the dull yellow moon of Big Ben's clock face. "Get him back! For God's sake get him back!"

"I can't. He's gone off the line." The older man began to grope his way across the darkened room. "Why?" He stumbled over the end of his bed and winced with pain but he forgot to curse. "Why should I? He's gone. What the hell's happening?"

"*That's* what's happening. Look." The young man pointed across the Park. He began to re-focus his field glasses, and he grunted. "Oh my God. The bloody light's on again."

"Don't be stupid. It can't be. That wasn't the idea." The older man stopped talking as he reached the window.

"We'll have to tell him. Where is he? At the Kras?"

"Yes. Room 352. Stop it." The older man shouted. "Leave that phone alone."

"But we'll have to tell him . . ."

"Not from here . . . Let's get out. We'll send a signal from down river. Something's gone wrong."

The younger man began to grope his way towards the bathroom door. "He'll blame us," he said. "He'll blame us. You know he will." He was talking in a voice of muted panic.

* * *

"Information Room, Scotland Yard," said an unnaturally cheerful voice. "Can I help you?" As he spoke, the Duty Sergeant glanced at the wall clock. *3.10 a.m.* He entered it in the log. Only four and a half more hours to do.

"Yes," said the telephone. "Can you see Big Ben from where you are?"

There was a short silence. When the Sergeant spoke again he sounded less cheerful.

"Sir," he said. "This"—and he stressed the word—"is the Information Room, Scotland Yard."

"I know it is. It's some information I want. Can you see Big Ben from there?"

The Duty Sergeant put one elbow on the desk and prepared for a long conversation with the inevitable nightly nut case. At the same time he pressed the correct button and a small blue flashing light went on behind the information desk. *Trace call* came up in lights on a panel beside the switchboard operator down below.

The voice on the telephone spoke again. "Tell your switchboard operator not to bother to trace. Tell him it's the operator at 930-6240. The Houses of Parliament."

"Oh!" The Duty Sergeant felt and looked doubtful. "How do I know that?" he asked. This was a new one, and it sounded dangerously clever.

"You don't know. I'm just telling you. I'm also asking you if you can see Big Ben." The voice had a catch in it as if its patience was being exhausted. Then, after a short pause. "Look at it this way, Constable . . ."

"Sergeant . . ."

"Sergeant. Which is the one building in London from which you cannot *possibly* see Big Ben? That is, if you're inside?"

"Inside what?"

The voice on the telephone began to speak a little louder, higher up the scale. "Inside the building," it said.

The Duty Sergeant pulled himself together. "I don't know who you are, sir," he said, "but I have other work to do." He prepared to put the receiver down.

"Don't cut me off," said the voice. "This may be important, Sergeant. I am in the GPO switchboard room in the Houses of Parliament. Five minutes ago some nut from the Regent's Park area rang me to say there was something peculiar happening on the Clock Tower. Please look at it and tell me if it's O.K. I just want somebody to *look* at it." It sounded increasingly plaintive.

The Duty Sergeant grunted into the receiver, put it down on the table and walked over to the window. He raised the venetian blind, pushed his face up against the glass and peered over the forest of pinnacles and chimneys on the block of buildings in

Tothill Street. Big Ben's clock was still where it should be. He walked slowly back to his desk.

"It's still there," he said into the telephone. He said it triumphantly as though he alone had done it. "As a matter of fact it says 3.12 a.m."

"And it's lit up?"

"Naturally. Bright and clear." He paused. His brain measured out the logical process. "Otherwise I couldn't see it." He sounded pleased with his reasoning. "And so is the light above it."

"Thank you Sergeant," said the voice. "You're quite sure the top light's on?"

"Quite sure. What's unusual about that?"

"Nothing at all—when the House is sitting. It just happens that the House rose five hours ago." The telephone went dead.

*   *   *

"What do you mean you can't raise him?"

"Just what I say. I can't raise him." The switchboard operator was beginning to get angry. "Shall I ring the Serjeant-at-Arms and tell him?" It was the Ultimate Threat.

"Blimey no!" Albert Glass jumped as his own voice rang along the Speaker's Corridor. "He's probably gone to the gents. I'll go and look for him."

"Do that. And when you find him tell him some joker's left the lantern light on."

"Good Lord!" Glass hesitated. "It wasn't on when I came in at midnight. Are you sure it's on now?"

"Ring Scotland Yard if you don't believe me—but find Tom Rendle first."

Albert Glass put the receiver down quietly beside the dim blue pilot light. For fifteen years, as a Night Custodian in the Houses of Parliament, he had lived a nocturnal life of total and unaltered routine in dark and silent corridors. He wondered about Tom Rendle, a new man but so far as he was aware, a reliable one, who knew as well as he knew himself that you don't go to the lavatory on this job without first warning your oppo. It was a breach of the basic law. He automatically tried the door to Mr Speaker's residence. It was locked, as he knew it would be. He glanced along the Ministers' Corridor to his right. It was silent and deserted. He shone his torch along the right hand wall. So far as he could see, the doors were all closed. They were, he assumed, locked.

He set off along the main corridor towards the Oriel Room door of the Commons Library. As he walked, the light from his torch flickered over the leather bindings of the vast collection of Parliamentary Papers which filled the left-hand wall from floor to ceiling, and his footsteps were muffled in the deep pile of the carpet. The only sound in the world was the faint jingle of keys on the chain at his side.

He tried the Library door, and found it locked. So far so good. He turned right and set off along the old Ways and Means Corridor. At the far end through the glass panels of the doors, he could see the Members' Lobby lit by the pale blue light from a single pilot bulb. David Lloyd George's statue in the far corner of the Lobby looked unnaturally tall and menacing. Glass found himself wondering for the first time in his life what he would do if the statue started moving. "Tom!" He suddenly shouted. "Tom Rendle!" and began to walk more quickly, fighting down a desire to run. The name echoed round the corridors, but there was no answer.

He burst open the door to the Members' Lobby and as he did so, a dark shadow slipped out of the Ways and Means Corridor behind him and into the Oriel Room of the Commons Library. The door clicked as the key turned and the latch dropped but Albert Glass was too far away to hear it.

He started to shout again as he turned right from the Members' Lobby and down the narrow staircase beside the lift. If the lantern light was on, he was thinking, maybe Tom Rendle was in the switch room, the central master control room beneath the Commons Chamber. By this time he was almost running and his torch light flashed and bobbed ahead of him. He had begun to hear his own breathing.

He stopped suddenly as he turned the corner. Ahead of him, the door to the Control Room was open a few inches and the light was on inside.

"Tom! Tom Rendle!" He uttered the name in a hoarse whisper as he pushed the door open. The long narrow room was brightly lit, and it was empty. The panels of instruments and switches stretched out twenty feet in front of him. He walked slowly past them to the control desk at the far end of the room. Two of the switches were down, their little red indicator lights bright against the pale green of the panel. He read the enamelled legends beneath them. *Lantern* and *Chamber (main)*.

He switched off the lantern light and turned slowly to the swivel chair at the left-hand side of the control panel. There was one easy way to make sure whether the main ceiling lights were on in the House of Commons on the floor above, but he had to force himself to look. Thrusting his mounting fear and apprehension behind him, he sat in the swivel chair, put his eyes to the shaped eyepiece of the submarine periscope and his hands on the control bars projecting from each side. At first they slipped on the smooth grip and he wiped them on the front of his tunic. Then he carefully turned the twist grip focusing device and looked down into the Chamber, slowly scanning the benches along the Government side to his left, sweeping past the Speaker's Chair and down the Opposition benches to his right. The House was brightly lit, empty and totally quiet.

He was half-way through a gentle sigh of relief when he saw the top of Tom Rendle's head. His navy blue uniform cap was on at a jaunty, cheerful angle. Most of his body was hidden by the back of the Serjeant-at-Arm's bench on which he was sitting, but one arm was hanging down over the carved wooden arm-rest and his fingertips were resting on the floor. Even from the periscope eye, up in the ceiling of the Chamber above the Public Gallery, it was clear from the way he was sprawled that Rendle was dead.

Slowly and deliberately Albert Glass unwound himself from the periscope and stepped over to the control panel. Without showing a sign of the panic he was fighting down, he pressed one finger on each of the switches in turn, and within twenty seconds the whole building was a blaze of light. The last switch of all at the top left of the panel was labelled *Whistle*. He pressed it and the Westminster factory hooter sounded the *Who goes home?*

Tom Rendle was not listening.

* * *

"The last time there was a murder in the Commons,"* said Vice Admiral Sir Robert Hancock, the Serjeant-at-Arms, as he nibbled an Osborne biscuit, "was in 1812. *Then*, the House lay the blame on the Serjeant of the day. This time I suppose they'll blame me." He shrugged his shoulders. "There's room on the wall for another picture, I suppose."

"Don't be bitter, Hancock, don't be bitter." The Clerk of the House took a sip of coffee. He knew as well as everyone else round the table knew that the portrait of the Right Honourable Spencer Percival, the only murdered Prime Minister of England, was, by an unbreakable and malicious tradition, hung on the wall of the Serjeant's room. The collective memory of the House of Commons is occasionally unkind. "Anyway, Spencer Percival was killed in the Lobby and not in the Chamber." The Clerk had begun to look more relaxed, and his face had lost the withdrawn vacuity of a man looking around in his own head for precedents. He helped himself to some more coffee and resolved to congratulate the Catering Manager. Where else in London but the House of Commons could breakfast be served at the drop of a hat. Even Tom Rendle's hat! The thought brought him back to the matter in hand. "The Serjeant of the day was invited to resign," he said.

For a moment, the Serjeant-at-Arm's face lit up at the prospect of resignation. His ears twitched as they heard the trout rising in some distant idyllic backwater. "With a golden handshake," he suggested.

The Librarian looked up from his scrambled eggs. "Not golden, my dear chap, silver-gilt."

There was a sudden, heavy silence. The Clerk broke it as he stood up. "We are all," he said, "fools."

Within two minutes they were standing, all three, in Mr.

---

* It was on the 11th May 1812. The murderer, a man called Bellingham, described as a madman, was rushed off to execution within the week.

Speaker's office. In front of them, open and empty, was the box which for a little more than three hundred years had been used to store the silver-gilt Mace of the House of Commons between sittings.

The Serjeant's long face grew three inches longer as his chin hit his chest, and his lips began to wobble. "My God," he said. The ultimate in outrage had occurred. "My God. It's gone!" He looked wildly round the office as though looking for a starting point at which to pick up the scent and his nose had begun to twitch.

The Clerk, a scholarly man, made things worse. "It had, I suppose, to happen some time," he observed. "After all, maces were designed to club people with."

"But not this one," said the Serjeant. His voice had something like a sob in it. He turned the box over to see if the Mace had got lodged underneath. The idea was laughable but he was not laughing. He stood up. "This is serious," he said. "Serious."

"I find it easy to agree, Hancock." George Kissen, the Librarian, leaned against a filing cabinet. His urbanity was beginning to slip. "I imagine the custodian chap, Rendle, would agree too." He paused. "If he could."

The Clerk of the House moved towards the door. "Don't be foolish, Kissen," he said angrily. "The fellow's dead." He looked at his watch. "What a hell of a time," he grumbled. "Half past seven. I suppose we ought to report this to the Inspector. I think he ought to know."

The Librarian had a red face, and he was obviously getting cross. "You report," he said. "Tell him he's looking for a man carrying a Mace. It ought to simplify his search." Then a new thought occurred to him. "I hope he finds it soon." He looked more cheerfully at the Clerk. "Otherwise someone's going to look very foolish when the House wants to sit at 2.30."

The idea of the House sitting without its seventeenth-century Mace did not occur to any of them.

"Good Lord," said the Serjeant-at-Arms. The thing was getting really out of hand.

* * *

"But it's ridiculous." Inspector Denny thumped the Table of

the House. "Why the Mace? Who the devil would want to steal a Mace?" He thumped again and the fancy handles on the Opposition Despatch Box rattled in a little genteel way, as though they were used to it.

"Who indeed!" Sir William Olsen looked round guiltily. As Clerk of the House he had no right (and especially not in that Place) to utter such heresies. He steered the conversation into safer channels. "I suppose it's worth a lot of money," he offered. "Anyway, it's the only thing in the whole building worth stealing." He moved past the Speaker's Chair and out of the Chamber into the Ministers' Corridor. The Inspector fell into step beside him. This was not easy; the Clerk's steps were short, quick and fussy.

"Valuable enough to justify murder, Sir William?"

"Good Lord, no." The Clerk stopped suddenly, as an entirely irrelevant thought struck him. "Rendle," he said. "How long had he been working here?" He poked Denny's chest with one finger. Although it was a pudgy finger, it made Denny wince.

"I understand about six months, sir," he offered.

The Clerk nodded. He began walking again. This time it was almost a trot. "Quite!" he said, "Quite! and you know where he came from?"

"The Royal Naval Barracks, Portsmouth."

"Exactly. And by special arrangement. He came in at the special request of the Minister of Defence Technology." Olsen stopped again. "I know because they arranged it through me." He looked about him to make sure the corridor was empty. "Maybe the stealing of the Mace was incidental," he offered. "I think you ought to speak to somebody across the way." He waved his arm vaguely in the direction of the Central Lobby and Whitehall beyond, and turned left into his own office. He closed the door quietly but firmly. Inspector Denny looked thoughtful as he turned back towards the Chamber. He had already spoken to somebody "across the way", and that somebody had sounded very angry indeed.

"Come round," he had said on the telephone. "Be here by ten o'clock with a full report. There's a Cabinet meeting at eleven.

And by the way, Inspector," the voice had almost whispered it, "come in by the back gate. Through Treasury Passage. I'll see you're expected."

The Inspector was composing his full report as he turned left into the Chamber where, he assumed, the cleaning-up operation would by now be more or less completed. You can't leave blood around on the floor for Question Time—especially since the rules of procedure would probably prevent anybody from officially noticing it, even if it got on the Serjeant-at-Arms' silk stockings. He clicked his tongue in disbelief at the strangeness of the institution. After six years in command of the special corps of police in the Houses of Parliament, he still found it hard to understand its manifold oddities. With some reluctance he shook his mind back to his draft report. If he was *really* honest with himself he would admit that he was embarrassingly out of practice at this kind of thing. Whatever else his job did (and it had its points) it did not equip him for criminal investigation. Ritual and ceremonial don't count much in the sordid business of blood-groups, finger-prints and the sifting of evidence. Now for the first time he found himself wondering whether his daily performance in the Central Lobby (however mellifluous and impressive his "Hats off, Strangers") was really enough. He stopped in his tracks as the thought struck him. "Hats off, Strangers! Hat off, Tom Rendle!" He looked down the length of the Chamber to the little group of men scrubbing and cleaning and polishing the woodwork round the Bar of the House, and threw his mind back to his first horrified examination of Rendle's body. His skull had been viciously crushed. There was a hole in it you could have put the end of a Mace in. Denny almost retched as he remembered it. And he remembered something else. He, Denny, had had to remove Rendle's cap to see the nasty hole; and the cap wasn't even dented. Bloody on the inside, yes, but on the outside clean and new.

* * *

"Exotic," said Christopher Pallister to the man who stepped towards him out of the fog. "Real exotic. Especially in November." He sniffed the cold damp air as he put on his quotation voice. "Dusty maps of Mexico dim as dreams and soundings of the bay of Panama." He shivered, and bent down to lock the door of his Mini. He dropped his key in the muddy gutter.

"You've got your geography all wrong. It's Cathay Street. Wrong continent." Tom Slaughter's teeth chattered.

Pallister shrugged his shoulders as he stood up. His key fob was wet and slippery with mud. "It's also bloody cold," he said. "Fancy calling this dump Cathay Street. I came along Jamaica Road. Romantic!" He pulled his overcoat collar up to his throat and shivered. "They're still here?" he asked. He looked vaguely in the direction of the River Thames hidden by wharves.

"Yes. Thanks to the fog. They were ready to move off a couple of hours ago but they couldn't get away."

"Good old London fog." Pallister blew into his hands. "Tell me all."

"Not here," said Slaughter. His MI5 training reared its head. "Too risky." He set off along Rotherhithe Street. "And too chilly," he added. "Let's go somewhere warm. I've made a friend."

The saloon door of the Angel opened even before he knocked. "Don't stand knocking," said a man's voice. "It's ready for you. I've done you two eggs with it."

"What about George Lemon?" Pallister asked as they stepped into the warm room.

"He's doing the watching." Slaughter drew the curtains back. "Keeping an eye on them." Outside, twenty feet below the saloon window, the Thames was sliding slowly past like a river of black oil. An empty lighter, moored off King's Stairs creaked as it swayed sluggishly on the tide. "Nice morning for watching. So long as it's somebody else doing it." Tom Slaughter laughed and rubbed his hands together. He walked over to the table. "Coffee. Hot coffee. Marvellous," he said. "I've been here over an hour."

"I'm sorry," said Pallister. "As soon as I got your phone call I had to consult Pierce." He stood up and did an elaborate salute. "And of course he had to consult Malplaquet." He saluted twice. "Takes time, you know."

"I see," said Slaughter. "Have a sausage."

Pallister drew up to the table. "What time did they leave the Hilton?" he asked as he began to eat.

"At five to four, A bloody M."

"With baggage?"

"Sure. And they paid their bill."

"What excuse did they give?"

"Said they'd been ordered back home by their boss who'd rung them up."

"And had he?"

"Someone rang them, certainly. At nine minutes to three." Tom Slaughter fished around in his pocket for his notebook. Stationery issue MI5/42173. He sucked his front teeth clear of sausage and egg and settled down to report.

"The call came through at 2.51 from Amsterdam. Brook answered immediately, on the first ring. And said who he was!"

"In English?"

"No. In German."

"And you got what they said?"

"Yes." Slaughter grinned. "For the simple reason that they didn't say anything."

"Come off it."

"It's true. We recorded their conversation." Slaughter corrected himself. "Their silence. You could hear them breathing at each other for damn near ten minutes."

"Expensive form of communication."

"Sure. I've worked it out. Fivepence a breath."

Pallister had stopped eating. He pushed his fingers through his bush of sandy hair (which looked none the better for it) and walked over to the window. "The fog's lifting," he said. Across the river he could see the dim shapes of warehouses and derricks on the Wapping shore to the north.

"At one stage Brook started speaking but the chap in Amsterdam cut him off sharpish." Slaughter joined Pallister at the window. "Then they went on breathing steadily at each other." He brightened. "Maybe it's a new form of code!"

"Maybe. You say you've got a recording. You'd better get to work on it." Pallister started putting on his coat. "It's clearing quickly," he said. "I'd hate them to get away. Did Enver use the telephone at all?"

"No." Slaughter went back to the table and finished his cup of coffee. "I can't guarantee that he didn't take over from Brook to do a subtle spell of breathing though. It would be hard to tell one man's breath from the other."

"And how did it end? A few kisses and night-night?"

"No. Brook spoke. In fact he almost shouted." Slaughter read from his notes. "*Zwölf Sekunden um Punkt drei* ... there was a bit more but I didn't get it."

"But you did record it?"

Slaughter nodded. "It's back in the office." He started working his way into his heavy overcoat. "Come on," he said. "I've already paid for this lot." He shouted his thanks towards the kitchen.

"Twelve seconds." Pallister muttered it as they walked along Rotherhithe Street towards Bermondsey Wall East. "On the dot at three o'clock." He looked around him in quiet wonder at the grimy streets with blocks of modern flats between the warehouses. The flats were beginning to look old before their time. "People live here," he said.

"Sure," said Slaughter. "Sometimes you can hear 'em laughing." A dog barked in the distance and an old man went past on a bicycle. He was wobbling a bit but whistling. "Makes you think," said Slaughter.

"Twelve seconds." Pallister had gone back to his thoughts.

"Oi. Right turn."

They turned down towards the river past the ancient public lavatory on the corner. It hissed insolently as they passed it.

"It's getting colder," said Pallister.

"Just wetter." Slaughter shivered, making a bubbling noise with his mouth. "Sweet Thames run softly," he murmured. It ran softly with a lazy, oily motion.

Their footsteps changed note as they stepped on to the wooden bridge to the landing stage at Cherry Garden Pier. Up river, to their left, they could just see the red guiding lights on Tower Bridge. The outline of the bridge was faintly discernible. A rat plopped into the water beneath them, and the fog, lingering in the greasy piles of the landing stage, smelt sour.

"They left the Hilton at five to four you say?" Pallister watched Slaughter's nod. "And came here straightaway?"

"No. They called at Westminster, but we don't really know why. They went straight down into the underground car park in Abingdon Street opposite the House of Lords..."

"I know the one. It's open day and night. Did you go down?"

"Lemon did. I was driving the car. He got there just in time to see them leaving again. They were there about five minutes."

"Was anybody with them? Down there?"

"Lemon isn't sure. He thinks he saw someone getting into another car. Then he came belting back to warn me they were coming out again. And we followed them. Over Lambeth Bridge, south of the river, Waterloo roundabout, the Borough, Tooley Street, Jamaica Road, Cathay Street to Chambers Dock."

Slaughter pointed up river. Two hundred yards away, against the quayside under a line of derricks lay a dirty grey coaster. Her sides had once, a long time ago, been white. She was wearing her riding lights. "*Olga*'s the name," said Slaughter. "Registered in Odessa. All above board as far as we can tell."

"Apart from our friends Brook and Enver."

"As you say, they're *below* board." Slaughter laughed at his own wit as he led the way down to the landing stage. "Let's see how George Lemon is doing. *Olga*'s asking for the river pilot."

Pallister had to show his Ministry of Defence Technology pass before he got what he wanted.

"It's irregular," said the man in charge of the landing stage.

"Sure it's irregular," said Pallister. "I'm an irregular fellow."

"That's bloody funny." The man was not amused. He rang for instructions from his boss in the Port of London Authority's operations room. "Tell him to ring the Ministry of Defence." Pallister spoke over the man's shoulder.

The man put the telephone down. His face looked as though the sun was going to break through it. "They did," he said. "They've never heard of you."

Ten minutes later, the steamship *Olga* churned her stern out into the stream and slipped away from Chambers Wharf. As she moved past Cherry Garden Pier she sounded her foghorn. The PLA man in charge of the landing stage looked proudly out into the river, as though aware of the master-pilot's touch on the whistle. "That's my brother-in-law," he said. "Fred Armytage. You can always tell."

Christopher Pallister swore and set off at the double for a telephone he had seen in the Jamaica Road. George Lemon, a disappointed man, had to be persuaded not to push the PLA man into the water. This persuasion took several minutes, at the end of which *Olga* had turned away to starboard past the Surrey Commercial Docks, and as they looked for Pallister in Jamaica Road, they heard Fred Armytage's fog-horn receding down river towards Gravesend and the Nore. It was sounding a masterly obligato.

They could not find Pallister.

* * *

"About four hours ago, I would say." The doctor walked over to the wash-basin, stripping his rubber gloves off as he went. "Give or take half an hour."

"That makes it about 3.0 a.m." Inspector Denny worked it out quite quickly considering the hour of the morning and the confused state of his mind. "And the weapon, doctor? What kind of weapon?"

"Big." Dr Ramshaw rinsed the lather off his hands and carefully examined his nails. "Big, heavy and extremely blunt but..." he hesitated.

"But what?"

"But with some nasty sharp edges."

Denny nodded. He glanced in the direction of the door. Two West Indian orderlies were wheeling Rendle's body back to its refrigerated drawer in the mortuary. They were abnormally silent. He waited until the door had swung to behind them.

"The House of Commons' Mace is missing, doctor."

Ramshaw nodded without hesitation. "That fits," he said. Then he looked a little doubtful. "I've a confession to make." He stepped over to Inspector Denny and looked up at him. "Actually," he said, "I've never seen it. Just photographs. I take it it's fairly heavy?"

"Sixteen pounds near as dammit."

"Ample." The Doctor went through the motions of smashing a

28

high lob at the net. "Ample." He nodded. "It certainly made a bit of a mess of him." He smiled courteously. "Must go, Inspector. Breakfast's served at eight o'clock. I'll just about make it. Look for that Mace." He nodded again. "You'll find it a bit bent," he said. "And very bloody."

* * *

"The bloody idiot." Christopher Pallister stood at the tall window in Malplaquet's office in Whitehall. "The world," he said, "is full of bloody idiots." He looked down into the Home Office courtyard two storeys below. "The fool said he had no authority to stop a ship leaving its berth once it had got its clearance papers!" He clicked his tongue so hard it hurt.

"That may be true, of course." Marcus Pierce in the armchair beside the fireplace put the tips of his fingers together as he spoke. As a demonstration of judiciousness it was impressive and extremely irritating. Pallister turned his head round slowly in time to get the full benefit of the performance.

Malplaquet saw the expression on his face and wagged a finger. "Now, now, Pallister," he said. He picked up a telephone and gave a number. His finger had stopped wagging and was poised over the scrambler button.

Pallister left him to it and turned to face the outside world. Down in the courtyard there was movement as the Cipher Office's Night Duty shift ended. One Civil Servant's motor-car had just reversed in the half-light into another one's motor-car, and the two Civil Servants were addressing each other in firm but genteel terms. For a moment Pallister felt cheerful and realised that it was the first time he had felt like smiling since the *Olga* started on her journey down the Thames. So he smiled.

"What I want to know," said Pierce, from the armchair, "is why twelve seconds?" His fingers were still pressed together. His thumbs, side by side, were holding up his chin, his first fingers were resting on the bridge of his nose. He looked like a Brahmin in some ritual of welcome. "Why twelve?"

Malplaquet grunted a thank you into the telephone and put it down. He made a few notes on the pad beside his blotter and then suddenly yelped as though stabbed in the head by an idea.

His pale moon of a face wobbled with excitement and the sight of it made Pallister move over to the desk. He sat down and said "Sir!" encouragingly.

Pierce also seemed to feel that something was on the move. He put his hands down from his face, sat up and looked conscientiously alert. He refused to say *Sir* on principle. "That was Sorensen," he suggested. He was on safe ground. Sorensen's voice on the telephone had a quality of rare penetration.

"Sorensen it was. A good chap." Malplaquet beamed at Pallister and for a brief moment his latent humanity cracked the surface of his face. It did not last long. "He says you rang him." Malplaquet nodded his approval at Christopher Pallister, "and asked him to trace the phone call from Amsterdam. Well, according to the Central Security Agency in the Hague, it was made by a man called Causter (at least that was the name he registered as) from his bedroom, room 352 in the Grand Hotel Krasnapolsky in the Dam, Amsterdam."

"Ah!" said Pierce, a slave to his memories. He looked up at the ceiling and sighed. "The Kras," he said. "The good old Kras."

Malplaquet disregarded the noise. "He booked the call at 2.30 this morning. He was put through at 2.50 and the call lasted until 3.01."

Pallister nodded. "It makes sense," he offered, meaninglessly.

Malplaquet allowed himself a dramatic pause. "Then having ended his call to London at 3.01 this fellow Causter made four more international calls in a row and then finally one extra call inside Holland." He looked up quickly to see that he was still carrying his audience with him, and grunted a quiet grunt of approval. Both Pallister and Pierce had pulled chairs up to his desk and both were scowling with concentration. Pierce's face had also developed a periodic twitch. Malplaquet who had seen it before, looked back at his notes with a slight shudder.

"They have no record of the call he made *inside* Holland, the last one. They don't record local calls." He sniffed at this notable example of continental insufficiency. "But they *do* know the places he rang *outside* Holland." He looked up again. "You're twitching, Pierce," he said in a cold voice. Pierce did a gargantuan twitch and took control of his face. "Go on," he said. "Sir."

Malplaquet went on. "Listen," he said.

Pierce made a little groan, and extended it into a noise of respectful encouragement. Pallister sighed. For a moment he thought of cupping one of his ears with his hand as a gesture of intense concentration but thought better of it. Instead, he increased his air of respectful expectancy. His head was almost buzzing with the effort.

"First." Malplaquet's pale moon face looked triumphantly omniscient. "Karlsruhe 26615—the Kaiserhof Hotel." He waited until Pallister had written it down. "Got that? Second, Milan 88.33, the Grand Hotel Duomo." He nodded as he saw Pallister spelling it properly. "Third, Brussels 17.62.90, the Astoria Hotel." He paused a moment, then ticked the places off on three fingers. "Karlsruhe, Milan and Brussels."

Pallister looked up from his notebook. "That's three," he said. "You said he made four calls. Where was the other?"

"Forget it for a moment. It doesn't fit into the pattern."

"Pattern," said Pierce. "What pattern?" His chin had come out as far as it could and he sounded cross.

"Tut. Tut," said Malplaquet, separating the tuts. Then again, "Tut. Tut." He read out the place names again with aggravating preciseness. Then he smiled as he saw the light dawn slowly on Pallister's face. His rather wispy eyebrows had gone up in surprise and his tongue was pushing one cheek out in consternation.

He began to nod in time with his thoughts. "Karlsruhe in West Germany... Milan for Ispra on Lake Maggiore and Brussels for Moll in Antwerp Province." He grinned across the desk. "They're the Nuclear Research Centres of Euratom. They're all there"

"No. You're wrong." Malplaquet looked a bit superior as he picked the telephone up and began to dial. "Not all of them; there's one missing." He held up his hand as the telephone clicked in his ear. "That Sorensen? Malplaquet here again. Scramble please." He pressed the button and waited for the thing to start its moaning. "There's a pattern in this telephoning business, Sorensen, as you may have noticed." He looked blandly at the ceiling as he said it, making it obvious that his words were due to courtesy rather than conviction. Then he stopped talking and slowly went pink. "Oh," he said. "I see. Thank you, Sorensen. Splendid work. Splendid." He seemed to have difficulty with the word. "The ceiling needs washing, Pierce," he said as he unscrambled the telephone and put it down.

Pierce disregarded the side issue. "Sorensen beat us to it," he said, showing his teeth in way of a smile. "A good chap."

Malplaquet avoided Pierce's eyes and looked at Pallister. "That's the one you forgot," he said. "Sorensen got round to it. Petten. It's on the North Holland coast near Alkmaar. Apparently there's only one hotel, called Het Wapen van Petten—the Petten Arms—and somebody in the Krasnapolsky Amsterdam put a call to it at 3.30 this morning. It all adds up."

"To what?" Pierce asked slowly. There was a long cold silence.

"You said there was another international call." Pallister jumped into the silence and Malplaquet looked infinitesimally grateful. The expression did not last long.

"Ankara," said Malplaquet. "Believe it or not, Ankara." He looked down at his notes. "The Bulvar Palas Hotel, Ankara."

"Ankara?"

"Ankara. Turkey. Where the atomic energy does *not* come from." Malplaquet spread his hands elaborately.

"But why Ankara?" Pallister got up and walked back to his place by the window. "It's ridiculous." He thumped the wall in exasperation, but only once because it hurt his hand.

"Very interesting," said Marcus Pierce. He looked likely to assume his pose of Great Thinker again. But then quite suddenly he looked alert. "Let's look at this from the beginning," he suggested.

Malplaquet nodded. "Back to Enver and Brook in the Hilton Hotel."

"No." Pierce held up one hand. "Further back than that. Preston Northcott rang me from Bonn early yesterday. He said he'd been tipped off that two undesirables, Brook and Enver, were on their way to London. And would we keep an eye on them."

"Why. Did he say?"

"Some German security business. No details. Not on the telephone anyway. Northcott's reporting via the diplomatic bag. All he said was—please keep an eye on them."

Malplaquet looked hard across the room. "Pallister slipped up," he said. "He let them get on board the *Olga*!"

Pallister nodded, but said nothing.

"So these two beauties shifted from the Hilton in the middle of the night." Pierce disregarded the interruption. "Why did they do that, do you suppose?"

"Operation completed, I imagine." Malplaquet sounded very doubtful. "Or, more likely, plans changed at the other end."

"In Germany? How did they know?"

"No. In Amsterdam. The call came from Amsterdam."

"But the person who rang from Amsterdam did not pass information. All that happened was that Brook said *Twelve seconds at three o'clock*." Pallister stared out of the window. The courtyard was filling up as the day shift came in to the Ministry of Defence Technology's department.

"Right," said Pierce. "So someone here in London must have passed information to them. How? Did Enver and Brook get any other telephone calls at the Hilton?"

"None at all. The only call they received was the one from Amsterdam."

"Earlier in the day I mean."

"They didn't book into the Hilton until 7.30 p.m. the night before. They went straight there by taxi from the airport."

"The taxi-man?"

"Just a taxi-driver. George Lemon had a word with him. He put the fear of God in him by showing his pass and accusing him of overcharging them."

"Which he had done?"

"Of course."

"Did they have any callers then?"

"None. None at all. Not even room service. They brought their own drink with them. They left half a bottle of *Bokma Jonge Jenever* under the bed. Half a bottle! Just dropped it and left. Which suggests they left in a hurry. Which we know they did."

"Bokma's a Dutch drink. That ties up with Amsterdam rather than Bonn."

"You *can* buy it in Bonn."

"Lift boy?"

"All the lifts in the Hilton are automatic."

"Receptionist?"

"Nothing unusual. Tom Slaughter stood beside them at the desk as they booked in. He got room 2514, the room next to them, and he watched their door until they left early this morning."

"The window?"

"No point in watching that. It's twenty-five floors up. And no balcony."

"I see what you mean."

For close on two minutes, the only sound to be heard was the distant hum of traffic in Whitehall and the rattle of Malplaquet's finger nails on his blotter as he played the Burletta from Bartock's sixth string quartet, accurately, in his head. Pierce had almost reached the point of dropping a filing cabinet on Malplaquet's right hand when a pigeon landed on the window sill. Pierce's mouth opened.

"Impossible," said Pallister. "According to Tom Slaughter, the windows in the Hilton don't open."

"Then somebody must have sent them a smoke signal from St James's Park, or an Aldis lamp from Buckingham Palace..."

As he spoke, Marcus Pierce smacked his hand down with a crash on Malplaquet's desk. Bartok's Burletta jumped the groove and Malplaquet uttered a sudden cry of anguish. "Pierce!" He made it sound like an imperative.

"Buckingham Palace..." Pierce's eyes were shining. He turned towards Malplaquet, who had begun to sweat as any good Civil Servant must do at the idea of getting involved with the Palace. "Steady, Pierce," he tried to growl it, but it came out as a squeak.

"Do you know Amsterdam?"

Malplaquet shook his head so quickly that his face was blurred. It looked like a photograph of the full moon out of focus.

"In the middle of the city, there's a large central square called the Dam. On one side is the Grand Hotel Krasnapolsky and on the other side, opposite, there's the Royal Palace. The Kras overlooks the Palace."

Pierce let the intelligence sink in. Then he spoke again. "Do you remember Brussels?"

Malplaquet had a fixed expression on his face and his eyes looked glazed. "Astoria Hotel," he muttered, "rue Royale . . ."

"Exactly." Pierce was riding high in triumph. "Along the road from the Royal Palace," he said. "I'd take bets that the top floor windows overlook the Palace."

Malplaquet swallowed noisily. "What are you getting at, Pierce?" he asked. His face suggested that he knew.

"A wicked Republican plot." Pallister offered the ultimate in catastrophe. He stared across the room at Marcus Pierce, the little prophet of doom. Then he drove the pin into his complacency. "Karlsruhe," he said. "Do you know Karlsruhe in that well-known modern republic, West Germany?"

Marcus Pierce looked deflated. "No," he admitted. He shrugged his shoulders. "It was just an idea," he said.

"I know it." Christopher Pallister decided to rub it in. "The Kaiserhof Hotel in Karlsruhe is in the Market Place. And the only thing it overlooks is a peculiar pyramid in red granite. It's the tomb of the first Royal Duke who built the place." He paused for dramatic effect. "He died in the middle of the eighteenth century."

"Congratulations." Malplaquet had got his voice back to normal. "Karl-Wilhelm Markgraf von Baden-Durlach," he said slowly. He was obviously dredging it up from the Middle Period of his expensive education. "But you've forgotten something Pallister," he went on. "The Kaiserhof also overlooks the grand-ducal palace in the *Kriegstrasse*. And that's now the Supreme Constitutional Court of the Federal Republic."

The pigeon on the window-sill made a meaningless observation in morse code, and a charwoman dropped a bucket in the corridor outside. Malplaquet's face suggested relief. The outside world was once more coming within reach. He looked at his pocket watch. Ten to eight. He felt he had been in his office all night.

"Twelve seconds ... *Zwölf Sekunden um Punkt drei!*" Pallister murmured as he tapped on the window. The pigeon panicked, jerked its neck at him, defaecated hurriedly and took off for the Department of Economic Affairs and a bit of peace and quiet.

"At three o'clock precisely." Pierce had lost his enthusiasm for a Palace revolution. "Something happened at three o'clock this morning. I wonder if we shall ever know?"

"Find the man who contacted Brook and Enver in the Abingdon Street car park," suggested Pallister. "He'll tell you." No one was listening.

Malplaquet breathed a long explosive burst of a sigh. His cheeks quivered as he blew towards the ceiling. It still looked dirty but he decided to ignore it. "Back to question number one," he said. "Why was that call made to Ankara?"

"And why twelve seconds?" Pallister put his forehead against the window-pane, and as he did so, Big Ben, a hundred yards away across Whitehall, began to strike.

"Eight o'clock," said Pierce. "Let's know what's on the news." He stepped across the room and switched Malplaquet's wireless set on.

"It doesn't work," said Malplaquet. He was right.

* * *

The Minister of Defence Technology, the Right Honourable Desmond Bassington, M.P., had shaved the left-hand side of his face when his wife thumped on the bathroom door.

"It's George," she said. "On the telephone."

Bassington prepared to attack the other side of his face. He got his razor in place, then relaxed his chin. "Which George?" he asked. He put his chin back at the ready, then he relaxed again. "We have several," he said.

"The one in Richmond Mews."

"Oh!" said Bassington. If his Parliamentary Private Secretary George Tiffany (an idle man) was up at eight o'clock (and on the telephone at that), something important had happened. "I'll be out in five minutes. Tell him I'll ring him back, dear."

"I've already suggested that but it's too urgent. He's down at the House and he says the lines will all be engaged by then."

Bassington winced as the razor moved too quickly down to his chin. A blob of shaving cream with a red streak in it fell on his bare stomach.

"At the House? What the devil for?" For a wild moment he had the idea that something had gone wrong with his watch. He peered through the steam at it. "It *is* only eight o'clock isn't it?"

"Just after, I can hear the News is on. They're saying something about the House. Shall I tell him you're coming?"

"Yes please. Tell him to hang on." He rinsed his face, dabbed it with a towel, left the bathroom and walked with his customary dignity along the landing. In the distance he could hear the radio in the kitchen and his curiosity mounted as he recognised the voice of Timothy Woodman, the BBC's Parliamentary Correspondent. He held on to his dignity as he pulled his dressing gown around him. It was when he heard the name Rendle that he forgot he was a Minister of the Crown and ran the last five yards to the telephone.

"You're wanted," said George Tiffany. "At the office at the double. All hell's let loose. Tom Rendle's been killed and Austin Lombard's been arrested on the airport at Athens."

* * *

The green light went off as Timothy Woodman came to the end of his report. He relaxed and lit a cigarette as, five miles away in the Television Centre, the newsreader picked up the story. *That was our Parliamentary Correspondent Timothy Woodman speaking from our Westminster Studio. Now here is the rest of the new in brief . . .*

A voice came over the headphones as Woodman fitted them back on his head. "Thanks, Tim. A nice piece. Go and get yourself a fried egg. David's on his way down . . ."

The voice stopped short. At the other end of the line Woodman could hear a confused clamour of voices and rattling typewriters. The Duty Editor's bark rang out from the far end of the Newsroom like the voice of impending doom. "Hold him," he was shouting. "Hang on to him."

"I'm still here," said Woodman.

"Good." The Duty Editor sounded hoarse with excitement as he came to the talk-back microphone. "Excellent stuff, Tim. How about doing a special piece (sound only) for the World Service?"

"O.K., Eric. Give me five minutes. Same order?"

"No. Switch the order round. Start with Lombard, then go on to Rendle."

"Rendle's dead. As dead as they come."

"Agreed. But Lombard's an M.P. arrested by a friendly power. And still alive, I suppose."

"O.K. I'll switch it round. Give me five minutes."

"Sure..." The Duty Editor paused for a moment. "Is the story going to move before the 1.25 bulletin?" he asked.

"Certain to. The No. 10 Press Conference is at 11.30. It's sure to come up. I'll be there."

"Make sure it does please. And then get back there to do a piece to camera for 1.25. O.K.?"

"O.K. I'll give you a call when I'm ready to record. Give me five minutes." Woodman took off his headphones, picked up his cigarette and settled down to re-shape his report.

The Duty Editor at the Television Centre beamed round the Newsroom. "Tim's good." He said it loudly with an air of proprietorial virtue. "And I take credit for it." He turned to one of the sub-editors who was too young to tell him he'd heard it all before. "Took one glance at him," he said, looking back into the dark corners of his memory, "and told him to take his beard off." He laughed at his own wit. "It's all right," I said, "wearing the old set of whiskers in the Library of the House. They expect it there, the greyer the beard the better. But you can't wear one on the box. The BBC," I said "is *respectable*." He laughed again.

"Fancy that," said the young sub-editor. He was a young man who would go far.

*   *   *

Eugene Malplaquet's face went pink with the effort to stifle a yawn. His lips trembled and his back teeth chattered slightly. He stood up. "Over the way," he said, using the Senior Civil Servants' euphemism for Lyons' Tea Shop. "You stay here please, Pallister. I don't suppose anything will happen, but you know where I am if it does." He dusted the early morning crop of dandruff from his shoulders and reached for his hat and umbrella. The door burst open before he reached it.

"Oh here you are!" Richard Tranter, Desmond Bassington's Principal Private Secretary glared round the room. "I've been trying to get you at home." He looked unusually dishevelled, as though he had thrown himself into yesterday's shirt. "My Master wants to see you. And you." He turned and glared accusingly at Pierce. "Now." He turned to go, and as he did so he seemed to sense the atmosphere of unnatural calm. He turned to face Malplaquet. "You've heard the news, of course." It was a statement expecting the answer yes.

Nobody spoke.

"You know Rendle? Tom Rendle?"

Malplaquet nodded. "I ought to. It took me three months to get him his job in the House."

"Well, he's dead. Murdered during the night."

"Good God!" Malplaquet's careful equanimity left him. "Where?" He sat down.

"In the Commons Chamber."

"What happened?" Malplaquet looked stunned.

"We're not sure. But the Minister wants to put you in the picture. We'd better hurry."

A sudden thought struck Pallister as Tranter led the way out of the office. He called after them. "At what time was he murdered?"

"My dear fellow!" Richard Tranter stopped so quickly in the corridor that Pierce walked into his back. "What an extraordinary question!"

"Three o'clock this morning?" Pallister refused to be impressed by Richard Tranter's beautifully modulated outrage. He watched Tranter's chin drop and got his answer.

He turned back into the office, walked over to the telephone and stepped into the most carefully planned and potentially the most dangerous coup in British security history.

*   *   *

"What on earth do you mean, Charles?"
"I said somebody has stolen the Commons' Mace, sir."
"But they can't. It belongs to Her Majesty."
"They have done, sir, I'm afraid."
"Have you looked for it?"
"Of course."
"Dragged the river?"
"They're doing that now."
"Who are?"
"Scotland Yard."
"Where else have they tried?"
"All over the building. They're in your office with me now."
"Well, it isn't in my office. Is it?"
"I didn't say it was, sir. They are; and I am."
"Why?"
"Ringing you up."
"That's very thoughtful of you, Charles. Do you want me to come and help look for it?"
"Good Lord, no, sir."
"You're just ringing to tell me, eh?"
"Partly that. Partly to ask you for another."
"Another Mace? Good heavens, they don't grow on trees, you know."
"No, sir."
"Wait a minute. I don't suppose they're using the one in Guildhall. Will that do? Tide them over, eh?"
"Splendidly, sir."
"Very well, Charles. I'll speak to the Lord Mayor. You arrange a Guards escort. It's the Coldstream's spell of duty. You can trust *them*."
"Of course, sir."
"But watch it. Watch those Commons fellers. Don't want them to make a habit of it. They lost a Mace once before, you know!"
"They'll need it by 2.30, sir. They can't sit without one.

"2.30 today? Today?"

"Yes, sir. In five hours from now. Just less than that."

"Rushing it a bit, aren't you? Serve 'em right if they couldn't sit. Teach 'em to be more careful."

* * *

The Assistant Commissioner (Crime) leaned forward across his black leather desk and barked. Inspector Denny, four feet away and in direct line of fire, jerked his head backwards so quickly that it hurt his neck, and an Alsatian dog out in Victoria Street, twenty feet below, started wagging its tail.

"I don't give a twopenny damn, Denny, you don't go to No. 10 on your own again. Ever!" The Assistant Commissioner took control of himself with a great effort. "If anybody goes, it'll be the Commissioner. And then only if the Home Secretary goes with him." The idea threw a cloud across his eyes. "Politicians!" he said, making it sound like a swear word. He looked down his long nose at Denny, putting him into a true perspective. "What did you tell them, for God's sake?"

"I showed them this report, sir."

The Assistant Commissioner made a faint moaning noise. "You showed them this report!" He wagged the typescript in front of Denny's face. Even in motion it could be seen to be badly typed, with carbon smudges.

"I *gave* them it, sir."

"So I see." The Assistant Commissioner paused. "You even gave them the top copy." This time when he raised his head to look down his nose he allowed his mouth to fall, and stay, open. When he spoke again he seemed to be having trouble with his words. "You saw the Prime Minister?"

"No, sir. One of his secretaries."

"God!" The Assistant Commissioner managed to utter the word wholly in his throat. It expressed exactly the ultimate in outrage. He turned to Detective Superintendent Macaulay and jerked his head three-eighths of an inch in Denny's direction. "He gave one of the secretaries the top copy."

Macaulay made a grunt of tactful agreement. "I'd imagine the secretary would show it to the P.M., sir." The remark did little to cheer any of them up. Macaulay took the matter a little further. "I imagine the P.M. would see it anyway if he wanted to."

It triggered the Assistant Commissioner off again. "That," he said, "is our trouble. Now look here, both of you." He leaned over his desk and stared at them both in turn. He seemed to be not much impressed with what he saw. "We are in the murder business. Rendle was murdered in the one place in the whole world where we can't work according to our own rules. Politicians are bad enough anyway but bunch them altogether on their own premises and what do you get?"

"Trouble," said Denny.

The Assistant Commissioner looked at him with a little more respect. "Trouble," he echoed it. If Denny's knee had not been on the far side of the desk he might well have tapped it approvingly. "Trouble. And that's something we can do without."

His eyes were dragged momentarily to the out-tray, in which lay a single document, the draft report on crime in the Metropolis for the preceding twelve months. He sighed. Then, very briskly, he started to brief Macaulay.

"You're used to this kind of thing, Macaulay. You've been involved with this lot before..."

"Not exactly the same lot, sir. There's been an election or two since then!"

"Don't quibble. You know the form. You know how difficult they can make it for you..."

Macaulay nodded vigorously but said nothing.

"Take this thing over and bear this in mind. I don't mind what you do—within reason, that is—but keep the bloody politicians out of it."

* * *

"I don't mind what you do, but keep the flatfooted police out of it." Desmond Bassington turned away from the tall graceful window at the west end of his office. In normal times, the view over Horseguards Parade towards Downing Street and Storey's Gate was pleasing and impressive, but these were not normal times, and Downing Street looked ominous in the November light. He knew what kind of reception he was likely to get from the Prime Minister later that morning and he swallowed hard as he looked round his room. "Keep them out of it," he said and flashed his teeth at the four men who were sitting along one side of the long mahogany table.

No one spoke and no one moved.

Bassington walked slowly the length of the room, and managed to give the impression that he was wearing robes of scarlet and ermine.

"Within reason, that is." He flashed his toothy smile again and Richard Tranter, a scrupulously loyal private secretary, nodded on cue. Once again he reminded himself to tell his Minister to get rid of either the smile or the teeth or both. The Minister must be the only one from one end of the Ministry of Defence Technology to the other who didn't know that his smile was known as the Ultimate Deterrent.

It was Eugene Malplaquet whose patience was the first to crack. "It won't be easy to keep the police out, Minister," he offered. "After all, Rendle *is* dead."

"Don't be foolish, my dear chap." The mechanical little smile was supposed to reduce the size of the wound; it just made it deeper and nastier, and frayed at the edges. "Of course he's dead. And of course the police must find out who killed him. All I insist on is that Rendle's connection with the Ministry is kept dark." Bassington looked along the line of faces. "And I mean dark. Keep it dark."

"The Clerk of the House, for one, knows all about it, Desmond," George Tiffany said. "And so does the Serjeant-at-Arms."

"I've no doubt they do. They're not likely to talk." Desmond Bassington crossed two fingers. "And why should they talk? As far as they're concerned Rendle was killed trying to stop someone stealing the Mace."

"He was killed at three o'clock this morning." Marcus Pierce spoke for the first time. He looked at Malplaquet for help.

"And what does that mean?" Bassington looked hard at Pierce. He was genuinely astonished. "You look tired, man."

"We all are." It was Malplaquet's chance to mention how early he'd reached the office. Bassington was not impressed, but he looked less and less assured and less and less patronising as he listened to the story of Enver and Brook and the message they had passed to Amsterdam.

"You'd better be quite sure of getting them off that ship then. But be careful." Bassington sat down and shook his head. "It was a coincidence, this three o'clock business. It *must* have been! How on earth could two men in the Hilton Hotel be connected with Rendle?" Bassington stared at each face in turn. "Quite," he said as they remained glumly silent. "I suggest we talk sense." He sat at the table and opened the red despatch box.

"Lieutenant Commander Austin Lombard, M.P." It was Richard Tranter who brought them back to reality. "The telegrams are all on top, Minister, with his file." He hesitated a moment. "There's his letter there as well." He leaned over and started to fish around in the box.

Bassington looked on the point of smacking his hand. Instead, he grabbed a letter on House of Commons notepaper. "The letter." He turned to George Tiffany. "You may not know this, George," he said. "More trouble. If I know the External Secretary." He looked quickly up to the ceiling in a gesture of resignation. "He's going to get himself involved in this Lombard business."

"But naturally. He can't see a British M.P. arrested abroad and not do anything about it. Or Mr Speaker will want to know why."

"But that's the trouble." Bassington looked at his watch and stood up quickly. In five minutes he was due at No. 10, and the Prime Minister was unlikely—especially in the circumstances—to welcome him warmly if he was more than two seconds late. For that matter he was unlikely to welcome him warmly full stop. "That's the trouble, George. It was at the suggestion of Austin Lombard," he tapped the letter in his hand "that we got Tom Rendle into the House of Commons as a custodian. He actually recommended Rendle. They worked together in the old days in the Special Weapons Division in HMS *Dolphin*."

As he spoke, Bassington started making his way towards the door, leaving Richard Tranter to stuff the papers back into the despatch box. "I'm worried," Bassington said. "Austin Lombard

44

was doing special work for us in Greece and Turkey. He was on his way to Ankara."

The words fell on the meeting like the sound of a cracked bell. Malplaquet and Pierce looked at each other. It was Malplaquet who was the first to find his tongue. "The Bulvar Palas Hotel, no doubt?"

"Certainly. He was due there today."

Bassington had opened the door. He turned round and spoke again. "I'll have a word with the External Secretary before the Cabinet Meeting. I'll tell him to handle it with his Department's customary delicacy."

He was obviously a worried man. He forgot to flash his teeth at them.

*   *   *

"*Civis britannicus est.*" As he proclaimed the words, the External Secretary slapped his hand down hard on a file of papers bearing the name (done in a thick legal black letter) of Lieutenant-Commander Austin Lombard, D.S.O., M.P., R.N.(retd). His cigar jumped an inch in the ash-tray beside him and Sir Ramsey Pinfold, the Permanent Under-Secretary, jumped a little more than that in his chair at the other side of the table. Apart from a little noise of outrage and impatience, Sir Ramsey remained silent. He had heard every External Secretary in the past fourteen years (and there had been quite a number) say it at least once each, and the edge was beginning to wear off. Apart from that, he knew very well that the External Secretary was due at a Cabinet Meeting within the next ten minutes and this was certainly not the moment to choose for a discussion on Palmerstonian principles even if those principles still applied, which he doubted. He shook his head gently.

"It's not as easy as that, I'm afraid, Foreign Secretary."

"Why not?" The Secretary for External Affairs had begun to bridle. For a moment or two his eyes looked as though they were about to load their muskets and charge. "Who do these Greeks think they are?"

"Just Greeks." The Under-Secretary let it sink in. Then he spoke the dreaded words, "Special Security."

"Oh," said the External Secretary. The muskets drooped. He looked down at the thick file of papers. "He seems to have got about a lot."

"Import-Export Corporation. London Division. It seems to work all right as a cover."

"Cover for what?"

"Ministry of Defence Technology."

"Oh, my God. That *will* complicate things." He stood up. "I'll be seeing Desmond Bassington this morning before the Cabinet Meeting."

"Indeed you will. You're due at No. 10 in five minutes."

"Good Lord!" The External Secretary jumped up. "I do wish you'd warn me. Give me those papers—no, get Cedric to put them in my red box." He set off towards the door at the far end of his vast office. "I can't help thinking," he said, "that we ought to try to keep Defence Technology out of it. Without upsetting them, of course."

*   *   *

"I reckon you're as near to her right now as you ever will be." The police driver took one hand from the steering wheel and pointed vertically upwards. George Lemon's brain did a double take as his eyes followed the driver's finger. He had a quick vision of the M/V *Olga* above them speeding down the River Thames with Enver and Brook lolling around in the captain's cabin, drinking duty-free Scotch and eating cheese-rolls. His stomach rumbled sympathetically. "If she's got as far as this," he said, "she'll get right away. How far is it to Tilbury?"

"Not Tilbury," said the driver. "Gravesend. Four and a half miles. She'd probably do it in twenty minutes."

"We could have beaten her if we'd gone straight to Tilbury." Lemon started to grumble.

"Sure." The driver slowed down as the lorry ten feet ahead of them shifted gear to start the long, slow drag out of the Dartford tunnel towards the toll-gate at the southern end. "Sure. And you'd have looked a proper bloody charley waving at her as she went past. The only thing she'll stop for is to drop the pilot. And the pilot-boat operates from Gravesend, not from Tilbury. Don't ask me why."

"Have you ever seen Tilbury?" The driver's mate in the front passenger seat seemed to come out of a daze. "My Aunt Lily lives in Tilbury." It seemed to explain everything.

George Lemon leaned forward and put his chin on the back of the driver's seat. "Your bell," he said. "Why not use your bloody bell." He tapped the driver's shoulder with one finger.

"No point. He's doing his nut. If he hears the bell and stops altogether we're stuck for keeps. I doubt if he'd ever start again." He edged the nose of his car out into the northbound lane and then brought it back again swiftly as a petrol tanker swung past, missing them by a foot.

"Then ask Scotland Yard if they've any news." Lemon's voice was beginning to sound like a lament.

"I can't," said the co-driver. "We're out of contact." He jerked his hand upwards. "Thirty feet of water and fifty feet of Thames mud. It can't be done. Out of radio contact. Oy! Oy!"

The left side of his head thumped the window beside him as the car swerved out suddenly to the right and curved round the ancient lorry. In seven seconds they were doing fifty up the long slope towards the open air half a mile ahead of them. "Made it," said the driver. "Four feet to spare. I bet that chap in the Rover nearly gave birth. As soon as we're out, get them on the blower, Arnold. Tell them we'll be there in ten minutes' time, barring accidents." He grinned at Lemon in his mirror, but Lemon wasn't listening.

"If they get away, they'll use my guts for braces," he was saying. He shrugged his shoulders, as if he'd stopped worrying about them.

* * *

The Right Honourable Alex C. Beasley, M.P., the Prime Minister, glanced up from his sheaf of papers, leaned forward over the green baize cloth on the Cabinet table and looked to his right. Everyone at that end of the table seemed to have given in except for Kathleen Kimmis, the Minister of Health and Social Security. She was sitting at her usual place at the far end of the table near the double doors which lead into the Secretaries' Room. She avoided Beasley's eye and went on doodling with concentrated ferocity on the blotting paper spread out before her. Her hair was immaculately set (high office had certainly revolutionised her appearance) but it managed somehow to give an impression of bristling anger and the parts of her neck which the Prime Minister could see were scarlet. He could hear her ball-point as it savaged the blotting-paper.

Beasley's eyebrows looked less aggressive now that they were going grey, but they were still heavy and thick, and they still met across the top of his nose. As he peered up from underneath them he gave the impression he was going to growl. Instead he cooed. It was easy "We are agreed, then?" He allowed himself a tiny smile of triumph and let his eyes sweep down the length of the table, coming round full ellipse to the Chancellor of the Exchequer sitting beside him on his left. One or two Ministers nodded as the Prime Minister's glance swept past them, but only one of them, the Lord Chancellor, said anything. What he said was "Congratulations", which pleased the Prime Minister and infuriated Mrs Kimmis. Only one person there however noticed that, as he spoke, the Lord Chancellor was looking at the wall high above the Prime Minister's head where, for well over a hundred years, the portrait of Sir Robert Walpole has hung. "It was obvious," said Sir Laurence Squire, the Secretary to the Cabinet, later to one of his assistants. "Absolutely obvious. He was congratulating Walpole on devising the ground rules. No votes to be taken. He's an old scoundrel."

"We *are* agreed then!" The Prime Minister turned to his right and nodded to the Cabinet Secretary who nodded back. He had already noted the fact on his papers. He had seen it coming.

"Lunch," he said, quietly. "You asked me to remind you, Prime Minister. You have to leave within the hour." He used his soft voice, the one he used for Cabinet Meetings and on no other occasions.

"Thank you, Laurence." Alex Beasley made his tidy sheaf of papers even tidier, tapping them with the rigid palms and backs of his hands, using them like butter pats. Then he spoke. "We haven't much time left I'm afraid. I apologise to the Minister of Transport and the President of the Board of Trade. We shall have to postpone their departments' items on the agenda." He looked up, caught the Minister of Transport's eye and looked angry for a moment as he saw relief and pleasure there. "The rest of the meeting we shall devote to three separate and very exceptional matters which have arisen this morning. The Cabinet Secretariat has prepared interim papers for us." He turned to Sir Laurence Squire, "I suppose they're ready by now. Have them brought in, please." He turned back to the meeting. "We'll adjourn," he said, "for five minutes. Please don't go far." He stood up, turned left (away from Mrs Kimmis), walked round the table and over to the window, as the chatter broke out about him. "It looks peaceful enough," he said to no one in particular as he looked out over the walled garden behind No. 10 to the Horseguards Parade, the Admiralty building and the Mall beyond. Carlton House Terrace was managing to glow cream and gold in the thin November sunlight, but wisps of fog still lurked beneath the trees in St. James's Park.

"Here they come." The Prime Minister turned away from the window and glanced at the elegant clock on the mantelpiece beneath Walpole's portrait. "Dead on time," he added admiringly. "Three minutes to eleven." As he spoke he held the green brocade curtain further back from the window and watched the Household Cavalry as it turned out of the Mall towards the parade ground for the changing of the guard.

"It looks peaceful." He smiled as he said it again to no one in particular. And no one answered.

Later, a number of them recalled the time and the words, but by that time there was nothing to smile about.

* * *

"It's very unusual you know; very unusual." George Kissen, the Librarian of the House of Commons stood up rather reluctantly. "I think I ought to ask the Speaker's Secretary." He moved slowly towards the door of his dark little office off the Speaker's Corridor. "I think he ought to know." The tone of his voice suggested that the Speaker's Secretary carried the same rank as the Archangel Gabriel but with longer seniority.

"It really is important, sir." Christopher Pallister fell into step beside the Librarian but the space was too narrow and he tripped over a large green leather settee which, incongruously, fills one side of the Librarian's room.

"Are you hurt ...?" The Librarian began. Christopher Pallister swallowed hard and did his best not to show his impatience. "There's a Cabinet Meeting on. It's just begun ..." He got to his feet.

"Your Minister knows you are here?"

"No, sir. He's at the Cabinet Meeting." Pallister looked quickly round the room. "Have you a scrambler?" he asked. "I'll ring No. 10." He had noticed that it was safe to make the offer. There was no scrambler.

"Good Lord, no." The idea cheered George Kissen up a little. If this young man proposed to ring No. 10! He opened the door and set off, rather briskly for him, along the Speaker's Corridor. "Plaster, you say?" He turned and addressed his guest kindly as they walked past the Parliamentary Papers published during Gladstone's first administration.

"No ... Pallister ... Christopher Pallister."

The Librarian nodded an economical nod. It acknowledged the authorised version of Pallister's name as well as the one-finger salute which was given to them both by the custodian on the main door to the Library. The brass-bound door rattled as they pushed it open. It always rattles.

"The House isn't sitting, of course, otherwise you would have to wait outside," said George Kissen. He looked a little mystified to find the room totally empty of people, and then a thought assailed him. "Coffee," he said in a hoarse whisper. "They've all gone to coffee." It seemed to do something terrible to his personality and he trotted—almost, indeed, ran—into the Reference Room on his right. He stopped just inside the door. His face had gone a mottled red and his voice seemed to have left him. He summoned his forces and in a few seconds he got his voice back. "There's nobody here," he said with great reluctance through his front teeth. He hissed the sibilant and made it sound like several.

A hoarse shout a hundred feet behind him, at the other end of Library, made him turn; and as he did so his face went redder still. The paler mottles on his skin caught up with the general background. "Not to shout," he shouted. Pallister watched with awe as the Librarian lifted a foot as though he was going to stamp it, like Rumpelstiltskin in a different context. Then he uttered a short moan and put his foot down slowly. "Good God," he said. He ambled across the Oriel Room, past the doorway leading to the first of the four large Parliamentary rooms.

"It's covered with blood," said Inspector Denny. "It's covered with blood." George Kissen stepped aside and an outrageous procession of three uniformed policemen went past him, across the Oriel Room, to turn right through the door and into the Speaker's Corridor. The door swung to behind them and as it did so, it rattled.

A Library Clerk was wiping his hands on his handerchief. "Blood," he was saying quietly. He had gone very pale indeed. "Blood." He said it again.

"Take him across to the cloakroom." The Librarian watched them leave the Library, one of them actually retching, the other one seeming likely to. "Where was it?" he asked. "Ah, Maxwell!" He seemed suddenly relieved to find himself alongside at least one friend.

"Sir," said Maxwell. He was eyeing Pallister carefully. He nodded infinitesimally. He obviously took him to be another policeman.

"Plaster," said the Librarian. "He's from the Ministry of Defence Technology. Tell him what he wants to know if you can." Kissen turned away to follow Inspector Denny and the blood-stained Mace.

"It was behind the biographies in the Old Silent Room," Maxwell called after him.

Kissen had reached the door and he stopped suddenly. By then his face had gone back to its pale urbanity. "Where did you say?" The question had a note of anger in it. "Where?" The red glow was on its way back.

"Behind the biographies," said Maxwell with a curious air of aggressiveness.

"Oh, no!" said the Librarian. "Not again!" He hurried

through the door, and Pallister waited for the rattle of Pugin's brass embellishments. They rattled. He turned to Maxwell. "Pallister," he said. "Christopher Pallister. You don't remember me."

Maxwell shook his head. "Should I?" he asked. He made the bald question sound courteous.

"No, I don't see why you should. In the old days when I was a Librarian in the Ministry of Defence I heard you speaking at the Library Association. *Edwin* Maxwell isn't it?" Pallister stepped into the "A" room as Maxwell led him to an armchair. "I haven't much time," he said and he told Maxwell about the Cabinet Meeting.

Edwin Maxwell looked at his watch. "Ten to eleven," he said. He curled himself into another armchair and gave the impression of being a long coiled spring. "You think we can help you," he suggested.

"Deposited Papers," said Pallister. "I once heard you say that the only really secret documents you keep here are among the Deposited Papers."

Edwin Maxwell nodded but said nothing. His eyes were very wary.

"Can I see them?"

"Good Lord, no." Maxwell did not move but his eyes opened a little wider with surprise. "Get yourself elected to the House of Commons and you can see them as often as you want." He paused. "Until then . . ." He shrugged. A lock of hair had fallen down over one eye. He seemed not to have noticed it.

"If I were an M.P. could I *borrow* one?"

"To read here in the Library. Not to take away."

"Would you know if one had disappeared?"

That did it. "Do you know that one has disappeared?" Maxwell had totally shed his langorous air of polite conversation.

"Not really." Pallister remembered the Cabinet Meeting again. "But please hurry and check for me." He stood up.

"Why?" Maxwell hadn't moved.

Pallister took a small notebook from his pocket and flipped the pages. "On 24th April this year the Minister of Defence Technology, my Master, deposited a secret report in the Library here. It's announced in *Hansard* for 25th April. It happens to be a very important document referring to secret defence equipment being tested in Turkey."

Maxwell was nodding. "I remember it." He stood up slowly. "Naturally. We don't get very many."

"You've seen it?"

"Of course I've seen it. They *do* trust us, you know." He grinned. "*We* can even read them."

"Have you seen it lately?"

Edwin Maxwell nodded. "Yes. But we'd better check," he said. "I had it out a few days ago. A Member wanted to read it."

"Which Member?"

"That is a question I would not normally answer," Maxwell said. "But in the special circumstances . . ." He looked round as though fearing the wrath of God or perhaps worse, the wrath of the Select Committee on Privileges, to thump him on the back of the head. Nothing happened. The only two Members in the "A" Room were thirty feet away. They had their heads close together and had clearly involved themselves in some secret plot or contrivance. "It was Lombard," he said. "Austin Lombard, Member for Birmingham East."

"You see what I mean?" Pallister's eyes were shining. "It's five to eleven."

"I see what you mean. Wait here please. I'll get the keys." Maxwell turned round and hurried with astonishingly long strides the length of the Library, and out through the small door in the Old Silent Room.

Pallister wandered over to the window and looked down on to the Terrace. It was empty and it looked cold in the pale winter sunshine. The flower tubs, empty and unvarnished, made the place look desolate and forlorn. The river was running swiftly with the tide. Everything seemed curiously muted and silent. A police car broke the stillness with its strident two-tone siren as it gathered speed over Westminster Bridge. Pallister did not hear Maxwell's return.

"Come next door, please," Maxwell said. "Into the Oriel Room."

Pallister followed him and watched as Maxwell ducked down

behind a desk in the corner of the room to unlock a cupboard. It opened very easily on a half turn.

"It's an ordinary cupboard," Pallister said, appalled.

"It's a *locked* cupboard," Edwin Maxwell looked up at him. "It's as safe..." He stopped. The cliché had suddenly acquired a special incongruity. He grunted. "Here's the list of deposited papers," he said straightening up. It was a simple quarto book in marbled boards, very old, very thumbed and three-quarters full. He opened it at the last page of entries. "Noah," he said.

"Shh!" Pallister looked round quickly.

Maxwell frowned but disregarded him.

"Number 1712 of 24th April," he read out. "That the one?"

"Of course it's the one." Pallister nearly shouted it. "Sorry," he said.

Maxwell ducked down again and put his head into the cupboard. After ten seconds of peering and grunting and rummaging, he straightened up again.

"Noah." This time he whispered it obligingly. "Operation Noah." He smiled cheerfully. "It's here. False alarm." He sighed with happy relief. It had not been stolen.

"Thank goodness for that," Pallister said, but as he said it he felt strangely flat. The Cabinet Meeting could go on uninterrupted, and his moment of importance and glory was up the spout. He watched Maxwell as he flipped through the numbered pages of text, maps and diagrams and checked the seal on the front with its embossed Ministry number. "All O.K.? Many thanks for the trouble," he said. He tried to sound grateful.

And then he saw it. The wintry sunshine striking through the phoney English Gothic windows of the Oriel Room shone on the staples down the left hand edge of the document. "Hey!" This time Pallister did shout and the two Members in the next room looked up guiltily. "Those staples," said Pallister, "are copper plated."

Maxwell seemed unperturbed. "They often are..." he said. And then he stopped. "I see what you mean. There's a rust mark behind this one." He tapped the document. "Red rust, peculiar copper." He brought it to within nine inches of his nose. "Just a minute. Let's look at it properly."

He strode over to the information desk, taking the report with him, opened a drawer and took out a reading glass. Twenty seconds later he looked up. "You're right," he said. "The original iron staples have been removed. These copper ones have been put in the same holes. Nearly."

"You have a photostat machine here?" Pallister's eyes were glowing with excitement.

"Of course."

"Accessible to everyone?"

"To everyone on the library staff."

"And to Members?"

"If they know where to find it, down on the ground floor near the door leading to Speaker's Court, *and* if they have a key to the strong room we keep it in, *and* if they know how to operate it. It's a proper photostat machine, not one of those ... oh!" He stopped and pulled an angry face. "I am a fool," he went on. "There are two small Xerox document machines. One's down below beneath the Chamber near the public interviewing rooms. All sorts of people use it—M.P.s, Members' Secretaries, Party officials, journalists ..."

"And the other one?"

"In the Library of the House of Lords." Maxwell waved his hand expansively. "Along the way."

"Far?"

"No; beyond the Members' dining-room."

"Locked up?"

"I don't suppose so. It wasn't the last time I saw it." As he spoke, Maxwell shrugged his shoulders elaborately. "Why should it be locked up? They don't have any secret papers." He looked down guiltily at the Noah Report. "We've boobed," he said. "I ought to tell the Librarian."

Pallister looked grim. "I should." He started buttoning his coat. "You've boobed all right." He stretched out his hand. "May I look at it please?" He grinned as Maxwell's hand tightened on it. "O.K." he said. "Look at the last page for me. What's its number?"

Maxwell looked up confidently. "Page 29," he said. "Why? Is some of it missing?" He began to look anxious again.

Christopher Pallister's grin had gone. "Then you're not the only one who's boobed. I've just remembered. That's the authentic report. The one which we made up in the Ministry to deposit here in the Library, the harmless one, had only 28 pages..."

Maxwell's eyes popped out in outrage. "You meant to mislead the Members..." His voice was still rising when it ran out of steam. His lips went on wobbling in an unseemly and silent tremulo.

"Of course," said Pallister, "we tried to, but we boobed. This one's the original, authentic thing." He said it grimly. "It's hot stuff. I'd get it locked away somewhere if I were you. And I *mean* locked away." His normal veneer of civility cracked open. "Not in a bloody little boot-cupboard. That," he said, stabbing at it with one rigid finger, "is hot stuff."

* * *

"It's the hot line, Prime Minister." Malcolm Rawnsley, the Principal Private Secretary, whispered it into Alex Beasley's right ear, and tried not to sound too excited. "Stand-by alert. They're coming through in three hours' time, at one o'clock."

"Which way?"

"The Kremlin." The Secretary's whisper sang its way round the Cabinet table. He swallowed noisily.

Alex Beasley reached out his hand to the silver box in front of him and selected a cigar. He cut the end off with elaborate deliberation and the faint crackle from the cigar could be heard at the far end of the table. Rawnsley suddenly realised that he was still poised rigidly over the Prime Minister's shoulder, like some attendant evil spirit. He relaxed, stood back and fished in his pocket for a match. As usual, he went to the wrong pocket, and Empery, the External Secretary, beat him to it. He leaned across the table and flicked his lighter. "It may be about Lombard, Alex," he said.

"Is it?" The Prime Minister turned quickly to look up at his secretary. "Did they say?"

Malcolm Rawnsley swallowed hard again. "Noah," he said quietly. The continued silence told him immediately that the word had been misinterpreted. "Operation Noah," he added. He said it, diffidently, in italics.

There was a squeak of dismay and anger from William Empery. "How on earth do you mean?" he asked. "They don't know about Noah!" His eyes were almost pushing his glasses off.

A hollow laugh came from the far end of the table and the External Secretary whipped round. The Secretary for Economic Expansion was staring at the silver chandelier. The whole Cabinet table was reflected in the silver and from where he sat he looked the biggest by far. This never failed to delight him. He looked delighted.

"It is not," William Empery said icily, "it is not in the least funny. Operation Noah is top bloody secret, I tell you!"

"*Was* top secret it seems." The Prime Minister sighed and shook his head. The heavy lines on his face had gone deeper, as though the fabric was beginning to crack. He turned back to his secretary. "I'll take the call in here," he said. "Warn me when it's coming through." He watched Malcolm Rawnsley make his way to the door and turned to the Cabinet Secretary on his immediate right. "I'm cancelling the rest of the meeting, Laurence," he said. "We'll meet again tomorrow. Please arrange it."

He turned to look round the table as Sir Laurence Squire began to collect his papers. "We'll call it a day," he said and held up his hand as the murmur of conversation started like the bursting of a dam. "I'd like the Secretary for External Affairs, the Home Secretary and the Secretary of State for Defence Technology to stay behind. Thank you."

He drew hard on his cigar and ran both hands through his hair. His long boney fingers were trembling a little. "Blast," he said to no one in particular and stared out across the Cabinet table at the silent and peaceful world outside. "Blast. If it isn't one thing it's another."

Then an idea struck him. He looked up and caught the eye of the Chief Whip as he made his way towards the door. "Stay behind please, Gilbert," he said. "We're going to need your help. I've just had an idea."

Gilbert Dace shepherded the other Members of the Cabinet through the door (murmuring the kind of encouraging noises that

57

Chief Whips go in for), nodded to the doorkeeper, watched him close the red baize outer door and then closed the inner door himself. The latch dropped with a firm noise of finality as the Chief Whip turned to join the group of three men sitting opposite the Prime Minister in the middle of the long table.

"Noah," said the Prime Minister. He stared at the papers on his blotting pad. "Noah. It's a stupid name. Who the devil thought of it?" He shook his head sadly.

William Empery looked up. His mouth said nothing but his eyeballs were eloquent.

"Oh," said four voices in unison. And then again, "Oh!"

* * *

ZK 14 calling WH 10. ZK 14 calling WH 10. We are taking up station ahead of you and will escort to Trinity House Pier, Gravesend. All traffic junctions alerted. O.K.? Over.

George Lemon leaned forward as the escort police car shot out of the lay-by half a mile ahead of them and took up station, all lights flashing. "Thank God for that," he said. "We might even make it."

"We might at that." The driver nodded to George Lemon in his driving mirror as he flashed his spotlight at the car ahead. He looked more relaxed and at the same time more alert. "I was wondering how I'd find the blasted place," he muttered. "Call 'em and tell 'em to step on it, Arnold."

WH 10 to ZK 14. Am receiving you loud and clear. Step on it, we're right behind you. Over.

"It depends on what you mean by 'loud and clear'." George Lemon leaned forward as the engine began to scream drowning the crackle of the radio receiver, and the car surged forward into the slip stream of the escort car. "You realise you're breaking the law," he said. "Not that it matters."

"Right," said the driver. The rev counter went up three points. "Too right it doesn't."

ZK 14 calling WH 10. Important message for Rastus follows: over.

George Lemon sat up with a jerk. "Tell 'em I'm listening. This means trouble." For the first time he began to appreciate that they were in a situation of extreme emergency. In thirteen years with MI5 he had only once before been addressed by his disposable code-name. And on that occasion two men had been killed, one of them very nastily less than two feet away from him.

Rastus receiving. Arnold spoke into the microphone. *Over.*

Magnus calling Rastus. Quarry now approaching Black Shelf on Fiddler Reach two miles upstream from Gravesend. Known maximum speed twelve and a half knots. Quarry has signalled she does not, repeat not, intend stopping for pilot boat. Will slow down to transfer pilot but not, repeat not, stop. Boarding warrant in hand proceed independently. Over.

"O.K. Acknowledge." George Lemon spoke to Arnold. "Tell him I'm glad to know he's still alive." Ever since he separated from Tom Slaughter in Rotherhithe Street and made his way to Jamaica Road to rendezvous with the police car, he had assumed "Magnus" to be loafing in the office, or, more likely, eating his way through ham rolls in the front parlour of the Angel at Rotherhithe. He grinned. "Remind me to apologise to him," he said. Then a thought struck him. "I'll need help. If she slows down to put the pilot off, the chances are I can board her." He had stopped grinning.

The driver grunted. "Got a gun?" he asked. "We're moving in." The signpost indicating the slip road to Gravesend loomed up swiftly. "Here we go." He stabbed his brake twice and dropped speed to just below fifty, flicked into intermediate hold with the little finger of his right hand, and swept round to the left still behind the escort car.

"No gun," said George Lemon. "I don't need a gun."

He was wrong.

*   *   *

"You're wrong, Robert. I tell you you're wrong." Geoffrey Pond, the Prime Minister's Press Secretary, stared across his large ground floor room in No. 10. "You're a stubborn bastard, aren't you?" The smile that came with the words stopped before it reached his eyes. He began to look very angry.

"Sure. And why not?" Robert Maryon, the Political Correspondent of the *Daily Mail*, carefully balanced a spent match on the end of his thumb, put the nail of his index finger behind it and took aim. "I always get there in the end. As you know." He raised his eye from his thumb and winked before going back to the elaborate operation of taking aim. "Rendle," he said, his eye cocked at a ridiculous angle. "Rendle died in the Chamber and I want to know what the P.M. thinks about it." He paused and flicked the match. "Blast." He grinned cheerfully at Pond sitting grimly at his desk. "Why don't you get a bigger ash-tray, Geoffrey?"

Pond disregarded the match on the blotter in front of him. "O.K." he said. "Rendle died in the Chamber," he paused. "It's nothing to do with No. 10. Go and ask the Lord Great Chamberlain or somebody about it. I tell you it's nothing to do with us." He glanced round the packed room. The *Times* man was doodling on the back of the *Daily Telegraph* and the man from the *Guardian* was looking angry and impatient.

"A fat lot of good that will do." Timothy Woodman nodded his head. "His Lordship's not coming in today. He's got a date with a horse."

A dozen heads shot round. "Who says?" The *Times* man had stopped doodling. He stared at Woodman and growled a gentlemanly growl. "You've been trying to get him on the telly." It was the newspaperman's ultimate in insult, and it seemed to please him.

"As a matter of fact," Woodman's wide face went still wider as he grinned, "that was the general idea. I *did* try to speak to him." He looked round the room defiantly. "I've got a news bulletin at 1.25. I've got to fill it. And it seems Geoffrey here isn't inclined to help." When his eyes reached Geoffrey Pond, there was no hint of pleasure in them. "Give us more about Austin Lombard then, Geoffrey, and we'll play the Rendle business down."

Geoffrey Pond put his elbows slowly and deliberately on his desk. "Get this." He spoke first to Timothy Woodman. "It's not my job to find a story for BBC Television," he said. "And I refuse to play along with anyone else." This time he looked hard at Maryon. "The Lombard business is a different sort of thing altogether. That's very much a No. 10 matter. As soon as we have anything on him from Athens you'll hear about it either from the Foreign Office or from here. But, I repeat, we've damn-all to do with Rendle." He started putting the papers straight on his desk as a signal that the press conference was over and the man from the *Express* stood up at the back of the room. As he did so, he glanced through the fine mesh curtains behind Pond's head in time to see a large black car pull up at the main door of No. 10.

"Ah ah!" he said, stirring it up a bit. "Assistant Commissioner, Crime! No doubt come to tell the P.M. that Rendle's nothing to do with No. 10."

Twenty heads turned to look out into Downing Street and the *Morning Star* fell over the *Sun's* briefcase. The usual crowd of rubberneckers on the far pavement had begun to rustle with excitement, their heads moving about like corn in a gentle breeze, as the car door opened. Then, as though switched off by some finger on a main switch, they returned to their stolid and silent immobility when they failed to recognise the Assistant Commissioner (Crime).

"Lumpenproletariat," said the *Western Gazette*. "They don't know what they're missing!" He shook his head with an elaborate show of wisdom.

"Nor," said Robert Maryon, "does the *Western Gazette*, it seems." He tapped his pipe on Geoffrey Pond's desk. "Better come clean, Geoffrey," he said. "That chap who came across from the F.O. archway as the car drew up was Christopher Pallister from MI5. They're all arriving at once, aren't they? Gathering of the clans."

He sat down again in the best of the large leather armchairs. "Methinks the young gentleman from MI5 looked a bit flustered," he observed as he began once more to poke at his pipe with another match. "I thought they were all trained to use the back door." He hesitated and started puffing with vigour. "Or the tunnel from their little underground lair." His eyes were bright with cheerful malice as he peered through the thick fog of tobacco smoke. "And talking about looking flustered, Geoffrey ..." He grinned and settled back in his chair. "You're beginning to look like a man in search of a lost D-notice." He was the only one who laughed but the noise made the policeman on the pavement outside turn and look curiously at the curtained window.

* * *

"Do they give you danger money?" The captain of the pilot launch kept his face rigidly straight as he said it. He was peering up-stream with the pale November sun behind him. "There she is," he said, "the stupid sod. Going like the clappers."

George Lemon nodded. "He must be mad," he said. He shivered suddenly and crossed his fingers in his overcoat pockets. "How do I get on board?" he asked.

The captain telegraphed an order, and the diesel engines roared. He glanced quickly at the north shore a quarter of a mile away and took a quick instinctive sighting on the tanker repair jetty alongside Tilbury docks. Then he spun round and sighted his position on the Railway Pier at Gravesend to the south-east. "Ready for her," he said. "She's got to take this channel." Then he turned to George Lemon. "You bloody well jump," he said. "And you make it nippy or else." He stared upstream. "She's busting her guts."

The *Olga* looked enormous and menacing even though she was two hundred yards away. She was high out of the water and riding her own bow wave as though she was chewing her way through the river. They could hear the steady rhythmic thump of her engines. "Three thousand tons and in the hands of a bloody maniac." The captain shook his head and repeated it. "A bloody maniac."

"He's beating hell out of her!" The cox'n at the bows of the launch looked appalled as he spun round. "Christ," he shouted at the captain, "she's changing course." He clambered back towards the high bridge and cracked his shin on the winch as the launch suddenly veered to port. He cursed as the launch turned in a sharp circle and he slipped on the deck as she heeled over.

"The bastard!" The captain screamed it against the noise of his own engine and the surging pulse of the *Olga*'s motors. "She's trying to ram us."

George Lemon looked up at the *Olga*'s bridge as she swept

past them a few feet astern. Two men in filthy grey overalls leaned over the side and shouted words he couldn't make out. One of them spat into the water. The launch began to rock violently in the *Olga*'s bow wave and the engine roared again. "Stand by!" The captain shouted the words in a kind of chattering frenzy. "She's going astern!" It was a long incredulous wail.

The powerful screws of the *Olga* churned at the water and a heavy clanking noise, intermittent and like the splitting of iron bars came from the *Olga's* stern. "He's out of his bloody mind!" The captain of the launch almost sang it as he gathered speed and started overhauling the *Olga*. They began bobbing about in the wash that slapped against the overhang of the launch's bows.

"There's Fred." A deckhand leaning out over the side of the launch shouted over the roar of the engines. "Fred Armytage." As he spoke the name a rope ladder came down from the *Olga's* poop deck and Fred Armytage, the river pilot, waved them on frenziedly. The *Olga* was still moving through the water at seven or eight knots. "Oh, the bastard, the clever bastard." The captain shook his head with reluctant admiration. The launch was shuddering with the effort of her engine as she very slowly overhauled the *Olga*. "He knows I'm full out. He's holding her speed down till Fred can jump. Oh, the clever one." The captain turned to George Lemon. "You can't do it," he said. "As soon as Fred Armytage jumps he'll be away like a bullet."

"I'll have a shot." Lemon swallowed hard. "There's a warrant to board her. It's important, captain."

"I suppose you know what you're doing." As he muttered it, the captain was easing his launch gradually alongside the *Olga* and three feet clear of her starboard side. Suddenly he shouted his orders and the deck hand at the port bow took the rope ladder neatly in the claw of his boat-hook. He braced himself against the launch's gunwhale and took the bottom rung of the ladder in both hands. The hook went over the side. "Clumsy bugger," shouted the captain, but he shouted it admiringly. "Well done, Victor."

As the captain spoke, Fred Armytage came down the ladder as if the devil wearing spurs was perched on his collar-bone. As he jumped the last three feet into the well of the launch, George

Lemon made a grab at the ladder and swung into space. He winced and howled as he came with a jarring thud against the iron plates of the *Olga*'s side and howled again with pain as he swung away and came back hard on the rebound. As he managed to get his foot on to the lowest rung, the *Olga*'s engines started up again. He could feel the power of the screws as a kind of tingling in his fingers and he began to shiver with sick reaction and fear as he started to climb.

The pilot launch swung clear in a broad sweep to starboard, leaving George Lemon bumping and swaying his way to the *Olga*'s rails.

The captain of the launch was shouting as he curled away out of danger. "We'll have the bastard," he screamed. "Hang on, lad, hang on. We'll get him off the Nore!" The last word sailed away on a dying fall as though being torn from the captain's throat. "Nore! Nore!" It was the only word George Lemon heard as he dragged himself over the *Olga*'s cold grey iron side. He slithered face forward towards the plates of the deck and threw his hands out to take the shock of his fall.

It was at that moment that a heavy boot kicked him in the angle of his jaw.

* * *

The awful and simple truth was that panic had gripped him by the ears, nose, throat and eyeballs. Christopher Pallister shifted his bottom on the leather seat of his chair and went unprofessionally pink at the thought. He had run, or practically run, into the front door of No. 10 of all places! Panic, according to the simple conventions of his MI5 superiors, was a thing you discarded in the first three months of your probationary training. He glanced round the waiting-room and hoped that the other people would ascribe his pink flush to reflection from the handsome red carpet which had obviously been laid there to impress the Prime Minister's visitors. No one seemed to have noticed either him or his dilemma, and Pallister began to feel a bit better. The Duke of Wellington (done in marble) looked arrogantly unconcerned from his little niche in the corner, Winston Churchill (done in paint) looked dependable and aloof in his Air

Force blue track-suit, and the uniformed door-keeper beside the red baize door into the Cabinet Room managed to look at the same time alert and infinitely bored, as if this kind of thing happened all day and every day, around the clock. Which, thought Pallister, it probably did with knobs on.

He was not alone in the waiting-room and he was obviously not the only one who was wondering what he would say when he stepped through the red baize doorway and faced the Prime Minister. Fifteen feet away from him, at the other side of the room, there was a young man who was presumably an airline pilot. The four gold stripes on his sleeve and the BEA badge on the cap balanced tremblingly on his knee were, however, hard to reconcile with his totally bald head, which was shiny and slippery with, it seemed, sweat. You could almost lay it down as a principle; airline pilots are never bald. This one was bald.

The man next to him (with an empty chair between them) was a cold-looking fish, rather dapper, who looked as though his underpants under his beautiful charcoal grey suit ought to be cut like cavalry breeches. He was the chap who had arrived at the door of No. 10 in a large black police car, three seconds before he, Pallister, had burst almost at the double out of the Foreign Office archway and belted across Downing Street. And he was the one who had caused both the policemen outside to salute (one of them had almost saluted with both hands in an excess of spontaneous subordination) and had caused the two policemen inside to go as rigid as goalposts, practically twanging with deference. One of them had breathed the word "Commissioner." Well, thought Pallister, you can keep him. *Wonderful. Counsellor. The almighty Boss.* He sang it *con brio* inside his head.

This, sadly, reminded him of his own boss, Malplaquet, the smooth-faced comedian with the air of infinite wisdom. And what Malplaquet would say when he heard that Pallister had called on the Prime Minister instead of sending him, Malplaquet, a memo in duplicate (and on the *blue* form) was nobody's business.

Correct that. It was Pallister's business and he applied himself, not before time, to rehearsing his own side of the conversation which he was, sooner or later, bound to suffer.

It was like this, sir. I know that the Minister of Deftech ...

He could imagine Malplaquet's face as he heard the word Deftech. It would be pale and puffy, like a pudding in a cloth. And it would grimace with Malplaquet's superior brand of revulsion.

Don't call him by that stupid term, Pallister. The Minister may like it. I loathe it.

Yes, sir ... *No, sir* ... *I knew he'd deposited the Noah papers in the Commons Library* ...

So did I. (Cold, this.)

Yes, sir. Of course. So I went to see if they had been tampered with.

(Grunt.)

They had.

(Louder grunt here, with a little one from Marcus Pierce hovering round in the background just to show he was following the conversation.)

They'd been photographed.

Carry on, Pallister. (Getting a bit warmer now.)

Yes, sir. There's a Xerox machine in the Library of the House of Lords. So I went along to see the Librarian, a nice old gentleman.

He would be.

He is. He said that to the best of his knowledge, the machine had been there for years but it didn't often get used. Actually he apologised for the amount of dust on it. You see, he hasn't got a very big staff ...

But when you got there, no dust, I suppose?

That's right. No dust.

Any fingerprints?

I'm afraid not. It had been wiped clean.

But it had definitely been used?

Quite certainly. And recently.

By one of his staff, perhaps?

No. He sent for them all and asked them. There are only four.

Any of the Peers? ...

I suggested that, sir. The Librarian giggled a bit at the idea.

Pallister's reverie was interrupted and he jumped as the door to the Cabinet Room opened. A young man, an under-under-under secretary if ever there was one, pushed his head into the waiting-room. It was a beautifully groomed head covered with disciplined fair hair.

"Commissioner," he said, lisping slightly but with great charm. "The Prime Minister will see you now." He almost bowed from the waist. "He's sorry to have kept you waiting."

Pallister doubted the truth of this but it surely struck home with the Commissioner. He stepped two paces forward, pulled his jacket down at the back, and actually smiled broadly as he strutted across the red carpet, carrying a black morocco briefcase under his arm. It was patently empty, or it contained, at most, one tissue-thin piece of paper with top secrets on it. Pallister glanced across at the airline pilot, who was showing signs of thinking that the principle of first here, first served, a beautiful and essential principle in British democracy, had been grossly outraged. The young man from the Cabinet Office noticed it too.

"Assistant Commissioner, Crime in brackets," he said softly, explaining all. The pilot relaxed and offered a quick grin. His bald head got shinier.

The grandfather clock beside him did an experimental wheeze and then struck a throaty twelve-thirty as Pallister shuffled back into his imaginary conversation. He got there just in time to imagine Malplaquet breathing a deep sigh of relief. *Thank God*, he was saying, and then again for emphasis *Thank God we didn't put the authentic Noah papers into the Commons Library*. His lips would be pale, paler than usual at the thought in his mind.

We did.

There would be a long pregnant silence, as they say, and then Malplaquet would start clucking like a Rhode Island Red and flapping his hands, big pale hands, like sheets of canvas in a high wind. And there would be moaning from Pierce, a ground-bass of consternation.

"Mr. Pallister." The smooth young under-under-under-secretary had crept up beside him and Pallister jumped. "The Prime Minister will see you now. Please come in." The tone of voice suggested that the young man was sorry to interrupt Pallister's sleep.

"I was thinking," said Pallister.

The young man smiled and the airline pilot laughed out loud. It was a rough noise, obviously uttered, in part at least, as a protest against further flouting of his sense of fairness and propriety.

It was not until much later that Pallister recognised the young attendant's finesse. He felt himself steered through the two doors, inner and outer, heard his name announced, and found himself responding to a firm but courteous left-wheel turn through ninety degrees. Before he realised what had happened he was looking the length of the Cabinet table which stretched it seemed into infinity. The young man disappeared and Pallister never saw him again.

The Prime Minister nodded curtly at Pallister and then seemed to put him from his mind as he turned papers over and drummed irritably on the green baize cloth with his fingers. Four other Ministers were at the table, scribbling phrases and collating pieces of noted information, working on drafts of some kind or other. It was Desmond Bassington who looked up. He nodded to Pallister to take one of the mahogany chairs at the table. Then they all seemed to forget him again.

"The time fits exactly," said David Orchard, the Home Secretary. He seemed very pleased with himself. Nobody else looked pleased with anything. There was a long silence.

"It's taking shape into something very nasty." It was Alex Beasley who broke it. He turned to Christopher Pallister. "This is very unusual, young man. You insisted on seeing me. Why?"

Pallister took a deep breath. "Because I think I know why Rendle was killed, Prime Minister."

That brought all their heads up from their papers. Bassington spoke first. "You assume you have all the facts?"

"I think so. I'm sure it concerns Operation Noah."

The Prime Minister held up his hand as Bassington opened his mouth. He nodded slightly as Pallister said Noah again.

"Why do you say that?"

"Because I think someone got a message out of the House of Commons during the night as soon as he'd secured a copy of the Operation Noah papers from the Library of the House."

"Zwölf Sekunden um Punkt drei," said the External Secretary.

"You'll be interested, no doubt, to know that according to the Chief Commissioner from the Yard who has just been reporting to us, Big Ben's light went on for a few seconds at three o'clock this morning. It was noted by a police constable."

"For twelve seconds?"

"That is the theory. The constable didn't count them."

"It fits exactly." The Home Secretary was persistent. He meant to get full credit for the admirable deductive reasoning made by the Metropolitan Police. "Shrewd man, the Commissioner."

"And all," said Desmond Bassington portentiously "to no avail." He smiled a superior smile. "The deposited papers in the Commons' Library are a blind. Anybody who steals them will find..." At that point he stopped and stared at Pallister's expression. "Oh!" He went very pale.

By the time Pallister had finished they were all very pale indeed. They were still pale when Malcolm Rawnsley came in from the Secretaries' Room next door. He spoke quietly to the Prime Minister. "Kremlin," he said. He picked up the special red telephone on a small table.

As Pallister left the Cabinet Room (for some reason he found himself walking on tip-toe over a rust-red floor that seemed to stretch for miles), the Prime Minister was listening carefully and Rawnsley was standing by to take notes. The expression on the Prime Minister's face was black and getting blacker.

*   *   *

Alex Beasley put the receiver down precisely and carefully on its rest and waited until the remote electronic moan had faded into silence. Then he looked up at his Secretary. The question was in his enormous eyebrows. They were moving slowly.

"Transcript in about a quarter of an hour's time," said Rawnsley. "They'll be typing it in relays. I'll bring it in immediately I get it."

"Thanks, Malcolm. Tell them not to bother much with all the preliminaries." Beasley turned to the External Secretary. "It takes them five minutes to get under way, as you know. Fifteen different ways of saying Good Morning." He paused and helped himself to a cigar from his silver box. William Empery noticed that his fingers were trembling. "The telephone's heavy, Alex," he suggested.

Beasley smiled and acknowledged the gesture. "And hot, William. Very hot." Then the smile left his face. "You can assume," he said, "that Noah is blown. Totally and absolutely blown." He paused a moment to light his cigar. "And they've known about it for the past year. They also know why Austin Lombard was on his way to Ankara."

The Minister of Defence Technology blew a gusty sigh. "Is there anything they don't know?" he asked.

"Certainly!" Beasley looked slowly round the meeting. "Certainly! They don't know why Rendle was killed." He paused again and blew some smoke towards the chandelier. "Any more than *we* know. He's only been dead ten hours and they know as much as we do. But they do have a suggestion and that's why Vossilof rang. He said it was too dangerous and too cumbrous to put it through the ordinary channels." His eyes came to rest on the External Secretary. "Don't look so outraged, William," he said. "There's a lot more in what he says than you'll admit. He says we're going to be in trouble in the next fortnight with Operation Noah unless we do something about it. He says we have until the 1st December. And the trouble, they are convinced, could start anywhere in the Euratom countries or Turkey. They're inclined to think it's Amsterdam or Ankara."

Outside, the clock on the Horseguards chimed 1.30. Six seconds later, Big Ben's ponderous half-hour chimes brought up the rear and, as though waiting for them to signal his entrance, Malcolm Rawnsley stepped into the room. "You won't forget Captain Pendower of BEA, will you, Prime Minister? He's out in the waiting-room and he's been there nearly an hour." Rawnsley stepped up to the table and looked at his notebook.

"The Lord Chancellor has stood in for you at the Tabula Luncheon. There'll be sandwiches and coffee for five in the Pillared Room at 2.0. I'll make it for six if you want to invite Captain Pendower to join you. I've warned Mr Cann and he's bringing a sherry in as soon as you give him a ring. And then don't forget you should be down at the House at 2.30. Mr

Speaker will be making a statement about Rendle and you'll have to say something, and there's a private notice question down about Lombard." He lowered his voice. "The BBC say they propose to bring in the cameras for live transmission of the Speaker's Statement and then of Question Time, and the Leader of the House has agreed."

"What you mean is that I ought to be there?"

Rawnsley's answer came without words. His shoulders went up slowly and came down quickly.

The Prime Minister nodded his thanks. "Ask the Captain to join us in the Pillared Room, please."

He led the way out of the Cabinet Room past the teleprinter machine in the lobby and up the long dog-leg staircase with its collection of engravings and photographs of British Prime Ministers from Walpole to Blackburn. Not for the first time, he noticed that they looked increasingly harassed as the centuries went by; and he wondered what kind of a showing he would make when his turn came to join the gallery. *Rough*, he thought, and he sighed. "They all had their Noahs," he said as though consoling himself and Winston Churchill looked ready to growl as he stepped past him.

The Pillared Room managed to look cosy in spite of its size and the elaborate magnificence of its furnishings, gold and pink and apple green. "As I said before..." Beasley murmured it as he walked over to the window, picking up a sherry from Mr Cann's tray and nodding his thanks. "It all looks so peaceful." St James's Park seen from the first floor of No. 10 is graceful and serene like the back cloth to some eighteenth-century masque. The gold brocade curtains moved only slightly as his arm brushed against them. "Peace," he said, just as Captain Pendower was ushered into the room. He looked startled and his mouth moved silently. He appeared to be saying "Peace", as though taking part in a ritual.

* * *

Beasley brought them down to business as the plate of sandwiches went around.

"I take it there was no way of preventing them arresting Lombard, Captain?"

"None at all, sir. They were quite clever about it. They announced on the blower from Athens control that there would be a delay of one hour before we could take off for Istanbul, so we let everyone go ashore to stretch their legs or something." Pendower was still sweating but not too much to prevent him from holding a plate.

"And they arrested him at the barrier?"

"Not really. They waited until he was kicking his heels at the bar. And they waited until the plane was refuelled and we were ready to leave."

"Delicate methods?" Beasley offered.

"Not at all, sir. They just wanted to get him on his own. There was nothing delicate about it."

"Who was with him?" William Empery nearly choked himself on a piece of tongue, the long end bit, that had slid out of his sandwich and was on its way down his throat.

Captain Pendower waited until the External Secretary was wholly with them again. "Lucille," he said. His bald head seemed to have got a little wetter again. "She's a sweetie. One of our stewardesses. Real name's Lucy French."

"I thought they weren't supposed . . ." It was the Home Secretary being a bit legalistic. He felt he owed it to his office.

"They're not." Pendower looked as though he felt himself a bit of a heel telling tales out of hours. "They do." He tried to laugh off the myriad foibles of humanity and dropped a piece of bread. By the time he had picked it up (it had gone part way under a very nice deep settee covered in green brocade) the whole party was poised to listen. "It's as well she joined him," he said. "Or he couldn't have given me the message for you." He turned to look at Beasley.

No one spoke, but no one chewed either.

"This is where it gets a bit embarrassing," Pendower was certainly embarrassed. "Lombard had got pretty friendly with Lucy between Rome and Athens (they both got on at Rome), and so as soon as he said 'lend me your lipstick ducks,' she upped and lent him it. He bent down and scribbled his note against the front of the bar on a left-luggage ticket he'd got in Rome. With lipstick. Then without turning a hair (according to Lucy) he got up, leaned forward and pushed the ticket down inside her blouse." Captain Pendower indulged himself with a noisy short giggle. "Not far down," he said out of some strange deference to protocol. "But far enough for it to disappear."

"Trust Austin." The Home Secretary looked mean for a second or two. He clucked enviously.

"And just then the Greek police, three of them, came into the bar. Lombard must have seen them coming. They're toughs you know, sir. My god they're toughs. Real thugs." Pendower's face had gone wholly serious. "As soon as they started moving in, Lombard said 'Push off, ducks. Be a good girl. Give my regards,' he said, 'give my regards to my friends the backward M.P.' That's what he said" Pendower's voice trailed off. "Backward M.P." He said it weakly.

The Prime Minister held his hand out for the message. "I'm glad he calls me his friend," he said. "It always helps."

The ticket was little more than two inches by one and a half; its number was F/NR 72272 and it had regulations printed all over in what appeared to be a rough and ready one-point typeface. And on the back, Lombard had scrawled his message in rough crude characters.

NOE DIVLIST KALDEC ADMIN ARMEN

It was smudged, the deep red lipstick running to the edge as though bleeding on to the hand that held it. Alex Beasley removed his thumb and seemed surprised that it was still clean.

"It must have left its mark on Lucy." The Home Secretary looked demure and it was terrible to see. Captain Pendower laughed obligingly. The others disregarded both of them.

They were still staring at Lombard's message when the Prime Minister's Secretary slid into the group. For a big man, he had a remarkable skill at unobtrusive infiltration. He was in the middle of the group, moving on castors, before anyone noticed him. "It's after quarter past two," he said to the Prime Minister. "Speaker's in the Chair"—he looked carefully at his watch—"in thirteen minutes, and your car's standing by."

Alex Beasley turned to Pendower. "Sorry about this, Captain," he said. "But I imagine you know what it's like living to somebody else's timetable." They shook hands. "Thank Lucy for me, please, and keep this very dark." He handed the message to his secretary. "Put a copy in the box along with my notes on Rendle please—and get the original across to the Cipher Office." Then a sudden thought struck him and he pushed his fingers through his thick mat of hair. "Better get a comb," he said. "You're sure the BBC cameras are on?" Malcolm Rawnsley nodded and held out a neatly pressed black tie. "After all," he murmured, "it *is* colour television."

*   *   *

"I am . . ." Eugene Malplaquet stopped. He kept the telephone to his mouth but addressed himself to the world at large. He formed his large fleshy lips into a kind of funnel and sucked some air through it noisily. His eyeballs rolled upwards and homed sightlessly on the shabby Victorian cornice of the MI5 head office. He began again, using more voice. "I am surrounded," he said, "by some very, very, very stupid people." The second syllable of the last word came out as a sort of lengthened yodel.

Christopher Pallister came through the door in the middle of it, recognised it and turned to go out again.

"Pallister!" Malplaquet shouted it and the man at the other end of the telephone yelped. "Shut up, Slaughter," said Malplaquet. He shouted again for Pallister and glared at him as he walked slowly into the room. Marcus Pierce was sitting on the window-sill, enjoying it all silently. "You as well, Pierce," said Malplaquet. "Shut up."

By now the silence was complete and Malplaquet left it that way for a few seconds. Then Slaughter spoiled it from the other end by asking if he was there. "Yes," said Malplaquet, "I bloody well am," and Pierce's head came up with a jerk. It was only the second time in his long career in the department that he had heard Malplaquet swear. (The other time was when he heard he had been given the MBE in the same list, years ago, as some singers called Beatles.) This was obviously serious. He went over to the extension telephone, picked it up, and waited for it. Pallister stepped over to stand beside Pierce. He held his ear out and hoped.

"Now," said Malplaquet breathing in steady gusts, "say it again, Slaughter."

Slaughter's teeth clicked to attention as he got ready to use his reporting voice. "The *Olga*," he said, "got away. She sailed straight past the pilotage control depot."

Malplaquet looked across the room at Pierce and said, "You see what I mean?" Slaughter disregarded it and went on to report the loss of George Lemon, last seen going down the Thames Estuary at twelve knots.

Pierce could see a battle going on behind Malplaquet's face as the interests of Service efficiency struggled with an inclination to rejoice at Lemon's loss. The Service won.

"I'll get on to the Admiralty," Malplaquet shuddered as he said it. *Please we have lost one of our MI5 operators.*

"Don't bother." Tom Slaughter's voice suggested he was full of understanding. "The Duty Officer here..."

"Where's there?"

"At the Thames Navigation Service at Gravesend. He's already asked the Navy in Chatham to send a gunboat."

The crude imperialistic phrase struck home. "Oh," said Malplaquet. "Tell them to be careful." He paused. "Publicity," he murmured. He meant Parliamentary Questions.

"They can't."

"Can't be careful! They've got to be."

"Can't send a gunboat. They say they haven't got one handy. They say they're sorry."

There was a long silence.

Malplaquet's face was wholly blank. If there was any thought going on behind it, it was causing no ripples.

Marcus Pierce came to the rescue. "Stay where you are, Tom," he said briskly into the phone. "We'll go into conference and ring you back when we come up with something." The warm word "conference" brought a touch of colour to Malplaquet's cheeks. "Right," he said, his voice almost vibrant with relief. "Good idea." They all three knew what was meant, and all three telephones went down slowly, together.

* * *

The Lord Chancellor's Senior Clerk waited, almost without breathing, for the inevitable. He lifted the Wig out of its silk-lined box and held it out five feet seven inches from the floor and with the empty space for his Lordship's face held towards the door. The inevitable came. "Capital," said the Lord Chancellor, a man of quite literal fancy. He stepped forward swiftly from his chair, ducked beneath the full bottom and brought his head up in one economical movement. "Capital, Bassett," he said. "Sir," said Bassett.

A man of unusual sensibility, Alfred Bassett could never be persuaded to go to a bullfight during his annual visit to the Costa Brava. Once when rather tired he confessed that he would expect the bull to rush head down towards the matador's cape, come up the other side of it, and say 'Capital!'

"Ah!" The Lord Chancellor was showing signs of overdoing it. "Excellent!" He pressed the sides of the wig to his neck, and shivered. "It's cold out there." He waved his left hand in the general direction of the outside world and drew his black and gold robe tightly round him. "Bassett," he said. He smiled as his long grey face went slightly pink; it was the warmth getting to work on it. "Bassett, I'm inclined to think that the Prime Minister is welcome to it. All these official lunches. As you young people say: he can have it." Bassett, who was fifty-four, smiled wanly. He watched a shadow come over the Lord Chancellor's face. "The food perhaps, sir?" he offered.

"Indeed no. Food good; wine excellent. Both are always good at the Merchant Moneylenders' Hall." The shadow lifted for a moment or two as the food and drink were recollected in tranquillity. Then it came down again, down past His Lordship's chin. "It was the people." He nodded agreeing with himself. "It was the people. I have a strong feeling that they resented my being there in place and room of the Prime Minister."

"Sir," said Bassett. The Lord Chancellor acknowledged the expression of outrage. "I mean it," he said. "A rather superior collection of people. The Chairman was a Chartered Accountant or something from Purley." This seemed to explain almost everything. He was nodding as though about to give utterance to a Judgement.

He was interrupted by a light tap on the door.

"That," said Alfred Bassett, just as he said it every Sitting Day so earning his salary, "that will be the Serjeant." It was, and the Lord Chancellor moved towards the door. As he walked he turned to Bassett, who bowed. "You may not believe it, my dear Bassett, but I told them the story about Lord Chancellor Thurlow and the two chickens."

Bassett found it very easy to believe; it was safe to say that the Lord Chancellor told it to everybody. He tried to hide his disbelief. His Lordship tapped Bassett's chest as he walked past it. "They did not think it was funny. They gave the impression they knew it." He went out along the corridor, shaking his head in disbelief so that the wig swayed from side to side. In front of him was the Serjeant-at-Arms with the Mace on his shoulder; behind him walked an attendant with the Great Seal in an ornamental bag. Bassett went back into the room and, for some ill-conceived reason, he hit the lid of His Lordship's wig box hard with the flat of his hand. It fell shut with a tinny thud and one of the hinges broke.

* * *

The dive bar door of the Red Lion in Derby Gate, S.W.1, is set on at an angle. The effect was to force them into single file as they came through it. Pallister at the rear, had a sudden, incongruous idea as they approached Whitehall twenty yards away that he should place his right hand on Pierce's shoulder, that Pierce in his turn should put his right hand . . . The idea, rich in perfectly justified implications, caused Pallister to laugh out loud. Immediately, Malplaquet turned round and smiled benignly at his little black-coated army. Then he tipped his hat (a black one) to the red lion fifteen feet up the wall on the corner of the building. The lion disregarded him and went on staring heraldically into one of the upper windows of the Welsh Office, its face twisted into a snarl of malevolence; its eyes, appropriately, sticking out like hatpegs in a Rhondda chapel. They marched on.

"It is marvellous," said Malplaquet over his shoulder, "it is marvellous what a couple of Stan's pork pies will do." He tapped the middle button of his coat with the flat of one hand. "Marvellous."

"Gin," said Pierce. "Pink gin." He said it with the rancour of a man who, for no really good reason, has stuck to light ale.

Malplaquet pretended not to hear him. As a diversion he said "*Avanti*." A hundred feet away, on the far side of Whitehall, the front door of the Home Office, open wide as usual, was beckoning them like an attack of toothache. "*Avanti*." He obviously liked the sound of it.

The warden on traffic duty at the junction of Whitehall with King Charles Street recognised them and stopped them. He signalled the traffic on eagerly and his face glowed with a flood of pleasure. The flood lasted until he ran out of motor-cars. Then, reluctantly, he signalled them to pass over to the other side. It was then that Malplaquet saw Preston Northcott of the West German office in Bonn standing waiting for them on the far side of the road. His smile was wiped from his face. Pallister grunted a two-note grunt at the back of his nose. "Back to it," he said. "Here we go." They wheeled left into the dark cavern of the Home Office.

None of them spoke until they were in Malplaquet's room and Northcott was settled in the guest-chair. A big man (a bit over size for MI5 really), he filled it. He started patting his pockets in search of his thick dossier of papers, and found them eventually in the pocket he had patted first. "That's the way it goes," he observed brightly. "Always the way." He nodded, agreeing with himself.

"Who paid for your trip?" Malplaquet believed in getting the admin points behind him first.

"H.E. did."

"Ah!" Malplaquet looked relieved. His Excellency had a fine record of parsimony. "Good. And why are you here? You could have put your report in the bag."

"Not all of it, I couldn't." Northcott looked pointedly at the electric fan above the door. "Better have the fan on." His face had a prim look on it.

"You can't," said Pierce beginning to whine a bit. "It's bloody cold."

"You don't know a thing!" said Northcott. "You ought to spend a winter on the Rhine." He looked delighted at having got this side-swipe in. "Anyway," he went on, "you know the rules. No fan, no story." He smacked his lips and his hands together simultaneously. As a demonstration of obstinacy it was perfect, and Malplaquet, recognising a highly developed skill, smiled, nodded to Pallister and said "Fan." Ten seconds later the noise was a few decibels, and only a few, short of deafening. "That's rather good." Northcott was impressed. He then began to shout to compete with it. "Enver," he said. "And Brook. Dangerous."

Pierce shivered, not because they were dangerous but because he was cold.

"You've got them," Northcott went on. It was a statement, not a question.

Malplaquet was guarded. "We know where they are," he said.

"Good. I'm very glad to hear it. They'll be very relieved in Bonn," Northcott leaned forward in his chair and tried to tap Malplaquet's knee. He missed it because Malplaquet moved it. "Seditious," he said. "They've a pretty good idea that Enver and Brook were behind the Karlsruhe riots last autumn."

Three pairs of eyebrows went up at the mention of Karlsruhe. "It keeps coming in," said Pallister.

"What does?" Northcott sounded suspicious. "You're hiding something."

"Not really," Malplaquet waved his white hands. He looked like a priest trying conciliation. "Carry on. Why Karlsruhe?"

"Because that's where it started," said Northcott, "years ago. In the Schwarzwaldhalle. The first meeting of the NPD after the war. Enver and Brook organised it."

"Oy! Oy!" Pierce suddenly caught up with his Current Affairs. "That's all old hat," he observed. "The NPD was made illegal in 1970. If not before."

Northcott nodded. "1970 it was," he said. "And they went underground. That's when they founded their international cover organisation, Tabula."

Malplaquet groaned. "Nuts," he said. He sounded very rude. "They're a lot of nuts." That sounded better. "As pure as driven snow and about as dangerous."

"You think so!" Northcott looked hard at Malplaquet. "Tell them that in Karlsruhe. And Petten and Moll." He looked

79

pleased as the place-names struck home. "You've heard of them?" He managed to sound very patronising.

"Certainly." Pallister looked up from his notebook. "And we also know about Ankara," he said.

Northcott looked deflated, as though his rug had been dragged away. "I see," he said. "And you know they have a cell in Turkey?"

"Sure." Pallister took a long shot. He looked very triumphant. "They operate from the Bulvar Palace Hotel." Northcott's face told him he'd hit the bull.

* * *

The first Division Bell of the day was sounding as the Prime Minister's car drew up at the main entrance to Westminster Hall in New Palace Yard. The policeman on the door saluted. "Prayers, sir," he said.

"Good." Alex Beasley looked relieved. "Five minutes. Plenty of time." He turned to wait for his Secretary. "You're sure about the precedents, Malcolm?"

Malcolm Rawnsley was guarded. He pushed open the heavy glass and wooden door. "According to the Clerk it's the third. Spencer Perceval, M.P., John Salterno, M.P., and now Thomas Rendle."

"It's not bad." Beasley looked around the great Hall as they walked briskly towards the Cloisters and the Members' Lobby beyond. "Not a bad record. Three murders in six hundred years."

"Three murders we *know* about." Like most people who walk through the vast enclosed space of Westminster Hall, Malcolm Rawnsley was aware of its menacing air of calm. "If these flagstones had voices..."

"You read too many detective stories." Beasley spoke quite sharply and Malcolm Rawnsley grunted. "Chance would be a fine thing, as they say." So far as he could recall he had managed to read one book in the past three years. He pushed open the door to the Members' Lobby. As usual on any sitting day, it was crowded with Members and Lobby journalists. Alex Beasley looked round quickly, mainly to see if there was anyone he wanted to avoid. "It's about as well we've never gone in for assassination," he said. "It would be pretty easy."

"That's what Guy Fawkes thought."

"And the late Mr Bellingham." The Prime Minister grinned cheerfully. "I wonder how many of these chaps would like to shoot me?" He nodded across the Lobby. "Bob Maryon, for example."

"More likely to use poison, I would say."

"He does, my dear chap. He does." As he spoke, Alex Beasley looked up at the clock at the apex of the Churchill Arch. "It's taking a bit longer than usual," he said. "The Speaker's Chaplain is obviously making the most of it. A death in the Chamber was bound to slow him down."

* * *

"Stand by, Tim, we're on the air. Caption's up, Presentation announcement now on. Stand by—coming to you in ten seconds from ... now. Ten ... nine ... take your cue from the picture ... seven ... six."

Richard Wentworth, the BBC's duty director in the control room specially built into the corner of the Star Chamber Court between Westminster Hall and the House of Commons' Chamber, waited for the Presentation announcer's out-cue. Timothy Woodman, the Parliamentary Correspondent across the way in the College Mews Studio, on the edge of Westminster Abbey precincts, took his "deaf aid" out, sniffed his nose clear, licked his lips and watched the monitor in front of his desk. As he moved, the remotely controlled camera moved with him, slowly, like a great lazy animal watching its prey. He was alone with the all-seeing eye. The Presentation caption faded out; immediately Woodman leaned forward, imparting his urgency into the single lens of the camera and began to speak. His picture came up as he began.

"The death of Mr Tom Rendle, one of the House of Commons' custodians—brutally murdered during the night in the Commons own Chamber. That, and the unexplained arrest of one of the M.P.s, Mr Austin Lombard, Member for East Birmingham, are the main talking points this afternoon in the

Commons' Chamber. At this moment"—Woodman elaborately looked at his wristwatch—"Mr Speaker's Chaplain is leading the House in daily prayers..."

Like a good professional, he felt rather than saw the cut on the transmission screen. Prayers over, Wentworth had cut to his main camera, giving a wide angle view of the Chamber in time to catch the Division Bell and the first shout of "Speaker in the Chair," "Speaker in the Chair" as it resounded round the Chamber, the Lobbies, the Library and the Committee Rooms of the House of Commons.

"Camera 3 get me the P.M., mid-shot as he comes in. He'll come from behind the Speaker's Chair... pan round with him to the front bench. Oh blast!... He's come in the other end past the Serjeant-at-Arms. Get him for me, Charlie, nice work." Wentworth made the cut to Camera 2. "Now take him along to the front bench. Lovely. Stand by, Walter. I'm coming to you again, very wide. As the Speaker stands up, I'll cut to the P.M. then you zoom in and I'll come back to you for the Speaker in close-up."

"Order. Order." The Speaker spoke quietly as he got to his feet. "As Members of the House know, I have to announce the death of one of the House's servants in especially tragic circumstances..."

"Stand by to pan right to the Bar of the House. Pan around. All except Camera 1." Richard Wentworth watched his six monitors intently waiting for reaction to show in the close-up pictures. "I want small group shots of reaction. Hold that, Roger!" He cut to Camera 4. "Very nice. Now I'm coming back to the Speaker. I'm on Camera 1. Now give me the Serjeant's Chair. That's where Tom Rendle was killed. As the Speaker mentions it, I want to cut to it. Here it comes, Roger." He cut to Camera four.

*   *   *

"Somebody's been proper busy with a scrubbing brush." Robert Maryon leaned forward in his chair and glared at the television screen. He pointed with the stem of his pipe and a thin column of smoke rose from the mouthpiece. The air in the

Lobby Correspondents' Library was already thick with smoke and very stale. "I'm disappointed," said Maryon. "What's the good of having colour television if you can't see the blood?"

The *Guardian* man sniffed expressively, looked angry, but said nothing. "Be careful, Cecil." Maryon growled a warning without taking his eyes from the screen. "Too much working on the *Guardian* hath made thee an angry old man." Cecil Bradshaw sniffed again, this time so much louder that it made him cough.

"P.M.'s up." The Lobby Correspondent of the *Mirror* looked critically at Alex Beasley in big close-up. "Very proper," he said. "Obituary expression perfect I would say, *plus* black tie. Oh, *very* proper. He thinks of everything."

"Do you think so?" Maryon was disinclined to give Beasley the credit. "I bet it was one of his secretaries."

Cecil Bradshaw got out of his chair near the doorway, strode aggressively across the room and turned the volume up with an angry twist of the knob. It was obvious that he was recalling the day, long ago, when the Lobby was peopled by gentlemen.

"Words! Just words!" Maryon shouted it almost, competing with the sound amplifier. "You notice he's not making any promises to find the murderer. Not our friend Beasley! Not on your telly!"

"And why should he, for God's sake?" The man from the Westminster Press Agency turned from the set to glare at Maryon. He had an angry flush on the part of his face not covered by beard. "Why the hell should he? He's not a policeman." He turned back to the set as Mr Speaker called the Leader of the Opposition. "Oy! Oy!" he said. "That was short and sweet. Now let's see what the boy will make of it."

The Right Honourable Eric Lockwood made quite a lot of it and even the Lobby was impressed. "That's silenced 'em," said the man from *The Times*. He sounded delighted.

"Something has, certainly." The *Mirror* looked hard as Richard Wentworth cut to a wide angle picture, panning around the Chamber past a sea of grave, silent faces, sober, reflective and almost numbed.

"That was rather clever, you've got to admit it." Cecil Bradshaw started making a note or two. "Not a word of criticism of the Government. Not one word and yet the whole bloody issue's been delivered at Beasley's feet like a sack of potatoes, and unwashed at that."

Robert Maryon had a glint of malicious pleasure in his eyes as he watched the screen. "I'd like to see how Beasley's reacting; why the devil doesn't the ... ah!" As he spoke, Richard Wentworth in the Television Control Gallery cut to a mid-shot of the Prime Minister with a serious-faced crony or two beside him. "That's got him worried," said Maryon. "I haven't seen *that* for a very long time. Beasley's making notes! I'd give a lot to see what he's written. He's probably decided to give Lockwood beta double plus for content and performance."

"That's that, then." The *Times* man turned away from the television screen. "They're going straight on to Questions." He stood up and made for the door. "A cup of tea, Cecil? There'll be nothing doing until the Private Notice on Lombard. We've a good half an hour. *Two* cups of tea."

Robert Maryon was still concentrating on the screen. "What's he up to now?" he breathed it.

"He's talking to the Clerk. Why the hell shouldn't he?" Cecil Bradshaw was still irritable.

"No reason, Cecil my old cock. Except that Prime Ministers don't often have a chat with the Clerk. Not at the Table anyway, as you flaming well know. Point one. Point two, they're talking about poor old Tom Rendle."

"How do you know that? Going in for lip reading?"

"Don't be stupid, Cecil, and use your loaf." Maryon spoke very slowly as though puzzled. "Something peculiar's happening. They're arguing about something written in that file he had open at the Despatch Box."

"And why not for goodness sake! Notes about Rendle's career, about the work of the custodians, about the ..." Bradshaw had started waving his right arm about in an expansive gesture of mock oratory. He looked angry when Maryon interrupted him, and his arm came down slowly.

"Stuff it," said Maryon. He jerked his head towards the screen. "The Clerk's leaving the Chamber with him. Explain that." His nose almost literally twitched with frustrated curiosity, then he turned back to look at Bradshaw. "Who got Rendle his job here? Do you know that? Olsen did. Sir William Olsen, the Clerk himself. Something's cooking." He got up slowly. The *Times* man seemed to have forgotten his cup of tea.

*   *   *

The Clerk sipped his cup of tea in the Prime Minister's room off the Corridor behind the Speaker's Chair. It was, he was ready to admit, a nice room; the tea however was less nice. He shuddered delicately, put his cup down, smiled courteously and said "We are, I suppose, rather rare these days, Prime Minister."

Alex Beasley grinned cheerfully, but said nothing.

"Indeed," Sir William went on, "I am the only one." He blushed delicately at the phrase, with its overtones of immodesty. "Nowadays Classicals are rare. We always seem to go in for PPE men." He picked his cup up again to cover his confusion and it rattled a bit on the saucer. Then he became more brisk. "Why do you think Lombard put it in Latin?"

"Because he didn't want the Greek police to understand it if it fell into their hands." Beasley explained how the coded message had been hidden and Olsen laughed a dry academic laugh. "The Classics help," he said. "Throughout the whole of Classical literature there have always been policemen with big hands." He paused a second. "And always secret messages being put down bosoms." He went pink again; this time with recollected experience from a dimly lit past. "May I see it, please?" He coughed a little cough. "The message I mean, of course, not the bosom."

"But of course." The Prime Minister handed him the copy of Austin Lombard's message. "Lombard's a good classical scholar?" He put it as a question.

"Certainly," Olsen nodded vigorously. "A very good one. Craven Scholar."

"The year after you, I understand."

"Two years," Olsen looked up from the piece of paper. "His was a very good year, I'm told." He tapped the sheet of paper. "KALDEC is the clue I suppose?"

"That and NOE."

"NOE? That's certainly Latin. It's Latin for Noah." Olsen raised an enquiring eyebrow.

Beasley nodded. "Noah. That's right. It's the code word we use for a very important military operation."

"I see. And KALDEC is of course *Kalendus decembres*. The first of December."

Alex Beasley nodded again. "So far I'm with you." Now the rest. By the way, the date, the first of December is very relevant and important also. I discovered that two hours ago."

"Good." Olsen began to look as excited as his character, his office and his training would allow. It almost began to show as a warm glow. He appeared to have forgotten his tea. It was as good a way as any to avoid drinking it.

"ARMEN is not, I imagine, a mis-spelling for 'Amen'." He glanced at the Prime Minister. "No. I thought not. In that case it's an abbreviation. There's no Latin word *Armen*. Oh!" He jumped as the penny dropped. "It's Armenia in eastern Turkey."

"That fits also." Beasley looked reasonably modest. "I'd got as far as that myself but 'Admin' and 'Divlist'... ?" He shrugged his shoulders even more modestly.

"ADMIN." Sir William Olsen shook his head slowly. "I suppose this is copied exactly. Spacing, I mean?"

"I imagine so. It was scribbled very roughly. Lombard hadn't much time." Beasley leaned forward. "What are you suggesting?"

"IN. It could be a preposition, of course. IN ARMENIA. That would make sense." The Clerk sounded confident then he groaned slightly and the light of his enthusiasm went out. "No! ADM." He pronounced it as a contraction of ADAM. Then he brightened. "Adam. That's Turkish for a man. 'A man in Armenia'."

"Could be." The Prime Minister sounded lukewarm. He pushed his hand through his thick greying hair leaving it a bit like a haystack in a wind. "Could be. But I doubt whether Lombard would bother..." He sighed.

"ADM." Olsen spaced the letters out. "Madam," he said. He had a distant seeking look on his face as though he was hunting through a dead alphabet for long forgotten words.

"It's over there." Alex Beasley pointed across the room. "A dictionary. I had it brought from the Library."

"Mr Lewis and Mr Short!" The Clerk lost forty years as he murmured the names. He almost trotted over to the side-table, as though going to meet an old friend. His hand was reaching out when a strange noise behind him made him stop, transfixed. For a moment he felt like Lady Macbeth holding her hand out for a dagger.

It was the Prime Minister who had uttered a wail of anguish. He was pressing the buzzer on his desk and shouting loudly for his principal Private Secretary. He stopped shouting as Rawnsley and two policemen burst into the room. "Oh!" he said to the policemen. He looked faintly foolish. "False alarm," he said. "I pressed the wrong button." He waved the policemen out of the room and turned to Malcolm Rawnsley. "Get Desmond Bassington," he said. "As quick as you can. It's ADM," he said. "In Armenia. Sir William got it."

"Good Lord." Rawnsley stepped quickly to the scrambler telephone. "Good Lord. ADM in Armenia." It sounded like a kind of crazy password. Sir William Olsen touched the dictionary as though it were a talisman of normality.

Quite suddenly he noticed the silence in the room, and he turned round. Alex Beasley was sitting at his desk staring out into space and absolutely motionless. His heavy face was drawn and grey, as though sagging under the weight of his thoughts. The silence seemed to last for several minutes, until Olsen noticed that he was holding his breath. He let it out with a gusty noise which seemed to bring Beasley back to reality. He looked across his desk at the Clerk. "Thanks, Sir William," he said. He grimaced. "Thanks for the bad news."

Olsen looked inclined to ask him not to mention it. Then his curiosity peeped through. He raised one eyebrow hopefully.

"Atomic Demolition Munitions." The Prime Minister seemed to realise suddenly that an explanation was due. "Atomic Mines we call them. Land mines remotely controlled and fitted with atomic warheads. ADM is the American name for them."

"In Armenia, of course."

"Yes." The Prime Minister looked troubled. "Damned things. This is big trouble."

Olsen walked over to the door. "I'll take the dictionary back," he said.

"I'll be very grateful." Beasley's voice was flat and sombre. "Give a thought to the other thing, please. 'DIVLIST'. It sounds more parliamentary. More in your line than timebombs or remote-controlled atomic mines."

Sir William Olsen, who had seen a succession of Prime Ministers handling—with more or less success—Parliamentary timebombs, nodded. "Much more in my line," he said. As he spoke he had to jump smartly to one side. The Minister of Defence Technology burst into the room and brushed past him. "This is trouble," he was saying. "Noah and ADM." No one noticed as Olsen closed the door behind him.

* * *

"Where's she bound for? Did anybody ever say? Does anybody know?" The Duty Officer stood at the window with his back to the Operations Room, on the Gravesend foreshore, and stared out over the river towards Tilbury. "Fog's coming down again," he said. "That might help." Lights were glowing like dark yellow lanterns among the derricks on the far shore nearly a mile away. "Depends which way she's going, of course. She might be sailing out of it."

He turned round, pushed his peaked cap half an inch further off his forehead and looked down at Tom Slaughter on a low chair beside the chart-table. "Do they ever tell you chaps anything?"

Tom Slaughter looked glum. He shook his head sadly, and said nothing. Then his knobbly red face brightened a bit. "Under her name, at the back . . ."

"Stern," said the Duty Officer.

Slaughter refused to be drawn into ship talk. "At the back, it says Odessa."

"Sure. That's where she's registered. We knew that. It's in Lloyds Register." The Duty Officer nodded across the room at an enormous black-bound book on a special table. Slaughter had a quick impression that it was a kind of professional altar, but the flowers were missing.

"Oh, that," he said and the Duty Officer's face darkened. He seemed likely to growl if pushed any further. "That's probably where she's bound." Slaughter felt silly saying it. "That's probably where she's going," he added with a shade of defiance.

"Oh yes?" The Duty Officer sounded rude in a polite sort of way. "Where were you born?" he asked.

"Halifax."

"When are you going back? Just because your birth's registered there it doesn't follow that . . ." He left it in the air.

"Oh." Slaughter smiled a thin smile. "I get you." He turned away from an unprofitable conversation and stared at the telephone on the Duty Officer's desk. He gave the impression he would like to give it a cuff. "Conference," he muttered. "Pierce said they were going into Conference!" He gave his head a little jerk of disgust and uttered a single grunt of disbelief. "I'm hungry," he added, and his stomach moaned.

The Duty Officer looked at his wristwatch. "There's a Joe Lyons up the road. They're still open. They make jolly good steak puddings."

Slaughter's stomach started cheering at the sound of the words, but he shook his head. "I bet the bastards have forgotten me, but Malplaquet said he'd ring me here. I'd better be around if he does." He settled back in his chair.

"Tongue!" It was the Duty Officer's Assistant who spoke. It sounded as though he was offering Slaughter an alternative diet, and Slaughter's eyes glowed. But not for long. The Assistant was on a different tack. He looked up from the chart of the Thames Estuary and tapped it lightly with the pair of dividers in his left hand. "She's just approaching the Tongue Lightship," he said. "That is, if they're still belting her along at twelve and a half knots. Alternatively, if she's turned north, she's just off Knock John."

In spite of his troubles Slaughter looked impressed. He got up and stood beside the Assistant Duty Officer, peering at the chart on the sloping table. "There." The Assistant pointed with his pencil. "According to Trinity House she was sighted by the coastguards at Eastchurch as she approached Oaze deep. Then they lost her. She could either turn north-east-by-east past the Mouse to Barrow and Knock John or she could carry on past Shivering Sands to Tongue."

"It seems a bit congested." Slaughter looked hopeful. "All these buoys and lights. With a bit of luck she might hit something. Hoy!" He poked his finger suddenly at the chart and the Duty Officer uttered a mild shout of dismay. Slaughter disregarded the noise and poked again. "There's an aerodrome," he said. "Look. Leysdown aerodrome in Sheppey. They could bomb her."

"Sure. They're still in territorial waters. We *always* bomb ships in territorial waters." The Duty Officer made a ridiculous dive-bombing operation with his right hand and buzzed like a horsefly.

"What makes you think they have any bombs?" His Assistant looked blandly innocent. "Or aeroplanes," he went on, warming up a bit. "Or pilots?"

The Duty Officer stopped buzzing to laugh—for a very short time—at his assistant's wit. Then he stopped laughing and started buzzing again.

Tom Slaughter shook his head and his face was red with anger. He turned and walked over to the observation window. Outside, two storeys below them, life was proceeding with leisurely normality. Close inshore a tug was moving past the Royal Terrace Pier and the captain was shouting cheerfully from his bridge at a girl from the Harbour Master's office. A seaman up forward started laughing until he almost choked and the captain looked modestly pleased at the effect of his wit.

Slaughter spoke over his shoulder. "The trouble is," he said, "you chaps," he waved his arms to encompass the whole port of Gravesend, "don't know Enver and Brook." Something (and not only the anger) in his voice silenced the Duty Officer. "We *ought* to be bombing them," said Slaughter, "but I don't suppose we shall. They're trouble, big trouble. And there's another thing." He turned and glared at the Duty Officer. "They've got George Lemon." He walked slowly over to the desk in the middle of the room. No one spoke for half a minute and all three jumped when the telephone began to ring.

90

Slaughter got to it first. He listened for three seconds before handing it over to the Duty Officer. "It's the Ops Room at Trinity House." He turned away and went back to his chair. "I bet they've lost her for good," he grumbled.

The Duty Officer's face was grim and unsmiling. He made a short growling noise as he scribbled on the report pad. "I'll read it back," he said and glanced at Slaughter before he began.

Message from Tongue Lightship received 1507. Ship Olga *hove to at 1453 two cables south of Tongue. No message transmitted. Boat lowered on port side and abandoned. Olga now proceeding full speed on course 108° E × S ½ S. Man in boat apparently ill or dead. Am investigating forthwith and will report. Message ends.*

The Duty Officer acknowledged receipt and put the receiver down. "I see what you mean," he said but Slaughter did not speak.

*   *   *

The Secretary of State for External Affairs tapped on the Prime Minister's door, opened it, stepped inside, closed the door, put his back to it and swore for nearly a minute.

Alex Beasley waited with mounting impatience. "How does that help?" he asked. "For goodness sake!"

"It helps me!" William Empery wiped his long face with his handkerchief. His hair, which he wore too long, was in great disorder. "You ought to have been there," he said.

"I was," said Beasley, "in spirit. I take it they gave you a rough time."

Empery nodded and walked over to the window. "The whole bloody House went for me. Both sides. Legge, Franks, Poston *and* Bligh. Apparently they're close friends, Bligh and Lombard." He turned round. "Did you know?"

"I think I did. You managed to stall, I hope!"

"Of course. But Bligh warned me he's going for my guts." William Empery grinned a rueful little grin. "Not that I find anything new in that. People are always going for my guts." The long lines from his nostrils to his mouth made him look more and more like a disillusioned basset-hound but less cheerful. "I always thought Bligh was a gentleman though."

"He is." Alex Beasley looked angry for a moment. "If Hubert Bligh went for you, he had good reason. You must have said something pretty hard to upset him." He wagged his hand to silence Empery who had started gobbling with indignation. "I've known Hubert Bligh for twenty years. We've always glared at each other across the House and sometimes we've said rough things about each other—but I'd trust him further than I would most people."

"Including me, I suppose?"

"Don't press me, William." The Prime Minister showed signs of beginning to blush. "Anyway, you'd better get used to Bligh. I've sent for him."

"Who?"

"Bligh. Sir Hubert himself. *And* the Chief Whip."

"Ours?" Empery was getting sour.

"Ours." Alex Beasley did not rise. "*And* Desmond Bassington. *And* the Secretary of the Inter-Parliamentary Union. He's called Steed." He looked up at the clock. "They're due at four o'clock, in five minutes."

"And why all this? Why Steed?"

"I've had an idea." Alex Beasley leaned back in his chair. "What's the date, William?"

"The sixteenth. Why?"

"That gives us two weeks and one day before the first of December KALDEC. We're going to need some pretty unconventional help. And Steed's part of it. He doesn't know it yet. He won't know what's hit him."

*   *   *

"He's in a mess." The cox'n of the Trinity House launch from the lightship peered through the swirling grey mist. "I reckon he's had it. He looks dead to me."

"He's bleeding. He can't be dead." The seaman up forrard held his twelve-foot boat-hook at the ready. "But he's in a bad way."

"Right. We'll take him in tow. Stand by to go round to port

and we'll come up alongside him. Get into the boat, Dusty, and try not to rock it. We'll need a cradle to get him out. As soon as you pass us the painter, see what you can do to stop the bleeding." The cox'n steadied the launch, dropped the revs and crawled, crabwise on the tide to come alongside the *Olga*'s small boat.

"It must have been a nasty accident," Dusty muttered it as he prepared to slide into the boat. "Poor sod," he said. "He'll be lucky to live."

George Lemon lay motionless in the bottom of the boat. Blood was oozing stickily from a gash in his neck below the angle of his jaw. "He'll be lucky." Dusty Miller muttered it again. He slid so carefully into the boat that no one heard the scrape of his seaboots on the bare wood of the thwarts.

"Bloody good, Dusty. Stand by; we're moving off." The cox'n slipped the engine into gear and slowly pressed the launch through the water in a big circle. Three hundred yards away, the Tongue Lightship, at anchor in the fairway, looked tiny and her flashing beacon glowed with a dull yellow light through the mist.

They were within twenty yards of the lightship, moving sweetly through the water, swaying gently on the ground swell, when George Lemon actually died.

* * *

At that moment, Sidney Firth, had been dead for almost exactly twelve hours.

"We thought he'd gone home early. We never thought..." The manager of the underground car park looked down at Sidney Firth's body covered with a car rug of incongruously bright tartan wool. He shuddered and his face was pale.

"Why? Did he often go home early?" Detective Superintendent Macaulay asked the question casually. He was looking through the wide glass walls of the office to the parking shed beyond, with its slim pillars of painted concrete. There was a strong smell of stale exhaust fumes, and a gas fire was blobbing in the corner. A very tall man, Macaulay had a feeling that the low ceiling was bearing down on him.

"Never. He was a good man." The manager hesitated. "He always did the night-shift. He said he preferred it that way. Gave him time to think, he said." The manager dragged his eyes away from Sid Firth's boot which was sticking rigidly out of the blanket.

"What made you find him? Looking for him?"

"No. Why should we? I tell you, we thought he'd gone home. We found him by chance."

"O.K., O.K." Macaulay found himself getting irritable, as he often did these days. He grumbled to himself as he walked away from the manager's desk and stepped out of the office. He glanced left up the ramp that led to College Mews and the crazy political world of Westminster. "Ambulance here," he said. He turned to the Sergeant who had come up beside him. "Get him away," he said. "And get me a report by five o'clock." The Sergeant was on the point of saying it was impossible when he noticed Macaulay's expression. He said nothing.

Macaulay turned about and wandered into the main parking area. A couple of dozen cars were dotted about on the painted grid. The manager came up behind him and spoke with diffidence and a kind of desperation. "We're usually pretty full by this time of the afternoon. Especially when Parliament's sitting. We get a lot of visitors. But we're having to turn them away, of course..."

Macaulay disregarded the manager's nervous prattle, and walked round to the right towards the exit door marked *Pedestrians*. "That's kept open all the time?"

"Naturally." The manager showed a little burst of spirit. "Customers. You can't keep customers out, can you?"

"Or murderers apparently. What's through there?"

"Lavatories and the staff wash-rooms."

"Anything stolen?"

"No. Nothing. There's nothing to steal. Mops, a bucket or two..."

"O.K., O.K." Macaulay was unfriendly. "And why the cages?" He waved his arm to the right. Five of the parking bays along the righthand wall were enclosed in grilles of expanded aluminium on heavy wooden frames.

"Lock-ups," said the manager. "Special customers. They're sliding doors that can be locked." He pointed to an old but well-kept Bentley tourer standing diagonally across the parking grid as though pushed or driven there in a hurry. There was blood on one of its tyres. "That's usually in the first bay." He pointed. "We found Sid underneath it. He'd been pushed there after he'd had his head knocked in." The manager showed signs of being sick again. "We saw the wrench first. It was sticking out by the front wheel against the wall. A big Mole wrench with blood on it. The police sergeant took it."

"Of course he did." Macaulay watched without curiosity as the men from the Cannon Row murder squad went about their work, down on their hands and knees in the lock-up parking bay. One of them was poking about with a pen-knife blade in a patch of sticky black oil. "It's bloody cold." Macaulay stamped his feet and the noise echoed round the concrete walls. "The murderer'd be wearing gloves if he had any sense." He turned back to the manager. "Make sure your men co-operate," he said.

The manager nodded. "Of course I will. It's nasty." His eyes behind his thick glasses were miserable and afraid.

"It always *is* nasty." Macaulay watched him walk slowly and reluctantly back to his office as though dreading to find Sid Firth still there on the floor beneath his tartan blanket, cold and stiff, and with one foot sticking out at an incongruous angle.

"Nasty." Macaulay muttered it to himself as he pulled the heavy wooden doors open. The air outside was damp and cold but he breathed it gratefully as he climbed the stone steps and surfaced on Abingdon Street Green. "Stinks," he said to the world around him. "You always have stinks," and he pulled a face at the abomination of his job. The polished bronze voluptuous shapes of Henry Moore's sculpture on the Green did nothing to cheer him up and the sight of the Houses of Parliament across the road made him scowl with anger and frustration. He measured the distance in his mind. Two hundred feet from the Houses of Parliament to the car park. Two men killed within hours—maybe within minutes of each other—and less than a hundred yards apart. Killed, moreover, in the same way, by a heavy crunch on the head, one from a steel wrench and the other from a silver-gilt Mace. There surely must be some connection. The difficulty was how to prove it; and having proved it, how to nail the man (or men) who did it.

He felt at a loss where to turn. He looked up at Big Ben towering up beyond the petrified forest of pinnacles on the phoney Gothic Palace, and noted the time with a grunt of anger. A quarter past four on a grim November day. If he followed routine, and indeed logic, he would descend on the Houses of Parliament with his squad of highly trained detectives and start from scratch again. Questions here, questions there. *What time did you leave the House last night? Did you go down into the car park across the way? Did you see anyone leave the building during the night or very early morning?* Brushing propriety to the side and privilege to the winds. That would be the normal thing to do in any normal place. But this wasn't a normal place. It was out of bounds. He laughed a scoffing laugh and a young woman walking briskly past him shied away with a faint squeak of surprise and fear. Macaulay raised his hat in apology and went pink. He stopped, turned his back on the Houses of Parliament, and leaned over the railings beside the Jewel Tower, the sad remains of the Medieval Palace of Westminster. He lit his pipe slowly and then flicked the spent match quite deliberately into the dark water of the moat. It brought one of the fat lazy fishes to the surface for a flicker of investigation and a single ripple moved sluggishly across the pool. "Poor stupid sucker," said Macaulay and then he grinned as he realised how well the cap fitted.

Behind him, the traffic moving westwards along Millbank and the Albert Embankment had begun to build up, and the pitch of noise was mounting like a dynamo slowly working up to full output. But he became aware of a different and separate noise over and above the hum of traffic. He turned slowly and swore. A group of about twenty men with one girl among them were pounding across the road diagonally from the St Stephen's door of the House of Commons. They were descending in a compact body on the Abingdon Street car park as though the smell of blood (literally the smell of blood) had reached them in the precincts of the Houses of Parliament.

They were the crime reporters and a handsome bloody lot at that. Macaulay felt almost sorry for them. For the past twelve hours, they had sat around uselessly in the back yards and waiting halls in and around the Houses of Parliament, totally disarmed by the heavy hand of authority, twitching and fulminating at their own powerlessness and filing meaningless nonstories to their editors. Now, having been prevented from sucking dry the story of Tom Rendle, they were on the scent of Sid Firth. He took a quick look at Big Ben; nearly four o'clock. Just time for them to get the stop press column in the later editions and make their several peaces with their news editors.

He turned his back on them, pulled his hat down over his eyebrows and stared at the Jewel Tower, trying to look like a tourist in the non-tourist season. Every one of these beauties, young and old, knew "Macaulay of the Yard" (Macaulay blushed as the phrase passed through his mind) and he knew what life would be like for the next half-hour if any one of them recognised him. He saw to it that they didn't.

He was lucky. No one saw his face as they rushed in their Gadarene and undignified way across Abingdon Street Green. He turned to watch them as they hurried away from him (as any tourist might have done, indeed) and felt sorry in turn for the manager of the car park. Maybe, if he thought quickly enough and saw the mob coming, he would be able to escape into one of the lock-up cages. Twenty-three baying hounds on one side of the grille, one car park manager at bay on the other side. Macaulay leaned on the railings and enjoyed his little piece of visual fancy. Then he snapped out of it. Not twenty-three, twenty-two! One of them, an athletic young man, who had slowed down to take up the rear position, had stopped. He waited for the whole phalanx to disappear down the slope into the car park and then he turned to the right, opened the iron gate beside the moat and hurried down to the heavy oak door let into the wall of Westminster School grounds alongside the Abbey. There was nothing on the door to identify it, but Macaulay knew it well as the Westminster radio and television studio of the BBC. *Anything to be first* he muttered. Maybe that's what it's all about. Maybe the BBC reporters had fixed the whole nasty story on their own doorstep in the interests of the goggle box! He shook his head sadly at the unbalanced state of his own mind and set off briskly for Victoria Street, his own office and sweet reality. He discovered his mistake about a week later, and by that time, nobody was putting flags out.

* * *

"I'm glad you felt you could come, Hubert. I need your help." Alex Beasley took Sir Hubert Bligh by the arm and steered him into the smaller ante-room. As though on a signal (which in fact was not needed) the two typists left the room by the far door. Neither of them spoke.

"You've got them well trained, Alex."

"Sure. As soon as I raise my left eyebrow, women always leave the room." Beasley walked over to the window and looked down into New Palace Yard. The mist was thickening into fog and the gas lamps beneath the catalpa trees made them stand out eerily, their leafless branches bending down to the flagstones as though weakened by the hand of winter. The cobblestones on the Westminster Hall side of the Yard glistened in the light from the policeman's box.

"You want my help." Sir Hubert spoke a little stiffly, and the Prime Minister turned round slowly. "I *need* it, Hubert." He too had begun speaking with a little more constraint than usual. "I need it. We're heading for trouble and I need your help." He grinned suddenly as he watched Bligh's reaction. "It's not political, Hubert. And I think you'll find nobody in your Party will object. Lockwood won't, I'm sure. You're not expected to join the Government."

Bligh grinned with relief as he sat down at one of the small tables. "Tell me more, Alex." He held a hand up. "Wait a minute, before you start I want you to know that if you've asked me to come to stop me attacking William Empery about this Austin Lombard business, you've had it and you can save your breath." His face was set as though he'd been steeling himself to make the point. "I just want to start on the right foot."

"On the contrary. It's *because* you attacked Empery that you can help us. Lombard's safety depends on whether you can join me."

"Then I'll help. But there's a hell of a lot I want to know..."

"Of course... come in, Malcolm."

Malcolm Rawnsley nodded gravely to Bligh as he stepped into the room. "Urgent, Prime Minister. And relevant." He passed a folded paper to Beasley. "They're all there next door," he said. "Steed's just arrived."

Beasley nodded absent-mindedly as he read the message. "Good God," he said. "I'll be in. Give us two minutes." As the door closed behind his Secretary, Beasley stepped across the room. "This is all part of it, Hubert." He held the paper out and waited for Bligh to put his spectacles on. "It's on the move."

There were five messages on the slip of paper, four of them typed with the curiously large typeface machines affected by all offices in the House of Commons. The fifth had been scribbled by hand. Bligh's jaw dropped as he read

> *Top Secret: Prime Minister and Need to know only.*
> 1. Submarine *Valiant* S102 and Guided Missile Destroyer *Hampshire* making rendezvous 40 miles east by south of North Foreland. E.T.A. 20.15 will contact *Olga* and intercept at first light. If *Olga* refuses signal to stop, will open fire on orders of Secretary of State for Defence. Consequences accepted.
> 2. Car Park Attendant Sidney Firth murdered in Abingdon Street Car Park 0300 today repeat 0300 today Thursday. Time established by autopsy.
> 3. Two bodies thought to be Germans Enver and Brook picked up on sandbank two miles down river from Gravesend. Not identifiable badly disfigured. Certainly not long dead. Metropolitan Police River Division request instructions.
> 4. George Lemon, MI5 investigator C 613 recovered dead from small boat abandoned by M/V *Olga*, see (1) above. Trinity House request instructions.
> 5. H.M. Ambassador in Athens reports Austin Lombard M.P. taken to secret destination and incommunicado.

Recommends protest in strongest possible terms. Requests further instructions.

Bligh passed the paper back to the Prime Minister. "A lot of it's meaningless but count me in. I don't know that I relish this gunboat and sub stuff. And I don't know what *Olga*'s up to." He tapped the paper with the back of three fingers. "Three dead men"—he made a quick count—"four dead men..."

"... and one this morning in the Chamber..."

"O.K., five dead men. Obviously something pretty unpleasant's going on, and if I can help, I will. But the most important thing from my point of view is this business of Austin Lombard." He paused. "He's a very good friend, you know. I don't want him making the score up to six."

"I understand. Let's join the meeting and I'll fill some details in." Beasley walked over to the door and held it open for Bligh. "We have to bring pressure on Steed," he said as Bligh stepped past him. "I want him to send you to Ankara—and points east—*without my knowledge*."

* * *

"Scrofula," said the younger man, making conversation as though on a casual encounter. His eyes took in the marvellous proportions of the Banqueting Hall. "The King's Evil," he went on. "A tubercular swelling of the neck and throat." He shuddered delicately and leaned back in the deep leather chair. "It puts this place into proper perspective. However beautiful it may be, and of course, it is. By far the most beautiful room in London. In England, perhaps." He looked old and wise, a man of the world and saddened by its absurd incongruities, as he raised his arm and pointed to the superb ceiling fifty feet above them. "That fat woman, for example..." He hesitated and glanced towards the window that looked out on to Whitehall and the Horseguards Parade beyond. He frowned with exasperation as he saw the uniformed attendant was still within earshot and walking slowly towards their end of the room. "She's called Abundance, on account, one assumes, of her bosom."

"Big," said the other man. He took his hat off and balanced it on his knee as though making an act of salutation. His pate, revealed, was large and shiny and fringed with an abundant fuzz of white hair like candyfloss. His tone was encouragingly conversational as though he, too, knew the attendant could hear every word that was spoken.

"But beautiful," the younger man went on, "if you like that kind of thing. She's been there about three hundred and fifty years. Looking just like that. Smug, self-satisfied and busty." He spoke the last word a little louder to test the attendant's reactions and groaned a quiet curse as he saw the man's head turn towards them, his pale face coming to life with a flicker of curiosity. "And for a century and a half all she saw was a weekly procession of miserable, scrofulous, pustular peasants stretching their swollen necks out for the King of England to stroke them back to health." He bared his teeth with disgust. "Imagine those dirty necks," he said. He looked slowly round the very beautiful room. "This is where it all happened," he said. He seemed to have forgotten the attendant. "Or their dirty feet. My God. Just think of their dirty feet." He paused. "Once a year the King washed them. In this Hall. Here. A whole bloody row of dirty feet!"

"So they chopped his head off." The older man, too, seemed for a moment to have forgotten their charade of casual encounter. "Chopped his head off." He repeated it with a sibilant hatred, and started as the attendant spoke loudly into his ear.

"Don't forget to look at King Charles's Window, gentlemen." He had shuffled up silently on the polished pinewood floor and was pointing vaguely towards the far end of the Banqueting Hall. "That's where they built the scaffold for his execution." His voice trailed off with embarrassment, as though he had helped in the building and had had plenty of time since to think better of it.

The two visitors, the only ones in the whole of the large Hall, grunted without enthusiasm, offended by his interruption. The attendant's face dropped and there was a long silence as he walked away discouraged, to take up his post again beside The Window. He was muttering it seemed, or chewing his tongue as he reverted to his state of sad apathy.

The two visitors watched him go and waited for him to reach

the far end of the room, a full hundred feet away. Then the younger man spoke first. "Blast the man," he said. "You got the packet off?"

"Of course I did." The older man waved his arm vaguely towards Trafalgar Square a quarter of a mile up Whitehall. "All night post-office." He smiled a sour smile. "You've got to admit, they make it easy."

"Good." The other hesitated. "They went into a panic, you know."

"Who did?" The older man almost barked it.

"E. and B. They reported to . . ."

"Careful. No names please." The hat, carefully balanced on his knee fell to the floor and he muttered as he bent down to pick it up. "No names."

"They reported it on the phone to C . . . and they saw the light go on again. I had to put it on again."

"Good Lord, it was you."

"Of course. I'd had to hit Rendle. Rendle was on to me. Us. Once I'd done that I needed to cause a diversion."

The older man scrubbed his hair in agitation. "That's a different matter," he said. "I thought it went according to plan. But if E. and B. panicked." His eyes opened wide as the thought struck home. "Where are they now?"

"They made for the *Olga*. At least that's what they said as they left the car park."

"I wouldn't like to be in their shoes." The older man went silent for a moment, as though contemplating the ultimate in vengeance that would surely strike them. "I suppose I'd better go. Give me a few minutes to get away. I'll ring you if I need to see you again."

"Where?"

The older man went into a reverie. "First it was the Tower; then Apsley House. Next time we'll make it Unity House. I confess I haven't seen the Epstein yet." He smiled meanly. "We can meet accidentally looking at it and contemplating the dignity of labour. Then after that Lancaster House, and, on the 30th, in the crypt of All Hallows." He stood up to leave. "They don't know what's happening, I hope?"

"Why should they?"

"The Prime Minister didn't turn up at the lunch. Instead, we got that bloody old fool Shawthorne." He pronounced it, inaccurately, as two words, splitting the 'th' into its components.

"I don't think that means they know anything. As far as they're concerned, they've just got two nasty murders on their hands."

"*Two*! Why two?"

"The car park man was awkward. He wanted to know why E. and B. wouldn't pay him. They said they weren't staying. He took their number. So I had to deal with him." His wide face got wider with pleasure.

"That could turn out to be a bit of luck. Keep their mind off the real thing." The older man got up to go. "It's a *very* beautiful room," he said loudly. And then, more quietly, "I'm looking forward to dining here. And that will be the day."

* * *

"Not an eye remained open to weep for the dead." Alex Beasley was careful to avoid anything like a quotation voice as he said it slowly, quietly, flatly; and its very flatness made it sound all the more revolting and horrible. Gilbert Dace, the Chief Whip, a little firebrand of a man, not given, one would have thought, to excessive delicacy, was seen to shudder and the Prime Minister nodded in agreement. "They're terrible words." He looked across the room at Bernard Steed, "I've got to start a long, long way back," he said, "because I want to convince you..." He left the details unspoken as he walked over to the long table in the middle of the room. "I want you all to look at this map."

"Impressive." Coming up behind, Hubert Bligh spoke for most of them, though not for Desmond Bassington who was managing to give the impression that he'd made the map himself in the odd moments between his other duties at the Ministry of Defence Technology. He nodded with a judicious air of responsibility. William Empery had assumed the mantle of the old Foreign Office superiority. If there weren't any Foreign Affairs there would be no need of military maps, and his eyebrows said so.

"Turkey," said Beasley disregarding them both. "There's quite a lot of it." He stood looking down at the table, on which were spread the fifteen sheets of GSGS 4830, the military map of Turkey with parts of Soviet Transcaucasia, Persia and Syria, published in London in the nineteen-sixties by the War Office and the Air Ministry. The Prime Minister's table, twenty feet long and six feet wide, was almost totally covered by a glowing spread of bright yellow, orange and brown, ringed by contrasting blue representing the Black Sea, the Aegean and the Mediterranean.

"That's a lot of mountains." Bernard Steed spoke for the first time. He was a little bristling man with a good deal of pomposity in his voice and his manner.

"It's an extremely mountainous country." Beasley tapped the paper appreciatively as though giving it full marks for being the right shape and colour. "The whole central plateau of Turkey," he said, "is higher than the Alpine passes."

"And cold." Gilbert Dace shuddered again, but this time for a different reason.

"Much of the year, *very* cold. Right now—" Beasley turned and looked hard at Hubert Bligh, "right now it is very, very cold indeed." He edged along the table to lean over the Trabzon sheet at the top north-east corner of the map. "Especially here," he said. Again he tapped the map and the paper rattled like the skin of a kettle drum. "Batum, the Soviet port on the Black Sea." He slid his finger along the dotted line of the Soviet-Turkish border south east across the Trans-Caucasian range, tapping the peaks as his finger passed them. "Twelve thousand feet," he said, "another here, fifteen thousand"—five quick taps—"all these over ten thousand. And down here," he paused as though about to produce something rather special out of a bag, "Mount Ararat, seventeen thousand feet. Ararat's in Turkey. And across the frontier on the Russian side there's Alagos, over thirteen thousand feet."

The External Secretary began to fidget to show that all this was beginner's stuff, and Desmond Bassington had withdrawn (for much the same reason) and was lighting his pipe with great sucking noises at the other end of the table, two or three feet north of Istanbul. The Chief Whip glared at him and then returned to the Caucasus where the Prime Minister was labouring his point a little for Hubert Bligh's benefit. "Absolutely impossible," he was saying, "absolutely impossible as military terrain. A two hundred and fifty mile border with Soviet Russia, over which you'd have great difficulty driving a donkey." He paused for dramatic effect and William Empery sighed a quiet sigh, changing it into a cough as Beasley caught his eye. "Except for this." Alex Beasley spanned an octave with one hand on the high Anatolian plain east of Kars. "The Kars Gap," he said "and we're back where we began. *Not an eye remained open to weep for the dead.*' It's a quotation from a Turkish manuscript of the thirteenth century. It's about Ghengis Khan and what his armies did to the people of Kars and the whole of Armenia. They all came through here. First the Seljuks, then the Golden Horde, and Tamburlaine the Great." As he recited his catalogue he swept his hand through the Kars Gap from east to west, his fist clenched and his fingers white at the knuckles. "Then the Russians." Again his fist went through the Gap. "Four times in the last century and a half. So Turkey decided to join NATO, and the Kars Gap became the Western Powers' frontier—militarily speaking—with Russia proper. There's another NATO frontier with Russia in the north of Norway, west of Murmansk, but this is by far the more vital. The Kars Gap is *our* frontier with Russia."

Hubert Bligh grunted. "I think they're wrong," he said. "Quite wrong."

"Who are wrong?"

"The Turks." Bligh began to look uncomfortable and angry at the same time. "You said there were no politics involved in all this, Alex."

"I said there were no *Party* politics involved. And there aren't. I happen to think the Turks are wrong too. But I live in London. And London's nearly three thousand miles west of the Kars Gap. You can see their point surely?"

Bligh nodded without enthusiasm. "And where do I come in? I've got to persuade them to love the Russians. Is that the idea?"

"Certainly not." Beasley shook his head violently. It made his shock of hair even more untidy. "For one thing it's impossible. Can I take the thing further?" He waited for a reluctant nod before he went on. Again he turned back to the map, stabbing it with one finger. "Somewhere along here," he said, "and I certainly don't propose to say exactly where, there are ADMs buried in the mountain sides. Atomic Demolition Munitions. Atomic mines. This"—he swept the area with the flat of his hand—"this is a vast minefield full of atomic war-heads."

"Christ Almighty," said Bligh, and Steed blinked several times in horror. "No!" he said inadequately. He nearly added that he didn't believe it; then he noticed Beasley's eyes. He did believe it.

"The Russians know it." Alex Beasley looked up from the map and his face was very grim indeed. "And what is more, everybody who matters east of this point knows it. Persians, Afghans., Tibetans and Chinese. Ever since Mao died, you'll admit the Turkish fears have been justified. Now, because of these mines, they're a bit more secure. The whole area," he slapped the table hard and the sound rang round the room like an explosion, "is mined and ready to go up at the touch of a lever. And don't ask me where that lever is."

"Kars would go up as well, of course, if they all went off." The Chief Whip almost whispered it.

"Sure." The Prime Minister shrugged his shoulders. "That's how they want it."

Bligh was still looking mystified. "You still haven't said where I come in."

"You come in here." He touched the map. "In Erzurum. And, of course, Ankara." Alex Beasley turned to Bernard Steed. "With your help. Not mine. Erzurum's a hundred and twenty miles this side of Kars. On the Anatolian plain. And I think *someone* ought to get to know the new Ataturk Technical University there. And who better than you, Hubert?" The Prime Minister's eyes slid to watch Steed's reaction. "I think there ought to be a Parliamentary Mission to Ankara. *Arranged independently of the Government* by our friends in the Inter-Parliamentary Union."

"Ah!" Bernard Steed suddenly saw all. A look of enthusiastic obstinacy rose into his eyes and he looked extremely pompous. "I don't think it's on, Prime Minister. I'm afraid the IPU Council would never agree. As you know, they're very jealous of their independence. They're flat against dictation, by anybody. And if I might say so . . ."

". . . especially against dictation by the Government." Beasley finished the sentence for him. "In that case I'll expect you to persuade them. And if it will help, I'll tell you the rest of it." He waved them over to a small table against the window and pressed a bell-push. "The photograph please, Malcolm." He called it out before his Secretary's head appeared in the doorway. He turned and looked hard at Steed. "We have until the first of December," he said as he sat down beside him. "It's not a lot of time."

"Indeed," said Steed. "It's impossible. I couldn't arrange it even if I were allowed by my Council."

Beasley seemed unperturbed. "You'll find it possible, I think . . . Ah, thank you, Malcolm. Pass one to Mr. Bligh and one here to Mr. Steed. This is your cue, Desmond."

Desmond Bassington waited until Bligh and Steed had had time to examine the photographs before he spoke.

"Operation Noah," he said and scowled at the External Secretary. "An embarrassing title."

"I think it's rather good," said Steed and William Empery warmed to him. "That's Mount Ararat surely in the distance." The fact explained all.

"And the aeroplane." Bligh seemed more at ease now. Here was something he *did* know about. He looked across the table at Bassington. "Vertical take-off. Straight-forward enough. Vertical and horizontal jets. Looks like an ordinary S26X. What's unusual about it?" He had that curious look of innocence on his face which had so often disconcerted his political opponents.

"There's nothing unusual unless you get underneath. Then!" Bassington made a pantomime gesture of astonishment. "The vertical push engines," he said, "are a blind. A pure blind. The plane never leaves the ground without going through the motions of using those jet engines. And they make a hell of a noise." He paused for fully five seconds. *But they don't mean a damn thing. The plane is entirely propelled vertically (up *or* down) by a new

107

anti-gravitational device. It will take off at great speed in almost total and utter silence."

"Good God!"

"God and Rolls-Royce between them," Alex Beasley offered. "I sometimes think you can't have one without the other. And I'm not the first Prime Minister to think that."

"It's staggering." Bligh looked across the table at Bassington. "Your people?"

"Of course. With Turkish engineers involved too. It'll make the Concorde obsolete. As you can imagine."

"Which is part of our trouble." It was Empery's turn. "Somebody's going to have to tell the French. Me I suspect."

"If they don't learn about it on the 1st December," Beasley broke in. "Now we really are down to brass tacks. Somebody is on to this. *And* on to the Atomic Mines. With a bit of luck we've got in early enough to stop them. And that's why I want Hubert Bligh as head of a totally independent mission out in Turkey. We'll look after the other places involved in Western Europe. The Euratom research depots come into it too. But we have to stay *officially* clear of Turkey."

"How much of this can I tell my Council, Prime Minister?" Bernard Steed had begun to look and talk much less pompously.

"None of it. None at all. It's out of the question."

"I thought so." Steed hesitated. "But there's one thing." He seemed a little diffident. "It's not the Kars Gap that worries me. It's the credibility gap." He looked hard at the Prime Minister. "You and I know very well that the Inter-Parliamentary Union is independent of your Government and of every other Government." He looked across at Gilbert Dace who was scowling and nodding. "The Chief Whip's expression confirms it. He's tried now and then to force his nominees on our delegation lists. And he has failed. If I say no, there's nothing you can do about it. Nothing!" He grew four inches upwards and two from back to front.

"Excellent," said the Prime Minister. "And perfectly true."

"But the Turks don't believe it. Nor do the French. Or anyone else for that matter. If Sir Hubert leads a delegation out to

Turkey, everybody in the world—if they think about it at all—will assume the British Government is behind his visit."

"Of course they will. In fact I've already checked with the Turkish Ambassador in London. And he thinks it's a splendid idea. I'm not worried about *them*. The people I've got to worry about are much nearer home than that. There's still a lot to tell you to put you in the picture." The Prime Minister's manner had suddenly become much more grave. "Five murders. Maybe more than five. The arrest of a British M.P. in Athens. The theft of the Noah documents in London. Some of these things (but not all, thank God) are known to the British press. *I*, the Prime Minister, send a high-powered group of M.P.s to Ankara and Erzurum. What do the press do?"

Steed's expression answered him. "The Lobby," he said.

"The Lobby," the Prime Minister agreed. "It's the Lobby I'm thinking about."

"I see." There was a long pause. Outside, the telephone bell was loudly summoning (and failing to bring) a taxi to the Members' entrance and a helicopter was fanning its way along the river. Across to the right, outside the Westminster Underground Station, a newsvender was shouting something about a second Westminster murder, and the fast traffic on the embankment motorway could be heard humming westward.

"How soon can Sir Hubert go?" asked Bernard Steed. He had two of his pudgy fingers crossed under the table.

II

"Battersea Power Station, the Houses of Parliament, Fortnum and Mason's, St Paul's Cathedral, two other churches (one Roman Catholic, the other bombed)..." Kaya Mersinli paused and lit another of his Yeni Harman cigarettes. He blinked across the room through the smoke and smiled disarmingly. "Your Central Office of Information have great imagination, Hubert Effendi. All this was two years ago on my first day in London. Oh," he grinned broadly, "I forgot! The London School of Economics also. Great stuff! !"

Bligh groaned gently and opened his eyes. "So you take it out of me," he said. He in turn smiled to take the edge off it. "The Grand National Assembly, the President's Residence..."

".... but of course, sir."

"... of course, the Roman Baths, the Temple of Augustus, the Ataturk Mausoleum..."

"... Naturally..."

"... Naturally. Old Ankara and the Citadel and the Hittite Museum." He waved his arm, brought his watch into line of sight and did some arithmetic which made his eyes stare foolishly for a moment or two. "All, my dear chap, in six hours and a half." He sat back and did a demonstration of exhaustion.

"But not including lunch, sir."

"Ah!" Bligh settled deeper into his chair. "Yes. There was lunch." He tapped his waistcoat (the maroon one) gently in salutation. He belched very gently and directed it courteously down his nose.

"And soon," Kaya spoke slowly, "there will be dinner." He went on without a pause. "That's why I came to speak to you, Bey Effendi."

Bligh sat up at something in his tone. "It's not dinner-time yet." His voice rose with his alarm.

"No, not yet." Kaya Mersinli seemed oddly embarrassed. "We shall call for you later. I came to tell you."

"And you want me to tell the others?"

Kaya shook his head with great sadness. "They will not feel like dinner, sir. They are too sleepy." His eyes beneath the sadness had a crafty look in them. "Mr Cott has cancelled the visit he was going to make to the Ankara Palas Casino."

Hubert Bligh leaned forward and tapped the coffee table with one rigid finger. "That, Kaya Bey, is absolutely out of the question. Everybody who travelled in the plane with us from Istanbul to Ankara knows that Richard Cott..."

"He is too sleepy. He has gone to bed. He is snoring."

"And Mrs Tronder?"

"Bed." Kaya blushed a little. "My colleague, Miss Fatma, assures me she has gone to bed." He paused. "They have *all* gone to bed. They are all very, very sleepy."

Bligh looked alarmed. "They aren't sick?" He made to get up, though what he could do about it was doubtful.

"Not sick." Kaya raised one hand. "Very sleepy." His face brightened. "They will be very fine tomorrow morning. Breakfast of cheese and olives and jam made with rose petals. I have arranged it." Then he smiled broadly. "Richard Bey will find a beautiful casino with a lovely cabaret at Izmir. The Büyük Efes Hotel is famous..."

Bligh was wide awake now. "We are *not* going to Izmir, Kaya Bey."

"*We* are not, I agree."

"What have you done to Richard Cott?" The question was spaced out in capitals.

"He is sleepy. Raki..."

"He drank less raki than I did. And Elizabeth Tronder?"

"Orange juice." The crafty look was back again.

"You doped them! My God, you doped a party of M.P.s! British M.P.s!" Bligh found his voice going up like the lark ascending. "You did," he said lamely. His voice came down again.

"It was the only way." Kaya Mersinli suddenly became brisk, as though having to admit the truth had absolved him from his embarrassment. "They will come to no harm, Bey Effendi. We assure you of that. This," he went on sternly, "is Ankara. Guests in Ankara are never harmed."

"Just doped." Bligh muttered it. He was wondering what would happen in London if a whole group of M.P.s were found to be doped. The idea began to appeal to him, so he brought the shutters down quickly. Kaya was doing some more fast talking.

"They were all asked before they went to sleep what they would like to do tomorrow. We *had* to ask them." He was insisting on some strange inverted protocol. "We gave them a real choice—to go to Izmir for the Trade Fair; to go to Zonguldak to the Black Sea coal mine..." he paused dramatically, "or to go to Erzurum to see a horse farm." Again the crafty look. "To go to the Erzurum meant travelling overnight. And it is very short notice for sleeping compartments."

"But Elizabeth Tronder *loves* horses."

"To her we say a snake farm." Kaya beamed with exuberant triumph. "Three of them go to Izmir for the Trade and the belly dancers; and the others all go to Zonguldak for the coal mines."

"I can't see Elizabeth going for the belly dancers." Bligh's voice was stern. "And I happen to know that she loathes coal mines."

"To her we say gold mines."

"You haven't got any gold mines."

Kaya Bey's shoulders came up slowly until they almost pushed his ears up. "That," he said, "is very sad."

Bligh gave it up. "Do they know where *I* am going?"

"Of course. To Erzurum to see the horses. That we told them."

"I hate horses."

"You will not see the horses, Bey Effendi."

"And we travel tonight?"

"We travel tonight. We found there *was* a sleeping car on the Orient Express after all." Kaya was beaming happily again. "Wagon-lits first class." Then he came clean. "There was one for me too," he said as he stood up. "But now we have a lot to fix." He glanced at his watch. "In about an hour's time a car will pick you up here and we shall have dinner with Major Kemal Karadeniz," he said. "One day he will be a Gold Star General."

He bowed gracefully before he left.

* * *

The car when it arrived, exactly an hour later, looked as though it ought to be wearing dark glasses. It was long, low, black, shiny, powerful and American. On it were two flags, one Turkish which was floodlit, the other a NATO composite which was not. It was standing, arrogantly well away from the kerb, and against the flow of traffic in the Ataturk Boulevard, facing south and the smart hillside suburb of Çankaya. Although it was standing motionless with its near door open, it had all its headlights on at full beam. It was not a diffident motor car.

Bligh acknowledged the salute of the driver and stepped into the vast warm cavern. He also stepped into something which, much later, in the decorous bottle-green club chair surroundings of the House of Commons' Smoking Room, would seem like a curious dream.

He smiled to himself and felt foolish as he found himself wondering what his wife, Helen, and more embarrassingly still, what his son Richard back in Dulwich, S.E.21, would think if they could see him doing the Pasha in the middle of the plain of Anatolia. Then he relaxed on the principle of rape-impossible-lie-back-and-enjoy. He laughed out loud and then changed the noise into a cough in case the driver, several feet away, thought he was transporting a dangerous nut-case and turned round to deal with him.

The driver was far too busy driving silently and fast along the middle of the well-lit boulevard. He did a smart (and in the circumstances, dangerous) eyes right as he passed the Ataturk Mausoleum, glowing with floodlights up on the hill to the right of the boulevard, and then settled down to some serious grand prix stuff. It was a cold, crisp, clear evening and the passers-by beneath the bare trees and the concrete lamp standards looked apathetic and tired, their faces little white smudges against the black of their defiantly western clothes. No one seemed to be smiling.

The boulevard curled away to the left. Bligh remembered it from earlier in the day as the road out to the President of Turkey's official residence and, alongside it, almost within screaming distance, the villa which houses the British Ambassador and his cohort of smart young men whom the Public Schools Commission seem so powerless to suppress. He found himself hoping he was not in for another of those stand round evenings with glasses of gin (the Gordon label, export variant, picked out in gold) talking about Twickers and the infamous All Blacks who weren't, when the car swung away to the right, climbed an impossible hill and stopped suddenly. As it stopped, it did a kind of curtsey on its front springs, then levelled off with a sigh. As though operated by the sigh, a wicket door opened in a concrete wall alongside the car and Kaya Mersinli came out. In one hand he held a glass of gin, in the other he was holding a pistol.

It took Bligh several minutes to get over that pistol—the fact that it turned out to be a fanciful cigarette lighter angered rather than relieved him—and as a result he missed much of what Kaya Bey was saying as they made their way into the house. He did notice, however, that the other man, over by the vast picture window, said nothing at all. He looked like a large guardian angel (dressed in a greenish-khaki) looking down over the city of Ankara deep in its protective hollow and making sure it behaved itself.

Major Kemal Karadeniz was one of those army officers who delegate everything (and conversation especially) to well selected subordinates, and Kaya was apparently saying all that needed to be said. The Major was waiting, it seemed, for a vital telephone call from Bodrum on the coast of the Aegean Sea and until he got it he was keeping quiet. He was courteous (and he smiled once) but conversation limped rather heavily for several minutes. Bligh, a member of a society which exists only by, through, with and from talk, found it unusual and, he was forced to admit, rather restful. And then the telephone rang and the Major took command. From that moment on, whenever the Major moved, Bligh had a feeling of air rushing past him in a hurry. Three strides he was at the telephone, in two seconds he had growled some Turkish words into it. Ten seconds later he said some more Turkish words (more resonant these were), put the receiver down without appearing to take aim, slapped his hands together and said "O.K. Operation completed. We go."

For the next few days Bligh had a feeling he was moving pretty helplessly in somebody else's slipstream.

* * *

Two thousand miles away, in the middle of Amsterdam, Marcus Pierce realised he was on to something though, regretfully, he didn't know what. He picked up the telephone and booked a call to Malplaquet's office in Whitehall. With a bit of luck (if that was what he meant) Malplaquet would still be there. But he did it with extreme reluctance because he knew Malplaquet was going to make a bit of a nuisance of himself.

"Ten minutes delay, I'm afraid." The switchboard girl spoke English in the best Roedean manner, so Pierce exercised his little bit of linguistic protest. *"Dank,"* he said fluently and put the receiver down. He then stared at it. Since he was in Room 352 at the Grand Hotel Krasnapolsky (and since there was no other telephone in the room), it was, presumably, the beginner and begetter of their troubles. This is where Monsieur or Mijnheer or even Mister Causter had sat to hold his deep-breathing colloquy with the London Hilton, four days earlier. What good this knowledge did him, Pierce had not yet decided. Maybe it would come later in the form of a revelation.

It was a nice room, he thought; large (a suite rather than a room), comfortable, airy and warm, and done from floor to lampshade in the expensive, soft brown tweed which is woven by Scottish peasants from the wool of seventeen specially pampered rams which live on the slopes of Mull. In choosing to operate from the Grand Hotel Krasnapolsky, Causter showed that he had taste and, obviously, money. Pierce's expense sheet rustled in his pocket and he thrust the thought of it quickly from his mind.

He walked over to the window. His memory was right about one thing anyway. The Hotel Kras looked across the Dam (a peculiar name for a square rather like Trafalgar, but smaller and a lot drier) on to the Royal Palace, an impressive seventeenth-century building, but lacking in charm. He decided, however, not to mention this fact to Malplaquet or to anyone else because the hall porter down below had told him that for fifty weeks in every year the Palace was empty. As the hall porter spoke, Pierce thought of pointing out that this was an oddly uneconomic way of using desirable city property. Then he remembered Holyrood House. These were dangerously revolutionary thoughts for a civil servant, so he stopped having them. Instead, he watched a pair of trams clanking and crawling their way past the National Monument—the "stick of chalk", he'd heard it called—and pondered on his odd and apparently meaningless mission. At that moment he heard two things, one loud, the telephone bell ringing on his bedside table; the other soft, a kind of scraping noise at the connecting door (which was locked) to the next room. As though someone, knowing he had booked a call, was going to be around to hear what he said.

So he said nothing, holding the receiver to his chest and stretching his ears out as far as he could towards the door. After a time he became aware of Malplaquet's voice, coming from near his breast-bone and it was shouting rudely at him. He tried to disregard it, picked the telephone up (it was one of those telephones you can carry about the room with you) and took it into the lavatory, where he pulled the chain and started talking into the telephone mouthpiece in a hoarse whisper at the same time.

The effect on Malplaquet was immediate, so immediate that Pierce filed the knowledge in his mind for future possible use. It caused Malplaquet to stop talking.

"Are you there?" Pierce asked him.

"Where," said Malplaquet, "are you speaking from?"

"A lavatory. And there's somebody at the door."

"Well, put the engaged sign up." This observation by Malplaquet made Malplaquet laugh out loud.

Pierce ignored the noise and the advice. "I'm in Causter's room," he said.

"Good. Is he there?"

"I'm in the room he was in the other night. Room 352 at the Kras."

"Call it by its proper name, that's a good fellow." There was a short silence. Pierce noticed the cistern was full so he pulled the chain again.

"It sounds like an expensive room," said Malplaquet, who had an ear for such things.

"It is."

"Well, don't stay in it long."

"I'm going to Petten tomorrow."

"Excellent. The quicker the better," said Malplaquet. "Those are the pips. You'd better let that chap in. Only decent." He rang off.

Pierce took the telephone back into the room and put it down carefully. The scraping at the connecting door had stopped, but there were faint noises coming from the next room. They sounded extraordinarily ordinary.

He decided to take the bull by at least one horn, opened his door quietly, turned into the corridor, walked up to door 353 and knocked hard. He had to knock again before someone opened it.

"Heek?" (or some such interrogative) said a very tall and

formidable woman with a very high bridge to her nose. On it was a pair of thick spectacles. From where Pierce was standing they didn't seem likely to fit accurately in front of her eyes, and she looked down at him disconcertingly from underneath them.

It took Pierce less than half a minute to decide that she was ignorant of the English language, and ignorant of any malicious eavesdropping. He apologised politely and went back to his room. She bowed, closed the door, took off her glasses and muttered "Stupid little man," before she went back to the seat near the communicating door.

It was when he reached his room and saw the telephone that Marcus Pierce remembered that he had forgotten to report to Malplaquet his discovery that during the night someone seemed to have been messing around with his papers. For a moment or two he thought of ringing up again but then he thought of the cost, and then he thought what Malplaquet would think of the cost.

He flapped his hand in disgust towards the telephone and decided to go out for the night on his expenses. He found it was raining heavily.

* * *

A few flakes of snow, tiny, hard and brittle, were tapping at the window of his sleeping-car as Bligh went through all the motions of the British traveller in the outer darkness. His trousers went into the trouser press, his jacket followed his Melton overcoat into the wardrobe on hangers made for noble and upright giants, some of his teeth went into a tumbler and the others were brushed until they almost glowed with heat. The only thing he couldn't do (and this disappointed him, rather) was to put his pocket watch on the special little let-down shelf of navy blue plush beside his bed, but it reminded him to wind the watch on his wrist. The Wagon-Lit is the only unchanged and unchanging thing in a swiftly changing world, and he found to his concern that he liked it even though the heat was almost unbearable, and even though the stink from caked layers of Anatolian dust deposited over decades on to steam pipes too hot to touch was peculiarly nauseating. He had already tried opening a window but had been forced to accept the fact that it had been shut for forty years and was not likely now to give way to anything less positive than a laser beam. He gave it up and decided to sweat. The sheets and the towels, he was delighted to see, were marvellously clean and white. For the first time he was willing to admit that he might enjoy himself.

He was wrong.

He even began to feel he might offer to put his shoulder to the wheels up the longer, laborious gradients. The Orient Express is not a notably fast train after it leaves Istanbul for the long thousand-mile drag across the Anatolian plateau and Bligh, his eyes shoved up against the window, began to see why, as they toiled round bends in the track so sharp that he could see both the driver and the fireman at work on the footplate a dozen or so coaches' length ahead of his sleeper.

The train seemed to stop far too often at small stations which seemed to stand alone on vast areas of silent desert. But there was nothing silent about the men and women and children on the stations, shouting, screaming, laughing, crying, wailing, singing as they piled into the coaches ahead of him. He found himself tutting with unbelief until he remembered he was the Honourable Member for a Metropolitan Division, seven miles from Westminster and on a Southern Region suburban line. At London Bridge, he saw the same thing happening every day at the rush hour.

The thought reminded him (for the first time that day) that he was here in this vast Victorian anachronism of a train, behind a monstrous ancient engine as hot and noisy and steaming as a dragon from the pits of hell, because *and solely because* he was a Member of Parliament, an envoy extraordinary, separated from his fellow Members in Ankara by simple, but effective, trickery and crawling out eastwards to a destination unknown and unimagined. It occurred to him (rather late in the day) that no one in London, certainly not his wife, certainly not the Prime Minister who had engineered it all, not even the British Ambassador in Ankara or any of his clever young men knew where he was or where he was going. Any more than he did himself.

Then he noticed that he wasn't actually, at that moment, going anywhere at all, because the train had stopped, presumably at another of those stations. He realised that it had been motionless for some time. He wiped some steam off the window in a little oval and peered out into the darkness of the Anatolian night. As his eyes reached the window, another man's eye reached it from the other side. Bligh withdrew and said sorry, but the other man kept on looking. He had an angry eye, the eye of a deprived have-not looking balefully at them. The have, moreover, was standing like a Charley, sweating, in his vest and pants and with only some of his teeth *in situ*. Bligh sat down to get out of the man's line of sight, and shut his mouth tightly. It was then that a loud and authoritative knock came on his door. By the time he got his teeth in, and a woollen dressing-gown on, the knock had come again but this time it was louder and it went on longer. He opened the door wondering what to say and how to put it in Turkish. He grinned with relief as Major Kemal Karadeniz and Kaya Mersinli stepped into his cabin. But neither of them grinned back. There was obviously something on their collective mind.

* * *

The Prime Minister grunted, signed his name in red ink, and added a rider in his tiny squarish hand. *Minister of Education to try again. Bring up in Cabinet.* He threw the offensive document on to the large pile of signed papers on the table to his left. "That can't be the last one," he said. "It's not in accordance with the Rawnsley doctrine." He looked up at his Private Secretary and grinned. It was not a very genial grin. "Always end on a cheerful note. Ah!" He looked down at the octavo slip of paper which Rawnsley had slid on to his blotter. "That's better. Remind me to congratulate her. Better still!" In the corner of the paper he wrote EXCELLENT! ! ! in capital letters and still in red. "Do you ever feel you're working for a Headmaster, Malcolm?" Beasley smiled, this time more cheerfully. "Of an Approved School," he added.

He leaned over and peered into the scarlet despatch box. "That's the last one." He got hold of Rawnsley's coat sleeve and looked at his watch. "We've done rather well," he said. Then suddenly, and quite loudly. "Blast that watch." He stared at it.

"In thirty-three seconds that nasty little date-figure is going to click over, and we're into another day. One day nearer the first of December." He looked up and stared at the long green brocade curtains drawn across the windows of the Cabinet Room. But he did not see them. "Hubert Bligh's taking his time, Malcolm. I think we ought to send him a signal."

Malcolm Rawnsley started pushing the pile of papers back into the despatch box. Someone else could sort them out in the morning.

"It would help, of course," he tried to say it nonchalantly, "it would help a lot if we knew exactly where he was."

* * *

"Kayseri," said Kaya Mersinli as he stepped through the narrow doorway behind the Major. He jerked his thumb at the black outside world behind him and closed the door. "A famous city," he added.

For a few seconds they stood close together in a straight line, filling the narrow space between bed and washbasin, with Bligh looking at the Major's face and Kaya Bey looking at the back of the Major's head. After a bit, Bligh thought of inviting the Major to sit on his bed. It was then that Kaya was able to see, and did see, the eye at the window. He lunged past Bligh, smacked the window with the flat of his hand and shouted some rough words in Turkish. When he took his hand away to smack the window again, the face had gone. In a flicker of ineffable understanding, Bligh realised he would never see that eye again, and felt rather relieved.

"There is snow in Erzurum," said the Major. It was not simply a conversational gambit. It clearly meant something.

Kaya offered a gloss. "It means we shall possibly be late," he said. He knew damned well they'd be late. He paused. "But also the others may not be able to land." He offered no further explanation. His thin white face looked very unhappy.

"We telephoned," said the Major as a kind of prompt. He nodded his head towards the city of Kayseri in the dark outside.

"Yes," Kaya agreed with him. "We telephoned. The Russians are very angry. They say the first of December will be too late."

He spread his hands. "And the American Colonel in Erzurum, he also is very angry. He is sending telegrams, always sending a lot of telegrams, to Washington."

"But no answers." For the first time, the Major showed signs of pleasure. It did not last very long. One short sharp blast of amusement and then silence again.

Bligh decided that the philosophy of wait and see (however honourable its precedents) was getting him nowhere. "Why the American Colonel?" he asked.

"He has the key." It was as simple as that. Kaya seemed to accept it totally. For a moment or two Bligh had an odd feeling that he was involved in some remote and meaningless charade. "The key," he asked, "to what?"

In reply, Major Karadeniz enacted a vast upheaval, flinging his legs and arms about and uttering a loud and throaty roar. It was impressive. If ever there was an atomic explosion, this was it.

"I see," said Bligh. "And where *is* the key?"

The Major did not reply. Instead he left it to Kaya, whose pale face went longer. And pink. "That," he said, "we do not know. They do not tell us." For the first time, Hubert Bligh really knew what the State Department meant in simple terms by the phrase non-proliferation.

* * *

"He has, how you say it? been making the water like that for more than three hundred and fifty years. Everybody love him. He is the oldest citizen in Brussel." The girl's voice was a lot less attractive than her appearance but Christopher Pallister was glad she had spoken. She looked very pretty in the back glow from the flood lighting.

"Fancy that," he said. "It's a long time." The chubby bronze boy was certainly making the water. "A long time." Pallister said it again because he didn't know what else to say. It was the first time in his life that he had been spoken to by a pretty girl while watching a statue urinating.

"You have a statue in London . . ."

"Several I would say. But they do not make water . . ." He did a quick run-down in his mind for the sake of accuracy, *Oliver Cromwell, Dr Samuel Johnson, Charles the First, Sir Walter Raleigh, Ernest Bevin, Queen Victoria*... "They do not make water." He felt he was on pretty safe ground, so he said it with authority.

"In the circus at Piccadilly." The girl divided the word into four distinct syllables.

"Ah," he said, "Eros."

"A naked boy."

"A *nearly* naked boy." Pallister was firm. "He has a loincloth." He assumed this was so, though he had to confess he had never really noticed. "He is shooting an arrow," he added severely. There is a time and place for everything.

"People put clothes on our little Manneken Pis," said the girl. "It is a Brussel tradition. The soldiers dress him as a drumming boy; the students, they dress him as a schoolboy. There are many different vestments in our museum." She looked eager and very attractive. Any moment now and she would be inviting him to go with her to the museum or something. Pallister began to glow at the prospect.

Then he put his stupid foot in it. He nodded at the statue. The flow of water was constant and vigorous. "The scientists," he said for something to say, "they ought to dress him in yellow protective clothing..." He grinned foolishly. "For the Atomic Age," he added.

Then he cursed. Within three seconds she had turned away and was lost in the crowd along the Rue du Chine. He cursed again, aloud, scowled at the micturating little manikin and turned to make his way back, through the Grand Place, and along the Rue des Colonies to his hotel, the Astoria in the Rue Royale.

He was walking morosely past the gilded facade of the town house of the Dukes of Brabant when he remembered where he had seen the girl earlier in the evening—in the marble-paved vestibule of the Astoria Hotel. He doubted whether she would be there when he got back.

*   *   *

In Karlsruhe four hundred and sixty kilometres away to the south-east as the autobahn runs, Preston Northcott of the West German office had the first break-through.

Later, and not unnaturally, he himself put it down to his judgement, intelligence, flair, percipience, acumen and perspicuity, depending on who it was he was talking to. But the fact remains that he had two strokes of luck within a few minutes, at a time when he had practically given up hope. Malplaquet, when he heard about it, was forced to admit (and you could see the trouble it was causing him to do the admitting) that Northcott's knowledge of the terrain and of the lingo had helped. But he, Malplaquet, put *that* down as a tick on his, Malplaquet's, own tally sheet for having the judgement, intelligence and all the other things to assign Northcott to West Germany instead of allowing him to loaf around in Westminster. Northcott was reduced to consoling himself with a rare proverb from North Rhine-Westphalia which he translated as "you can't smoke your ham and still sit on it". It had been tiny consolation.

Northcott had had a bad day, long, tiring, and apparently wasted. Until the strokes of luck came. The day began all right early in the morning. Karlsruhe in Baden-Wurtemberg is an attractive town, as all tourists who have motored through the Rhine Valley know. Unlike most of the Rhineland towns it lies back from the river (though its suburbs are stretching out now to touch the eastern bank) and for this reason it has an almost rural quiet and charm. Apart from this, the terrible devastation of the Hitler war has now been completely repaired, and the place is as good as new. Northcott knew it well (the hundred and ninety miles from his office in Bonn, with superb autobahn all the way, and a reasonably fast car on his slopchit, made Karlsruhe almost one of the nearer suburbs of his official "parish") and he had accumulated quite a number of useful contacts there. He also had the advantage (recognised reluctantly as such by the London office, who paid him seven and six a day for it) of speaking German almost flawlessly.

On the other hand, to add a spice of novelty to what might have been a fairly run-of-the-mill operation, he had never before stayed at the Kaiserhof Hotel in the Marktplatz. His expense account was normally at such a level of generosity that he had to manage with something rather lower in the scale—with a *Pension* at the bottom near the end of the month, and a *Gasthaus* at the top on pay-day plus one or two. The Kaiserhof has, and deserves, three obelisks in the Varta *Führer durch Deutschland* and four stars in the AA Continental Guide. He enjoyed it; and especially the four different kinds of cold sausage on his breakfast plate—a sausage, he assumed, for each star. The Germans, he reflected as he chewed, have a scrupulous logic.

So, in a different way, had Malplaquet. In spite of the expense (which must have done damage to his digestion and to his whole personality) it was Malplaquet who had suggested that he stay there because one of the original telephone calls made by Causter had been made to the Kaiserhof. The fact that the man who took the call (in room 74) had registered as Herr Schmidt (and why not? there are two million of them at least in the Rhine Valley) and had given his address as in an imaginary suburb of a town that didn't exist, would suggest to most people, though not to Malplaquet, that he was unlikely to be still sculling around in the Kaiserhof four days later. Northcott had, in fact, looked for Herr Schmidt. The chambermaid (for a consideration) had let him into Room 74 while its overnight occupant had been having his breakfast downstairs, and he had looked very carefully indeed so that he could put his hand on his heart when, with the other one, he signed his report to head office.

After the sausages, he had gone out. Although the weather was not very pleasant, the place was. He had made a lot of enquiries. The Police Department in Karl-Friedrich Strasse had been co-operative though useless, and the other police stations in the Schlossplatz and the Beierthaimer Allee had been sympathetic though, in the end, no more useful. He had even been to the fire station.

He saw the château, which he already knew to be beautiful, with its bold, fantastic fan-shaped lay-out, and he visited both the constitutional courts with pleasure but without success. Looking back on it, he didn't really expect to discover anything in the Castle or the Courts, but he had been told to look, and so look he did.

He even motored out north into the wooded out-back where the Euratom atomic research centre had been sensitively part-hidden. But it might have been wholly hidden underground for all he saw of it. The policeman on the gate had been granted powers to stop him even from using the car park, and use those powers he did. Northcott was very angry at this, though he ought to have known better than to say what he did to the policeman. It was the friends he had made earlier in the Police Department (the one in the *Schlossplatz*) who got him out of the mess, but not even they could get him into the grounds. He had to write later in his report that he had seen what he took to be a Nuclear Reactor from a distance of an estimated five hundred metres (he expressed the distance in metres to impress Malplaquet with his European *Weltanschauung*) and a mysterious tall structure like a pipette of concrete, steel and glass with a cylindrical bubble in the middle of it, from about a kilometre. Neither of these turned out to be notably secret. Later he was able to send Pallister a picture postcard of both of them which he bought in a shop down by the zoo. He did not see any point in going into the zoo.

He ended up late in the evening in a beer-hall just round the corner from the *Schwarzwaldhalle* and that is where it happened. It was dark by this time, and far too cold for him to sit out in the open beside the lake. The hall itself had intrigued him all day and he had spent half an hour inside it. He was forced to admit that he agreed with everything everybody said about it. It is large, very. It has a strange but attractive shape, like an oval box the top of which has been left out in the rain (which of course, it has) so that it has warped or, as they say in Rudden, West Riding, skellered. It is like an oval biscuit tin which has had its lid thumped in the middle. Glass, steel, plastic, concrete and beautiful is the way he described it. But that wasn't all, of course. It resounds with memories and one of the memories is the *Horst Wessel* song.

Northcott knew, of course, from his security friends in Bonn, that Enver and Brook were the two people who, years ago, in June 1966, organised the first conference of the Neo-Nazi party, NPD in that very hall (indeed he had been sent back to London to report this and other facts about Enver and Brook to

Malplaquet), and he would have had to be a very insensitive person indeed (which he wasn't really) not to feel the ghostly presence of von Thadden and Thielen and behind them, on the platform of the Schwarzwaldhalle, the sick and sickening shade of Adolf Hitler, as the NPD brought the Nazis to life again on that hot June night.

He was feeling despondent (and with very good reason) when he went into that *Bierhalle*. He looked up when the waiter eventually reached his table, and he ordered a Polly water.

In his report later he admitted that he and others could speculate until his dying day (or theirs, as he put it) as to why on earth he did that, because he normally loathed the stuff. One reason is that after two days in London with three visits to the Rising Sun in the Euston Road, where they sell Tetley's Beer, he felt disinclined to go back to the thin stuff served as beer in German beer-halls. Another reason, much more disturbing, was the insidious effect on him of the *Schwarzwaldhalle* and that distant night in June.

The row in the beer-hall was deafening (an English pub that got anywhere near as noisy as a German beer-cellar would find its name on a petition organised by the Noise Abatement Society) and the seven or eight men and women at his table were singing and sweating hard when he casually gave his order. When he said he wanted a Polly water they suddenly stopped singing (though they went on sweating) and looked at him with special interest. A queer bond was suddenly and eerily forged. The waiter's expression did not change, but his eyes glinted for a fraction of a second. Appollinaris water, from a natural mineral spring in Rhenish Prussia, was Adolf Hitler's invariable drink; and in the NPD Polly water is holy water.

Quite suddenly, Northcott knew he was on to something, and he blessed the magnificent good fortune that had made him sit at that particular table and order that particular drink. It was not until later that the thought occurred to him, sadly, that the same thing might well have happened at any other table in the place. The second stroke of luck came later.

Because he spoke German perfectly Northcott could, and did, spend a full hour talking loudly and singing more loudly still, and although he did not actually claim to be a fully paid-up member of the NPD from Hamburg he did have the wit to suggest it, by using the sibilant esses and the soft fluffy effs and vees of the Hanovarian from Lower Saxony. And it worked.

His companions (there were five men and three women when he came to count them) did not sing all the time. Sometimes they talked and at least once they whispered. That was when another man arrived, looking screwed up with anger and disappointment. It is safe to assume (as Northcott did) that the man did not notice the stranger amongst them, because he leaned over the table and whispered urgently *Enver und Brook haben sich im letzten Moment gedrückt. Sie haben ins Gras beissen müssen.*

It was first the man's manner which alerted Northcott, and then the names, though they were whispered, struck his eardrums as though they were hitting an alarm-bell. It was in this way that he heard what had happened to Enver and Brook, because when he left London the two corpses found in the Thames near Gravesend had not been identified. When he wrote his report in the middle of the night, he added a translation for Malplaquet and for anyone else who might be interested. *Enver and Brook,* he wrote, *have chickened; and they've been bumped off.*

Almost immediately the whole party left the beer-cellar—some of them left their beer unfinished, which is very rare among Germans. Northcott left just behind them (as soon as he could, in fact, without giving the game away), but they got into a car and he had to let them go.

He went back to his seat at the table, more to make notes about the people and what they said, than to finish his Polly. It was then that he had his second stroke of luck. Under one of the chairs at his table he found a packet which had contained matches. Like a fool, he picked it up with his great fat sweaty thumb and fingers instead of using a pair of tweezers (which he didn't have) or a handkerchief (which he had). On the packet, in blue, white and gold, was the symbol of Euratom, a circle with a dot in the middle of it, representing the nucleus, surrounded by the interlaced eliptical paths of three neutrons. Underneath in bold capitals KARLSRUHE.

Preston Northcott knew he was on the move. The beer-hall

and all it represented and the little packet in his hand became suddenly very menacing.

*   *   *

"Charley Peace," said Malplaquet, as Preston Northcott's voice came over the line.

"Oh." Northcott hesitated. It seems unlikely, but it was not inconceivable. He had already had two wrong numbers, one in Swindon, the other in, of all places, Slaithwaite. He thought of putting the telephone down, looking for another telephone booth with a better telephone in it, and starting again, and he groaned. It was far too late to go hunting round the back alleys of Karlsruhe. One thing was certain. If he went back to the Kaiserhof, that hall porter, the one with half an ear missing, would be sure to listen in. He had an incongruous little thought and then shuddered at it. If the hall porter put *that* ear to the telephone it would very likely disappear into the little hole.

"Charley Peace." Malplaquet said it again, but this time he laughed a little to show that it was one of his jokes. "It's what it means, isn't it?"

"What is?"

"Karlsruhe." Malplaquet spaced the syllables. His laugh went quieter, as though he had wrapped the eiderdown round himself, and had got it mixed up with the telephone receiver. "I'm in bed," he said. The word bed came through loud and clear as though he had suddenly wrenched the eiderdown free.

"Lucky you. I wish I was."

"It's very late, you know."

"Of course I know. It's also late where I am. It's also very important."

"Right. Hang on." Malplaquet had stopped laughing (for which Northcott was grateful) and his voice sounded brisk in a subdued sort of way. "I don't want to wake my wife. I'll put this receiver down and go to the other one downstairs." The receiver scraped on something hard; there was a little tinkle and a half-stifled squawk of annoyance. "Bang," said Malplaquet's voice thinly, as though through a million miles of space, "goes my Famel."

Northcott found the next two minutes extremely embarrassing. There was Mrs. Malplaquet (who would ever have thought there was a Mrs. Malplaquet anyway?) lying, innocently he assumed, in her little world of sleep, while he... it was all very indelicate. He wished Malplaquet would hurry up, and began to wonder what kind of stately mansion he had managed to provide himself with in Streatham. He had just got to the point of visualising Malplaquet shuffling along vast marble halls like the ancient beadsman (and, he hoped, as cold) when Malplaquet's voice came up.

"Shoot," it said.

Whenever Malplaquet slipped into his generally outdated and always cosy vernacular, Northcott (and Pierce and Pallister as well for that matter) found it hard not to laugh. This time he did not laugh. Instead, he told the story of the Schwarzwaldhalle, and Malplaquet listened. At the end they both put their receivers down quietly and thoughtfully. They both knew they were unlikely to sleep peacefully that night or for several nights to come.

* * *

Sarkisla... Sivas... Kangal... Kemah... Erzincan. The towns rolled by like snails on the road to eternity. Nothing changed. The ground was bare and brown, and drifts of snow had begun to form in the gullies. The mosques, one to each town and village that slid past them, seemed to sink lower into the ground as the night passed and the day wore on, becoming more and more like beehive fortresses, low, impregnable and dark. Their minarets were thicker and lower than the soaring slender columns in the western cities, as though the winds from the east were too strong for them and had left them stunted. And all the time, far away on the northern sky-line were the snow covered peaks of the Pontic Taurus range.

The night passed quickly. In spite of the heat in his sleeper cabin (and possibly because of the bottle of raki in his overcoat pocket) Bligh slept soundly, waking for a moment or two occasionally when the train stopped in stations or slowed down on gradients. Once or twice he got out of bed, ran his finger across the window to clear the glass, and looked out on the empty world of the Anatolian plateau. Each time it looked the same, the broken earth reaching to the northern skyline and there, unchanging like the repeated pattern on a frieze, the white mountains running parallel with the Black Sea coast fifty miles beyond them.

The day passed more slowly. Their compartment was comfortably warm, the food excellent, the drink soporific, the coffee rich and thick and sweet, the view from the window magnificent, with mountains, ranges of them, at both north and south of the central plain. But the tempo was infinitely slow. Kaya Mersinli did his best now and again with conversation but it meant little—guidebook chatter which began to bounce off Bligh's mind and eventually drove the Major out into the corridor. Neither Kaya nor the Major would speak about the things that mattered most to Bligh, and the phrase "atomic mines" which Bligh used once and once only, stopped their conversation for almost two hours.

Alex Beasley in London (years ago!) had said it would be cold. He was right. He had said it would be mountainous and strange and beautiful. Right again. He had said he, Bligh, would enjoy it. Within reason, right again. He had said he would get every possible help from the Turkish Government and the Army. Again, within reason, right once more. He had said that, once out in Turkey, *Operation Noah* and the business of the atomic landmines would be made totally clear to him. Wrong. Bloody well wrong! Up to now all that had been made totally clear to him was the fact that he wasn't being told. He began to sulk a bit and Kaya Bey found it harder to keep the conversation going, though he went on trying. The Major, as usual, was no use at all. It was quite obvious that he was one of those men who could not sit and do nothing gracefully. And sitting there in the Orient Express for twenty-four hours was bearing down hard on him. And on all of them.

The only time the Major's eyes came to life were when Kaya Bey mentioned a place called Erzurum, and then for a moment or two there was an excited flurry of talk. Both of them spoke as if their troubles would be over when they reached this magical city.

Bligh suddenly realised that, as far as they were concerned, he was a piece of valuable merchandise which they had been instructed to deliver in good condition to Erzurum. He presumed that if their troubles were over his would be too. And that is where he too was wrong.

* * *

Report, Pierce 2391. Petten North Holland.
Reactor Centrum Nederland ...

Marcus Pierce stared at the words he had written, but he did not see them. He put his pen down for the twentieth time in half an hour, shivered as he pulled his dressing-gown around him, got up from the tiny bed-side table with its beautifully embroidered and laundered linen cover, and walked the three paces to his bedroom window. The man was still there, sitting in his car at the entrance to the garage across the way.

The cobbles of the side street were wet with rain, and a tin sign advertising some brand of engine oil or other was swinging and rattling a little in the wind that came up the street from the sand-dunes. The whole thing could be, and probably was, totally and absolutely innocent—like the rest of Petten and the Nuclear Research Centre a mile up the main road towards Dan Helder with the island of Texel beyond. The whole day had been devoted, as far as Pierce was concerned, to a public demonstration of innocence and Pierce found himself half wishing that he had written and posted his report earlier that evening, as soon as he got back from the Research Centre. It would have been simple. It could have gone *en clair*, on the back of a picture post-card with plenty of space to spare for rows of kisses. *Having a good time but shall be glad to get back. Love, Marcus.* To Malplaquet that would have meant simply damn all to report.

He had even bought a postcard at the bar downstairs. He turned back to his table and fingered the card, his mind uneasy at the implications. It was a glossy black and white panoramic view of the village of Petten with the belfry of the new church close up on the right (it is one of those which look like a hose-drying tower in a modern fire station; a self-conscious concrete statement of the church's contact with earth and reality) and in the middle, beside the cobbled road, a shabby open space roughly covered with grass, a village green without its cross or its fancy maypole. Pierce had seen twenty like it in England, each of them duller than the last. The thirty or so gabled houses with their TV aerials were almost identical, each with its prominent dormer window and its white painted woodwork, solid Burger houses of the middle sort. And at the far end of the village green you could see, facing the camera, a long two-storey building which looked like a row of houses, except that every ground floor window opened to the ground and the whole row had to make do with a single, central chimney stack. It was the Petten Arms. *Het Wapen van Petten*, the only hotel for ten miles around and the only one within easy reach of the *Reactor Centrum*. All Pierce had to do, to complete the picture of unimpeachable innocence, which was to put a cross (which he did absentmindedly) at the top of the left of the hotel and curl an arrow around to the side of the building, opposite the little garage and filling station with its swinging sign. *X marks my room, see you soon, M.* He scribbled it angrily and went back to the window. The car was still there and the man still in it. Pierce shrugged and went back to his doubts.

The postcard had started them off in his mind. At the bottom left, rather crudely printed, was an odd legend, *Petten, North Holland Plein 1945*... The Square, 1945. It had not struck him at first as being unusual. He had sipped at his whisky and ginger, and had smiled non-committally when the landlord's wife, a cheerful, friendly young woman had said, as she handed it to him. "She is not very beautiful place, hey?"

Then two sips later he saw the date. He looked up at her. "1945," he had said. Just that date. For a fraction of a second her eyes went hard and cruel and then she brushed the matter aside as a disagreeable fact of life, far better buried and forgotten. "The Germans," she said. Then, more brightly, "This is the *new* Petten."

Pierce looked round the long cosy room, its tables warm and inviting with their scarlet table-cloths all set for the evening meal; the stove in the middle of the room with logs two feet long blazing in the hearth, the American bar behind him flashing with chromium, the polished wood, the indoor plants, the deep red curtains and the long plank table running down the middle of the dining area, its end so near the stove that blisters had started to cluster on its legs. It could be anywhere in post-war Europe. Anywhere. But it was here on the North Holland coast.

He knew the answer before he put the question. "The *old* Petten? ..."

The landlord himself answered it as he came through the door from the kitchen, uttering a crude guttural noise in his throat. A Dutch word maybe, but its meaning had no land frontiers.

The landlord jerked his thumb violently towards the far end of his dining-room. Beyond the wall lay the dunes, hillocks of sand rising in places to forty-feet, an immense height in contrast with the flat wet inland plain. "A mile away," he said, "you can still find the stones if you look for them. Some people," he leaned over the bar and pushed his face to within eighteen inches of Pierce's nose, "some people forget. At the Reactor." Another jerk of his thumb. "Some of them forget." Then he grinned, as though aware of the warning coming from his wife's eyes. "We have to live here." He drew himself a glass of thin local beer, wiping the froth off the top with a stick of wood, and poured it swiftly down his throat, as though subconsciously he was putting a fire out that was beginning to burn in his belly. His voice became more conversational. "There was a Petten four hundred years ago, they say," he paused. "But I am the oldest native of the place. I was born here, in the *new* Petten," he said. He was very little more than thirty years old, thirty-five maybe. "The old ones," he went on, "those that were still alive. They came back. But they remember their town across the sand dunes." Again that jerk of the thumb.

Pierce put his glass on the bar counter. "I'll have another whisky," he said. "This time with the oldest native and his wife." They had all laughed but there was a strangeness in the laughter. Pierce had looked at his watch, picked up the picture postcard and taken the key to his room. "I must write home," he'd said, the out-of-season tourist ready to chat in his meaningless tourist sort of way. When he got to his room he saw the car in the street outside his window and the man in it, waiting and watching.

That had been an hour ago, and he was still there. Waiting for

133

the garage hand? Waiting for some private assignation? Petrol maybe? Just waiting? Wasting time? Loafing? Pierce had no means of knowing. All he did know was that he had seen that man earlier in the day but then he had been dressed in the bright yellow overalls and the elaborate space-helmet equipment worn by those whose job it is to move around in the "hot" radio-active areas of the Nuclear Research Centre.

That visit to the Research Centre in its way, had been the strangest thing Pierce had ever done. From the beginning, as the official car picked him up at *Het Wapen van Petten*, he felt he was moving into a separate existence, a totally new world, which, of course, he admitted he was. Trained to observe the strange, the inexplicable and the unnatural, he had spent six hours switched on like a finely tuned piece of electronic equipment. And the overall impression? One of rational normality imposed on the abnormal. With normality coming out on top.

"Guard dogs, electrified fences, a control system of identification, a para-military force of security men. What more do we need?" Dr. Cornelis had answered his question. "Have another sherry, Mr Pierce." He grinned with a hint of mischief in his eyes. "It is not radio-active, I assure you."

Pierce took another sherry and walked over to the window of the Director's office. The window seemed to stretch for ever in both directions. Ahead of him, the North Sea was as flat as a pewter tray, to his right the sand dunes and the sloping, manmade banks of the polder dykes spread out to touch the black of the sky; to his left, a few copses of fir trees and more dunes covered with tall thin wispy grass. "You are wide open to the world," he said. Somehow he'd imagined the *Reactor Centrum* to be in a fortress area with walls twenty feet high and a front gate like Wandsworth Prison, but holding people out rather than in.

Dr. Cornelis smiled. "I studied in Cambridge," he said. "I often travelled through your fenlands. It felt like home. You're not suggesting that anyone who wanted could wander into the RAF stations in East Anglia." He helped himself to more sherry. Pierce waved his hand slightly. "No one can get in then?" he asked.

"No one can get in if we want to keep him out."

134

"But if he has right of access?"

"Then no one can keep him out." Dr Cornelis hesitated a second or two. "What you are implying is that someone who works here is, or could be, Mr Causter?"

Marcus Pierce spilled some sherry on his tie. He made a great effort. "Clumsy," he said.

"My fault." Dr Cornelis smiled again. "You don't think I would have let you come in, if the Counter Espionage Division hadn't told me the whole story?"

Pierce had no answer. He drank the rest of his sherry in case he received any more shocks. One came almost immediately. "We have a man in the Centrum here called Causter." Dr Cornelis seemed remarkably calm in the circumstances. He leaned forward and pushed a ring-book personnel file towards Pierce. "He's on grace leave. Doing a sabbatical year in Princeton in the States. He's been gone at least three months." He pointed at the last entry. "Here's the date he went."

"And he's still there?"

"Of course. I knew you'd ask me that so I spoke to him an hour ago. He said he was in bed, asleep. I have no reason to doubt him. It was 6.15 a.m. Princeton time."

"Thorough," Pierce thought. "Everything's so bloody thorough." He began to love the Dutch.

"Someone was using his name then?" he suggested.

Cornelis spread his hands. "It seems possible, though I can't see why."

"Could he do any damage?"

"Who?"

"The man who used Causter's name."

"Of course he could. Anybody could. Inside. But why should he?"

Pierce disregarded the question.

"What kind of damage?"

In reply, Cornelis put another question, and as he spoke he walked over to a large plan of the Research Centre on the wall of his office. "When they showed you round this morning, I take it they took you into the High Flux Reactor?" He put his finger on the Reactor complex at the rop right of the plan.

"Yes."

"You looked down into the Reactor itself?"

"I did." Pierce, a man of the world, nodded nonchalantly, as though it was the kind of thing that happened to him every Thursday, but the glow in his eyes gave the game away. He came clean. "Impressive," he said. "Very impressive." He doubted as he spoke whether he could ever forget the experience. "It's hot!" The young guide-technician said, somehow managing to put the inverted commas round the word. *Hot without heat*, he meant. Hot with radio-activity. The water in the enormous cylindrical tank, like a big pressure cooker, was totally and absolutely motionless, and glowing like a dark blue silvered mirror, as though a hundred fathoms deep. The gantry on which they stood had been rolled back to a safe distance from the controlled nuclear reaction taking place at the far side of the tank and twenty feet down below the surface of the water. Down there, a fire of enormous intensity was raging without a ripple of movement and burning with a dazzling blue incandescence. A brighter and more vivid blue than Pierce had ever imagined.

"Impressive," Dr Cornelis agreed. "It could blow up," he said. "Anyone who knew how to do it could . . ." He left the thought unspoken. Pierce got its full meaning.

"And the purpose?" he asked.

"Just destruction. Everyone in range would die very unpleasantly." He let the idea sink in. "Including the man who did it. He could do it *only* from inside the reactor complex, inside the radio-active area. There would be no point . . ."

"We are, you mean, if this is true, looking for a mad scientist?" Pierce was despondent.

"Of course," Dr Cornelis said. "Like me." He held up one hand as he saw Pierce's reaction. "We're *all* mad. In one sense. Obsessive. But we're not mad in the way you mean. Thank God. Every man who works here—and it's true of all other nuclear research centres in the world—every man here has the knowledge to destroy mankind. And himself." He smiled. "We leave that to the politicians," he said.

"Do you have many here?"

"Politicians? Some. They are harmless enough. Debating

society politics." He laughed out loud. It was a surprisingly coarse noise, entirely out of keeping with the elegance of his appearance. "That is never done inside the radio-active area. When they have their political meetings, they do it in safe areas. They have to have their fun." The idea amused him.

That had been the end of it. Pierce had been vetted carefully for radio-activity and had been delivered to the security men on the gate. And now, confused, irritable and in an icy bedroom, he was shivering, in more than one sense, out in the cold. He stared once more at the title of his report, picked up his pen, hesitated, put it down again and went looking for his dinner. As he left the room he looked once more out of the window. The man was still there. By now he must be very cold indeed. It was little consolation to Pierce.

* * *

The train whistled with triumph as soon as it had stopped. "Erzurum," said Kaya Mersinli as if he had invented it, and Bligh half expected him to whistle in triumph too, until he remembered that for undisclosed theological reasons Turks never whistle.

"The Christians who once lived in this part of Turkey..." Kaya had got back to his guide-book jag. He really must have put in an awful lot of work.

"The Armenians..." Bligh saw no reason why he shouldn't say the word even if it stuck in Kaya's gullet. It helped his peevishness.

Kaya nodded and took the word as said. "They said that the place where we are standing was the Garden of Eden."

"Oh!" Bligh found it hard to comment politely. He looked out of the window and found it harder still, so he began checking his belongings. He had only one small case, so that didn't occupy him for long. "I wish," he said, changing the subject, "that I had been warned to bring a Balaclava helmet." For a second or two there was silence between them and Bligh's mind raced back to the Crimean War in his school books. Was Balaclava a place you didn't mention to Turks? He was half-way through considering this problem when he realised that neither Kaya nor the Major knew what he meant by the term. He described one, using his hands, as they made their way out on to the platform.

"Yaşmak," said the Major. He nodded with understanding as though a lot of things had been made clear to him. Then he stiffened and did the most elaborate salute Bligh had ever seen, including those in the annual ritual on Horse Guards' Parade for which, as an M.P., he had had free tickets for the past twenty years and more.

Bligh stiffened too though he didn't salute. Coming towards them on the cobbles of the station platform, and scattering the mob of passengers and their piles of baggage as though they were fitted with an invisible snow-plough, were six men. At their head strode a tall and extremely handsome officer in the Turkish Army (later Bligh got to know him well as Colonel Mustafa Tuna) with a grim, aquiline face and an air of arrogant authority. Beside him, and marching in step with him, was another tall man wearing a short sheepskin coat and a white astrakhan cap. Behind them were four others, apparently lined up in strict order of seniority. Even the one in the rear was marching as though hand-picked by Allah.

Kaya Mersinli was grinning now in open triumph, showing his teeth in a transport of delight. "They got here first," he chanted. "They got here first," and he almost clapped in enthusiasm. Obviously his own mission was now totally completed. Major Kemal Karadeniz was breathing heavily through his nose as though approaching a convulsion of subordination and his arm was still trembling in salute.

Bligh just stood, appalled and totally unable to believe his eyes. The man in the white astrakhan cap was Lieutenant-Commander Austin Lombard, D.S.O., M.P., R.N.(Retd.), the Honourable Member for Birmingham East.

* * *

The Right Honourable William Empery looked out at the motionless traffic in the Cromwell Road and went red. He bent his head down over his papers and tried to cover his embarrassment. It was bad enough for a Minister of the Crown to be caught in a traffic jam, it was unbearable to be recognised as such when caught in one, and the girl in the rather old repainted MGA alongside had just waved at him. She was now obviously telling the young man in the passenger seat who he was, and she was clearly finding it funny. He made a note in his mind to speak to the Minister of Transport about the traffic, though he doubted whether that would help. He already knew, he felt sure, about the Cromwell Road. In the meantime, he made the best of it, smiled his best smile at the girl (which made the young man mad) and pressed the little blue button. He was glad he had decided to use the new Wankel-engined Rolls-Aston (it was the one they had bought to celebrate the third successive, if small, movement of the Balance of Payments into the black), because of its strategically placed blue button. He pressed it and watched (with dignity) as the second window came up between him and the angry young man. Being of polarised glass, and set accurately at 90 degrees polarity to the other piece of glass, it had the effect of putting a shutter between himself and the outside world. The young man swore, William Empery lost a vote for his Party at the next election, and the car stayed, locked, in the traffic jam. Empery sighed. The only answer was to move Dorney Wood, his official country residence, lock, stock and barrel, especially barrel, to Hampstead Heath, and then he could use one of the new London Transport helicopters.

He was in the middle of this revolutionary thought when the telephone rang. He lifted the receiver. "Empery," he said. His voice distorted into a quacking caricature of a human voice went out into space.

"William." He recognised the Prime Minister's voice. "I've had an urgent telegram from Hubert."

Empery grunted. He knew only one Hubert, but better be sure.

"The Knight," he said. He sounded like a Scotsman making an assignation.

"Yes. He's with Austin! !" There was a long pause. "Got that?"

The Secretary of State for External Affairs grunted again. This time the grunt had a different note; it went up at the end.

"It's true, apparently." Alex Beasley was taking a risk over the air but it was a slight one. Only M.P.s remember Members' constituencies. "East Brum," he said.

Empery got it. But he got it wrong. He had a vision of two British M.P.s in cells side by side in a Greek gaol. "Bloody hell," he said. "Some more Private Notices!" And, not without reason, his loathing of them got into his voice.

The Prime Minister sighed across radio space. "He must have got out," he said. "Hurry back and look into it please." The line went dead.

"Hurry back, he said! ! !" William Empery made a loud scoffing noise as he put the telephone down. "He's also cracking up. What he meant is that Bligh must have got *in*."

He shook his head sadly and looked at the date on his watch. "First signs," he said as he took out his cigarette case.

"23rd November." He muttered the words into the microphone hidden behind the five artificial Embassy Tipped. "Beasley showing signs of confusion. Is this the beginning of the end query. Must talk to Bassington. Very disturbing." His long face showed no signs of disturbance, however, and he smiled as he put the cigarette case away. One day this would make quite a nice chapter. He patted his pocket, pressed the blue knob again and looked out at the outside world.

They were still in the Cromwell Road and the girl was still there. And laughing.

* * *

A de luxe hotel, the most central, the quietest, the most up to date in Milan. Eugene Malplaquet read the blurb as he waited for his coffee to arrive. He saw nothing in it to complain about— and he was in a complaining mood. Only a de luxe hotel with aspirations to a couple of bonus stars over and above its regulation five could possibly think of buying the little ormulu table inlaid with black glass on which he had laid his gloves. He looked down at them, glanced quickly round the graceful little room, and turned them over so that their less shabby sides were facing upwards. It was certainly quiet, so quiet, it occurred to him, that you could have heard a ten thousand lire note drop, and it was infinitely quieter than Milan Cathedral fifty yards away in the Piazza del Duomo. The hotel was also, so far as he could tell, almost empty. The room in which he was sitting (and trying hard to give the impression that MI5 insisted on his living the life of a twentieth century *condottiere*) had only three other people in it—not counting the three big men dressed as bar-attendants. The young woman in an outrageous pink creation, was an extremely costly piece of Italian merchandise he decided until he heard her speaking English with a Scottish accent. A shrewd observer, he then decided that she was an extremely costly piece of Scottish merchandise. Very good indeed, he nodded to himself, for the Balance of Payments. The men, both of whom seemed to be host to the young woman, were grey little men, with dark grey suits and pale grey faces. They both looked as though they owned a million acres of Southern Italy but they did not seem to be enjoying it. The younger man who was standing at the bar had a blotchy face. He was making a short drink last a long time and appeared interested in nothing but what he was drinking, a yellow liquid that seemed to hurt as it went down.

Then Malplaquet's coffee arrived, and with it his bill. He looked at them both and shuddered. His lips moved but no sound came out. Then he got his glasses out, put them on, leaned over the table, and located the coffee cup over there by his left glove. It was the smallest cup he had ever seen in his life and the coffee was about two centimetres deep in the bottom of it. The bottom of the cup was also the smallest bottom of a cup he had ever seen in his life.

The bill (which was also on the table) was a big one and Malplaquet paid it with exaggerated reluctance, wondering as he did so how he was going to disguise it on his expense account. *To entertaining seven Italian journalists in the Grand Hotel Duomo, Milan.* He doubted whether it would wash and decided to make it eight.

The waiter pushed the change towards him, without letting it get too near, and watched Malplaquet's mouth with interest. It was moving as though in silent prayer.

"*Cameriere* ..." said Malplaquet after one or two false starts.
"Signore?"
Malplaquet gave it up and went back to English, which he

spoke loudly and with clarity. "Young man," he said, "what you need in Italy is a Prices and Incomes Board."

"*Si, signore,*" said the waiter. He picked up nearly all the change, bowed his thanks, flicked an overlooked crumb from the ormulu with his very clean napkin and went back to the bar.

"*Americano?*" asked the blotchy faced man who was leaning on it. He took a long drink from the glass in his hand, but he kept his eyes on the back of Malplaquet's head.

"*Inglese*," said the waiter. They both shrugged their shoulders.

They were shrugging them when one of the under-managers* arrived and leaned over Malplaquet as though offering sympathetic counsel. He spoke quietly and in exquisite English and only an occasional word crooned its way over to the bar. *Ispra ... Maggiore ... car ... Sestri Levante ... Autostrada del Sole ... Hotel Astoria ... Thank you.* The waiter near the bar shrugged his shoulders once more and went back to his boredom. The other man finished his yellow drink so quickly that it made him cough.

Malplaquet polished off his coffee in one determined sip and stood up. When he followed the under-manager to the door, the man at the bar followed them without appearing to hurry.

* * *

Marcus Pierce examined page four of the newspaper again. It was meaningless (or nearly so because the Dutch language when printed looks very much like the Dutch language when spoken) but he had to do it. Otherwise he would look as though he was listening, which was what he was doing. The newspaper, a local one, had been printed twenty miles down the road at a place called Alkmaar. It seemed to have an editorial bias towards cheese and its technology.

The dining-room of the Petten Arms was fairly full, though one or two of the tables—like his own for that matter—had only one person at them. The landlord and his wife were obviously far too busy to talk to him, and the meal was becoming something of an exotic gamble. The young girl who was serving him off and

---

* They are at a fixed ratio of one under-manager to ten residents, a system which also works well at Eton.

on was a pretty young thing about fifteen years old who had obviously been rustled up in Petten to meet the evening rush hour. Her only word of English was, dangerously, yes; and he was having to order his courses by hit-and-miss. *Snert* had turned out well and certainly better than he expected, as a kind of soup with sausages in it, and the *Blinde vink* went down very agreeably indeed, though he was not normally devoted to stuffed veal. What worried Pierce was the fact that *Vruchtensla met Slagroom* when it came might turn out to be some slight and trivial sweetmeat which would go down in thirty seconds even if he did chew each mouthful thirty-two times. Worse than that, if it was crunchy he would find it even harder to hear any names of people or places which the seven people at the long middle table might let fall. Three of those people, to his certain recollection, worked at the *Reactor Centrum*.

When they arrived (they all came together) and he recognised three of them, he'd got a bit of a shock and had nearly choked on a piece of sausage in the *snert*. But then he realised that he had been partly warned by the landlord to expect them. That was earlier in the evening when he came down, frozen, from his bedroom not quite sure whether his mounting persecution complex should be taken seriously or not. The central table had been laid for a meal for eight people (he never knew what happened to the eighth) but more than that, it had also been laid for a council meeting of some sort. At one end there was a formal kind of lectern with a gavel beside it (obviously for the chairman) and there were leather mounted blotters instead of table mats. "Very often we have them." The landlord had led him to a glass case at the end of the room by the door. It was full of sports trophies (silver cups and salvers and the like), gavels and signed photographs, highly polished and meticulously stacked. "It is good," he added. "They eat, they drink, they talk." His broad face blossomed into a big smile. "Then they pay." He pointed to the long table. "Tonight," he said, "we have a table-meeting."

And here it was, happening; and he couldn't tell a bloody word they were saying. He found himself getting irritable (especially when the *Vruchtensla* stuff turned out to be fruit salad with cream and hardly any cherries in it). He was working on what he would say to the next blasted amateur (or professional) etymologist who told him that the Dutch language is almost identical with the stuff they talk in Yorkshire, when he remembered what linguistic indignities he had suffered a few years ago when he spent some time in a dump called Rudden looking for a U2 aeroplane that never existed, and he began to understand.

"Kaffay," he said, enunciating distinctly to the girl when she came for his fruit plate. She did not understand. "Coffee," he said, resigning himself to non-communication.

"Ah! Coffee. Yes." She seemed delighted.

He actually had three cups of it, though it was not very good. The Dutch, he thought, still miss the East Indies. In the middle of the third one, the landlord came through from the kitchen and spoke to a small grey-faced man with long black hair—one of the people Pierce had recognised as coming from the Research Centre—and they went together back into the kitchen. One word (the first he registered) stood out—*telefoon*. All good hotels keep the telephone in the kitchen. He saw signs of a frustration complex building up in him so he took himself off to his bedroom again.

The man had gone but the car was still there. Pierce thumbed his nose at it and went to bed.

It was almost an hour later that he heard the car leave. He stayed in bed (it was far too cold to get out, and useless anyway) and cursed the noise it made, belting on to the highway, the *Groene Kustweg* north to the *Reactor Centrum Nederland*, or south towards Alkmaar and then Amsterdam beyond. He couldn't tell which, so he shrugged his shoulders with the eiderdown up round them. "To hell with them," he said, loud and clear. Then he put his head under the bedclothes and shouted it to relieve his feelings.

As he lay there shouting, there came a timid knock on his door. He sat up, quickly, just as James Bond would have done when the blonde came and knocked timidly on the door. "Come in," he said, using his strong masculine voice.

The landlord came in. He looked tired and he needed a shave.

"They have just gone," he said. "The telephone . . ." He sat at the foot of the bed and looked embarrassed, rubbing his chin.

"They talked about you on the telephone. I heard them. They spoke your name. I could not stay in the kitchen long. Mijnheer Groot from the Reactor told me to leave. He said the telephone call was private." The landlord looked distressed, partly at what had happened but mainly, it seemed, because he could give Pierce no details. Then, as an afterthought, he added. "I do not speak German very well." He looked up. "I do not *like* to speak German," he added.

Pierce did not press the matter. "It's good of you to tell me, Mijnheer," he said. Then he took a long shot. "Did you hear the caller's name?"

"But of course. It was Causter."

By the time they went to bed, the landlord looked very tired indeed and even more in need of a shave. But they had to give it up in the end. They never knew where the call came from.

* * *

"Distinctly cold," said the Clerk of the House, "for the bottom." He sat down with care and great dignity on one of the enormous leather couches which are unique (some red, some green) to the Houses of Parliament, though common enough in them. "The apotheosis," he remarked tapping the couch with one hand "of obesity." He held his hands out to the artificial fireplace. "They were designed," he went on, and his eyes began to glow like the coals in the phoney fire-basket, "in the days when beauty was measured in the roundness of the features and in the generosity of the folds of fat." His right hand, warmer now, stroked the leather beside him. "To say nothing of the depth of the *umbilicae*."

"In the Good Queen's middle years, perhaps?" For a moment or two the Prime Minister looked dreamy, as though ready to sigh for those genteel days when the First Lord of the Treasury had a decision to make only once every second day. In those days, conversation (even conversation of substance in this very room) always began with a few proper observations of irrelevant generality. He looked up at the wall of his room and caught the eye of Sir Robert Peel done in a rich dark velvety mezzotint. He turned back to the Clerk.

"You miss your gown, Sir William."

Olsen nodded thoughtfully. "Of course," he said. He had never denied being in the minority who opposed the idea some years earlier that the Clerks at the Table should stop wearing wig, tabs and gown and should be dressed like ordinary men and indeed (he flinched a bit) women. He looked down at his striped trousers and sighed. "The gown was warm," he said. "And the wig." He stopped stroking the leather of the couch and touched the skin of his head. "Warm." He said it again.

Good God, it's like hunt the slipper. Alex Beasley thought it but didn't say it. This had gone on long enough.

"And DIVLIST?" he asked. He pointed to the piece of paper in the Clerk's left hand.

"Ah, yes, the DIVLIST." Sir William's broad, red face glowed a little more than usual. "I think it means what it says."

The Prime Minister's face did not glow. Nor did he speak.

"You say Lombard wanted to fool somebody?" Olsen cocked his head like an ancient bird of prey.

"Yes, the Greek police."

"Then why not use a term which no other Parliament in the world uses? *Division List*." Sir William looked triumphant. "Especially since the rest of the message was in Latin. You agree?"

"Of course. We agreed that last time."

"Right. We put all the Latin into English. And the English we put into Latin." By this time the Clerk was showing signs of great animation. He fished around in his inside jacket pocket, pulled out a packet of papers and put them on the floor in front of him. Most of them were OHMS letters addressed to him at his penthouse flat up on the roof of the House of Commons. "Bloody income tax," he said.

The First Lord of the Treasury kept silent.

"Ah!" Olsen found a folded sheet of octavo paper. "A photocopy," he explained, "of an article in *Parliamentary Affairs*." He looked up like a willing gun-dog: he was almost pointing. "It's about the *Anonimalle Chronicle* of 1333-81. It's the first known account of a sitting of Parliament, when they met across the way in the Chapter House of Westminster Abbey." He paused for the sake of effect. "Lombard," he said, "wrote the article a year or two ago." He tapped it with a nicely turned finger-nail. "Very, very scholarly," he said. He looked round quickly though he knew there was nobody else in the room. "I'm thinking of putting it into Erskine May," he said. "As a supplement. Very useful."

"Divlist," said Beasley.

"Not mentioned," said Olsen. "Instead, as Lombard points out, they used a Latin term. *Tabula*. It means voting list or tablet. I think that's the word we want."

"Tabula." Alex Beasley said the word quietly, under his breath almost. He walked slowly to the fireplace, frowning at his thoughts. He glanced casually in the big mirror on the wall. In it he could see the long table covered with its green baize cloth, the richly upholstered arm-chair made for a century of Prime Ministers, and chandeliers at each end of the oblong room and, precisely positioned on the far wall, another tall, graceful mirror. "It goes on for ever," he muttered. The room was extended by the two mirrors into infinity. "Tabula, the writing on the tablet. I thank you, Sir William."

He strode briskly to the middle point of the table where the three telephones were positioned in a careful arc of a circle. He pressed a button marked Secretary and looked at Sir William Olsen. "Tabula," he said again. He looked grim.

Sir William Olsen looked delighted and bowed courteously.

*   *   *

"Leros. It's an island in the Dodecanese. With a large, and very largely involuntary, population." Austin Lombard turned his head and peered through the half darkness at Hubert Bligh, sitting on his right. "You've heard of it?" He spoke loudly in competition with the wind-noise and the steady roar of the car's wheels on the military highway.

"Of course I have. At one time it seemed to be in the news every day. It's where they keep their political prisoners."

"That's the place." Lombard tapped Bligh's knee. "Avoid it, Hubert, avoid it. The only good thing about it from my point of view is that it's only a few miles from Bodrum on the south-west coast of Turkey."

"Halicarnassus." Colonel Tuna growled it. "Halicarnassus."

Lombard's reaction was unusually swift. "Bodrum," he said. Bligh couldn't see his mouth as he said it, but he knew from the way it sounded that Lombard's teeth were clenched in a sudden spurt of anger. The back of his neck went rigid.

Bligh broke the quarrel up before it really began. "How did you get away?" He began to feel like a Greek chorus. The idea was, in the circumstances, inappropriate, so he pushed it from his mind.

"Ask the Colonel."

The Colonel showed his teeth for a moment or two in the light thrown back from the road by the car's headlights. "Top secret," he said. Then his voice took on the resonance of innocence. "And we found Commander Lombard." He laughed louder than was necessary and Bligh felt uncomfortable. Trust him to use Lombard's naval rank.

"Who told you he was there, Colonel?"

"Top secret." This time Tuna did not laugh.

"I did." Lombard gave no more details. "You haven't said, Hubert. Did Beasley get my message from that little fancy piece?"

"Lucille was her name."

"That's it. 'Call me Lucy.' Did he get it?"

"Apparently. Otherwise I wouldn't be here."

"And why *are* you here?"

Hubert Bligh suddenly saw red. "Because the Prime Minister bloody well conned me into it." He almost shouted it, though Lombard's ear was less than eighteen inches from him. He calmed down when no one replied. "God knows why I'm here. Beasley maybe knows. The Colonel maybe knows"—he nodded at Tuna who was looking arrogant and wise at the other side of Lombard in the back seat—"I don't."

"I do." Austin Lombard spoke quietly. He looked out of the car window. They were still moving swiftly eastwards along the superb military road that runs from Erzurum, the main military base in the Anatolian plain, towards the Kars Gap and the

Russian border near Leninakan. He glanced at his watch. "Three more hours," he said, "and we're in the danger country. It's 2.0 a.m. now. We go through Kars at about three o'clock. The local Vali has orders from Ankara to see us through without delay."

"Without stopping." The Colonel seemed to find it richly funny. Lombard leaned forward and tapped the driver on the shoulder. It must have been some form of pre-arranged signal because neither of them spoke. The car slowed down, pulled into the side of the highway and stopped. The heater fan went on humming like a dynamo notched down.

Colonel Tuna spoke curtly in Turkish and the driver bent under the fascia and came up with a mobile spot lamp. "This will probably do," said Lombard. "You need briefing, Hubert."

"Why here, for God's sake?" Bligh was indignant. "Why here in this God-forsaken place? Why not back in Erzurum?" He remembered the way they had made him rush his cup of ceremonial coffee in the Governor's office. "I am sorry, Vali Bey," Lombard had said, doing his commander officer on the bridge stuff. "We have a rendezvous to keep." They had all laughed, Bligh joining in through courtesy. And two minutes later they were in the car and moving far too quickly eastwards through the city.

"Isn't it obvious?"

"No, it's not." Bligh was beginning to get a bit irritated by all this man of action stuff. M.P.s are elected by their constituents to talk, to think maybe, to complain certainly. "What the hell's the idea?" He moved into phase three and tried complaining.

"Because nine people out of ten back there in the Vali's office speak English, even though it *is* with an American accent. This business is secret, Hubert, I do assure you. *Top bloody secret.*"

"Too secret for some Turks but not for others, you mean?" As he spoke, Bligh leaned forward and looked beyond Austin Lombard at Colonel Tuna. Their eyes met for a few seconds and then Bligh looked away. "I'm sorry," he said "that was not called for." He found himself trembling slightly and wondered what he had seen in Tuna's eyes.

The only sound in the car was the low harsh roar of the heater-fan, and then nearby, out in the dark of the night, they heard the long whimpering howl of a marauding wolf. The driver's actions were instinctive and immediate. He swung the spot-lamp which he was still holding to his left with one hand and his right hand flashed to a loaded pistol which lay on a shelf beneath the fascia board of the car. Bligh noticed that he was shaking, but the pistol in his hand was steady. The wolf had stopped howling. No one spoke as the beam from the spotlight slowly raked the broken rocky ground to the north of the road. "There it is," said Tuna quietly.

Kurt, the driver breathed it rather than spoke it, and the beam of light trembled. The wolf was about thirty yards away, crouching ready to attack, and its eyes glowed in the light. Then its head went up as it uttered a short savage snarl of defiance and fear, and it turned to slink away behind the rocks on the hillside.

Colonel Tuna leaned forward. He tapped the driver's pistol arm and spoke a sharp guttural command. He watched the pistol go back to its ledge. *"Peki, Peki,"* he said. *"O.K."*

Lombard touched Bligh's knee. "I have yet to meet a Turk," he said, "who didn't react like that to a wolf. With men they are brave; with wolves, they're cowards." There was something behind his words that Bligh found hard to understand. And then, appallingly, the Colonel spat. It was offensive in every possible way.

"Foolish Colonel," said Lombard. "Foolish."

"Christ Almighty." Bligh was shattered as the truth hit him. "Good God, Lombard, what are you up to?"

"Very foolish." Lombard said it again and Bligh saw that his pale, gaunt face was rigid with anger. His lips were drawn back as though he was having to restrain himself from some act of violence.

Bligh spoke quietly, rubbing it in. "Halicarnassus," he said, whispering it.

Lombard's face relaxed a little as he turned to look Bligh in the eyes. "That, too, was very foolish." He nodded. "They say the third time's unlucky." Then his voice changed and he became brisk. "It's also a very useful mistake, Hubert. You're beginning to see what you're in for. You're not likely to start imagining you're in the nice quiet respectable area you represent in Westminster are you? You're not in Brockley Park, South-east whatever it is. For one thing, that pistol's loaded. And so is this." He tapped his sheepskin jacket.

Colonel Tuna put his hand inside his coat and nodded. He did not speak to Bligh. Instead, he gave an order to the driver, who brought the spotlight round again to the map which Lombard was spreading out on his knee. Bligh recognised it but said nothing. It was the Tbilisi sheet of the military map of Turkey he had seen—God Almighty, less than a week ago—in Beasley's room at the House.

"We're here." Austin Lombard started the map-tapping business just as Alex Beasley had done. "Give or take ten miles. It's bloody hard to be certain until we reach Kars." His finger slid a couple of inches to the east.

"We passed Horasan two kilometres back," said the Colonel. He leaned over and pointed to a tiny place-name on the map, and Bligh was impressed. The Colonel certainly knew his terrain.

"O.K." Lombard nodded his thanks. "We go through here, the city of Kars (if you can call it a city), at three o'clock. Then we turn north to Melikoy . . . then west again!" He traced the route with his finger. "To Perkit about twenty miles further on. This . . ." Austin Lombard paused, rather overdoing the drama . . . "this is where the danger country begins." He looked up from the map. "How much did Beasley tell you?"

"He showed me the message. *ADM in Armenia.*"

"Good. This"—Lombard laid his hand flat on the map—"is Armenia. And here"—he ran a finger north from Perkit through the mountain range along the eastern shore of Lake Cildir to the Russian border, "and here are the atomic minefields." He paused again. "We are actually, at this moment, less than fifty miles from Kingdom Come." Lombard jerked his shoulders and uttered an explosive whistle through his front teeth. Only the lack of space in the back of the car seemed to limit the elaborate mime that Bligh had come to expect with any reference to the atomic minefield. "And Kingdom Come with a vengeance if one of our people makes a mistake."

Bligh thought carefully before he spoke. "Only if the mines have been fitted with detonators," he said.

"But of course they have, man. Why otherwise should that stupid fool Schutzbacker carry the key round with him? They say he even takes it into his bath with him."

"And to bed." Mustafa Tuna leered unbecomingly. "Clonk, clonk," he said and his eyes rolled. Bligh did not smile but Tuna didn't let that stop him from enjoying his thoughts.

Bligh remembered his earlier conversation on his way by train from Ankara to Erzurum. Kaya Mersinli had not named the American Colonel, but he had the same views about the key. "Schutzbacker's the American Colonel, I take it?" he asked, making sure.

"That's the one. American Liaison Commander NATO Eastern Command. With powers of a full General—and that essential key." Lombard grinned in the light of the torch. "He's the reason we rushed you out of Erzurum, Hubert. He might have seen me. He's expecting *you*. Beasley warned him through the NATO machine at Izmir. He's not expecting to see *two* M.P.s. He'd have a bloody fit."

Tuna grunted as though a fit is what he hoped Schutzbacker would very soon have. He grunted again as the idea warmed his heart.

"How do you mean, he's expecting me?"

"He's waiting for you. Here." Again the map tapping. Bligh peered down at Lombard's finger-nail. It was not very clean.

Kizilçakçak. The name came into focus. Lombard said it explosively, loosing the 'i's' deep down in his throat and spitting the *chak chak* out as though imitating a burst of gunfire. As he spoke he stuck his first and second fingers out and pointed them like a pistol aimed at Bligh's head. "*Kizil* means 'red'," he said. "The name tells its own story. It's on the Russian border. That's where you'll meet him."

"And you?"

"Not me. Nor the Colonel here. We have other things to do." They both grinned.

Bligh groaned. "I may be stupid," he said. "In fact I'm *sure* I'm stupid, but I can't get this right. Turn the blasted car round and let's get back to civilisation."

Lombard refused. "Out of the question, Bligh. Out of the

question. You took this on. As I did." His eyes had begun to glow in his gaunt pale face. "Hasn't it occurred to you, for God's sake, that what we're doing is for the sake of civilisation? Ours?" He paused almost as though giving himself a moment or two in which to cool down. Then he went on, using his voice flatly, as though consciously keeping a note of excitement out of it. "We've got a big job to do. And I mean 'we'. You and Tuna and me. Three more days and we're through with it. And then, my dear Hubert, you can get back to Westminster and put down your starred Parliamentary Questions about unmarried mothers in Tulse Hill."

Hubert Bligh grunted. The idea was curiously seductive. "Carry on explaining," he said. "Only start at the beginning."

An hour later, still on schedule, the car bumped along the broken cobbled streets of Kars. The sky ahead of them to the east had a faintly luminous glow which touched the snow-capped summits of the mountains, and inside the tumbled city the citadel on its mound stood out against the sky.

They were flagged through by the sleepy military guard on the main route to the east. Now they were moving into action, and now he knew more clearly what was expected of him, Hubert Bligh felt more settled, more secure and certainly more excited. Austin Lombard's briefing had been crisp and totally comprehensive.

Bligh did not realise, at that stage, that he was going to make one of the most phenomenal mistakes of his life. Otherwise he would have stopped the car (using that loaded pistol, if necessary, to do it), got out and taken his chances with the bitter cold and the wolf-packs of the Anatolian wilderness.

*   *   *

The inner door of the Cabinet Room opened so quickly that the draught blew the Lord Chancellor's agenda paper on to the floor. It swooped down prettily like a bird. He had to pick it up himself (a rare thing for a Lord Chancellor to do) and he grunted with the exertion. He was out of training.

The Chief Whip came into the room as though shot from a gun. He was hot and angry and obviously looking for trouble.

For a tiny man he had an incredible aura of energy and vitality.

"Ahhh!" said the Prime Minister. The only reason he did not look at his watch with ostentatious irritation was that he didn't wear one. One thing a Prime Minister never needs is a watch, since he is always surrounded by people who keep on telling him what time it is. The Home Secretary told him, and the Chief Whip bridled. His apology for his lateness was a meaningless growl.

"Trouble," he said as he sat down and got down to business. "Bloody trouble." It occurred to him that whenever he had to sit on the Cabinet Parliamentary Committee for the Leader of the House he always seemed to have trouble to announce. He frowned. He did not like it. You get a bad name.

"Lombard?" The Prime Minister had a nose for trouble. So had all the others. It seemed best for him to say the word. He did not say it with warmth.

"Lombard." The Chief Whip had lost a lot of his dignity as he sat down at the Cabinet Table. All the chairs in the Cabinet Room are the same height from the floor, on a well-established principle of average dimension. Big men gain in dignity, little ones lose it. Gilbert Dace was a very little one. "Lombard," he said glaring balefully at the Prime Minister. "It's a week since the announcement and a lot of chaps on both sides are starting to complain that we're doing nothing about it. The troops, in other words, are revolting." This is the Chief Whip's most regular joke (when away from the troops) but this time it was not meant as a joke, and nobody laughed.

"Anything to report from your people?" The Prime Minister cocked an eye at the Secretary for External Affairs.

"Not a thing. So far as the Greek Government's concerned, he's still under surveillance at an undisclosed address." William Empery put the last six words into inverted commas, and gave the word surveillance its full Diplomatic Service pronunciation. It still meant Lombard was in a secret prison.

"Still secret, different address," Alex Beasley said. "Why don't these people use the Embassy? Lombard must have known the trouble that's blowing up." He turned to the Home Secretary. "Did you see him before he left London?"

154

"No, but one of my people did. *And* the Board of Trade."

"What did he know about Operation Noah?"

"As much as most." The Home Secretary was cryptic. "Not much," he added. "His firm was involved to a slight degree in supplying materials. Import-Export Corporation."

"A bit chancy surely?"

"No. He always declared his interest. Do we know whether he's still in Greece?"

"H.E. in Athens thinks not. He thinks the Turks got him out of gaol and whisked him over to Turkey."

"That's chancy too."

Beasley shrugged his shoulders. "It happens," he said. "I don't suppose we'll ever stop it, unless we can put a buffer state down between the two of them. A broad one." He paused. "Thank God we're out of Cyprus," he said. "Nothing from Hubert Bligh, I suppose?"

"Nothing." William Empery was getting tired of being negative but there was nothing he could do about it. "The communications system is a bit on the weak side." You can always blame the communication system.

"They've got telephones."

"But no scramblers for overseas calls."

"Then Bligh's wise... what's funny?" The Prime Minister stared at Desmond Bassington, who had laughed.

"Bligh's wise," Bassington laughed again and then stopped. It was going to be one of those days. "It sounded funny."

"It isn't." Beasley turned to the Home Secretary. "I asked you to look into 'Tabula'. Found anything?"

"Plenty. It's a pressure group. All above-board, it seems. It's got international connections."

"Communist?"

"No. Just the opposite. The President's a Chartered Accountant from Purley."

"With no sense of humour." It was the Lord Chancellor who spoke. "I went there the other day for lunch. Instead of you." He looked at the Prime Minister. "I told them the story of Lord Thurlow..."

"Quite." Beasley had heard it.

"Like the 'Link' before the last war." The Lord Chancellor firmly believed that age meant wisdom, so his precedents tended to be old ones. "Sinister and dangerous," he said, and nodded wisely.

Alex Beasley looked up sharply. "You think Tabula's sinister and dangerous?"

"It wouldn't surprise me." The Lord Chancellor was very circumspect. "But I've no proof." More circumspect still.

"Has the Home Office?"

David Orchard shook his head. "None. We might try to get someone in."

"I don't see why not." The Prime Minister didn't sound enthusiastic. "But do be careful."

"We could raid it." Orchard looked blandly round the Cabinet table. "They've a place near Curzon Street. Rather plush."

"Not yet. Try infiltration first." Alex Beasley turned back to the Chief Whip. "We'd better say something about Lombard at the Party meeting. In the meantime get your chaps talking around the House. Put the troops in the picture. But not too much. I've a feeling this might turn out very nasty before we've finished. Right." He looked across the table at Desmond Bassington. "Euratom. Anything turned up there?"

"Traces of odd activity." Bassington hesitated. "Not a right lot you could put a finger on. But odd. Definitely odd." He looked a bit vague round the eyes. "They're scientists," he said. "They tend to be odd." He glanced round and looked ready to duck, expecting a howl of rage from the Minister of Technology. Then he relaxed when he realised she wasn't on that particular Committee. He said it again. "They tend to be odd. For one thing, in Amsterdam and Petten, our man was sure they were on to him. They put a tail on him. And in Karlsruhe, some of the local Euratom people knew about Enver and Brook being killed. Knew almost before we did. Anyway, we're following it all up."

"And the police?"

"Still working on it." The Home Secretary's voice had a ring of no confidence in it. Silence fell on the Cabinet Room.

* * *

"Did yer see Wipers?" Gordon the messenger made conversation as he opened the MI5 office with the three regulation keys. Christopher Pallister stood by the door impatiently. He felt he ought to be asking Gordon why the keys were kept, all three, on one bunch instead of being scattered as far about the building as topography permitted according to Regulation 7214/3216 MI5, *New Series*. He decided that he knew the answer he would get (full employment, he confessed, had its disadvantages) and compromised by asking what it said on the label. Gordon looked first at it and then at him. It took a long time. "Nothing," he said. He had a crafty look in his ancient eyes. "Dunt need to," he observed. "It says MI5 on the 'ook."

The door was now open. Pallister escaped inside and shut it. Then a thought struck him. He opened the door again and put his head out. Gordon was three feet away and engaged in the long slow process of turning to go back to the Reception desk. "Wipers," said Pallister.

"Wipers." Gordon echoed it. "Did yer see it?" He stopped turning round and started turning back.

"No. I'm afraid I didn't." Pallister, a courteous young man, gave it a moment's thought. "I probably flew over it though. Both ways." As if that made it any better.

"R! an interesting place, Wipers. Spent a couple of months there once. Yer ought to see it." He looked dreamy as well as rheumy.

Pallister took a deep breath. "Gordon," he said slowly and distinctly. "How did you know I went to Belgium?" He paused. "On holiday," he added.

"It's in the book. The aeroplane ticket book. *Mr Pallister,* it says, *Belgium.*" Gordon looked at Pallister's face. "It's all right," he said. His arm came out to console Pallister, who saw it coming towards him like the Kraken's top left tentacle. He sidestepped it. "I allus look it up," Gordon went on. "It said *Mr Malplaquet to Milan, Mr Pierce to Hamsterdam.* And *Mr. Northcott to Germany.* None of us could read it. A funny-named place."

"None of whom?" Pallister sounded daft saying it like that, and Gordon noticed it.

157

"None of whom?" he repeated it, cooing on the double-O and humming a rising note on the M. Then he paused. "Bloody cleaners," he said, and he started turning round again.

Pallister had just got inside the door when Pierce pushed his way in. "Chatting up the boys," he said. He threw his hat towards the hat stand. "Pick it up please, Pallister, that's a good chap. By God, am I glad to be back! Fifteen hours a day." He whistled the second half of a wolf-whistle to express his total exhaustion. "Must be getting old," he said. "Used to be able to do it without batting an eye."

Pallister looked at him venomously. He had intended himself to say sixteen hours. "I hope it rained," he said.

"As a matter of fact, it did." Pierce looked up from the deep chair. "Fifteen hours in the rain!" He was beginning to believe it himself.

The door opened. Eugene Malplaquet came through in time to hear what Pierce said. "You were lucky," he nodded. "Sleet." He went over to his desk. "Has the coffee trolley been round yet? Northcott's on his way up. He was arguing with a traffic warden who found him putting German money into a meter." He looked up as Northcott came in, fuming. "Let that be a lesson," he said. "Security. Now that traffic warden knows where you've been. You've got to be careful, Northcott."

Northcott smiled with utmost courtesy and at the same time murmured the three rudest words in the German language.

Malplaquet smiled back. "That's better," he said. He was all for Harmony in the Office.

* * *

Dah-di-dah-di; Dah-di-dah-di. "There it is." Colonel Tuna spoke rapidly to the driver, leaned over the front seat and picked up the spot lamp. The driver changed down and prepared to swing the car off the highway towards the flashing signals a quarter of a mile away to the left. He stopped as soon as they were off the road, and as the engine noise dropped they heard the crunch of ice beneath the tyres.

Tuna lowered the window and the cold wind struck him in the face. Bligh felt it almost like a high-voltage electric shock. Lombard cursed and pulled his sheepskin jacket round his ears. "Get on with it," he muttered.

Di-dah-di; di-dah-di. Colonel Tuna flashed the message-received signal by passing his heavy fur gloves across the face of the map, and in the distance a faint flicker of light made the O.K. *Dah-dah-dah; dah-di-dah.*

"We'll have to make a run for it. I don't suppose they'll wait long." As Tuna spoke, Bligh assumed there must be some kind of car or tank or cross-country vehicle out there hidden in the hills. Tuna suddenly seemed to glow with authority and Bligh realised for the first time the strange power of the man. "Got everything?" Tuna asked.

Lombard disregarded him and turned to Bligh. "You can trust the driver, Hubert. A picked man and a good soldier. He'll take the car up there along this gully about one hundred yards. Then he'll put all lights out as we leave and he'll keep them out until we signal you. Then away you go. Kizilçakçak's four miles away to the east." He spoke a word of command in Turkish; and began to check his gear as the car moved off very, very slowly over the frozen ground. "Keep the Russians busy as long as you can, Hubert. They enjoy it, and we need it. We're depending on you a lot."

The terrain was smoother than Bligh had imagined though they went down more than once with a dreadful crunch on the car's rear springs. The headlights were on at full beam, like twin searchlights. They rose and fell ahead of them. The car's engine was roaring as it moved slowly in bottom gear towards the end of the gully. Suddenly the sheer craziness of the operation struck Bligh in the stomach and he began to giggle uncontrollably to himself, bubbling and choking in his throat. His face was running with sweat. Lombard turned on him viciously. "Shut up, Bligh, for Christ's sake. Where the hell do you think you are? This is serious." The tone of his voice, high pitched and almost hysterical, made the whole thing sound even more ridiculous, craziness gone crazier, and Bligh began to laugh out loud, sucking air into his lungs as though his life was being wrung from him. He also felt strangely sick. The car kept up its slow, rolling progress and the driver's back was as rigid and firm as though he had been built into the machine and was part of it.

"You bloody, bloody English fool." It was Colonel Tuna who turned on Bligh. He seemed almost insane with rage. His voice had gone up two octaves and was forcing its way out of his mouth with a grating sound that made Bligh's stomach turn. In a split part of a second he realised that Tuna was practically on the point of having a fit. And then it happened. Tuna spoke a word that stung Austin Lombard into action. Bligh never knew what the word was, though he knew pretty exactly what it meant. And what happened next was clear to him too. Lombard brought his forearm up in a vicious jab into the Colonel's throat. "Third time unlucky," said Austin Lombard. "Unlucky for you, Colonel, you fool!"

Tuna's lips were set in a rigid line, and tears of sheer pain were dribbling off the end of his chin. And then very slowly a thread of blood crept out of the corner of his mouth. He must have bitten deep into his tongue. He said nothing (he probably could say nothing) as he brushed the blood away with the back of his gloved hand.

It was then that the driver stopped the car, turned round in his seat and shot the Colonel in the head.

"*Türk degil, Rum gavurudur,*" he said. His voice was cold and expressionless. He then put the pistol back on its special shelf and sat there, waiting.

Bligh never knew why he didn't panic. For one thing he had never before seen a man killed—even during the war he had managed always to be somewhere else when the bullets started flying. In the Artillery, he had of course been trained to use a pistol, but on the field the enemy was always impersonal, distant and invisible. Indeed, when he was being honest with himself, he admitted that he joined the Coastal Defence section of the Royal Artillery just for that reason. It was mainly through a refined form of cowardice.

He watched, stiff with horror, as Lombard leaned over Tuna's body to make sure that he was dead, and then opened the door of the car and gently pushed the Colonel out on to the ground.

For a second or two his foot jammed against the cill and Lombard had to force it clear with his own boot.

Lombard himself had assumed an air of cold efficiency. "I told him," he said with almost a tone of tenderness. "I said 'third time unlucky' when he swore at you."

Bligh heard his own voice. It seemed to be coming from the far side of the moon. "He swore in Greek."

"That's right."

"He *was* Greek."

"Of course. The driver realised it. He said, he's not a Turk, he's a damned Greek."

Bligh heard himself groaning. "I don't get it, Lombard," he said. "I just don't get it."

Lombard seemed oblivious of him. He was wiping blood from the seat of the car. "It's as well it's red leather," he said, almost to himself. Then he looked up at the driver, who was sitting rigidly at the driving wheel. Again Bligh was left out in the cold—quite literally so, because the door was still partly open and the night air was freezing. He was beginning to feel numb up the left side of his leg, either from cold or from shock, he couldn't tell which. He found himself wiping blood off his shoe with a folded handkerchief, then he took it by one corner and shook it free. He stared at it as he held it up; it had a geometrical pattern on it in red. He felt very old and sick and frightened.

Lombard was doing nothing to help him. Instead, he was leaning over the back of the front passenger's seat. And he was talking a low swift stream of Turkish that was rolling out of his mouth like blood from a wound. Bligh took charge of himself and tried to concentrate on the driver's neck and head. He was still sitting rigid at the wheel and staring out into space. Occasionally his head shook. *Yok*, he said; that is all. *Yok*. And then, at the end of what seemed like an hour, he nodded vigorously. *Evet* he said. *Evet*. Bligh knew at least (and almost at most) what this meant. *Yok* for "no" and *evet* for "yes" were the only two words he had needed to learn since that crazy moment years ago when he agreed to do as Alex Beasley had asked him. *By God.* He found himself reacting to his thoughts, and indignation started piling up like a cloud about his head. *By God, wait till I get back, Mr Prime Bloody Minister.* He felt better for it, but not much. He still felt sick.

Austin Lombard spoke to him as he sat back in his seat. As he spoke he began to collect his gear again. "Take Tuna's pistol, Hubert. I'll hand it in when I get out. He won't be needing it."

"You're going?" Bligh was ashamed of his reaction. He said it again, this time fairly quietly but still with an edge of panic. "You're going."

"Of course. I've no alternative." Lombard jerked his head towards the driver. "He'll keep quiet. I've just put the fear of Allah into him."

Bligh looked at the driver. He was sitting less stiffly now and his hands, gloves off, were held on top of the steering wheel, cupped together as though held to catch grace from heaven, in the praying posture of the Mohammedan. "He'll give no trouble, Hubert. That's certain."

Lombard was now talking briskly. "We carry on as we had planned. The driver got his orders from Ankara, and he'll carry them out. He knows that he'll be hanged if he admits to murder so he'll keep his mouth shut. He'll take you to Kizilçakçak and then it's up to you. Set off as soon as you can. It's bloody late." He looked at the luminous dial of his watch. "We've lost eleven minutes."

"Good God." Bligh leaned over and peered at the watch. If he'd said eleven hours instead of minutes he would have taken it without question.

"Better wait till I signal you." Lombard looked out into the night. "The sun will be up fairly soon but I want to get away in one piece. I don't fancy being left out there with one dead man and a pack of wolves." He put his hand on the door handle. "Don't forget, Hubert. Try the *Niet* stuff and keep them talking. The longer the better." He put his hand unselfconsciously on Bligh's knee. "Don't think about Tuna. He was due to die soon anyway. And it wasn't your fault." Again he looked at his watch. "It's November 26th, Hubert. See you in the Members' Lobby on the 3rd. And I'll stand you a lunch at Pruniers!" He took his hand away and opened the door. Bligh looked down at his knee;

where Lombard's hand had rested there was a patch of blood about the size of a tenpenny piece. When he looked up Austin Lombard was gone.

The engine was silent but the heater-fan was still humming, though now with a lower note. Ten minutes passed and Bligh began to feel panic on its way to his throat. Then he remembered Tuna's pistol and realised that Lombard had forgotten to rescue it. *Oh God*, he thought. So far, he had managed not to see Tuna's body, and the idea of touching it made him tremble. He stopped trembling when he thought of the wolves. Quite clearly he could do with that pistol. He swallowed hard, held his breath and stepped out of the car. He trod on Tuna's hand and heard the dead knuckles grinding against each other.

It was then that he vomited. He was still vomiting when a flash of light in the far distance caught his eye. He stepped forward three or four paces. "Lombard," he shouted, and a queer echo threw the word back at him across the valley. The light continued to flash in dots and dashes as though Lombard was still signalling, desperately perhaps, as the car which had been waiting for him climbed the hillside.

"Good Lord." Bligh spoke it out loud and forgot to vomit. The light had stopped flashing but he hardly noticed that. Against the very pale hint of luminescence in the night sky he saw a strange shape, an aeroplane of some kind with elliptical wings set out at a strange angle. It was moving swiftly northwards and climbing into the sky. The night remained as silent as the grave. In the distance, as though from a place ten miles away, he heard the thin noise of a night bird. But there was no sound from the machine in the sky.

He scrambled back into the car and slammed the door. *Evet. Evet.* He shouted it, his voice dry and hoarse, and immediately the engine roared. "Kizilçakçak," said Bligh as though he was in a London cab.

"*Evet, Bey Effendi*," said the driver and the car moved slowly round in a wide circle on the rough terrain. The early light of dawn was bright enough now for him to see Colonel Tuna's body, a black lump in a rough expanse of black humps. He took his eyes away quickly and then noticed for the first time that he

163

was holding Tuna's pistol in his hand. He leaned over to the front seat, picked up the spotlight and shone it on the pistol.

And then he found himself saying a short prayer. It was said partly for Colonel Tuna out there for ever in the Anatolian scrubland, partly for the nameless driver in the seat three feet from him, a soldier who had shot a senior officer dead, partly for Austin Lombard, M.P., last seen a thousand feet up above the plain of Anatolia. But mostly it was for himself. Bligh realised that he had made the phenomenal mistake of his lifetime. The pistol was a Walther P.38 (he read the name and number on it), and even Bligh knew it was the kind that German policemen, and German policemen only, carry in their belts.

* * *

"Well," said Eugene Malplaquet, a large smile on his large face, "they can't grumble at that!" He looked with pride at the neat assembly of figures on his desk. They were in four columns headed "Pallister", "Pierce", "Northcott" and "Self", and they were written neatly on the back of a pad of discontinued forms 27P13 (Pink). He sighed. They had been good forms in their day but someone had thought of some better ones. It was life. He looked up sternly and caught Preston Northcott's eye. "But there's one thing, Northcott," he said. "If you drank Apollinaris water, how is it you managed to spend DM 27.35 on hosp?"

"I drank a lot of it." Northcott was getting bolshie. "Bloody buckets of it."

"You must have swum in it." Malplaquet said it quite seriously. That's what the Accountant Officer was going to say anyway. "Have you got all the chits?"

"Yes, I have." Northcott looked pointedly at his watch. "Look here," he said. "I've to be at the airport in less than two hours. May I suggest you have a look at my report?" He wanted to get back to Bonn and that blonde on the Embassy switchboard. "Please," he added, late.

"But of course, old chap. Of course. We'll discuss the reports right now." Malplaquet took a long last look at the figures, smiled at them, and pushed them towards the end of the desk. Not *too* far. They ended up still well within reach for an occasional pat. "Your reports! They're all in, I hope. Triplicate?"

Three heads began nodding. "I put mine in last night," said Northcott. "Just before midnight." It was then that he had begun to think of the Bonn blonde. He remembered it well.

"Ah, yes." Malplaquet found the very thin sheaf of papers and looked at them without enthusiasm. "There's not much here." He held them up with one hand and hit them with his signet ring on the other hand. "Not much for the amount of money it cost."

"There wasn't much to report. I couldn't *prove* a single thing."

"No, but you could have *written* more. Instead of sitting around enjoying yourself drinking Apollinaris water..."

Northcott leaned forward. His imminent departure had made him exceeding bold. "Please," he said, enunciating it carefully, "do not call it Apollinaris water. I do not like to hear you calling it Apollinaris water. Nobody else in the whole world calls it that. They all say 'Polly water'." He stopped, and his brain could be seen to be counting his temper down. It got down as far as four maybe, when he thought of an addendum; "And," he said, "I did not enjoy doing it."

"You spent a lot of money on not enjoying it then..." Malplaquet's loosely constructed face had begun to tighten itself up. And a bit of colour was coming to it.

"If all the reports are short..." Pierce sounded like the Reasonable Man in the textbooks... "we might be able to get through them in time to write another report for Bassington before he goes down to the House." He had not been in the Civil Service for nineteen years and seven months for nothing.

"Ah!" Malplaquet's irritation expired in the face of bounden duty. He avoided Northcott's eye and began spreading the pieces of paper out. Nobody pointed out that his, Malplaquet's report about Ispra, was a very small one indeed. They all three remembered in time that Malplaquet's visit to Ispra had been little more than an overnight hop, and they didn't want to start undesirable comparisons.

"Northcott's. From Karlsruhe, Germany." The report, written in violet ink, made its way to the top of the pathetically thin pile; and Malplaquet's voice started a sing-song demonstration of public report reading. Every tenth word came out in full; all the others between them became a kind of meaningless rhubarb. "Karlsruhe ... *Schwarzwaldhalle* ... police ... atomic energy ... reactor. Ah! Here's the meat." He looked round the room to make sure everyone was ready open-mouthed to receive the meat. This time he read with exaggerated care. *I proceeded to the headquarters of the Karlsruhe Police (Civil Division) and reported what I had overheard in the beer-hall. I also informed them of the object I had discovered.* They undertook forthwith to investigate the people who were presumed to have come from the Central Reactor. This they did. I paid another visit to the Police at 12.15 on the following day. The people I had identified had been traced and both of them had, that following morning, left Karlsruhe on leave of absence. The leave had been approved well in advance by the Directorate of Euratom Administration, Brussels ...*

"Ah!" Malplaquet stopped his bravura performance and looked up from Northcott's typescript. "That," he said with relief, "let's them out." He began to do arithmetic on his fingers, and then stopped. "How much leave were they taking?" he asked, his eyes aglow.

Northcott was suspicious, partly because Malplaquet's logical processes often intimidated him, but mainly because he didn't want to give away the fact that the Karlsruhe police had not given him full details and, more to the point, it had not occurred to him to ask for them. "About a fortnight," he said. This he did know, but anything more detailed than that was beyond him.

"Splendid." Malplaquet was shining with relief. "That means they would be miles away from the Research Centre on the 1st December, which date, I may remind you, is the D-day—the December day, if I may put it that way—according to the Prime Minister. Good-oh." He prepared to read on. He was just working his vocal chords up to the required pitch of resonance when Pallister stopped him. "I'm not so sure," he said. His face had gone white with astonishment and excitement. "You're certain that's Northcott's report, not mine?" It was a purely rhetorical question. Even from where he was sitting, he could see the violet

* Annexe A. Pkt. matches, one in no., empty.

ink. "The thing is," said Pallister, "precisely the same thing happened in Moll." He looked across the room at Pierce and his face went whiter still with excitement when he saw that Pierce was nodding vigorously.

"Same in Petten." Pierce's thin precise mouth stayed open with a restrained kind of astonishment. He seemed to have come to life and was surprised at it.

"And in Ispra?" Pallister turned from Pierce to Malplaquet, who held a hand up. He looked like a bishop at the moment of benediction. "Yes," he said. "I admit the same thing happened at Ispra, but let's not rush it."

He was too late. Pallister was already rushing it. The telephone was quivering in his hand.

It took him seven minutes to get through to Brussels, four more to reach the Euratom Headquarters, five more to discover the young man who assembled, filled and administered the Euratom leave chits, ten more to give him the names (mainly because most of them, not unnaturally, were foreign, they had to be found in the several reports, spelled out to Pallister and then relayed to Brussels).

Then the young man said, politely, "Yes, what about them?"

Pallister said they, the British authorities, would like to know where all these people had gone to spend their leave of absence.

The young man was not an international bureaucrat for nothing. He repeated the request slowly, accurately and tonelessly. Pallister's foot was tapping on the floor as he listened to it all again. He was looking at the ceiling with an air of infinite patience, nodding occasionally and grunting to assure the young man that he was doing very well, considering the fact that he was foreign.

And then, suddenly, Pallister went stiff. The word the young man had used was actually a low form of Flemish but its meaning was quite clear.

Two hours later, Pallister was still on the telephone. The Belgian Minister of Posts and Telecommunications, the Director-General of Euratom, the Area Commandant of Interpol, the Chief of Police of Brussels and the third private secretary of the King of the Belgians had all become involved. In the face of such a mass of assembled authority, the young man threw the towel in, and Pallister got his information.

All the people concerned, it seemed (eleven of them, eight men and three women), had set off from their own bases and had assembled in the Euratom Headquarters in Brussels. As senior officials of Euratom (grade MA2 minus and above) they had travelled to Brussels from their several Research Establishments—Petten, Moll, Ispra and Karlsruhe—at one third normal fare, repayable by deductions from salary. Then, taking advantage of Sabena group travel (night flight), they had flown via Rome to Athens. At Piraeus they had boarded the Motor Vessel *Olga* bound via Istanbul and the Black Sea ports to Trabzon. "Was there," the young man asked, "anything else the gentlemen wished to know?"

"Yes," said Pallister. They wished to know what the hell they were up to.

The young man had taken that in his stride too. As members of the Euratom Geological Study Group (all the constituent groups in the European Communities have highly developed non-vocational facilities of this kind, of course) they had gone to make a seismological survey of the Northern Taurus range in Anatolia.

Once the brake had been forcibly removed, the young man had been hard to stop. He conceded that November is a cold month in Anatolia but, in an area which is notoriously susceptible of seismological disturbance (it is, of course, as he mentioned, in the middle of the Asian-East European earthquake belt), it is better to undertake such a study when earthquakes of severe proportions are less likely. And in any case (Pallister could visualise the young man two hundred miles away in the Rue Belliard, raising his hand to brush away his protestations of gratitude and satisfaction) the highest executives of Euratom are always encouraged to undertake expeditions which will exercise their bodies as well as their minds. *Mens sana,* said the young man . . .

Pallister thanked him, grimaced, put the receiver down in *media re* and fanned his brow. He then reported the details to Malplaquet, who had obviously been deeply impressed by the young man's bureaucratic *tour de force*. Pierce (who was hungry and therefore cross) pointed out that the geological group had played into their hands by insisting on group-travel to save money. This had hurt Malplaquet, who had a deep respect (both temperamentally and professionally) for parsimony, and he had gone into an extended tutting and twittering session which reminded Pallister (he had considered it carefully) of a budgerigar he had known when young.

The long delay meant that they missed getting their report in to Desmond Bassington. Preston Northcott missed his flight back to Bonn. He also missed the blonde on the switchboard. Eight months later she married a lance-corporal who was just finishing his tour of duty with the British Army of the Rhine at München-Gladbach and they went to live in Brighouse.

* * *

"What the hell..." said Sir Hubert Bligh as soon as he could speak. He picked himself up from the floor of the car and gently rubbed his forehead. *More blood*, he thought. The inside of the car was beginning to smell of it, and then he realised that the smell was inside his own head. *Oh what a bloody way to live.* The driver, to do him justice, seemed genuinely sorry. He was shrugging his shoulders and putting his hand on his heart in a desperate attempt at silent communication. In between, he was also rubbing his chest to show that he, too, had been surprised by the ambush. He irritably clipped the steering-wheel with the back of his hand for having damaged his breast-bone when he clapped the brakes on. As a gesture, it was self-explanatory but he overdid it and then he had to start rubbing the back of his hand with the front of his other one.

The door of the car opened and a pistol came in. The hand that was wagging it at Bligh was clothed in black, and so was the arm behind it. "Good God," Bligh muttered. "Batman."

He then took charge of himself with a great effort and said, slowly and distinctly, who he was. The pistol seemed unimpressed. It went on wagging up and down.

"Out," said a voice in English from outside the car.

Bligh got out with all the dignity he could call on. There wasn't much of it left because the past twelve hours had begun to tell on him. The man holding the gun was still unimpressed. "The others," he said. His English had a kind of mock textbook ring about it, as if the man was out of practice, or had never been in it.

"There are no others," said Bligh. He held the door open, politely, to let the man see. The back seat was empty if a bit untidy.

"Chertovshchina!!" said the man. He said it as though he meant it.

"Moskof !!!" shouted Bligh's driver. First a Greek; now a Russian! He dived immediately for the gun on the ledge beneath the fascia. It was getting to be a bit of a habit and it was a courageous thing to do, but it didn't do him any good this time. The pistol in the gloved hand hit him on the back of the head, once, hard.

"More blood," said Bligh. He shuddered and felt sick again. The driver looked dead but he was making bubbling noises with his mouth. Bligh found little consolation in this, though some. He turned to the man with the pistol. "What," he asked, "is the idea?" It was an incongruous question. It was obvious what the idea was. He, the Right Honourable Sir Hubert Bligh, M.P., Member of the Shadow Cabinet, Envoy Extraordinary of the British Prime Minister, was in a totally ludicrous situation, out in the wilderness between nightmare and reality, in a frozen lunar landscape, and shivering abjectly (more with cold than with terror, though with some of that too), as the prime object in a skilfully engineered ambush. One thing was certain. He was not out in the wilderness on his own. There were at least six men around him, all dressed in black, like mourners at a wake, but all holding pistols with an assurance which suggested they had been born holding them. Bligh put on a spurious air of nonchalance, though his voice was not very steady. "My case," he said. He pointed to the back seat. "My brief-case, please. The one with H.B. on it." As if there were half a dozen of them. That made him feel better.

"O.K." said the first gunman. He got the case out, felt it carefully to see if there was a gun in it and then stiffened. "I bring," he said. He had obviously found the late Colonel Tuna's Walther P.38.

"We go." The pistol (the one in his hand) started wagging again rudely and imperiously.

"Where to?" It was a perfectly genuine and reasonable question but it seemed to make the man angry. He said something in Russian and one of his colleagues jumped forward. Bligh flinched. The man grasped his shoulders, one with each hand, and turned him round so that he had his back to the boss gunman. Bligh waited for it. Nothing happened.

"Walk," said the man, so Bligh started walking. It was not easy. It was still more dark than light. The ground was rocky and frozen, with patches of ice and snow on which he slipped four times in the first fifteen yards. Each time he slipped, the man behind him said words in Russian which obviously meant clumsy, clumsier, clumsiest and then something much ruder. They scrambled rather than walked for about a hundred yards up a steep slope and, apart from Bligh's grunts of exertion and the scraping of boots on rough, hard ground, there was silence. As they breasted the slope, Bligh, out in front, had the shock of his life.

Twenty yards away on a flat space which had been cleared of stones stood a strange aeroplane with elliptical wings exactly like the one in which he had seen Austin Lombard leave the gully a few miles back on the highway from Kars. Beyond it, in the far distance, were the subdued lights of a town, a cluster of low squat mud hovels hardly visible against the foothills of the Trans-Caucasian range, the inevitable screen back-drop miles away to the east. As he stood there, he heard a rattle of gunfire and saw spurts of flame and then tracer bullets coming from the town and landing uncomfortably near them. Kizilçakçak, as he assumed, was living up to its name.

Bligh had never seen a group of men move more quickly. He himself covered the twenty yards to the plane in four seconds, but it was not until they were all inside, the door had been shut and locked and his seatbelt had been fastened, that he fully realised the incongruity of it. *He had been the last to reach it!* All he had needed to do was to turn round and run the other way, and he could have escaped. He blushed and hoped his friends would never hear about it. He looked out of the window to his left just in time to see a tracer shell thump into the car they had just left. He had the grace to thank Providence for allowing his legs to make his mind up for him, and then he thought of the young man who had driven him in the car from Erzurum, lying there, slumped down beneath the steering wheel, with blood oozing out of a wound in the back of his head and bubbles coming out of his mouth. The principal gunman freed himself of his seatbelt and joined him at the window. He shrugged his shoulders so vigorously that the one nearer to Bligh hit him on the cheek-bone. "War," said the man, "it is the war!" and as he said it, he howled with astonishment and alarm. His feet left the floor of the cabin and he shot to the ceiling where he stuck as though glued to the casing, looking very foolish and muttering what seemed to be obscenities in Russian.

Bligh, strapped to his seat, looked up at the gunman and then down at the burning car. It was by now a thousand feet and more below them, and still burning with a fierce white light. The voice of the man who was pinned to the ceiling was the only noise. "*Operation Noah*" thought Bligh. The anti-gravity invention. Eureka! And then he added, as an afterthought, "But what's the point. The bloody Russians have pinched it."

* * *

"It's five past eleven and the Gentlemen of the Press," said Miss Gloria Tooth in the Outer Office, "are mustered."

Geoffrey Pond, the Prime Minister's Press Secretary, thanked her politely. Inclined by temperament as well as by training to appreciate statistics, he added one to the number of times he had heard her say it. Three hundred and forty-three, he said to the wall, and his eyes rolled in exasperation. He pushed the door of his inner office open with unnecessary zeal and it hit the knee of the man from the *Evening News* who was sitting just inside.

"Naughty," said Geoffrey Pond as he heard what the man said. As he spoke, he put on his brisk press conference smile, and the assembled Lobby men groaned.

"You don't sound very cheerful this morning." Pond almost

carolled it as he threaded his way through the crowd of journalists who were packing his room from wall to wall. "I'm sorry to keep you," he said, lying.

"You have," said Robert Maryon from the *Mail*, "the look of a Press Secretary who has bugger-all to say but intends to say it nicely."

"Exactly." Pond decided to come clean.

"What's the position on South African gold?" It was the *Financial Times* man getting it in before *The Times Business News*. He was rushing it a bit.

"The Chancellor's making a statement." Pond smiled charmingly. "I think you'll like it."

The *Express* man groaned from his place by the bookcase. If the *F.T.* would, the *Express* was not likely to. He switched to surer ground. "What about the Falklands?"

"Speak to the Secretary of State for External Affairs." Pond was not amused. The *Express* man asked him about the Falklands about as often as Miss Tooth told him they were mustered. He pulled a face.

"What about the Rendle business? Anything moving?" Cecil Bradshaw of the *Guardian* put it in the tone of voice which suggested that he expected the answer no.

"No," said the Press Secretary. "Not yet, I'm afraid, Cecil."

"Or Lombard?" Robert Maryon knew very well that the Prime Minister *must* by now have seen the *Mail*'s story about rumours of Austin Lombard's escape from Greece.

"*Still* no news," Pond had no difficulty preventing his face from smiling. The *Mail* piece had given him a few very uncomfortable minutes earlier that morning with the Prime Minister. "Nothing to report. As far as we're concerned, the stories appearing in the press are without foundation."

"Stories!" Robert Maryon was affronted. "Story you mean." He surrounded himself with a lot of tobacco smoke.

"Bligh?" It was the BBC Lobby man, Timothy Woodman. "Our Middle East man understands that Sir Hubert Bligh has left Elizabeth Tronder and the others in Izmir and has gone off on his own somewhere."

Geoffrey Pond took a chance. "Off the record," he said, "do

you blame him?" The laugh that went up was partially successful. Neither of the women, neither the one from the *Scotsman* nor the other from the *Liverpool Echo*, even smiled. One of them tutted.

"Has he?" Woodman, blast him, was persistent.

"How would I know?" Pond put on a mock-indignation act. "He's not under the P.M.'s orders. You'd better put that question, as I've said before, to the Inter-Parliamentary Union."

"Crap," said somebody quietly but very distinctly. Pond let it ride.

"Is Bligh in touch with Lombard. Have they met?" Maryon was still angrily blowing smoke around. He spoke through his own smoke screen.

Geoffrey Pond had been in the business long enough to handle that one. "Unlikely, I would have thought. One of them's in Greece and the other's in Turkey." He dredged up a bit of geographical "O" level in support. "They're over two hundred miles apart," he said.

Woodman smiled sweetly. "Not," he said, "if you count the Greek islands. Leros can be seen from the Turkish mainland." He had a look on his face that suggested he'd gone on to do geography at "A" level.

Looking across the room at him, Geoffrey Pond suddenly realised with a flash of insight why Timothy Woodman was such a success on television. His face was unusually cast in the correct aspect ratio for the screen—three up and down, four from side to side. He looked infinitely smug, like the Buddha at the moment of beatitude.

So did Robert Maryon. "What's in the story about some secret papers being stolen from the Library of the House?" he asked with an expression of infinite innocence.

"On that," said Geoffrey Pond, spacing his words carefully, "the D-notice Committee has decided for the time being to slap a D-notice." The bag was now open, but the cat was still in it. He felt extremely relieved, and showed it. "Have a sherry," he suggested, then the noise started.

* * *

"*Dobro pozhalovali, Gospodin Deputat.*" The man who addressed him had, without any doubt whatsoever, the ugliest face Hubert Bligh had ever seen. It was constructed from the neck upwards in what appeared to be broad lateral folds of flesh and from twenty feet away it looked like a folded army blanket seen end-on. He seemed also, from that distance (the length of the room), to have no hair of any kind, no eyelashes, no eyebrows, no beard line. There were no means of knowing whether he was smiling or scowling, but his voice was resonant and pleasant, and his words sounded kind.

Bligh took a chance on reading the situation correctly. He bowed infinitesimally as a concession to foreign parts (and foreign parts was most certainly where he was) and spoke his visiting card. "Bligh," he said. "Hubert Bligh, Member of Parliament." Characteristically, he did not feel it was necessary to say which Parliament.

"Welcome, Sir Hubert," said the man. He stood up and began working his way round his enormous desk. It was about half an acre in area, and made of metal covered with flat grey paint. There were no papers on it but a lot of telephones and what appeared to be unusual electronic devices. "Kevork Ohannesiantz," said the man, "Colonel-General of the Red Army." He was an enormous man and his dark green uniform, square cut in fine cloth, made him look like a mountain-side in springtime.

With a shock, Bligh realised that the first two words the man had spoken were his name. Polite by nature, he was wondering how on earth he was expected to remember them, when the General spoke again. "Kevork," he said. He laughed richly (presumably at the mystified expression on Bligh's face) and said, "George. My English friends call me George." The laugh came again. "They seem to have difficulty with Armenian names."

You can, Bligh thought, say that again, but he didn't say it out loud. He also managed not to look surprised at the idea of George's having any English friends at all. This was unreasonable of him and he felt a bit ashamed, especially when the General said, "Millionaires' Row, Russian Embassy, Kensington Palace Gardens, W.8." He paused and looked as dreamy as his odd face would let him. "Very good." Like all foreigners he made it sound like *Ver goot*. He then went on to say "Kensington Palace, Ver' beautiful. Princess Margaret . . ." Words failed him, so he made a gesture, putting the end of his second finger against the end of his thumb and holding his hand up about eyebrow level, except that he hadn't any eyebrows. His face looked as beautiful as was in its power and Bligh got the message.

"*Ver goot*," he said entering into the spirit of it. Then, having made contact, the General shouted out loudly in Russian (or possibly in Armenian, Bligh could not, of course, tell which) and four men came into the room from a door at the far end. Each of them nodded at Bligh as he lined up beside the General's desk.

"My men," said George, and Bligh wondered if he was expected to inspect them, walking along the line and grumbling at their dirty buttons. One thing, however, was certain even at that distance. They did not have dirty buttons.

It occurred suddenly to Bligh that he ought to take a stand. "Where," he asked, "am I?" Too late, he realised that he sounded like a Victorian governess coming out of the vapours.

"Yerevan," said the General. He clicked his heels very slightly. "The capital city of the Armenian Soviet Socialist Republic." Then he relaxed slightly. "The oldest city," he said, "in the world. Please come and sit down." He waved at a comfortable chair near the desk. "You and I, Sir Hubert, have great trouble." He waited until Bligh had sat down and then he flicked his fingers twice behind his back. Almost immediately, one of his men stepped forward and put a large envelope into the hand that was doing the flicking.

"This," the General walked over to Bligh, "you want." He put the envelope on to Bligh's lap. "You look, then we talk." He turned round slowly and walked back to his desk.

The only sound in the room was the tearing of paper as Bligh worked his way into the envelope. Then there was the noise of a gasp as he took the document out. *House of Commons Library Dep. Paper 1712 24th April. Operation Noah.* It was a photocopy, and although it was legible throughout, it had obviously been copied in a hurry. Parts of it were very faint.

Hubert Bligh looked up angrily and opened his mouth to speak, but the General's voice got in first.

"You are about to make a natural mistake, Sir Hubert," he said. "A natural mistake to make, but you are wrong. We did *not* steal it from your House of Commons Library." He held up one of his big fat hands. "In Turkey," he said. "We found it in Turkey."

"Found? Found?" It was the only word Hubert Bligh could think of saying.

"Found. In the papers of Lieutenant-Commander Austin Lombard, M.P."

* * *

"This," said the Assistant Commissioner (Crime), "is a police department." He glared angrily around the long table. "And you ..." he swallowed hard as though he knew the words were going to hurt him ... "you are expert police officers." He lit a cigarette and took a deep swallow. He was right; the words had hurt him. He looked at the ceiling, avoiding the assembled eyeballs of his twelve top expert police officers. "We have," he remarked, "five dead men." He ticked them off. "Rendle, Firth, Lemon, Enver and Brook. All dead. For all we know all five were killed by the one man. Had you given that a thought, eh? ... eh? ... eh?" In the rather long pauses between one eh and the next, his eyes got noticeably more bloodshot.

Detective Superintendent Macaulay said they had given a thought to it. He looked away to his right, mainly to avoid the Assistant Commissioner's eyeballs. Instead, he found himself reading the advertisements on the sides of the red buses which were stuck, motionless, in Victoria Street outside. "We gave it a lot of thought," he said. "But it didn't help."

"So, instead, you got yourselves involved in all this international Euratom stuff?" The Assistant Commissioner wagged his finger as he raked the conference with his eyes, very angry eyes. It looked as though he was counting heads prior to a purge. "Where did it get you?"

No one answered.

"And now,"... he was warming up. He changed gear and

moved into top. "And now you're getting mixed up in MI5 stuff." He said it as though it was painful to say. "Not even in Europe. It's ... It's ... It's ..." His geography let him down.

Detective Superintendent Macaulay came to his help. "Asia Minor," he said. He never knew why he said it, quietly. "Asia Minor."

"Parse and bloody analyse it," said the Assistant Commissioner (Crime) at the top of his voice. A little tinkle came from the light bulb above him and later, when it was switched on, it stayed off.

"Turkey, then."

"That's better." The reference to Asia Minor had thrown the Assistant Commissioner's mind back to the Classical Remove. This, in turn, had reminded him that he was a fully equipped Gentleman. When he spoke again his eyes were less bloodshot and his voice had a straw hat on. "Right," he said. "Any ideas?" He looked round the table. It was called Involving the Other Ranks. Or, less offensively, Encouraging Participation.

There was a dead silence. He let it stay that way for quite a long time. Then he pressed a button on his desk.

"Switch on," he said. There was a click from a loudspeaker over the door. "Recording, sir," said a brisk voice.

"No names, no bloody pack-drill." The Assistant Commissioner always made a point of speaking in the vernacular at a time like this. It helped the technique for which he was locally rather famous, a kind of communal testimony of ideas. "Throw the ideas up and we'll knock 'em down. Now or later," he said. "The tape's running."

This time the silence was shorter. At the end of it, eleven throats were heard delicately clearing themselves for communication. The twelfth was Macaulay's. He was, as usual, stubborn and he intended to remain surly.

"Firth." The voice from the bottom of the table was hesitant. "Sidney Firth in the car park had a girl friend in the House of Lords' tea room. Where was she?"

"At home. Alibi proved. With her husband."

"The last parking ticket stub in Firth's pocket was timed at 0247. Who left at that time?"

"A Peer. He'd been to a private dinner party. All above board. Had his wife with him all evening. You have to take the word of a Peer when it's supported by a Peeress."

"Why?"

"Next question."

"How many others left after Firth died? Without handing in their tickets?"

"Seven. All accounted for. Five of them left their money on the counter. The other two *say* they meant to pay later. All O.K."

"Enver and Brook are supposed to have gone down into the car park at 0405 approx. Any blood on their clothes?"

"Yes. A lot. But not Sidney Firth's. Only their own blood groups. Established. All O.K."

"No prints on the spanner?"

"Correct. And none on the Mace either."

"When Rendle was hit with the Mace he had his cap off."

"True."

"Why?"

"We presume he was relaxing and had removed it. He was ex R.N. Sailors always use their caps as pillows."

"But he wasn't a sailor. He was a Chief Petty Officer."

"Old habits. I bet C.P.O.s do it anyway."

"When the Mace was found on the Library shelf behind some books, one Librarian said it was 'behind the biographies in the Old Silent Room' and the Chief Librarian said 'Oh no! Not again,' what did that mean?"

"An ancient tradition. Soon after the Chief joined the staff there was a notorious report published saying that M.P.s had been known to leave empty wine bottles behind the books.* Usually behind the nineteenth-century biographies in the Old Silent Room. The staff are very reticent about it."

"And what does that mean?"

"It means they're reticent."

"I mean, what does it suggest."

"It suggests that the man who put it there knew what he was

* H. C. Papers 1953–4 (184) p. 24. See also Osbert Lancaster's cartoon in the *Daily Express*, June 24, 1954.

doing *or* he accidentally found a good place *or* he wanted to implicate the Library staff."

"Were the Library staff on the premises?"

"One member of it was. In a little staff bedroom up in one of the attics. One of them always stays there when it's a late night."

"It wasn't. They closed down at 10.30."

"Unexpectedly. They were 'counted out'. Less than forty Members present. They were expected to go on. All night maybe. The man on the Library staff had made arrangements, so he stayed."

"So the murderer couldn't know much in advance that the coast would be clear at three o'clock?"

"He couldn't be certain. Not until 1030."

"That explains why the *Olga* left in a hurry. Half her cargo was left on the quay at Rotherhithe."

"Certainly. She went off at half-cock."

"Why didn't the Navy hold her?"

"They did. Once they'd caught her up in the Channel. But they'd no proof, so they had to let her go."

"They knew George Lemon was dead, surely?"

"No. *Olga*'s captain said that Lemon was still alive when they put him in the boat to be picked up by the Tongue Lightship crew. And that's true. Confirmed by the crew of the Lightship."

"How do the *Olga*'s crew say it happened?"

"When George Lemon was climbing on board. They say he struck his jaw on the rail as he climbed the ladder. That's confirmed by the captain of the river pilot's tug at Gravesend. And by Fred Armytage, the river pilot. Lemon certainly struck the side with a hell of a crash, but ... and it's an important but ... he climbed two or three more steps *after* he'd crashed against the side. It's difficult to prove though."

"Was Lemon known to be in MI5?"

"Possible. Who can say?"

"But surely they could have held the *Olga* on suspicion of the murder of Enver and Brook?"

"Nobody knew they were dead at that stage. They'd been dumped over the side on the way down river. Nobody saw them go over. There are some totally deserted reaches between Gravesend and Sheerness. They were found quite by accident on Blyth Sands. If a working party hadn't gone out to repair the Egypt light-buoy they'd be there yet. Stuck in the mud."

"But surely they searched *Olga* for Enver and Brook?"

"Yes. Stem to stern as they say. And they didn't find them. Naturally. They weren't there."

"That in itself was suspicious, surely?"

"Why? They only had one man's word for it that they'd ever gone aboard in the first place. George Lemon's."

"I see. And by this time . . ."

"Lemon was dead."

"Go back to the Librarian sleeping in the attic. Has he an alibi?"

"No. He just says he didn't know about it until he heard the pandemonium, the bell and the hooter when Albert Glass found Rendle dead. We can't budge him."

"What about Glass? Any alibi?"

"None. Naturally. We can't budge him either."

"What about journalists?"

"Several were seen about the place up to midnight. They'd expected to be late. So when the House rose early they stayed on to write their pieces."

"I suppose it was quite a stroke of luck for them. They could catch the earlier editions, and then push off home."

"Did they?"

"Did they what?"

"Push off home."

"They say so."

"No check on them?"

"Partly, but it's pretty negative. There's only one fixed point. The BBC Radio 1 and Radio 2 midnight newsroom. The BBC man, Timothy Woodman, did a short piece from the Westminster Studio about the House being counted out."

"Big deal."

"Steady. Privilege."

"Was it 'live' at midnight?"

"Certainly. We've checked.

"And did he see any of the other journalists?"

"Yes. Bradshaw of the *Guardian,* Maryon of the *Mail* and Forbes of *The Times*. They all saw each other."

"And after midnight?"

"They all went home. Or that's what they say."

"No check?"

"No check on any of them. Two of them also named an M.P. or two they saw about the place. We've a list of twelve. Including the Home Secretary, Sir Hubert Bligh from the Opposition Front Bench, and guess who?"

"The Speaker?"

"The Prime Minister!"

"Oy! Oy! That'd be a turn-up . . ."

"Steady. Back to it! The P.M.s Press man, Pond, was about as well."

"The journalists and the M.P.s. Could they get into the debating chamber where Rendle was found?"

"Of course. If they knew it was open and Rendle was in there."

"Do we know anything about Rendle's job? Before he joined the House of Commons' staff? He was a fairly new man, of course."

"Certainly we do. He was working with Commander Lombard, M.P., on special weapons."

"He was also acting for MI5."

"Sure. But that's secret. It's still secret. And true."

"Is it possible that Lombard had anything to do with Rendle's death?"

"Hardly likely. He was arrested in Athens the very same day as Rendle's murder. BEA are efficient but not all that swift."

"According to the reports from the Euratom Research Stations, the *Olga* picked up a group of atomic scientists in Athens. It's possible that she left London in a hurry to rendezvous with them."

"But of course . . ."

"And *not* just to clear out with Enver and Brook. As an escape route."

"Well, I think that's obvious. The fact that they ditched Enver and Brook means they weren't very important. They didn't treat them gently."

"Keep on Enver and Brook for a bit."

"O.K. What?"

"They *must* have seen the signal on Big Ben and reported operation completed."

"Yes. That's certain."

"Well then, which operation?"

"It's assumed it was the theft of the papers. The ones we aren't supposed to mention by name."

"O.K. then. Why was the Mace pinched?"

"Simple surely. A diversion. Nothing's more likely to divert the attention of the authorities than the loss of their flipping Mace. The Serjeant-at-Arms nearly had kittens."

"O.K. I'm with you so far. But once he'd stolen the Mace, why go into the Chamber?"

"God knows. I'd like to know why he didn't just fling the thing out of the Library window into the river."

"That's easy to explain. It's impossible. The windows are small casements. They're big windows but only small sections of them open. Say a couple of feet wide. And the Terrace is forty feet wide. You just couldn't sling the Mace that far. Not without space to swing it."

"Has it occurred to anybody that X didn't find Rendle in the Chamber? Maybe Rendle found X there?"

"So what? If that had happened, Rendle would have blown his whistle or something."

"Not if he knew X."

"Not if he knew X. That's true."

"And his cap fell off when the murderer started something."

"He could even have thrown it at him. A neb cap's very useful."

"You've forgotten something."

"What?"

"At this time surely the Chamber was in darkness."

"Then Rendle took his cap off to hold it as a shield against a bright torch. I think we ought to go back and do some experiments in the darkness with a torch. Late at night."

"If we can persuade them to rise early enough. They never seem to leave the bloody place."

"At 3.0 a.m. Fix that please, Macaulay."

"Certainly sir."

"*Olga!*"

"What about her?"

"She was registered in Odessa. Did she always work in the Black Sea?"

"Usually. This time she certainly did. She had to deliver her party of atomic scientists to a place called Trabzon."

"It's better known as Trebizond. I once read a book about it. By Rose Macaulay. It's very funny. Any relation?"

A snort from the top end of the table brought the meeting to an end.

* * *

Colonel-General Kevork Ohannesiantz demonstrated another of his grotesque smiles and said it again. There was no hint of a smile in his voice. "We found them in the papers of Lieutenant Commander Austin Lombard, M.P." He looked quizzically at Bligh through a slit in the folds of his face. "Perhaps you did not hear me, Sir Hubert. Your silence . . ."

Hubert Bligh grunted and hoped he sounded a good deal more nonchalant than he felt. "I heard," he said. Not for the first time in his life, he realised that there was some benefit to be gained from the gruelling he had received on occasion at the Despatch Box in the old days when he was in office. At least it taught you how to take a shattering blow without parading the fact that you were shattered.

"Your hands are shaking," said the General, as though making casual conversation. "You will have a whisky." He flicked his finger and thumb again and one of his young men went into action, as though that was the moment he had been waiting for all his life. *Regular bloody Stakhanovites.* Bligh found himself getting testy. "I don't drink whisky at this time of the morning." He looked at his watch, didn't believe it, screwed up his eyes and looked again. He groaned. It was still only a quarter to five. *What a very, very stupid way to live,* he thought. *If this is the way the Higher Diplomacy is developing, from now on you can bloody-well count me out.*

"I guess you don't often get such a shock at five o'clock in the morning." The General made the observation through deep rumbling landslides of laughter. "Teacher's," he said. The rumbling of laughter continued to roll round the room like thunder far away beyond the clouds on the horizon. "Teacher's. It makes the water taste better. Even Armenian water. The best water in the world." He began to pour. "Say when. We get it in bulk delivery from the Army and Navy Stores in Victoria Street, S.W.1. Such a wonderful, imperialistic name, Sir Hubert. Please say when."

Bligh grunted again and the General stopped pouring. "Thank you." Bligh spoke his thanks automatically, and waved a hand in irritation as though his mind was miles away, thinking of something Alex Beasley had said at the briefing session that took place days, weeks, perhaps even months ago before all this mad and stupid charade began. *Twenty-nine pages of vital secrets, but all meaningless without the last page,* Alex Beasley had said. "Your good health, General," he said without much enthusiasm.

Kevork interrupted him. " 'George', please, Sir Hubert, my English friends..."

"Austin Lombard...?"

"Alas no. I never met Mr Lombard." The General had stopped laughing and an eerie silence had fallen on the room. The four young men seemed to have stopped breathing. The document in Bligh's hand was trembling as he fought the temptation to open it at the last page. Then something in what the General had said struck him on the front edge of the brain. "You never..."

"I never met him..." The General emphasised the past tense of the verb. He shrugged his shoulders sadly and looked like some volcano about to erupt. "We found his papers in his coat pocket. A sheepskin jacket. By that time, of course, he didn't need the jacket. He was dead."

Bligh stood up slowly and put his glass down with great care on the General's desk. Even so, he spilled some of the whisky. "Dead?" The word sounded melodramatic in the extreme. Especially when he said it again. "Dead?"

"Dead. One bullet in the head." The General pointed with one stiff finger at his own hairless skull and made a little popping noise. "Dead. Now you will agree, Sir Hubert, that we have a lot to discuss. Austin Lombard is dead."

"Where is he?" As though he was in the casualty ward in St Thomas's across the river! *Must send some flowers. Oh Christ Almighty, it's all mad.* Bligh sat down again, and his stomach felt empty and queasy.

"You must listen, please, Sir Hubert. Please do not interrupt." Again that arrogant flicking of the fingers, four or five times like an obligato performance on the castanets. This time, one of the attendant young men stepped up to the desk and began to operate the dial of one of the pieces of machinery.

"What the . . ." Bligh began to protest as the room began to turn slowly. There was a dull humming sound as though the machine was starting to shift the whole building.

"Come here please, Sir Hubert."

The General walked over to the far side of the room, flapping his thick arms as though urging Bligh to victory at the end of his own personal three minute mile. Bligh stood up and as he did so the room stopped moving. Bligh staggered and felt inclined to blame the whisky. Then the humming began again, the lights in the ceiling went out slowly and the far wall of the room began to slide away to the right. "It's our own little Iron Curtain, Sir Hubert." The General shook with laughter as he stood silhouetted against an early dawn sky, and partly obscuring one of the most spectacular views Hubert Bligh had ever seen.

"The sleeping giant," said the General as Bligh joined him at the window. "Father Ararat." The General sounded faintly embarrassed. "That's what we Armenians call it. But it is no longer ours." He hesitated and Bligh had a feeling that he was controlling a deep and atavistic anger. He avoided the General's eyes and looked out through the plate glass window across the wide valley. Here and there patches of snow glowed in the very early grey light. Beneath them—it was obvious that they were high up in the tower of a modern building—lay the spacious avenues and parks of a city, presumably Yerevan. The streets were just beginning to come to life; lights were coming on here and there in the houses among the trees and one or two people could be seen as dim shadows walking along the streets slowly, as though they were not yet fully awake. A trolley-bus, brightly lit but almost empty, was disappearing towards the suburbs of the south. The only sound was that of a baby crying near at hand. It sounded very lonely. It could have been anywhere, anywhere in the world, but for one thing. Over to the left, south-east from the city, the whole horizon was filled with the towering, colossal mass of Mount Ararat, wholly covered with snow, deserted, treeless and bare. Beside it, to the left, stood the smaller cone, almost geometrically perfect, of "Little Ararat".

"It is a very famous view of the mountain, Sir Hubert. Known throughout the world. You have, of course, seen it before." A rumble of laughter made Bligh turn. Kevork's face was shining with delight. "Take another look, Sir Hubert, and think of our friend Comrade Philby." The General hesitated. "You remember him, naturally." He laughed again.

Bligh turned back slowly to look at the mountain. "I remember him," he said. His voice was flat. "He was here, I suppose?" He turned and looked beyond the General at the bunch of acolytes over by the desk. They looked solemn and respectful, as though at the mention of Philby's name the conversation had moved on to a higher plane, and their eyes were shining.

"He was here. In Yerevan. With his camera."

"Let us now praise famous men." Bligh said it as brightly as he could. He smiled charmingly at the General. "Do you mind," he asked, "if I wash my hands?"

The noise that came from the General's throat was not a laugh. His face was still shining but no longer with delight. He was having some difficulty in keeping his temper, and the air hissed through his teeth for a second or two before he spoke. "You have your joke, Sir Hubert," he said. "Look out there." This time it was nearly a shout. "And look at this!"

Bligh watched him as he plunged his great pudding of a right hand into his breast pocket and pulled out a wallet of crocodile skin.

"Gamage's," said Bligh. "Holborn, E.C.1."

The General disregarded him. He was fishing around inside

the wallet and grunting with impatience. "Look at this." He breathed triumphantly as he held a photograph about four inches from Bligh's nose.

Bligh smiled courteously. "Ilford Panchromatic," he said.

"You are a fool, Bligh." Kevork was getting really angry. "You are *all* fools." He pointed at the photograph with a very big stiff finger. "Philby had this picture on the wall of his office, Bligh, in London. For years and nobody noticed that Little Ararat was on the left." He began to cool down and the folds of his face began to look like a smile of sorts again. "He took the picture from here." He said it with a kind of proprietorial pride.

Bligh felt miserable. "I don't suppose you'll ever understand, General." He turned round to look at the mountain. It made a very pleasant change. "Everybody knew Philby had taken the picture himself," he said. "We assumed he'd also done the printing and enlarging. Knowing him, it was natural to assume he would print it the wrong way round."

There was a shuffling noise from behind him, as though the young men were getting restive. He went on looking at the mountain. "Inefficient," he said but his heart wasn't in it and it sounded thin.

A noise like a growl came from the General and the young men calmed down. "You are all fools, Bligh," said Kevork. This time he sounded more sad than angry. Then, surprisingly, the tone of his voice changed. "*We* are fools also, Sir Hubert." He came over to the window and stood beside Bligh. "Bigger fools, perhaps, than you." He said it almost in a whisper, as though afraid that his words might be heard by the young men who, in their own interests, ought to be spared his heresies. "You know, of course, that Father Ararat is no longer in Russia but in Turkey!" If he had had any eyebrows, Bligh knew he would have raised them in disbelief at the madness of his countrymen. "We *gave* him to the Turks." A deep sigh escaped from him, and it seemed to release him from his nostalgia. Once again he flicked his fingers and the room began to turn again to the right.

As the mountain slid away to the left, Bligh realised the purpose of the building they were in. "This is an observatory," he said. He watched Mount Ararat as it moved away.

"Correct. The Yerevan State Astro-Physical Observatory. We are just beneath the telescope platform." The General was brisk again. "But it's much more than that, Sir Hubert. Watch." He pointed out into the foothills of the Trans-Caucasus range. "That is danger country. Not no-man's land. Everyman's land." He managed to growl it without sounding silly.

The room was still turning slowly. Now they were looking due west into Turkish Anatolia. "Everyman's land. Turks, Persians, Kurds, Armenians, Russians, Americans and now," the General did a stiff little bow towards Bligh, "one Englishman." Bligh felt a little foolish as he inclined his head.

The machinery was still humming and the room was still on the move. The General stared out over the rough inhospitable landscape. He seemed to be seeking a landmark, some particular mountain-top picked out by the pale sunlight that was just beginning to come up behind them. "There it is." He flicked his fingers, and immediately the room stopped its progress. *He thinks he's God.* Bligh hid his thoughts and stared obediently along the line of Kevork's arm. "The danger country." It was Bligh who said it this time. In the distance, beyond the edge of the mountain range, he could see the beginning of the broad flat lunar landscape over which he had travelled with Austin Lombard and Mustafa Tuna and the sad, brave Turkish soldier who was burned to death in the freezing wilderness. "That's it," Bligh said. "The Kars Gap."

"Yes, the Kars Gap and the danger country." The General seemed to relish the phrase. "That's where we found Lombard."

"*How* did you find Lombard?" Bligh said it quietly, as though he was talking to some resentful delinquent. "How?" But the General would not be rushed.

"Come here." Kevork turned his back on the outside world and walked slowly back to his desk. "I will tell you." He waved to embrace the whole world. "I'll tell you a lot of things."

"And Lombard? You were telling me about Lombard."

"Lombard is just one of those things." As he spoke, the General was slopping more Teacher's whisky into Bligh's glass. Bligh knew he would not be heard if he spoke, so he kept his mouth shut. He also kept clear of the whisky. It had occurred to him that in the next few minutes he might well hear the reasons for his visit to the Caucasian Hinterland, and he needed a clear head.

"This map..." The General tapped a large almost wholly brown sheet on his desk. It obviously warmed his heart.

"Oh no! Not again." It was the same map. Bligh felt he ought to regard it as a familiar friend, but he found he had begun to loathe it. The two local sheets, Shahpur and Tbilisi, had been clipped together and were laid out flat on the desk.

One of the young men spoke for the first time. "They are very beautiful maps," he almost crooned it. "Very useful." The fact that he had spoken at all pleased Bligh. He had begun to think they had been recruited, trained and promoted to serve the mountainous and unlovely George simply because they were mutes. He smiled his approval at the young man and felt he ought to go across and pat him encouragingly on the top of his head, but he was too far away.

The General nodded in enthusiastic agreement. "Captain Andranik is right. Very useful." He tapped Bligh's arm. "Stanfords," he said. "Edward Stanford Limited, Long Acre, W.C.2." Bligh began to wish he would at least get one of the postal districts wrong.

"Look." The General got down to business and, as Bligh had expected, he tapped one of the extra dark brown areas with a fingernail. Bligh had come to the conclusion that they all did it. Open a map, put it on a table, and within seconds somebody starts tapping it with a fingernail. "Look closely," said the General. "The radar plot has been added." He waited until Bligh's face was near enough to the map for him to make out one or two tiny legends which had been added in red ink across the Turkish plain. Bligh could make nothing of them, because they were, of course, written in Russian and were about as big as a spider's footprints. Then the General spoke again. "Sit back, Sir Hubert. And listen." *God was at it again.*

"It is now the 29th November." The General seemed to be taking credit for the fact. He put his fingers together, doing a kind of uncle act with a cat's cradle.

"Surely not!" Bligh found it hard to believe. As far as he

was concerned, they were half-way through next January.

"I assure you it is. Two days, according to *your* evidence, from D-Day." General Kevork hesitated for the sake of effect. "But you and your Prime Minister are wrong. Wrong!" He thumped his desk which rumbled as though made of spare plates from an old battle-ship. "Today is D-day. Today!"

Bligh nodded wisely and managed, he thought, to give the impression that he wasn't in the least surprised. This, it occurred to him, was especially skilful because he didn't really know what the D-Day was about.

"I have spoken to Comrade Prime Minister Vossilof." The General waited for Bligh to show he was impressed, and seemed satisfied when he saw a little nod. "He spoke to your Prime Minister Beasley a week ago. He told him the danger would come earlier than expected. The first of December, said Comrade Prime Minister Vossilof, is too late." The General looked smug. "Comrade Prime Minister Vossilof was right." He seemed to be waiting for a standing ovation.

Hubert Bligh had no difficulty in agreeing that the General had the right to look smug, though he wished he could have looked more attractive doing it. The Russians (even the Armenian Russians) were obviously very efficient at this kind of paramilitary stuff. He allowed himself a split second to reflect that the trolley-bus he had seen working its way out in the General direction of the Persian Gulf would probably not run to time in contrast with... He thought of the No. 3 buses that ran though his constituency and drew a swift shutter down over his thoughts.

"I will tell Comrade Prime Minister Beasley," he said. The words sounded so daft that he said them again. *Too bloody true*, he added inside his head. *I propose to tell our Comrade Prime Minister a mouthful.* And the sooner the better.

"Good. He must realise by now how wrong he was." Kevork was overdoing the virtuous line.

"Very wrong," said Bligh. "How do you know it's D-Day today?"

"We can see." The General tapped the maps again. "We have plotted it."

To answer the question, General Kevork pointed at the ceiling.

"As I said, the Astro-Physical Observatory is much more than its name suggests. Much more."

"Radar?" Bligh felt he had to show he was with it. It was a nice technological thing to say.

"Of a kind, my dear sir. Of a kind." It was clear that Kevork was going no further down *that* road. "We plotted it. Now look." He leaned over the map and gave way only three or four inches as Bligh leaned over to join him. "Show me how, General." Bligh was doing his best to seem eager.

"Here ... and here ... and here ..."—more tapping with a forefinger—"are those stupid American atomic mines." The General took a deep breath, as though about to tell Bligh at length what he thought, first of the Americans, then of the mines. He obviously thought better of doing either because he let the breath out harmlessly without using it and Bligh congratulated himself on his escape. "We know exactly where the mines are located and we know that they are all fully operational. The mines are in Turkey but the switch which explodes them is held by an American ..."

"Colonel Schutzbacker."

The General nodded. "An American." He struck an attitude which made him straighten up like a defiant yak interrupted in rut. Hubert Bligh took his chance and got six inches nearer the middle of the map. "I understand," he said. He kept it at that for fear of sidetracking Kevork into an ideological discussion.

"We resented the idea at first." The General nodded judiciously. He obviously approved the resentment. "It suggested that we, the Soviet Union, would attack Turkey." He left a silence for Bligh to fill.

Bligh said nothing. He was thinking, in his reasonable way, what Her Majesty's Government would say if anyone laid some atomic mines between England and Scotland. Then he found himself warming to the idea and he dropped it. The General was talking again.

"So in return we threatened to train short-range ballistic missiles on all the Turkish cities. With atomic war-heads." Once more, a military man treated Bligh to a mimed demonstration of an atomic explosion. This time it was bigger and more explosive, simply because there was much more of the General than there had been of Major Kemal Karadeniz. A big man does that sort of thing much better. The effect was equally revolting, and vivid.

"But now..." The General's leathery face, which was only a few inches from Bligh's, assumed a look of exaggerated innocence but his eyes, or what Bligh could see of them, had a cunning glint in them. "But now..." He pointed once more at the ceiling. "We are much more sophisticated," he said. He put his face even nearer to Bligh's. "You know, of course, Sir Hubert, that we can control our most remote space-platform from the earth?"

Bligh nodded. Everybody knew it. The General began to warm up. "Even though it's hidden on the far side of the moon."

Bligh nodded again. "Here in Yerevan?" he asked. He felt he was on to something.

"Perhaps." Kevork realised he had gone too far. He nodded and said perhaps again. "Whenever we want," he said, "we can explode those atomic mines. Any one of them or *all* of them at any time, whenever we want."

A cold shiver went down Bligh's spine. "This," he said, "is very madness." It was a crazy way to put it, but it seemed perfectly sane as he said it.

"Today."

"What do you mean?"

"Today, Sir Hubert. D-Day."

"But you're mad, General."

"No. Just secure." To do him justice, the General did not seem elated. He pushed his lips out in an exaggerated show of reluctance. "Today it is."

Bligh left the desk and the map and the crazy General, and went over to his chair. "Where does Lombard fit in?" he asked. It nearly split him in two to ask it so casually.

"Where *did* Lombard come into it, you mean?" General Kevork snapped his fingers and one of the near-mutes lifted a suitcase on to the desk. Just a simple suitcase, "Revelation," said the General. "Harrods. Knightsbridge."

"S.W.1," said Bligh.

The General nodded twice. Once with approval at Bligh and

once as a signal to the man with the suitcase. "One sheepskin coat," said the man as he opened it, "one British passport, one watch, one wallet. All bloodstained." He seemed to be enjoying it. "All Austin Lombard's."

Bligh felt very sick. "May I take them?" he asked. *I enclose the deceased's personal effects.*

"I don't think you should." The General seemed sympathetic. He meant that he knew Bligh didn't really want to. "You can, of course, have the Noah documents. Those, too, were in his pocket." He grinned broadly. "We have, naturally, taken a photo-copy. We are rather good at that sort of thing. It's quite a lot better than the one Lombard was carrying."

"I don't understand." Hubert Bligh tried his best not to let it sound like a bleat.

"You will. Come back to the map."

Bligh was beginning to feel dizzy and he had seen as many maps as he wanted. Especially those. "Bring it here," he said. The tone of voice he managed to say it in, cheered him up a lot. He patted his lap as though the map was a small spaniel. Once on his knee the map would look devotedly up at him and wag its legend.

The General disregarded him and went on talking. "If you looked at the map, my dear Bligh"—the knighthood had gone, Bligh noticed. Even that made him feel better; the General was getting a bit rattled—"you would see two separate journeys across Eastern Turkey have been plotted with great care. One is from Trabzon, a sea-port at the eastern end of the Black Sea. The other began in Erzurum, it went, without stopping, through the town of Kars, and then drew off the road a few miles to the other side of a tiny frontier post called, rather childishly, Kizilçakçak."

"Who? . . ." Bligh got no further. The General was holding one great fat hand up in the air and was wagging it for silence. "One of the two expeditions—a party of atomic scientists from Europe, took two lorries from Trabzon and struck inland towards the atomic minefields. The other, the one from Erzurum, split up. It stopped here. Two people presumably left the car; two others continued the journey. One of them, a stupid young soldier in the Turkish Army is dead (through his own foolishness, may I add?), and the other, you, my dear Bligh, are here."

Again the General held his hand up for attention. "A moment, please. The Trabzon party is now exactly two miles from Lake Çildir. Please, Sir Hubert, I insist. The map. It is most important." George the petulant was even less attractive than Kevork the arrogant. He was stabbing the map with a stiff forefinger, and likely to work his way through it.

Bligh sighed. Actually, he almost overdid the bored-British-traveller-abroad line and one of the silent acolytes got a bit restive. He appeared to be looking for something to throw if the General flicked his fingers. Bligh made his way over to the map to find that the General's large forefinger was covering the lake. "Pardon me," Bligh peered down at the fingernail until the General removed it.

"At Cala?"

"Right. The Turks foolishly insist on pronouncing Cee as Jay. 'Djala'. That's where the party from Trabzon is. They have located one of the mines, but so far, we have evidence that they haven't got at the detonator. They're lying low until nightfall." The General laughed a rich laugh. "They will soon have a shock."

"Who are they?"

"You do not know, Sir Hubert?"

"No."

"Your Comrade Prime Minister does. He telephoned Comrade Prime Minister Vossilof yesterday."

"Well, he didn't ring me." Bligh took a deep breath. "And," he went on enunciating with special care, "he is not my Comrade bloody Prime Minister. When I get back to London . . ."

"Tut, tut, Gospodin Deputat, tut, tut!" General Kevork was deeply hurt. "That," he said, "does not sound democratic."

Bligh uttered a single high-pitched laughing noise which lasted one second. Then he breathed deeply, counted ten inside his head and managed to speak quietly. "Who are they?" he asked.

"Tabula."

"Tabula what?"

"Just Tabula. An international group of right-wing intellectuals with designs on the rest of the world."

"What on earth do you mean?"

"Just that. Designs on the rest of the world. Especially on Moscow and Berlin and London."

"My dear George! That is ideological crap!"

"It is true. And not quite so silly as you think. Soon they will have an atomic bomb. *One* A-bomb. *And* the means of delivering it.

"Noah! The Noah machine."

General Kevork nodded gravely. "Your aeronautical experiments near Erzurum are rather impressive and well known. To us, anyway. The 'geologists' have got one of your anti-gravity aeroplanes."

Suddenly a lot of things clicked in Bligh's brain, and he felt like kicking it for being so thick. Lombard had obviously been in contact with the Tabula Group and it was they who had picked him up from that roadside briefing-place between Kars and Kizilçakçak. He grinned cheerfully at the General. "And you have got control of another one?"

Kevork looked sheepish for one second and then angry for half a minute. "The anti-gravity machine was invented by us," he said loudly, as though he was trying to convince himself, and for that matter his team of silent attendants. He did not sound very convincing, nor did they seem very convinced.

"I see." Bligh smiled sweetly. He knew the expression did not suit him (Helen was always on to him about it), but that did not deter him. "I see. And Lombard was behind it all? That's the line?"

"Yes. He and Colonel Mustafa Tuna who travelled from Erzurum with you. It is Tuna who has kept us informed. He is still doing so. We have just had the final signal." General Kevork pointed to an elaborate piece of equipment like a miniature radar-screen on the far end of his desk. On it were patterns in green light. "Tabula is ready to move," he said. "So are we."

"Poor Austin Lombard." Bligh muttered it with real feeling. His mind, awake now in a way which suggested that he had spent a week in some kind of zombie state, was back on the Kars road. *Don't think of Tuna. He was due to die soon anyway.* That is what Austin Lombard had said as he stepped out of the car. *Take Tuna's pistol, Hubert. He'll not be needing it.* And he, Bligh, had taken the pistol; a Walther P.38. He shook his head; the whole thing was, in the strictest sense of the word, daft.

"Why were you angry, General? As I travelled from Ankara with a Turkish officer I was told 'the Russians are angry and the Americans are angry'." Bligh had begun to see sense emerging from the fantastic comedy.

"Because you didn't believe us. You thought Lombard was on your side. Just because he was an English M.P.! That he was rescued from Leros by the Turks to work for you. *We* knew different. We knew that Lombard was working with Tabula, that he meant to take command of the atomic mines and the antigravity machine. It was the *Greeks* who released Lombard. Tabula has a lot of friends in Athens."

"And Tuna?"

"Tuna is Greek. But he is against the Greek Government. Very much so. He will die bravely."

A bell rang loud and clear in Bligh's brain. "Why should he die?" he asked, suddenly afraid.

"This is war, Bligh. Maybe you don't realise it yet, any more than your Prime Minister does. This is war."

"And that's why Tuna killed Lombard. Because of this war of yours?"

"Of course. And it's why Colonel Tuna left the Noah document"—Kevork pointed to the photocopy on the floor beside Hubert Bligh's chair—"in Lombard's pocket. He passed a message to me personally and told me exactly where we should find Lombard's body. Two kilometres east of Horasan." The General looked impressed. "He is always accurate, is Colonel Tuna. We found Lombard's body at the side of the road exactly two kilometres east of Horasan." Kevork shrugged his shoulders. "The wolves," he said. "The wolves are hungry as the winter comes down. I do not think you would recognise your colleague Lombard".

Bligh shook his head sadly. Not too sadly, just sadly enough. "You buried him?" he asked.

"Of course. He was a sailor." The General was angry at

Bligh's veiled suggestion. The only people you don't bother to bury are civilians! Bligh felt cold, as though the night winds were beginning to bite.

The General's anger reminded Bligh. "Colonel Schutzbacker..." he began.

The General suddenly roared with laughter. "Why was the Yankee Colonel angry? We told him we were going to destroy Lombard. And we told him why. He is still angry, as you will see."

General Kevork walked over to the large window and flicked his fingers irritably as he went. The machinery moaned, and the window moved with the rest of the room, this time to the left. It went on sliding round, smoothly and without a semblance of tremor, as though moving in a bath of highly refined oil, until Ararat was in the middle of the landscape. "Very beautiful," said the General. This time the mountain looked even nearer in the bright clear light from the sun, its snow-cap dazzling, brilliant. "Very, very beautiful." Without turning round, the General spoke to Bligh. "Have another whisky, Bligh. It's very cold out there. And we have a date with Colonel Schutzbacker. We often meet to discuss our problems, we, the Turks and the Americans. This time we meet in Turkey. We are, as you say, playing away today. At Kizilçakçak." Then he turned round and his voice was less aggressive. "We need your help, Sir Hubert," he said. "The Yankee Colonel is a very stubborn man. He refuses to believe the Tabula story. We want you to tell him about Lombard: and we want you to identify his clothes and his papers. Especially the Noah document. Anybody could forge a passport, but only Lombard, surely, could have the House of Commons papers in his pocket." He beamed his revolting smile at Bligh. "That's all we need you for." He grinned broadly as Bligh nodded. "You will do it, then?"

"Of course, General. And then afterwards you will leave me in Kizilçakçak. I must get back to London, you know."

"But naturally. I hope you remember your rather unorthodox visit to Soviet Armenia with pleasure. Yerevan especially." He clicked his heels. "The oldest city in the world."

Bligh bowed as he put the Noah papers in his inside pocket, flipping the pages over as he did so. "Delighted," he said. "Really delighted." And he meant it. *Page 29 of the Noah papers, the vital page, had been removed.* "To Colonel Tuna," he said and drank his Teacher's, without water.

*   *   *

"Everyman's land." The General was rather pleased with his own *jeux d'esprit*. He said it twice, so that everyone in the plane would hear it, and looked down on the mountain range beneath them. It was a beautiful but very unfriendly tract of country, browner even than the maps.

"You can," said Hubert Bligh, "stuff it." He was immediately contrite, partly because it was a very rude thing to say, and partly because he could see that George had taken it as a personal insult. And whatever else George was, he was a reasonably kind and courteous host. Or was he? Bligh took the thing a bit further. *Tuna will die bravely.* Just like that, in the simple future tense. Not would die, *will* die. Ethically, of course, it was irrelevant that Tuna was already dead (though Bligh alone knew it), but Bligh was not really equipped to regard the matter in terms of ethical equation. For "Tuna" read "Lombard". That, Bligh was quick to admit, was a very different kettle of tuna-fish. Not even the joke pleased him. For "Tuna" read "Lombard". And Lombard, if Kevork had his way, might soon be a scattered mass (a very widely scattered mass) of radio-active carbon dust floating down from the bright sunlit sky of the Trans-caucasus. No man likes to think of his friend coming down as fall-out.

Bligh hadn't actually made up his mind about Lombard's complicity. To be perfectly honest, he didn't know whose side he was on. Austin Lombard had always been something of a rogue character, a latter-day Nelson or Lord Louis of the sixties. In the Navy, he'd built up a reputation for unorthodox activities which caused Their Lordships at the Admiralty (if that was what they were still called) to be rather relieved when he found and won for himself a seat in the House of Commons. For one thing, they mistrusted his rare and incredible skill with languages.* Everybody knew that he could have stayed at Oxford (and got lost) as a don teaching dead languages to a dying race of students. Instead, he took a commission in the Navy. That in itself made him exceptional. But it didn't automatically qualify him for a cell in the Tower of London as an enemy agent.

Then Bligh remembered the message which Lombard passed in the traditional spy-story manner to Alex Beasley. That surely meant he was working (however unconventionally) for H.M. Government. Bligh felt cheerful for a moment, until he realised that the message which Lombard thrust down Lucy's bosom was exactly the kind of cover story a clever agent for the other side would think of. Especially an extra clever one like Lombard.

But which other side? Tuna was obviously a rotten lot. By which Bligh meant he was willing to work for anyone who paid him well enough. That was quite obvious. The Colonel-General, "George" to his friends (to Tuna maybe?), obviously thought very highly of him. And so, it would seem, did the other side, the new fascist power-lust boys from the European atomic energy places. *Beware Greek bearing a Walther P.38.* Bligh nodded vigorously at his thoughts. But they didn't help him to explain Lombard's connection with Tuna. Once again, Bligh remembered Lombard's words. *Don't think of Tuna. He was due to die soon, anyway.* What on earth did that mean? Who was going to kill him? Lombard? The Tabula brigade? The Russians? The Turks?

Bligh gave it up and looked out of the window at the mountain peaks around them. By this time they were hovering over a deep ravine with sharp-cut edges and vertical sides that twisted its way through the mountains like a Colorado river in miniature. It was the kind of landscape that was devised specially for athletic mountain goats.

"Arpa Çay," said the General. "The Barley River; it's the border. That side Turkey, this side Russia," He grinned to show there was a laugh coming. "Sometimes, when it's in flood, the

---

* It was reported that when he was selected to fight the Election for Birmingham (East), the chairman of the local Party said, "Languages! Keep it dark, old boy. They might take you for a foreigner."

river changes its course and a bit of Turkey finds itself on the Russian side. Or a bit of Russia gets into Turkey. Then we have trouble. Big trouble. Bang. Bang." He roared with laughter and the aeroplane juddered under the strain.

Bligh sat there just shaking his head. He was revolted in a superior sort of way. *What a stupid, childish attitude! God help us.* His disgust was emanating from him like mist from a swamp.

He had shaken his head slowly about six times each way when one of the General's young men arrived with a rush and sat down beside him. Up to now, Bligh hadn't heard him utter a word, but utter he certainly did now. He was quite literally livid with rage, and bubbling a bit at the mouth. "You no like?" he asked. "You no like?"

Bligh stopped shaking his head. "I no like," he said. He stared into the young man's eyes at a range of about seven inches. They were brown, beautiful and bloodshot. Then quite suddenly they went stiff. Stiff eyeballs were new on Bligh, but these certainly went stiff and the young man's forehead came forward to hit Bligh quite hard on the bridge of his nose. It made his eyes water. The young man's eyes were glazed and sightless.

"Young," said the General, explaining it all as he hit the young man again on the nape of his neck. "Undiplomatic. Foolish." He followed these epithets with some more short, crisp ones in Russian or Armenian, rubbed the outside edge of his hand and smiled charmingly as he tipped the unconcious man into the aisle. "What you call a stupid bugger, eh?" Kevork was back on the agreeable sympathetic host touch and Bligh felt sick.

"Lavatory," he said in a weak voice. "Lavatory."

Kevork roared with laughter at this new manifestation of Anglo-Saxon invective (it was obviously a new development since his spell of duty in Kensington Palace Gardens, W.8) and ordered another of the young men to come and remove the body. As it was dragged away to some luggage compartment or other, Bligh found it easy to believe it really was a body and the young man had died. He never knew for certain. Other things started to happen, and he was ashamed later to admit that he never got round to asking. And he also forgot the lavatory.

One thing (and one thing only) stood out with certainty. Kevork depended on him, Bligh, to persuade Colonel Schutzbacker that "Tuna" and his band of amateur fascists were dangerous, and that they must be rounded up before they could grab the atomic mine. Once the Americans, the Turks and the Nato Command had been convinced (and not until then), Kevork's diplomacy would have succeeded. Nothing else in the world could possibly explain Kevork's three hours of concentrated velvet-glove charm, first in Yerevan and then in the plane. A man who could fell an over-zealous lieutenant with a delicately skilful karate flick, a man who could decide, in cold blood, *hours* before the event, that one of his privileged (and highly successful) agents should be blown into atomic dust, was not the man Bligh would have thought to ingratiate himself, without very good reason, with a British ex-Minister two thousand miles away from base. He looked upwards for inspiration, and got it. On the bulkhead above the door into the pilot's cabin was a little silver badge with two interlaced letter R's done tastefully in red enamel. It was the famous Rolls-Royce symbol. Suddenly, Bligh knew without any shadow of doubt whatsoever that he had a job to do. Kevork had been lying. The machine in which they were flying had been hi-jacked; and it had to be saved.

He had little time to work out a plan, because the plane was dropping swiftly on to a landing strip outside a low mud building which seemed half-buried in the ground.

"Kizilçakçak?" He pronounced the word, adequately enough, as a question.

Kevork sniffed and then remembered his manners. He nodded. "This is where we meet the American," he said. He managed to use a flat tone which hid his resentment; but then the mask slipped an inch or two and he added. "With his key!" He started a snort of derision, remembered what he was doing, stopped it half way down his nose and smiled. "Your friend," he said as the plane touched down. "Colonel Schutzbacker."

Bligh was feeling curiously elated as he stepped to the ground, and reached behind him for his travelling-bag. Like a bloody commercial traveller, he thought, as one of the young lieutenants handed it to him.

"Let me carry it for you," said Kevork but he said it without warmth. You can carry courtesy too far.

"Good Lord, no!" For a second, Bligh saw his plan collapsing. "An M.P. must have his carpet-bag with him." It was an inspired thing to say because Kevork found it meaningless. He was still trying to work it out when Bligh got the bag open. In between two pairs of dirty socks, his pyjamas (none too clean) and his new sponge bag (from Boots and Taylors, Brixton High Street, S.W.5), he found what he wanted. He took out Colonel Mustafa Tuna's Walther P.38, aimed it, and shot all six bullets at the anti-gravity plane two yards away from him. Surprisingly, he hit it with five of them; four shattered the complicated electrical gear on what he assumed was the engine, the other one made a hole in the fuel tank and some kind of blue liquid began to gush out.

"The death of Noah," said Bligh as he turned round to meet Colonel Schutzbacker. He felt a fool saying it, but he felt better for it.

"Turkish Government property, I presume?" Colonel Frank Schutzbacker knew very well what he was looking at. "They will be glad to see it returned." It was all so curiously formal and restrained until Kevork began to swear. He went on swearing for several minutes, using long low words, apparently in batches of ten.

"We shall be glad to escort you back, General," said Schutzbacker. "We can probably find a train." He was looking delighted.

Kevork took a deep breath and then, with great dignity he stepped over to the plane. The fuel was still dribbling out on to the ground. He stepped over the mess and into the pilot's cabin, disregarding the shouts of his attendants—now reduced to three. Two minutes later, he came out again, stepped over the patch of brown mud, turned round, lit a petrol lighter with deliberation and threw it into the fuel tank, dropping to the ground as he did so. Bligh, who had seen it coming, was already on the ground.

Once again, he found himself looking into Kevork's face at very short range. "That was a very foolish thing to do, General," he said. He was surprised to see that the General was smiling.

"Not as foolish as your shooting, Bligh. A wiser man would have put a bullet into the radio. You didn't. I was able to use it." By this time he was grinning broadly. "You forget that we took a photo-copy of your Operation Noah documents." He jerked his thumb at the blazing plane behind him. "And you forget what I told you about the atomic mine at Djala. This will be a very good experiment. At any moment the mine will explode. I advise you to stay where you are on the ground."

"And your man Tuna?" As he said it, Bligh knew what was going to happen to Lombard. He closed his eyes and put his forehead against the packed mud of the landing strip. The plane, ten yards away, was still burning and sending a column of black smoke into the cold morning air.

"He will die with the others," said the General. Lying on the ground, he found it hard to shrug his shoulders, but he managed it. "He is a soldier. He expects to die."

Hubert Bligh raised his head and looked at the General. He was appalled. "The man you call Tuna," he said, "is Austin Lombard, M.P. And in his pocket he has the last page of the Operation Noah document. Without that last page, the thing is useless."

"That was very clever of you, Bligh." The expression in Kevork's eyes showed that he meant what he said. "Very clever. But your man, whoever he is, Tuna or Lombard, will die Nothing can stop it. Listen."

The ground beneath them began to tremble as they felt the explosion forty miles away. Then it began to rock with a long thrusting, heavy motion. "Chain reaction," said Kevork. "This is an earthquake."

His voice sounded awed and hushed, as though he really thought he was God.

* * *

"There's been an earthquake, Prime Minister." Geoffrey Pond fell into step beside Alex Beasley and trod carefully over the smooth flagstones, green with moss and age. Too late, he noticed that he was walking on the Prime Minister's left. He had once worked out on squared paper that, because of the lay-out of the flagstone paths in the garden of No. 10, if you walked on the Prime Minister's right—on the regular, unchanged and unchanging line of route—you did seven yards less walking than the Prime Minister did. If, on the other hand, you walked on his left, you did seven yards more than he did. This, in an average year, came to four thousand eight hundred and thirty-two yards. Geoffrey Pond was not an athletic man, so he looked out for a chance to skip across to the other side without looking too silly.

Alex Beasley walked several paces before he answered, and then he addressed himself to one of the green copper domes of the Admiralty building far away on the north side of the Horseguards Parade. "I've got a Cabinet Meeting in three hours' time," he said, "with Grafton at my throat, there's a little matter of the U.N. decision due today, two African states are threatening to pull out of the Congo Agreement; and there's Arthur Kinman... And he comes and tells me there's been an earthquake." He did a right-wheel and Geoffrey Pond shot round behind to take up station on his right hand. "There are, my dear Geoffrey..." Beasley looked to his left. "Where the devil... Oh. There are earthquakes somewhere every seventeen minutes of the day and night." It was the kind of statistic he was good at. He looked pleased with himself.

"This one's in Turkey."

"Oh. That's different." Beasley stopped. "That's different. Bligh?"

"No details. But it was in the Kars and the Agri provinces. Near Mount Ararat. That's just where Bligh is, we reckon."

"Yes. Exactly. Why the devil doesn't he ring me up?" Beasley sounded exceptionally plaintive. He started walking again but this time less briskly. "Where's the report from?"

"Reuter's. Just come through on the tape." Pond wagged a few small sheets of teleprinter paper. The hand holding them was blue with cold. Unlike the Prime Minister, Pond was not wearing an overcoat. "Originated from the Anatolian Agency, Ankara."

"Well they ought to know! What about the Noah Research Station? No mention, I hope!"

"None. But there's a D-notice on that anyway. So it wouldn't be on the tape."

"What's the External Office doing? Anything?"

"The duty man's got a line booked to H.E. in Ankara. At least he can offer a few blankets. And some sympathy."

"How many casualties?"

"Nobody knows yet." Geoffrey Pond looked down at the tape. *A party of young scientists from Brussels are known to be in the area. Some anxiety is felt for their safety.*

"Hm! I wouldn't call it anxiety so much as curiosity. It would, of course, be very convenient." Beasley stopped dead in his tracks. "Good God... You don't think! It would give the impression of an earthquake." They stood there, side by side, under the evergreen to the right of the Cabinet Room, and neither of them spoke for twenty seconds. Geoffrey Pond broke the silence. "Some more coming." He turned round as he heard the patter of foot-steps on the path behind them.

Miss Tooth was bearing down on them with a piece of paper in her hand. "No. 10's little special harbinger," said the Prime Minister, who had noticed the expression on her face.

"I must tell her to get some stick-on rubber soles," said Pond. "She's waking the neighbourhood." He looked up at No. 11. The Chancellor of the Exchequer was standing at the window of his breakfast-room two floors up. He was in his braces. "Jack's getting fat," said the Prime Minister. "He's spending too much time on working lunches with the IMF boys. I must talk to him." He turned to Miss Tooth as she came up the straight. "Doom," he suggested.

She nodded breathlessly, and held out the teleprinter message. Doom was written across the line of her eyebrows and she was blowing hard, as though she had just brought the bad news on foot from Ghent to Aix. Far away to the north, Frederick, Duke of York, was gazing balefully from the top of his column, and a messenger in a navy blue suit appeared round the corner from the typists' room. His purpose was to tell the Prime Minister that Mrs Beasley wanted him to know that his breakfast was ready. He saw the expression on the Prime Minister's face and decided to let the coffee go cold unannounced.

"Trouble." Alex Beasley held the paper out to Geoffrey Pond.

"You'd better book me a call to Ankara and to hell with the scrambler. We'll have to rely on Prendergast's accent for security." It was a well-known fact that the Ambassador to Turkey spoke his mother-tongue as though he were chewing it. He turned about and made his way towards the back door of No. 10. As he set off, the clock on the Horseguards struck the half hour. "Half past eight, Prime Minister," said Miss Tooth, who was learning her job quickly and whose breathing was almost back to normal.

"Ten-thirty in Ankara, then. I suppose H.E.'s up and about. What do you make of it?" Beasley turned to Pond, who was still glaring at the tape as though it had done him an injury.

"I suppose it could mean any one of them."

"Except that Elizabeth Tronder and Cott and the others never went further east than Ankara. I'm afraid it means Bligh." The Prime Minister wiped his feet on the outsize doormat and stepped on to the black and white chequered marble floor of the lower hall. "Robert Maryon is going to make the most of it," he said. Then both Beasley and Pond, triggered off by Maryon's name, said the one word "Lombard!"

The Prime Minister ran up the flight of steps to the Pillared Room and the private staircase to his flat. The coffee was cool, but he hardly noticed it. Robert Maryon and the *Daily Mail* were much hotter.

Geoffrey Pond handed the tape to Miss Tooth. "File it, please," he said. "If ever a piece of tape meant trouble, this means trouble. Second thoughts. Type it and get it circulated in the Private Secretaries' Room." Gloria Tooth settled down to her typewriter.

Add Turkey earthquake. Local reports that British M.P. (not named) in Turkey missing presumed dead. Confimed no trace of geologists ex Euratom Brussels Ankara scientists in Department of Land and Regional Resources state no known precedent for earthquake so late in year. No prelim. warning received in Seismaxxxxx Seismological laboratory Univ. Erzurum. Mount Ararat thought to be in eruption.

0819 *ends*

"Bloody hell," said Miss Tooth. She managed to sound very ladylike, by over-emphasising the aspirate.

*   *   *

"But Hubert Bey Effendi, you do not understand. The Istanbul drivers are the best in the world." Kaya Mersinli smiled rapturously as the car (another of those long black things) swung its nose round to face Galata Bridge, turned sharp right, mounted the pavement, slid between a lamp-post and a tobacco kiosk, turned sharp left and came to a halt, nose down, at the head of the queue. The lights were red so the driver sounded his horn once to express his feelings. He then looked pleased with himself, wound down the window to his left, put out his head and acknowledged the applause. Hubert Bligh turned round with some diffidence and looked out of the rear window. The drivers of fourteen taxis and one private car were jumping up and down in their driving seats. All fifteen were sounding their horns, and all fifteen were shouting rough Turkish words. The din was appalling.

"They are disappointed," said Kaya. "They did not think of doing that." He leaned forward, patted the driver on his shoulder and said something complimentary in Turkish. "He is very clever," he said to Bligh. Bligh nodded. He felt he had to.

"Are many people killed in Istanbul?" Bligh felt mean as soon as he had asked it, and meaner still as Kaya Bey looked hurt. "You do not understand, Bey Effendi. They are exceptional drivers. Sometimes they bang, but not very much."

The lights changed and the car moved forward on to Galata Bridge. "You see," said Kaya, "no one is hurt." The two cars in the outside lanes had got their front bumpers locked, not much, but enough. Their drivers had got out and were addressing each other. Then they turned, stood shoulder to shoulder and advised the drivers of the cars behind them to be more patient. "They are friends," said Kaya. "It happens like that."

Bligh gave it up, and relaxed. What could the evening traffic of Istanbul do to upset a man who, in the past forty-eight hours, had seen a man shot dead at eighteen inches' range, had been ambushed on the plain of Anatolia, had paid a short (and involuntary) visit to the oldest city in the world, the capital of one of the Soviet Socialist Republics, had been shot at by artillery using tracer shells, had himself shot down an aeroplane of sorts (a bit of an over-statement that; how do you shoot down an aeroplane which isn't up?) had felt, rather than heard, the explosion of an earthquake? Totting them up in the warm rear compartment—as roomy as a sitting-room, it was—Bligh confessed that anything after that little lot had to be an anti-climax; the hard, rough ride in the cab of an army truck from Kizilçakçak back to Erzurum, the bumpy flight in an Air Force jet to Istanbul, and the meeting, in the unbelievably respectable fin de siècle dining-room of the Park Hotel in Istanbul, with Elizabeth Tronder, M.P., and Richard Cott, M.P., and the other faceless, nameless delegates on the Parliamentary Mission which he had first led and then deserted. *You've a bloody cheek, Bligh.* Cott had grumbled, *leaving it all to us. Seventeen official functions! Seventeen speeches.* Bligh shuddered as he visualised it all, the worthy chat about the New NATO, the cant talk about the democratic principles, the smoke and the drink and the lavish official hospitality. *Got out of it very nicely, didn't you? All to see a bleeding horse-breeding place.* (Cott had found that rather hard to say.) *That's your story.* Fortunately, Bligh had bitten his tongue in time to prevent it from saying it was, actually, Kaya Mersinli's story. And all the time, the Palm Court Orchestra played in the back-ground (vaguely, insincerely and unreasonably applauded at the end of each piece), with its gems from the first world war; *Tea for Two* as accompaniment, much out of key, unreal and like a dream, to his Scotch and soda with Richard Cott. He shuddered again.

 He sat up and pushed it all to the back of his mind, but not before he'd relished again the long silence that followed his last words to Richard Cott, as he pushed his way past him to join Kaya Mersinli in the long black car. "You might like to know, Cott," he'd said, "that what I've been up to concerns only three people, Alex Beasley, myself and Austin Lombard." He had paused, staring Cott in the face. And then he went on. "And Lombard was killed."

He laughed to himself, maliciously, as the car crawled its way across the bridge. Cott had looked incredibly foolish. Not only did his jaw drop; so did his top teeth.

"You are liking Istanbul," said Kaya Mersinli. He had heard the laugh though not the malice behind it.

"I am, Kaya Bey."

"We call it our magic city," Kaya said it wholly without self-consciousness. "This is the Golden Horn." He swept his right arm slowly to embrace the floating bridge and beautiful stretch of calm water. The water traffic was a confused mêlée of lights.

"And where are we going?"

"To meet our friend the Major. Major Kemal Karadeniz. He will be pleased to see you again and talk to you about what has happened."

"And why not in the Park Hotel? My room..."

"Impossible. Quite impossible, Hubert Bey Effendi." Kaya looked very embarrassed. "Mr Scrott..."

"Cott. He is harmless."

"But he must not know. And the lady, Mrs Tronder."

"Miss Tronder."

"Ah! She too must not know." He managed to give the impression he was blushing in the darkness.

The driver spoke to Kaya for the first time (his previous remarks had been made to pedestrians, the other taxi-drivers and, occasionally, to Allah). There was nothing sinister in what he said, he just made it sound sinister.

"We are nearly there." Kaya translated for Bligh. The traffic on the bridge was thinning out a little ahead of them and Bligh could see the hill beyond the foot of the bridge. Houses, very new and very old, trees, gardens, warehouses and shops were piled high as though shovelled together into a heap ready for Judgement Day, a black mountain silhouetted against the night sky, and brilliant with thousands of points of light. The whole antheap was surmounted by a mosque, a squat brooding dome on a turbulent city, its slender minarets picked out in lights. Bligh felt cold and alone as the car stopped half-way over the bridge, and the door opened. "Here we are," said Kaya as they got out.

He spoke to the driver, who nodded and drove the car back into the creeping line of traffic.

Bligh suspected a practical joke. From what Kaya had said they were to meet Major Kemal in some comfortable quiet place where they could speak secretly and hear comfortably. Galata Bridge is neither secret nor quiet. It is probably the most populated bridge in the world. Built on pontoons across the mouth of the Golden Horn, it floats on the water which runs past it down the Bosphorus from the Black Sea to the Aegean. But it is much more than a bridge. It is, above all, a long, floating landing-stage for the ferry steamers which are themselves the only bridge between Europe and Asia. And as such it is very busy late into the night.

"Down below." Kaya led the way down an iron staircase to a long catwalk beneath the road level, then along a broad gangway of heavy wooden planking. Bligh could hear the water slopping against the pontoons just beneath him, and over all there was a strong fishmarket stink. It was brightly lit and very busy as people rushed about to catch their ferry to Üsküdar or Kadiköy on the Asian side of the Bosphorous, or to the Islands in the Sea of Marmara.

A ferryboat was coming in to berth alongside, its hooter sounding arrogantly, and its searchlight sweeping its way across the landing stage. Bligh saw Kaya, a few yards ahead of him in the blaze of light. He had his hand on the open door of a small brightly painted hut leaning against the wooden verticals of the bridge. On the door, painted rather carelessly in gold, was the name first in Turkish, *Köprüalti,* and then in English for the tourist trade, *"Below the Bridge."*

Beside Kaya in the doorway, beaming a warm welcome at Bligh, stood Austin Lombard, M.P.

*　　*　　*

Eugene Malplaquet found he was talking to himself and it made him angry. He stopped outside a recondite little boutique which seemed to sell nothing but tin soldiers. He stared at a Royal Inniskilling Fusilier (late eighteenth century) until Christopher Pallister caught up with him.

"And what did she want?" Malplaquet led with his chin.

"Five pounds."

"I hope . . ."

"Certainly not. She says it's along here on the left, round the corner."

"I know it is."

"I was just making sure."

They set off walking again. Shepherd Market, Mayfair, is busy in the early evening as people make their way to the Curzon Cinema, round the corner in the main street, to the chi-chi pubs and dives in Park Lane, or to the Hilton Bar.

"The Hilton!" It seemed to hit Malplaquet on the forehead. He looked up at it and wondered how he had missed it earlier. "It makes sense," he said. "Enver and Brook must have made their contact here before they booked into room 2531."

"2513. How on earth do you prove that?" Pallister clearly resented the loss of his evening. Overtime is O.K. on foreign location; it's less rewarding in London W.1. His resentment was in both his manner and his tone of voice. "I know!" He affected a blaze of inspiration, as he walked along past the smart little tarted-up Georgian houses. "We go and knock on the door. 'May we speak to the London Manager of Tabula please,' we say. We want to join the outfit because the Home Sec says we have to. And we would like to know . . ."

"Finished?" Malplaquet stopped in his tracks and watched Pallister walking ahead, doing elaborate gestures of conversational civility. Then he moved quickly to catch him by the arm. "Stop. Who's that?"

Outside No. 71 there was a young man in the regulation uniform of the plain clothes policeman. He was clearly identifiable in the light from the open door and he was talking animatedly into what appeared to be an electric shaver in his right hand.

"It's one of the Special Branch men from Victoria Street. I know him. He's working with Macaulay."

"And he knows you. He's flagging you." Malplaquet began to walk quickly, making the only concession to urgency that he would permit himself. As almost always happened, he arrived several seconds after Pallister, a younger man, without the burden of official dignity. As he arrived, Pallister was already speaking to the Special Branch man. "You go and phone them from the Hilton then," he pointed along Hertford Street. "And we'll keep watch. You're sure he's dead?"

The young policeman nodded twice. Once in reply to Pallister's question; and once to acknowledge the arrival of Malplaquet. He then explained. "Battery's dead," he mourned. He shook the thing in his right hand.

The thing cracked and started screeching at him. "It bloody well isn't," said a rough male voice from inside it. "You're coming through loud enough to stop the blasted traffic in Victoria Street." The voice stopped speaking suddenly and then uttered a grunt. The man whose voice it was had abviously looked out of his window at the blasted traffic in Victoria Street. It started again, plaintively. "Do remember to press the listening knob. Do please."

"Yes, sir," said the young man. He sounded a bit desperate. "I'm at No. 71. Reporting death of subject. Will wait here. Over."

"O.K. Car on its way. Keep everybody out. And I mean everybody. Over."

He was too late. Malplaquet and Pallister were in.

"He's dead all right." Pallister did a regulation inspection of the corpse's eyeballs. He looked at Malplaquet. "It's the Tabula boss," he said. "He's a Chartered Accountant from Purley."

"And a lot of good that did him," said Malplaquet. Not even Chartered Accountants can do anything about it if someone hits them hard enough on the temple with an ebony ruler, cylindrical.

* * *

"I'm sorry to have missed your friend Kevork..." Austin Lombard stuck his knife into the steaming paper bag on his plate. "Marvellous cooks!" He smiled at Kaya Mersinli and nodded his appreciation. "'Sea-bass in paper'. It justified the Ottoman Empire and now it justifies the State of Turkey." He got to work delicately on the sea-bass. "I would like to have met him, I must admit."

213

"A strange man." Bligh was still busy with his fried mussels. They were plump and delicious. "He was in a terrible dilemma. Even I could see it." He looked up at Major Kemal Karadeniz on his right." There are ... I mean there were ... two of the experimental anti-gravity planes?"

"Three actually." Major Kemal spoke very quietly. "One we keep static for operational research, the other two are actually flying, or were. They were the ones the Americans and the Russians were interested in." The Major took a sip at his vodka and orange.

"In fact, so interested that they risked a major upheaval, an international incident, even a full war, to get hold of one?" Bligh threw it off casually.

"Not really. They did capture one. They said it violated their airspace and they forced it down. But I don't think they would have gone to such dangerous lengths if the strike force from Brussels hadn't turned up. The 'geologists' arrival drove them to action."

Lombard stopped eating, a fact which Bligh took, quite rightly, to be an earnest of his interest in what the Major was saying. Kemal hesitated, then began again with more urgency in his voice. "For the Russians, the Nazi background to these atomic weapon scientists was much more dangerous than an experimental aeroplane." He looked hard at Lombard. "Until the people from Brussels themselves got hold of one of the planes." The Major twirled the ice in his glass. "Then it became a different matter."

"Exactly." Lombard went back to his fish. "Exactly. Then of course the Russians stepped in." He looked up from his fish at the Major. "I imagine your security people are a bit hot round the collar." Then he went back to his fish again.

"Now," said Kemal, "they have no collars." He gave no more details. "The security was well organised to deal with local spies. It was never meant to handle a regular task force from outside. That we did *not* allow for."

"And the 'geologists' from Trabzon were considered a task force?" Hubert Bligh sounded very doubtful.

"Not really." The Major went deep red. "They were much

more subtle. They didn't come in with guns, they got help from inside the Research Centre. One of the experimental engineers." Major Kemal stared down at his empty plate. The pattern seemed to fascinate him.

"Turkish?" Bligh put as much understanding into his voice as seemed proper.

"No." Lombard interrupted quickly. "He was English, Hubert. It's a combined Anglo-Turkish research station. And that's where I came in. We were on his trail. I just got here too late because I was held up by the Greeks. It was Rendle, the man in the House of Commons, who put me on to him." Lombard lifted one hand. "I know all about Rendle, Hubert. I heard it from the other side..." His voice changed. "That was quite wonderful." He turned to the waiter and spoke in Turkish. Bligh assumed he said much the same thing to him because the waiter grinned and nodded vigorously as he took Lombard's plate away. "Try the Lady's Thighs, Hubert," said Lombard.

Bligh looked round the tiny restaurant. It was a quick involuntary glance and then he went pink.

"A sweet, sweet 'sweet', Hubert. The Turkish equivalent of the Englishman's rice pudding, but much more exotic."

"And sweeter." Kaya looked rapturous again. He probably had in mind the pudding he had in the London School of Economics, because then he shuddered.

Bligh shook his head. "No Lady's Thighs," he said. "I'd rather get down to details. I've promised to ring London at ten-fifteen."

"After the Division." Austin Lombard uttered a snort of a laugh. "It's a million million miles away," he said. "And I'm not going back to it—yet."

"Carry on, Austin. Forget the Division. I'm listening."

"The Tabula movement." Lombard lit a Turkish cigarette. "You know much about it?" He blew smoke at the ceiling.

"Very little, I'm afraid." Bligh meant he knew nothing.

"A European neo-Nazi movement which has been in existence for quite a long time. All over Europe. They've been rather clever in keeping their cover intact up to now. Unfortunately they tried to get at Thomas Rendle (and at me) some time ago.

We were doing special weapon research for the Navy at Gosport at the time." Lombard hesitated. "They offered us the world, Hubert. Quite literally that!"

"And you turned it down."

"But of course. There were rather disagreeable conditions."

"Political, I assume."

"But again, of course. Then I heard quite accidentally that they were striking high. All they needed, it seemed, was a couple of atomic bombs and something to deliver them with. That's all."

"Deliver them where?"

Lombard shrugged his shoulders. "Wherever it proved to be necessary. You don't need much imagination, do you?"

"So you decided to save the world."

"Sort of."

"On your own. Why didn't you tell the Government?"

"For a very good reason, Hubert. I don't know that you can trust any of them."

Bligh blinked. "What on earth do you mean?" He asked. "That's nonsense."

"Just what I said. How long have you been in the House?"

"Twenty-some years. Why? Do you doubt *me*?"

"I suppose I do." Lombard was quite serious. He went on, his voice low and harsh. "Do you remember a fellow called Philby a few years back? And Burgess and Maclean? And Kinman more recently?"

"Of course I do. But they weren't the Government."

"They were top Government advisers. Who was one of Philby's contacts at the Russian Embassy in London? You've forgotten. But you've certainly met him. It was Colonel-General Kevork Ohannesiantz." Lombard leaned across the table.

"He was asked to leave London," he said.

Bligh looked a bit bewildered. "He said his English friends called him 'George'." It seemed relevant before he said it, afterwards he wasn't so certain.

"Sure they did. But he didn't say who his friends were." Lombard looked mean. "Even you would have recognised some of the names, Hubert. Now don't get indignant. It's true, isn't it?"

Bligh gave way, a reasonable man. "I suppose so," he said and nodded judiciously. "So you decided to do what the Government couldn't do."

"Precisely. And as soon as I got away from London, they killed Tom Rendle. They didn't waste much time."

"Who killed Rendle? Do you know? The C.I.D. at Scotland Yard would love to know that. And since Rendle was killed, there have been quite a lot more."

"No. I don't know for certain. But that's up to them at the Yard. All I'm saying is that it could be anybody. Anybody from the P.M. down."

Bligh gaped. "It's the Mediterranean sun, Austin. You've been out in the sun."

"And you lot have been hiding under the blankets, Hubert. I'm staying here in the sun."

"You'll need your passport, which you probably know Kevork is holding."

"That or another one. I'll manage."

Bligh remembered something. "You went back to Tuna after he'd been killed in the car and left your passport and the Noah papers on him. I take it you removed page 29 first."

"Of course. I ate it! In the best tradition. Without sauce! We went back to Tuna as soon as you'd disappeared down the road to Kizilçakçak. We saw the Russians ambush you."

"We?"

"Yes, we. Two of the Euratom people and me. The two who met us in the plane they'd filched. They were a dedicated pair. One of them was the Englishman I'd come to winkle out."

"They're dead now?"

"Naturally. They went up with the atomic mine at Djala. I must say, the Russians handled the whole thing pretty skilfully."

"Except that they haven't got the anti-gravity machine. I immobilised it. With a few of Mustafa Tuna's bullets."

"Well. Well!" For the first time Austin Lombard seemed impressed.

"And since you had removed page 29 of the Commons' Paper, they don't have a complete blue-print either!"

"Well well again. You've got it all worked out, my dear Hubert." Lombard grinned and slapped the table . "Four brandies," he said very loudly. "We'll drink on that. One thing, Hubert. You said that Kevork was in a dilemma. What did you mean?"

"I mean he couldn't have both anti-gravity plane *and* destroy the party of geologists. He needed me to persuade Colonel Schutzbacker..."

"That's his name! The Yank in charge of the NATO minefield I take it?"

"That's it. Kevork needed me to persuade Schutzbacker to move against the Tabula people. And therefore to get me from Yerevan to Kizilçakçak in time to do the persuading he needed that plane."

Lombard nodded. "He could always fall back on the Noah document which I left for him on Tuna's body. I assume he thought it was complete."

"In the end, of course, he lost both. He had to leave the plane behind in Turkey because I shot it, and at the same time, he was forced to announce to the world that the Russians now know how to fire the mines by remote control. It's a remarkably interesting advance. He also lost a good agent in Tuna. You knew Tuna was on their side?"

"Of course I did. He left his Russian call-signs around one night, when he'd been on the binge. Moral, Hubert, don't drink. Ah. Here's your brandy."

As he spoke, Lombard looked at his watch. "Two more minutes," he said. He leaned back and called to the proprietor of the restaurant who was busy on the open charcoal fire, speaking urgently to him in Turkish. "The radio," he said to Bligh. "I rang the BBC in London this afternoon. I want to know what they put in their Turkish bulletin."

As he spoke, the radio came through with the BBC's signature tune, the Trumpet Voluntary. *Burasi Londra,* said a brisk metallic voice, *Avrupa yayinlari merkezi* ... Bligh left them to it and went to the lavatory.

"Blast them." Lombard's voice came through the thin wooden partition to where Bligh was standing. "Blast them." It came again, this time more loudly as Lombard burst through the door. "Not a bloody mention. For all they know, I'm still alive."

"And so you are. So you are." Bligh turned round to the wash-basin.

"That's the trouble." Lombard growled it and started to swear with extraordinary vehemence. "That's the trouble. I rang them to say that Austin Lombard, M.P., was dead."

*   *   *

"And of course, he's no more dead than I am. Or you are!" The Prime Minister's voice on the telephone sounded thin and a bit tinny. But he was, without any doubt, relieved.

Bligh spoke with vigour. "He's a lot less dead than I feel to be." He was much inclined to tell Beasley, there and then, on the public telephone, what he had been through in the interests of Her Majesty's Government, and Beasley obviously sensed it. "Later, Hubert," he said. "Later." The tone of his voice changed. "How is my friend Noah?" he asked.

"Sick. I shot him." Bligh was beginning to enjoy himself.

Beasley could almost be heard rocking under the inpact. "Just a moment please." Bligh giggled to himself as he imagined the Prime Minister in his room at the House of Commons pressing buttons left and right to get a second earhole stuffed against an extension telephone. He thought he heard a click, but that may have been his imagination. "You say you shot somebody?" The Prime Minister had obviously got his reinforcements disposed.

"Certainly," said Bligh. "I shot Noah. And I shot him where it would do him least good."

There was a faint sussuration at the far end, and Bligh smiled at the ceiling. He was enjoying it.

"Where are YOU?"

"In Istanbul, of course."

"I mean, where are you now?"

"In the Park Hotel, looking out over the most beautiful and remarkable view I have . . ."

"Never mind the view, Hubert. Give your telephone number

to my secretary... Malcolm..." The Prime Minister called Malcolm Rawnsley in the next room and Rawnsley (equipped by training as well as by intelligence) did a convincing "yes, sir" act as though he had just arrived at the telephone. Bligh had to admit it was done rather well. "I'll ring you back within the next two hours." Beasley was back. "Keep looking at that beautiful view. If you're not waiting within two yards of the phone when I ring back..." Beasley paused as his mind ran through the alternatives... "I'll send you to the House of Lords."

Malcolm Rawnsley took over. "Give me your number and your extension, please, Sir Hubert. We will pay for the call." The faultless Principal Private Secretary.

III

"I've just had a word with Hubert Bligh in Istanbul," Alex Beasley had just begun speaking when the door opened and Geoffrey Pond stepped, with exaggerated care, into the room. The Prime Minister grunted unreasonably. Pond was late for the meeting because he had had to come over from his office at No. 10 whereas the rest of them were within the precincts of the House. "I'm just saying, Geoffrey, I've spoken to Bligh in Istanbul." Beasley waited with an elaborate show of patience until Pond was sitting down at the table. "He's seen Lombard."

"So the Anatolian Agency was wrong." Pond did not sound surprised. He had a fairly fixed view of foreign news agencies.

"Quite wrong. Unless the M.P. they were talking about as being killed was Richard Cott or one of the others."

"It wasn't." Gilbert Dace, the Chief Whip, spoke from the far end of the room. He was leaning forward, which had the effect of almost putting his chin on the table. "They're all alive and kicking. The Opposition ones as well." His voice had a note of unchristian sadness in it.

"Right. The Anatolian Agency was wrong. Anything else, since, Geoffrey?"

"On the tape you mean?"

"Yes. Reuters or A.P.?" The Prime Minister occasionally

showed signs of chauvinistic prejudices as deep as those of his Press Officer. "Really reliable sources."

"Nothing. I had a quick look at the teleprinter before I set off to come across. But I could double-check."

"Do. As soon as we've finished. And find out, at the same time, what the BBC Newsroom did about a telephoned report they got from Istanbul that Lombard was dead."

"Who sent it?" Pond had been in the news business most of his life. *First principle, always query sources.*

"Lombard."

"Lombard!"

"Lombard himself. Apparently he rang the BBC from Ankara and reported it as an official flash from the Turkish Government."

"The newsroom would do nothing, I would say. They certainly wouldn't use the report until they'd got confirmation from another independent source. They couldn't possibly announce the death of an English M.P. on one unconfirmed report by telephone. Especially not from a foreigner."

"Is that invariable?"

"Absolutely invariable. When Mahatma Gandhi was assassinated, they refused to use the report until it had been confirmed. And the original report was itself broadcast by All-India Radio. You couldn't get a harder source for the death of Gandhi."

Alex Beasley grunted. "I suppose it's wise. Would they check back. To Turkey, I mean?"

"I think they'd ring the Anatolian Agency. It's a very close old-boy network."

"Anyway, do a check for me. Now . . ." Beasley put his forearm on the desk and made his points on his fingers. "Something has happened today. It hasn't been made public yet, and it certainly isn't on the news tapes. The agencies have all agreed to hold it for twenty-four hours. Another murder."

"Good God," said Geoffrey Pond. The words were rung from him not so much by the act of murder, but more by the fact that the news agencies were going to hold it. A thought struck him. "Robert Maryon," he said. "I bet he won't sit on it."

The Prime Minister was seen to cross two of his fingers for a second or two. "With luck, he won't know." He swallowed. "The murdered man was Rupert Hetherington." He looked round the room. "Means nothing? I'm not surprised. He was the London head of Tabula."

"Goodness me. The Solicitor from Pinner." The Lord Chancellor whistled a low judicious whistle.

"The Accountant from Purley."

"That's right," said the Lord Chancellor. "A man with no sense of humour. I once met him. Bald. Thin."

"And now dead."

"Oh dear. Poor man." The Lord Chancellor, the oldest man round the table, spoke the requiem.

"Who did it?" The Secretary for External Affairs looked across at the Home Secretary.

"Not me, William." The Home Secretary steered the conversation rather amusingly away from the Metropolitan Police and their insufficiency.

"We don't know who did it," said Beasley.

"Not yet." The Home Secretary put it in out of loyalty rather than conviction. "Not yet."

"That's what I want to talk to you about." The Prime Minister looked around the table. "I want to make a very unusual suggestion." The dead silence was not very encouraging but he battled on. "One thing's certain. The other two murders—Tom Rendle and Sidney Firth—here in Westminster were done by someone in the House of Commons."

"Or in the House of Lords." The Lord Chancellor felt he owed it to the Woolsack.

"As the Lord Chancellor says. I myself think it was an M.P. (from the Lords or the Commons) or alternatively an Officer of one of the two Houses; or it was someone else who works here."

"From the Cafeteria?" The Chief Whip had never been impressed by the quality of the buns.

"It could be." Beasley took the offer seriously. "I may say the Police are inclined to agree with me. Whoever it was, he certainly knew his way around in a way that only a Member or an official could."

"Or a journalist?" said Geoffrey Pond. He had long lost his

illusions about his trade. One kind of murder is no worse than another kind.

"A journalist! The idea," said the Prime Minister, "appeals to me." He had a dreamy look in his eyes, as though carried away by the beautiful thought. Then the look drained away and he sighed. "But I doubt it," he said "I doubt whether he'd have enough knowledge of the Members' end of the House. Any more than an ordinary Member could know the Upper Press Gallery or the Lobby. How many of us here know our way about up there?" He pointed vaguely beyond the Chamber to the area assigned to the Press. "Certainly not me." Nobody else spoke. "Except for Geoffrey Pond here." Beasley waited for Pond's reply. It was a simple nod.

"I'm not accusing you, Geoffrey. In any case I think he, the murderer, is older than you."

"That let's me out." The Home Secretary was fond of emphasising his youth. He was at least eighteen months younger that anybody else in the Cabinet.

"And brings me in." The Lord Chancellor said it jovially but without much success. Nobody laughed.

"Except that you are known to have an alibi."

"Good God. Alex, you mean somebody checked my alibi?"

"But of course. There'd be something wrong if somebody up top were left out. Undemocratic."

"Good God."

"Where's your sense of humour, Leonard?"

"Good God." The Lord Chancellor went on muttering it for quite a long time. After a bit, the meeting learned to live with it.

"Why old?" Geoffrey Pond obligingly put the question. "He seemed to have moved pretty smartly from one place to another." He grinned round the table. "No sign of gout," he said. Too late he realised it was the wrong thing to say at that moment.

The Lord Chancellor had grunted. He had begun to feel somebody was gunning for him.

"Order, order," said Beasley. He thumped the table; then, in the silence that followed, he picked up a small book from the book-trough on the desk in front of him. "You all know this, of course." He held it up. "You've all read it. It's Fell's Illustrated Guide to the Houses of Parliament. It's the first thing a new Member buys, as all of you know. So you can impress your constituents with your learning. We've all done it. This is my copy. I usually keep it at home." (He didn't say it, but presumably he meant, in the flat above No. 10 Downing Street.) "I've had it for twenty years and I can remember whole pages of it. Listen to this bit." He cleared his throat and seemed about to address Mr Speaker, Sir.

Since 1885 a light at the top of the tower, called the Ayrton Light after the First Commissioner of Works of that name, has indicated when the House is sitting at night.

On 24 April, 1945, after more than 5½ years during which it had been extinguished, Mr Speaker relit the light by pressing a switch beside the Chair . . .

Alex Beasley stopped reading and put the book down. "That was written over twenty-five years ago. Anybody reading it would assume that the light is operated by the Speaker from the Chair. But . . ." he looked round the table defying anyone to interrupt him, "recent editions of the Guide—as you know, they are always prepared by one of the Senior Clerks in the House— recent editions go on to say that, since then, the switch has been removed to the Control Room down below and Mr Speaker no longer operates it. How many of the younger M.P.s would go into the actual Chamber to the Speaker's Chair if they wished to put the tower light on? None of them. Older ones would, though. I would have done. I hope I'm making my point."

"I admit I've always assumed the switch was on the arm of the Speaker's Chair." William Empery decided to come clean.

One or two other growls of assent encouraged Beasley to continue. Geoffrey Pond took a sly look at his wrist-watch and then scratched the back of his hand as an alibi. He could see this going on for quite a long time, and it was already nearly 11 p.m. It started again.

"Who but a Member or an Officer would know where to find the Mace, when it's not being used. Who would know a good place to hide it? Who would know where to find the photocopying machines and the Deposited Paper cupboard? And the key for the cupboard? Who would know the side exits through the Speaker's Court and the Chancellor's Court?" The Prime Minister stopped suddenly.

"Any one of two hundred people," said William Empery in the silence. "I could name at least forty people, myself, who fit that lot. Couldn't you, Gilbert? He turned for confirmation to the Chief Whip. But Gilbert Dace was not listening. Instead, like everyone else but Empery, he was watching Alex Beasley's face. It had gone red with some kind of internal effort, the heavy eyebrows were twitching as though moved by waves of concentrated thought going on behind them, the eyes were glazed like the eyes of a man in a trance, and his mouth had fallen open. He was not beautiful.

The Lord Chancellor was just going to suggest that someone should get a first-aid box or call the Serjeant-at-Arms or phone for a doctor when Beasley's face began to move again. He began to speak, slowly. "By God," he said. "By God, I know who did it."

* * *

An hour later the meeting broke up thoughtfully, each Member with a particular and urgent job to do. The Secretary for External Affairs was to make sure that somebody on the Front Bench on the Opposition side of the House would put a Private Notice question about the Greek Government and Austin Lombard. Because such Questions have to be on some urgent matter in the news, some relevant news flash would be found and "leaked" by the Press Office at No. 10 to bring it within the rules of procedure. At the same time, the Lobby was to be alerted so that the political correspondents actually went into the Press Gallery instead of loafing about in their easy chairs watching the proceedings on their television screens in the Press Library.

The Home Secretary would make sure that the Metropolitan Police would surround the Palace of Westminster. And by "surround", the Prime Minister meant "surround". The river police would take the Terrace side. Appropriately, and with due decorum, the policemen (other than the normal Houses of Parliament regulars) would wear plain clothes and shoes, brown for preference.

The Lord Chancellor would make sure that his Right Honourable Friend the Attorney-General was in his place, on the day, on the Front Bench in the Commons. It would be inconvenient, to say the least, if something happened (as surely it must) that he ought to witness, and he were away on some less essential legal occasion. The Lord Chancellor found this matter especially intriguing. There are few precedents for an Attorney's being able to call himself as a witness in the Central Criminal Court.

Geoffrey Pond was to leak a fictitious story of Lombard's escape from Greece, being careful not to allow any credit to go accidentally or incidentally to Robert Maryon (of all people), whose earlier story (so near the mark) must be subtly discredited. Geoffrey Pond would find a way of doing it. Geoffrey Pond was buggered if he knew how.

The Chief Whip would approach Mr Speaker and recommend most urgently that the Clerk of the House be present in person. Admittedly, he usually was at Question Time, but would the Speaker make doubly sure please? No more details could be given, at the moment, but the Speaker should be told that the Clerk might well be needed to pronounce, off the cuff, on some rare and indeed unprecedented matter of procedure. As editor of the current edition of Erskine May,* it would be as well, one might suggest, for him to do a bit of homework in the meantime on the recondite (and normally unread) bits in the footnotes. It would also help, the Speaker should be told, if the Serjeant-at-Arms was there in person. No deputies, by request.

Malcolm Rawnsley, as the Prime Minister's Principal Private secretary congratulated himself as he put his coat on sleepily, on not having been assigned special duties (his ordinary ones were quite enough, thank you very much). He saw himself in his bed for a change before one o'clock in the morning, and this, on a Parliamentary sitting day, was almost wholly without precedent. The only job left to him, before slipping out through Chancellor's Court and down to the underground car park, was to arrange for a priority telephone call. He picked up the receiver

* The Twentieth.

in the Prime Minister's room and asked for Istanbul, Turkey, 274731, The Park Hotel.

"Good evening," he said, forgetting that it was nearly one o'clock in the morning in Turkey, "extension 417."

Sir Hubert Bligh was asleep.

Two minutes later the Prime Minister came on to the phone. It took him ten minutes to put Bligh in the picture, then Bligh went back to bed. Just before he went to sleep he noticed that he was shivering, though his bedroom was very hot.

* * *

Two hours later, at seven minutes past three in the morning (GMT), the telephone rang a few inches away from Malcolm Rawnsley's ear. He picked it up and yawned into it.

"Lucy," said a voice.

"Wrong number," said Rawnsley, whose wife's name was Kathleen. He put the telephone down and went to sleep again.

At nine minutes past three the telephone rang again. This time the voice said "That air hostess called Lucy..."

"Ah!" Rawnsley saw the light. "Ah. Lucille!" He said it loudly with a vibrant ring of recognition and his wife, Kathleen, woke up. She sat up in bed, took the telephone out of her husband's hand and put it down on its cradle. "You can stop that," she said and went to sleep.

* * *

At eleven minutes past three, Rawnsley, his hands poised like the talons of a bird of prey, picked up the telephone as it uttered its warm-up click. "I'm sorry about that, Prime Minister," he said. "Very sorry."

A woman's voice answered. "I wanted the Junior Carlton Club," she said accusingly, and rang off.

* * *

At twelve minutes past three, the Prime Minister and his Principal Private Secretary managed to make contact. They scrambled. "I've just spoken to Bligh," said Beasley. "And I've told him to get Austin Lombard incognito on a plane tomorrow."

"Today. It's well past midnight."

"So it is. Today then. It's just occurred to me. We don't want Lombard recognised by anybody on the plane. So I want you to make sure that the pilot who came to see us..."

"Glendower."

"Pendower. Nice work... and Lucy, the girl with the bosom, get a day off. That is if they are booked to fly the 10.05 Concorde from Istanbul. I don't want them on that flight."

Malcolm Rawnsley knitted his brows. This was not difficult to do, because they were trying to knit themselves. "How do I get them a day off?" he asked. "The plane leaves seven hours from now." His voice was rising in pitch.

"You ring the Chairman of BEA with my compliments and you tell him to get his finger out otherwise..." Beasley thought for a moment or two... "otherwise I'll get him shifted from BEA and get him transferred to the British Railways Board. And, incidentally, they leave in five hours from now. They're two hours ahead of us. So I suggest you get moving. Oh, and there's another thing, Malcolm. Bligh says Austin Lombard left his passport in Soviet Armenia, so ring one of those clever young men at the Consulate in Istanbul and tell him he's got to work Lombard through the Turkish Passport Control. Then get William Empery to have somebody waiting at London Airport to work him through at this end. The plane's due here at 2.15. Fortunately it's the non-stop Concorde and Bligh will come straight down to the House."

"You realise, of course, that Lombard will be recognised by those BBC news-hawks at the airport. They'll have him on the telly before he knows what's happened."

"Not if Bligh does as I told him. He's got to get Lombard a disguise."

"A false beard?"

"That's the general idea."

"And dark glasses?"

"That's it."

"He could wear a toga."

"No. That's going too far," Beasley hesitated. "I suggested a fez."

"But they don't have fezzes in Turkey any more."

"All the better. They'll think he's an Egyptian or something. Goodnight, Malcolm."

"Goodnight, Prime Minister."

Outside, in Blackheath Park, an owl hooted once as Malcolm Rawnsley staggered into the bathroom to prepare himself for his working day, beginning now.

* * *

The telephone operator in the cellar at No. 10 Downing Street was saying wakey-wakey and the telephone itself was half-way through its seventh pair of rings when Malcolm Rawnsley got a hand to it. The impression he gave was that he was asleep for the first six. He dropped the receiver and consolidated the impression.

He began to speak with great dignity. "Sorry," he said as he picked the receiver up, "to keep you waiting I was at the other end of the office."

"Ah!" said Geoffrey Pond from his office downstairs. He knew where the telephone was and he knew where the leather arm-chair was. He also knew it was not a very big office. "I was ringing on spec," he went on. "I thought you might have gone home." He was cooing it.

Rawnsley assembled his defences instantly, He knew from the tone of Pond's voice that, at any second, he was going to get the busy journalist line, the slaving for the public weal while the rest of the world is deep in sleep business. He nipped in swiftly, shed his dignity and shouted. "I was. I was in my bed." He dropped his voice as he began to get the echo back from the far wall. "The P.M. telephoned me at home. It was ten minutes past three." By now he was enunciating with scrupulous care. "I came back to the office where I am now. I have been ringing the Chairman of British European Airways. He, too, was at home and in bed. He asked me what time I thought it bloody well was. I told him I knew with absolute certainty that it was four forty-six in the morning. I had, I told him, heard, one minute earlier,

Big Ben. He told me to bugger Big Ben. He then went on to ask me why it was that Prime Ministers—all Prime Ministers—have the idea that they can ring perfectly respectable citizens up at four twenty-six in the morning... I told him it was four *forty-six*..." Rawnsley stopped talking as the Chairman's wisdom struck home. "Why do they?" he asked.

Geoffrey Pond sighed at the other end of the line and for a few moments they were in a state of absolute accord. Then Pond got back to business. "I imagine he's in bed," he offered.

Rawnsley blinked at the telephone. "That," he said, "was the whole point of the story. Of course he was in bed."

"The P.M., I meant."

"Oh. I see." Rawnsley took a quick look round the office. "Yes," he said. "He is. Why?"

"I think you ought to tell him we've made it."

"*You* tell him... Made what?"

"We've leaked the story."

"Which story?"

"The Lombard story. I've been on the phone for hours." Geoffrey Pond made sure it had sunk in. "Hours!" he repeated it. He plugged his weariness a bit.

"Tass?"

"Good Lord, no. They wouldn't touch it." Pond tutted in disbelief. "Considering the kind of stuff they do carry!" He lowered his voice. "Actually, I think they knew more than they should about the whole thing."

"It wouldn't surprise me. Who did it for you?"

"Rome."

"Gino no doubt."

"Gino it was. He's a good friend."

"Balls. He's after something."

"Could be! It's all a matter of give and take in our business."

"An exclusive with the P.M. for instance."

"Sort of."

"About whether he agrees that France should be re-admitted into the Common Market."

"Something like that."

"When she's got her economy on the right lines."

"I imagine that's the idea."

"You damn well know it is."

"I'd no alternative, Malcolm. Honestly. It took me two and a half hours to find him. He said he'd been out visiting a friend."

"I can believe that. I've met her."

"As it was, he was able to twist my arm. We only just got it on to the tapes in time for the last editions. But it worked. *The Times* has it on page one. Half-way down column eight. The *Mirror*'s doing us proud. Giving it a banner, LOMBARD M.P. SPRUNG BY JOHNNY TURK."

"Bully. With a Greek evzone in a skirt. On Leros Island."

"Sure. The skirt's always good for a giggle on the 8.10 from Tooting Bec."

"What about the *Mail?* Robert Maryon will be on to you."

"Any moment now. And the Greek Ambassador will be on to you."

"No doubt. You'd better send me all the tape."

"Sure. Shall I bring it up?"

"Don't sound so enthusiastic. Just read it."

"O.K.... ROME SNAP 0410 2nd DECEMBER ACC. TO UNCONFIRMED REPORTS FROM ISTANBUL THE BRITISH DEPUTY ALEXANDER LOMBARDO WAS RESCUED FROM GREEK POLITICAL PRISON ON ISLAND LEROS LAST NIGHT BY TURKISH NAVY GUN BOATS STOP GREECE EXPECTED TO PROTEST SECURITY COUNCIL, FORTHWITH LOMBARD ON WAY TO CYPRUS 0412/2

"Excellent. Why don't they get names right?"

"That was me. Sounds more authentic."

"Anybody ever tell you you're a genius, Geoffrey? Now you've to make sure Lockwood sees it. Leaders of the Opposition keep civilised hours, I wouldn't ring him too early if I were you."

"I shan't ring him at all. He reads his papers—especially on Thursdays. It's the National Gallup Poll day."

"The Greek Government's going to protest, you know. I'd make sure somebody gets the Question down and approved by the Speaker before the denial's issued."

"Good point. I'll ring Empery right now and tell him to get moving."

"You know what he'll say if you ring him now?"

"He'll say do I know what bloody time it is? And I'll say yes it's five-oh-five on a nasty cold morning that's likely to hot up later."

"We hope. What'll the BBC do about it?"

"They're already doing it. It's in the World Service bulletin already."

"What. Unconfirmed!"

"No. They rang me as soon as they picked the story up from Rome. I made the right kind of encouraging noises."

"Nice work. So long as they say the source is Rome and not you."

"They will. See you soon."

"Oh, Geoffrey. Oy! Oy!"

"What?"

"Did you ask the BBC about Lombard's alleged telephone call from Turkey?"

"Yes. But I didn't say it was from Lombard. Naturally."

"Naturally. What happened to it?"

"They didn't get it. They checked all the newsrooms while I waited."

"That's funny."

"They didn't think it was funny. They're having a post-mortem. The Centre desk at Bush House is in a god-almighty state. In view of the new story about Lombard, though, they're a bit relieved they didn't get it."

"I can see their point. Lombard dead followed by Lombard escaping. It's liable to cause confusion."

"I still think it's funny. Either Lombard's daft or they are."

"Or both."

"Or both. See you soon. I'd better ring Empery. Blast. The other phones are going. It's started! It's going to be one hell of a day."

*   *   *

"Help," said the Prime Minister. He smiled into the telephone. "I could do with your help, Eric." He made it sound as submissive as he could. It did not sound very submissive.

"Anytime," said the Leader of the Opposition. He made it sound as guarded as he could. It sounded very guarded. He transferred the telephone to the other ear and waited for it.

"I spoke to Hubert during the night. He's on his way back." Beasley spoke in a carefully off-hand manner.

"So I understand. He rang me an hour ago." Eric Lockwood looked up at the clock on his mantelpiece. He was not really the kind of man who would normally have a clock on his mantelpiece but this one, in the form of a polished riding boot, had been given to him by the Chairman of his constituency party, a regular visitor to the flat. By a rapid chain of primary associations his mind went back to the National Gallup figures in the *Daily Telegraph* which he had just been reading. He kicked it further under the table. "It's just after nine o'clock, so they'll be leaving Istanbul in just over an hour."

"He told you about Lombard, of course."

"But naturally. And it makes total nonsense of this story from Rome in the *Daily T* ..." He stopped and his feet moved in a natural reflex. "In *The Times*," he went on. Then he hesitated. "You're behind it," he suggested without rancour. As an ex Prime Minister he was aware of the realities of power.

"There's something in that," said Beasley entirely without embarrassment. "And that's where I want your help. I'd be glad of a Private Notice Question."

"I'll bet you would." Lockwood's eyes glowed behind his thick glasses. "It'd make me look a Charley."

Beasley was glad they were using the ordinary voice-only phone. The Vis-phone would have revealed his expression as he went on. "I didn't mean a question from you. I meant from one of your bright young men."

"Ah!" Lockwood warmed to the idea. After three seconds of thought he spoke rather eagerly. "Crisp," he said. "Jeremy Crisp."

Beasley kept his mouth shut. He had no intention of intruding on Lockwood's private grief.

"Crisp." The Leader of the Opposition said it again with even more determination.

"He's on the back bench."

"Of course..."

"I see... And Hubert Bligh. He should be back in time."

"Certainly. He'll follow Crisp up from the Despatch Box." Lockwood's long pale face assumed a touch of colour. "Judging by what he said on the phone, he won't give you an easy ride." His lips formed into a smile like the edge of a knife.

"I don't want one." The Prime Minister said it very sharply. "This isn't politics. It's just simply a case of murder. I'm after a murderer."

"I think you'd better explain that. Do you mean the Rendle thing?"

"Rendle and the others. Half a dozen dead men."

"Why didn't you say? If you'd only said that was what you were after."

Alex Beasley sighed into the telephone. "I would have thought it was obvious, Eric. There's nothing to stop me from getting up and making a statement and denouncing the murderer on my own..."

Eric Lockwood dropped his telephone receiver on to the table and it upset his breakfast coffee—

"Having trouble?" Beasley's voice was tinny. It appeared to be addressing an uneaten piece of toast with marmalade on it. Lockwood picked up the receiver, shook it free of crumbs and put it back to his ear. "Say it again," he said louder than he meant.

"Denouncing the murderer." Beasley enunciated it carefully. "Of course. He's in the House. He'll be there this afternoon. But I've got to flush him. He's got to give himself away. And for that I want the whole House involved. Get Crisp to put the question. Get Hubert to follow up on the Lombard business and you chip in on Rendle and the Noah job."

"Is that wise?"

"Wise? It's essential."

"O.K. I'll see it's done."

"Thanks, Eric. I won't forget this."

"Don't mention it, Alex. I shan't let you."

* * *

His Excellency the Greek Ambassador to the Court of St. James swore delicately and diplomatically in his own tongue. A highly intelligent man, he had made it his business to learn a good deal more about British Parliamentary practices than the average British elector, and when a Parliamentary defeat stared him in the face, he recognised it for what it was.

"The Question has been put down, Minister? I put it as a statement rather than as a question."

"Put down, accepted, posted in the Lobby of the House of Commons and printed on the Press Association tape. I see no way out, I'm afraid." William Empery, the Secretary of State for External Affairs, did his best to look contrite. "I suggest you have a word with Mr Lockwood. He may be persuaded to get his man to change it." He knew he was on safe ground to suggest it. The Leader of the Opposition would not dare to seem to give way to outside pressure once the question was in the newspapers. He looked at his watch as the sherry was brought in. "I'll have a word with the Prime Minister, of course, before he goes to the House, but he is very busy at the moment."

"That," said His Excellency, "I can easily imagine. I understand that he has been busy all the morning." He smiled a diplomatic smile and swore again into his glass, this time in a lesser known Macedonian dialect to be on the safe side. "I hope to see the results. At half past three, I understand."

"At half past three. After Question Time." William Empery inclined his head gracefully. "At four o'clock," he said, "we go on to the Pig Breeding (Miscellaneous Provisions) Bill. Second Reading," he added by way of explanation.

"Ah," said His Excellency. "That is a pity. At four o'clock I must keep another appointment. A pity." He repeated it.

"A pity." William Empery agreed with him. British democracy at work has occasional morasses of tedium.

* * *

"You can't be serious." Michael Griffin, the Head of BBC

News and Current Affairs (Television), looked up from the notes he had made. His eyes seemed in danger of exploding. "You just can't be serious." He was shaking with indignation.

"I can and I am. And it is." Richard Wentworth looked at the clock on the wall. "I have to be back at the House of Commons in an hour's time for camera rehearsals and I have to report everything O.K. to No. 10. by 2.0 p.m."

"You realise what he's asking us to do? In two hours?"

"Telling us to do..."

"It's impossible."

"O.K. It's impossible. You tell him. You pick up that telephone and tell him." Wentworth had begun to stutter a bit. "I spent half an hour this morning with him and Geoffrey Pond. He said if we can't do it, he'll ask ITN to come in as well."

"Ask?"

"He meant 'tell', he said 'ask'."

"He's out of his mind. If we do this, the whole of the Television Centre'll jam up. Does he realise that?"

"I don't think he's given it a thought." Richard Wentworth stuck his neck out. "If I were in his shoes, I wouldn't give it a thought."

Griffin blinked. "What the hell do you mean?"

"Murder comes first. Even before *Top of the Pops*." Wentworth glanced at the ceiling to see if it was likely to come down on him. He was glad he'd had his Annual Interview for the year; by the time the next one came round his heresy might have been forgotten.

"You think so." Griffin glared across his desk as he picked up his telephone. "You think so." He was shaking more than ever. "Get me Eunice in Planning," he said to his secretary. "It's urgent." He kept the telephone to his ear and had plenty of time to notice that his hand had gone white at the knuckles. He took a deep breath as his secretary spoke. "She's on the line." He plunged.

"I've got Richard Wentworth here, Eunice, from the Parliamentary Unit." He waited until Eunice's groan was spent. "It's the P.M. He's made a special request." He did a snort. "Don't blame me for it."

The telephone crackled in his ear. "I don't think you ought to say that, Eunice," he offered. But he said it without spirit; she had a point. "Moreover," he went on, "it's Top Secret. Nobody repeat nobody, has to know what's on. Nobody."

"Shoot," said Eunice. She seemed to have settled down.

"The Commons' proceedings to go on the air as usual..."

"O.K. That's easy."

"And recorded..."

"Yes, of course."

"At the same time," Griffin swallowed and glanced at Wentworth over the top of his glasses, "he wants the output of all six cameras to be recorded."

"All six cameras to be recorded."

"Each to be recorded on a separate machine."

"Each to be recorded on a separate machine. I see." Her voice, though calm, was gently climbing the register.

"And in secret." Griffin said it at dictation speed.

"And in secret." Eunice was writing it down. There was a zombie ring to her voice as she repeated it. "Not easy," she went on. "Not easy. Six videotape machines are hard to hide." A thought struck her. "They ought to have backing copies," she offered. "Perhaps?"

"That," said Griffin, "is the general idea. Twelve machines altogether."

There was a rustling noise for quite a long time, as though Eunice was maltreating a lot of sheets of paper, then her voice came up again. She was breathing a little more heavily than usual. "There is a soccer match from Crystal Palace, a circus being recorded from the London Pavilion, a special performance from the Colosseum Ballet and a transatlantic discussion programme in Studio 2. You will, I suppose, be telling the various producers that their recordings are cancelled. And do you mind if I listen while you are telling the Controller of BBC-1 that all his programmes are going up the spout. I could," she went on, speaking more rapidly now, "do with one big laugh."

Michael Griffin said nothing at all, so after a bit, Richard Wentworth leaned over the desk. "Tell her it's murder," he said.

"She knows it is," said Griffin. He held the receiver up between them to let Wentworth hear the noise that was beginning to come out of it. He then murmured a thank you into it, put it down carefully on its cradle, crossed his fingers and smiled a weak smile.

*   *   *

"If anybody gets out of this building between 3.30 and four o'clock..." The Assistant Commissioner (Crime) made a harsh noise with the back of his tongue and the front of his epiglottis. Then he drew the edge of his hand sharply across his throat.

"Yes, sir," said Inspector Denny. He looked, for an instant but no longer, at the eyes in front of him. "Not even the Speaker," he said. "Or the Prime Minister." Then he tried a joke. "Not even you, sir," he said.

It was a mistake. Denny saw it immediately. His red face went redder and he changed the subject. "I've got six men in the cellar," he said and waited for the glow of approval.

"What the hell for?" A short silence fell between them.

"It's a big cellar. Stretches for miles." The silence came back. "If he got down there we'd never find him."

"Get them back up again." The Assistant Commissioner (Crime) turned round and made his way with brisk little steps towards the Central Lobby. Just before he turned the corner past Oliver Cromwell's marble bust, Denny's prayers were answered.

"Let me see your pass, sir" said the constable on duty. He was a keen young man with an eye on promotion.

Denny nodded his approval and set off towards the North Curtain and the steps which led down into the cellar. "Come up out of there," he said to the man on the doorway. "Pass it on."

They only found five.

*   *   *

"The Black Hole of Calcutta must have felt roomy." Richard Wentworth allowed himself a shallow breath as he stepped into the Television Control Gallery in the courtyard alongside the House of Commons and closed the door behind him. "Fug," he said, and looked at his watch in the half-light from the row of television monitors. Forty-five minutes since the programme began (the first five minutes when the House of Commons is at Prayers are never televised) and the atmosphere was already as thick as pea-soup.

"You'll get used to it," said Bruce Mather from his seat at the control panel. He cut to Camera 1 and a big close-up of the Minister of Health and Social Security hit, if that is the right word, the several thousands of viewers on the Parliamentary channel.

"Cold," said Bruce as he searched his monitors for an alternative picture. "Even Kathleen Kimmis is cold. Yesterday's custard. Why don't they react?"

"They're saving it for later. They'll warm up then." Richard Wentworth found himself getting more and more apprehensive as the minutes rolled by. Another eight minutes of Questions. He hoped his nervousness was not showing. He knew from years of experience that a crew's morale could be damaged by nervousness in the gallery.

"Then we have Pig Breeding," Bruce Mather groaned. "Big deal."

"That's where you're wrong." Wentworth stripped off his jacket and loosened the knot of his tie. "Then," he said, cryptically, "it'll be murder. O.K., Bruce." He moved over to stand by his assistant's shoulder. "Cut to a wide-angle on 6, Bruce, and let me take over. I've some quick talking to do to the cameramen. Special action stations." He slid into the control seat as Bruce edged out the other side, looked up at the row of seven monitors (one from each of the six cameras disposed about the Chamber of the House and one, the selected one, for transmission) and began to speak into the microphone in front of his face.

"Wentworth here. I'm on Camera 6. Keep it like that, very wide, No. 6. But zoom in slightly if you can hear me quite clearly." Camera 6 zoomed in, "Good. Cameras 1, 2, 3, 4 and 5 acknowledge if you're getting me." The five cameras nodded their lenses and the pictures on their separate monitors moved up and down in acknowledgement. "Right. Listen carefully. We are changing the routine for a special reason. I couldn't tell you earlier because it was secret. And it still is.

"I'm going to come to Camera 1 now on a close-up of Mrs

Kimmis. This must be very nearly the last question. O.K. One?" He cut to Camera 1. "Now that's your shot. The Prime Minister will take over from Mrs Kimmis, Camera 1, big close-up on the P.M. But also keep an eye on Desmond Bassington, David Orchard, William Empery, Gilbert Dace, all on the Front Bench with the P.M. O.K., Camera 1. Government Front Bench. I'll cut to Camera 6. Now!" He pressed the piano switch in front of him and as soon as he was cleared, Camera 1 nodded. *Instructions received.*

Wentworth thanked him and turned to Camera 2. "A nice picture, 2. Remember you've got the Opposition Front Bench. Eric Lockwood. There he is. Before the P.M. gets up, there'll be an extra Question from Jeremy Crisp. He's the young man with freckles and the sandy little beard behind the Leader of the Opposition. Pan up and slightly right. That's the chap. Big close-up when he stands up. O.K.? We're shooting this in tight close-ups. Oh, Camera 2. The Member who's just come in behind the Speaker's Chair. That's Bligh. Sir Hubert Bligh. He looks pretty scruffy. Not too tight. He's sitting down. I'll want him later. Watch him for me.

"Now Camera 3. Instead of covering the Government benches below the gangway, I want you to give me shots of the Press Gallery. Repeat, the Press Gallery. Up above the Speaker."

The picture on 3's monitor lurched and wobbled as the Cameraman, hidden in his little cubicle in the wall between the Chamber and the "NO" Division Lobby, took the shock. Then the lens of his camera slewed right to the Gallery behind the Speaker's Chair. "Excellent," said Wentworth. "Got 'em. Keep on moving round until they begin to react. The Lobby Correspondents are in that middle line behind the Hansard shorthand reporters. The one you're on now, that's Cecil Bradshaw of the *Guardian*. He's not crying. He just looks sad. It's his normal state. Pan right. I don't know that one, but no matter. Pan along and I'll identify. That's the *Times* man, Forbes. Then *Western Mail*, *Sun*. That woman from the *Scotsman*. Hold that one. That's Robert Maryon of the *Mail*. Move on. Oy! Oy! there's an empty place. Good God, the BBC man's missing."

"No, I'm not. I'm here in the commentary box." Timothy

Woodman's rich fruity voice came over the inter-com from the glass sound-proofed cubicle beyond the Bar of the House, under the Strangers' Gallery. "I'm hearing you loud and clear. Trevor Trelawney's gone sick or something. And it's too late to get anybody else. I'll fill in."

"God. I wish people would tell me. I'm just the producer, of course..."

"Didn't have time..."

"O.K., Tim. Sorry I barked. You will talk to Camera 5 across the Chamber. O.K., 5? Excellent. I'll come to Timothy if any explanations are necessary. Though I imagine it will all go to pattern once it starts. Right. All ready. The Right Honourable Lady's sitting down any moment. I then come to Camera 6 with zoomed in close-up on the Speaker. All O.K." Wentworth relaxed his muscles.

"No. What about Camera 4?" The Senior Television Engineer pointed to the picture on 4's monitor, which was swaying from side to side.

"Oh hell. Sorry, 4. I want you on the Public Gallery. Very important. Especially the front two rows. I'll identify from the right. The first batch of eight in a line are Peers who've strayed from their own Chamber. The third from the right, the one with gold teeth, that's the Lord Chancellor, Lord Shawthorne. He looks a bit different in civvies. Loses a bit without the wig, don't you think? Pan left. Left. Left. Ah! That's an Ambassador. Blimey, they've turned up in force. Turkey first, then Russia then Greece. A nice little bit of history there. Oh, and that one at the end, he's the United States. Looks like a soap salesman. Someone says he *is* a soap salesman. Now, pan left, 4. Those are Distinguished Strangers and don't they look it. Six of them, three white, two black and a yellow. I dig the one on the left, Sheik of Arabee. It makes a very nice picture. Especially the gilt rope round his head-dress. Anybody seeing this lot would take it for the United Nations, not the great Mother of Parliaments. Talking about the Great Mother, Mrs Kimmis is sitting down. I wonder what she was on about?"

"You should listen more and talk less." Timothy Woodman's voice came up. He sounded very irritable.

241

"Blimey, was that transmitted?"

"What do you take me for?" The sound mixer sitting in the far corner of the control room was indignant. "But it was recorded. Along with Camera 5's picture."

"All videos running, Duncan?"

"All running."

"The P.M. said we were making history. I hope I don't make a balls up. Oy! The Speaker's getting up. It must be very difficult being so fat. I'm coming to 6. Cut. I'm on 6."

As Richard Wentworth pressed the switch on his control panel Mr Speaker, his large round face red and obviously damp beneath the arc lights and his full-bottom wig, went on to the screens of close on half a million television sets. Of the ten thousand people who were paying any kind of attention to it, four thousand switched over to the beginning, at 3.30, of horse-racing at Kempton Park. The others, six thousand in a population of fifty-seven million, stayed on to get the shock of their lives.

* * *

"Mr. Crisp. A question by Private Notice."

Jeremy Crisp certainly caught the Speaker's eye. It almost bounced off him. It glared at him as though defying him to start something, and start something he did.

He stood up as the Speaker settled his fat form back into his Chair. "Mr Speaker, sir," he said. "I want to put a Question to the Prime Minister, of which I have given him notice, about the reports in the Press that the Honourable and Gallant Member for Birmingham East has been rescued from a prison camp in Greece by the armed forces of a friendly Power." He hesitated a moment to get full benefit from the growl of anger that came from the benches around him. "I would also like to ask the Prime Minister why he did not give instructions for Her Majesty's forces to be used openly for this highly commendable purpose." the growls rose in volume as Crisp sat down, and a voice was heard from the Benches behind him saying "Which forces?" There was an unpleasant laugh. *Richard Wentworth cut to camera 6 with a wide-angle view of the whole chamber, then back to a close-up of Jeremy Crisp who had a look of malevolent triumph on his face.*

Alex Beasley stepped briskly to the Despatch Box. Too briskly. William Empery, who knew the signs, muttered rather too loudly, "He's not worth it, Alex," and Beasley smiled one short smile.

What's he got to smile about? Wentworth cut to Camera 1. Blast. Missed it. The smile had gone. Instead there was a look of calculated insouciance. This time it was the Press Gallery which read the signs. "Look out, Crisp. You'd better duck." For a moment or two, Cecil Bradshaw looked even sadder. He had a son about Crisp's age but without the beard.

"I am grateful, Mr Speaker, to the Honourable Gentleman the Member for Pemperley for putting this question to me." Alex Beasley looked blandly across the Chamber and put his tongue in his cheek quite deliberately. His eyebrows came together as he "selected" the next phrase, the one he had decided to use two hours earlier. "Partly," he said sweetly, "because it gives me a chance to tell the Honourable Gentleman that his friends in the Press are very rarely a source of impeccable accuracy..." The clear implication was that Members who believe what they read in the papers, beard or no beard, are advertising the wetness behind their ears. He waited for Crisp's irritation to show on his face. (*Wentworth got the frown of annoyance on Camera 2.*) Then he made a deliberate half-turn to his left and stared at the Lobby Correspondents up in the Press Gallery. "Partly," he went on again, "because it gives me an opportunity to wonder how it is that one national daily newspaper had such contacts in a not very friendly country that it was able to put out this rumour several days before it reached the rest of them." (*Wentworth, sensing the feeling of the House, cut to Camera 3 and panned along the row of Lobby Correspondents. Like everyone else who read his newspapers, he knew the man he needed. "Maryon. That's him. Centre on him, 3. Hold that. I'm going back to the P.M.," he said urgently. "But stay with that shot. I'll be back for reaction. Cutting now." He cut to Camera 1.*)

Beasley was turning away from the Press Gallery (and at the same time presenting his shoulder-blades to the Lobby Correspondents, a simple, symbolical act that he obviously enjoyed) as he spoke to the House at large. He leaned his left elbow on the Despatch Box as he pursued his argument. "When this sad and unprecedented business is over (a business of deaths and treason in its most dangerous form) I am confident that the House will want to know something about that particular newspaper's sources of information and methods of obtaining it."

On the word "newspaper" Wentworth cut to Camera 3. "Zoom in gently," he cooed into the gallery microphone. The picture was quite startling. Maryon's face was rigid and pale, then his lips began to move slowly* twisting in a demonstration of loathing which caused the cameraman to break the first and basic rule by speaking during transmission. "Bloody hell." he whispered. "Look at that then." "Hold it." Wentworth almost shouted it. He had a strange feeling that the Prime Minister's plan was in the balance. "Go in tighter if you can."

"Lockwood's getting up." Bruce Mather tapped Wentworth on the shoulder. "You'd better not miss him."

"Blast," said Wentworth. He cut to Camera 2 as the Prime Minister sat down and the Leader of the Opposition began to speak.

"I hope the Prime Minister will take this matter further," he said. He peered across the Table through the top half of his thick glasses. "This is the first time that he has even hinted at treason. And will he tell us more about the deaths he seems willing to dismiss in so cavalier a manner?"

Wentworth cut to Camera 1. "I'm back on the P.M." he said, "But hold Maryon on 3. It can't be long now."

"Certainly." Beasley looked very angry at the implication behind Lockwood's words. "We have evidence, from the Honourable and Gallant Member for Birmingham East who rang me from Istanbul, that an international organisation, which may or may not be known to Members of this House called Tabula..." He hesitated and looked round the Chamber. The silence was complete. If anybody knew of Tabula, the fact was being very

---

* There was, of course, no microphone near Robert Maryon at the time. Four telephone calls of complaint were received by the BBC's Duty Officer within five minutes, all from expert lip-readers. They all told the Duty Officer what Maryon had said, and they were all different.

carefully concealed. "Tabula," he went on, his voice flat and cold, "was behind the arrest of the Honourable and Gallant Gentleman. It was later instrumental in getting him released"—again there came a flick of a glance towards the Press Gallery—"to some degree, but not exactly, as was described in one of our national newspapers..."

Cut to 3. Wentworth caught Maryon's cynical smile. "Marvellous," he said as he cut back to a close-up of Beasley.

"More than this, it was Tabula which organised an abortive expedition against the Anglo-Turkish aeronautical research station near Mount Ararat in Turkey (about which it would not be in the national interest, British or Turkish, to say more), and it was Tabula which almost precipitated an international incident of dreadful consequence on the Turkish border with Russia."

Beasley stopped talking and surveyed the Chamber. Every single seat was occupied. Even the side galleries reserved for Members above the back benches were full to the aisles, a thing which Beasley had never seen before on any occasion other than Budget Night. Before beginning again he looked hard across the Table at Hubert Bligh. He raised one of his eyebrows and Bligh construed it accurately. "Everything O.K.," he said in a Parliamentary whisper and nodded.

Richard Wentworth saw his chance in the short pause. "Listen! Tim!"

"I'm listening." Timothy Woodman's voice came through quickly from the commentator's box beneath the public gallery. "I'm with you."

"Good, I'm going to cut to Camera 4 and pan along the line of three Ambassadors in the Gallery above you. Their faces are a proper picture. O.K.? Turkish, Russian, Greek, in that order. Will you identify?"

"Sure. Give me the picture."

Wentworth cut to Camera 4 and Timothy Woodman's voice went out over the air identifying the three Ambassadors. They looked like the original Three Wise Men hearing all, seeing all, knowing all and their faces were totally expressionless, until at the last second the Greek Ambassador sucked in a lungful of air

245

and blew it out slowly through his pursed lips. It told the whole story of his dilemma.

Wentworth grinned as he cut back to Camera 1. "Fine, Tim. You can relax."

"I've relaxed."

"... the Right Honourable Gentleman the Member for Lambeth Brockley..."

"That's Bligh. Coming to you. 2. O.K. Fine. I must say he looks rather pleased with himself."

"... confirms my description of the danger into which Tabula almost ran us, and would have run us, but for the resource and the public-spirited actions of two men, the Right Honourable Gentleman opposite"—Beasley was careful to avoid a Parliamentary solicism; he pointed at Bligh with his eyeballs rather than his hand. *Wentworth got there in time to catch the look on Hubert Bligh's face. "Made it," he said. "Nice work, Camera 2. A marvellous Close-up."*

It was while he was congratulating Camera 2 that he missed the moment he was waiting for.

"The other man" (Beasley went on), "is the Honourable and Gallant Gentleman, the Member for Birmingham East." As he spoke, the Prime Minister used his right hand to point to the public gallery. And, as the *Times* reporter said the next day, pandemonium reigned.

"Christ, what's happening?" Richard Wentworth cut to Camera 3 and Robert Maryon's face filled the transmission screen. He looked as though transfixed with horror. His mouth dropped open and his eyes were staring past the camera lens. And then he started to smile. And then to grin. And then to laugh.

"Wrong one! Wrong one!"

The cameraman on Camera 4 shouted it through the hubbub in the Chamber. "I've got him, Richard. I've got him. Public-Gallery."

"Oh God." Wentworth pressed the switch and cut to Camera 4. "Who the devil's that?"

"It's Lombard. He's dressed as a bloody Arab."

"Get in close, 4. Get in close. Where's he going?"

"He's moving along to the Members' Gallery so he can speak."

"My God, the Speaker's doing his nut."

"Richard! Richard! Quick, come to me." Camera 5 joined in. "Look at Tim!"

Wentworth moaned as he cut to Camera 5. "I'm lost," he said. "What the hell..."

Timothy Woodman had burst out of his glass-panelled commentary box and was fighting his way to the door of the Chamber. He had torn his earphones off and was flailing them around him like a chain mace. Two Members went reeling away with blood streaming from their faces.

"All cameras on Woodman." Richard Wentworth came into his own and justified his selection as Producer in charge of the unit. With four cameras he watched and presented Tim Woodman's last battle as the whole corps of Badge Messengers moved into action from the Members' Lobby. Within seconds it was over and the Serjeant-at-Arms marched solemnly to the Table of the House. Camera 1 followed him as he reported the arrest.

That is the reason why no one had an eye on Timothy Woodman as he was dragged past the Bar of the House, through the Churchill Arch and into the Members' Lobby. The bullet from his pistol, once it had killed him, ricocheted round the Lobby and chipped a piece of bronze from the statue of Ramsey Macdonald beside the door.

* * *

"You look rather good sitting there, Hubert. It suits you." Alex Beasley piled on the charm a bit and smiled across the Cabinet Table. "Change your party and I'll give you a job."

"You gave me a job, remember?" Hubert Bligh found it extremely hard not to sound sore. "It took three whole years off my life. Three years in less than two weeks." He glared at Beasley and then quite suddenly he smiled, and the smile took the years off again. "Three very interesting years, I must admit. You must meet Kevork some time." He reached out and took the whisky which Beasley had poured for him. It was a very large one and Bligh transferred his smile to the glass, looking rather foolish. "Bad habits," he said. "I shall blame you." Then the smile disappeared from his face. "It's *Teacher's*," he said accusingly.

"*Black and White*," said Beasley. "It seems more suited to politicians. A whisky, Lombard?" He held a glass out for Austin Lombard to take as he wandered slowly over from the window. The green brocade curtain was swinging slowly behind him. "It looks cold out there. English winter." He growled and shuddered. "Thanks." He took the whisky, then he jerked his head to take in the whole Cabinet Room and waved his left hand around him. "A nice place you have here." he said. "Cheers." He raised his glass to Robert Walpole above the fireplace and sat down at the table next to Hubert Bligh. "Hmm!" He made an exaggerated noise of admiration. "The chair fits me," he said. "Absolutely made to measure." He wriggled his bottom on the polished mahogany seat.

"Magic." Beasley spoke quite firmly. "They're magic chairs." He patted the one beside him. "They take on all comers. All shapes, sizes, textures, sexes, creeds, and politics." He began to spike a cigar and pushed the box across the table. Then he spoke again, his voice a little flatter and quieter. "It won't be long before I can add all races and all colours." He lit his cigar. "But not yet." He blew smoke towards the elaborate chandelier. "Not yet."

A short grunt of astonishment burst from Bligh's nose. He looked up quickly and caught Lombard's expression reflected in the polished silver of the cigar-box. He was looking arrogant and aloof. His views on race and colour were extreme and well known. The short silence threatened to stretch itself out uncomfortably, so Bligh broke it.

"Woodman," he said quietly. "How did you know?" He frowned across the table at the Prime Minister. It was called Tact.

"I'm supposed to know everything." Beasley sounded sour. "It goes with the furnishings." He paused. "Opportunity, motive. All the usual things. Fortunately Woodman gave himself away. In front of five hundred Members plus, and several thousand television viewers. It's about as well he did. I don't think I could have pinned it on him otherwise."

Lombard spoke without looking up from the dark green blotter in front of him. "Robert Maryon of the *Mail* . . ." He raised his head and stared across the table at Beasley. "He's going round saying you thought it was him. He says he's discovered that one of the television cameramen was told—on your instructions—to keep him in his picture on the assumption he was going to do something unusual." Lombard waited for the Prime Minister to speak, and when he didn't, he went on again. "He says it's almost certainly actionable."

"He does, does he?" Unaccountably Beasley laughed, but it did not sound very pleasant. "The idea of Maryon suing *me* for something I said is rich. Rich!" Beasley's smile got no warmer. "He can take me to court. O.K." He carefully put a cylinder of cigar ash in the middle of the ash-tray. "And then I can ask him in public how he got his story about your escape from Leros."

"I rather think that won't wash, Beasley. I imagine he'll go to prison rather than tell you his sources. It's been done before."

"Certainly it has.* In quite remarkably similar circumstances. You don't need to worry, Lombard. I'll keep that side of it out of the courts. If he is foolish enough to sue me."

"*Did* you suspect him?" Bligh seemed astonished at the Prime Minister's anger.

"Not seriously. For a lot of reasons." Alex Beasley shook his head vigorously. "But I did pass instructions that he should be carefully watched by the television cameras. And for a very good reason, Lombard. The seat next to Maryon's in the Press Gallery is usually taken, or rather *was* usually taken by Woodman. I couldn't very well tell a BBC Director to keep his eye on one of his own colleagues, could I? The chances were that if Maryon was in the television picture, Woodman would be as well. In the event, Woodman wasn't there at all. He was in the commentary box. I can't know *everything*, though I'm supposed to."

"Arrogance." Lombard uttered the word quietly.

"Arrogance also comes with the furnishings." Beasley did not seem to mind Lombard's tone.

* Reginald Foster of the *Daily Sketch* and Brendan Mulholland of the *Daily Mail* went to gaol for refusing to name their sources of information to the Vassall Tribunal *Times Law Report*, 5 February, 1963).

"What did Woodman actually say? I didn't hear." Bligh grinned. "I was too busy listening to you two."

"Listen. I've got it here." Beasley turned to a tape-recorder on a low table beside his chair. "It's a recording off the BBC's transmission. Fortunately the BBC sound man brought Woodman's microphone up as soon as the row started. He switched on and turned up the volume. His own voice, low-pitched and over-dramatised, came out of the machine.

... the other man is the Honourable and Gallant Gentleman the Member for Birmingham East.

Lombard cut in. "That's where I took my cue and stood up. I rather enjoyed it. I must say I was glad to get those whiskers off..."

"Listen. Listen." Beasley held up his hand as another voice, a very famous BBC voice distorted into a near-scream of rage and fear took over. *"My God, it can't be. It just can't be. It's impossible. They said he was dead. They said he was dead."* It died away to a harsh moan. There was a loud crash and a splintering of glass.

Beasley switched the tape off. *"They said he was dead."* He repeated Woodman's words, and turned to Lombard. "You rang the BBC from Istanbul."

Lombard nodded. "As I told Hubert, I disguised my voice."

"And you announced that you had been killed."

"That's right. I wanted it to get to Hetherington. I wanted him to hear it on the news."

"Why?"

"Because I was sure Hetherington was behind it all. He was the one who accepted me as a member of Tabula. If you want to beat 'em join 'em. That's the only way I could get on to them. I knew that Hetherington would skip the country if he thought I was alive and coming back to London. He'd spent a lot of time moving around Europe. He had plenty of prepared bolt-holes—Amsterdam, Milan..."

"Using the name Causter no doubt?"

"That's right. Causter was actually his second Christian name His mother's name, I suppose."

250

"And you didn't know about Timothy Woodman being involved in Tabula?"

"No. Absolutely not. He kept the secret very well. I hardly knew him anyway."

"But you did speak to Woodman on the telephone from Istanbul."

"I spoke to the BBC. I didn't know it was Woodman."

"Where did you ring?"

"The House of Commons. Naturally. the BBC has a permanent office there. I knew the telephone number. It's on the House of Commons switchboard."

"Of course. And you spoke to Woodman. *And he kept it dark.* He didn't pass the knowledge on to the newsroom. He then went round to Tabula head office near the Hilton, and bumped Hetherington off. He was wiping the slate clean. You were dead (or so he thought), so was Hetherington. So were Enver and Brook. So was Rendle. So were the Euratom scientists. They did die, I suppose?"

"Instantaneously and totally. Atomised, I presume."

"Leaving the field absolutely clear. Not a soul alive who could identify him. He could get away with it, sit back, retire and draw his pension from the BBC.

"Oh what joy!"

"Unexciting and a bit thin but quite a temptation in the circumstances."

"Go further back, please, Alex." Bligh came into the conversation. He felt a bit dull and put it down, rightly, to the whisky. "Why did you suspect Woodman?"

"You know me, Hubert. I suspect everybody." Beasley leaned forward. "You would have done, Hubert, if you'd been here. And if you'd thought it out."

"Why for goodness sake?"

"Because you've been in the House as long as I have. You came here as a backbencher when I did. Twenty years ago, when Woodman was working in the Library of the House. He was in the Research Department."

"I don't remember him."

"Maybe you didn't use the Library as much as I did."

"Possibly. Hoy!" Bligh woke up and shook his head. "Working in the Library doesn't make him a murderer. They've got some very nice chaps..."

"But working in the Library *did* give him all the information he needed. Where to find the Mace. Where to hide it. Where, above all, to find the Deposited Papers. Where to find the photocopying machine. Where to find the key to the Commons' Library." Beasley paused and looked first at Bligh then at Lombard. "Would either of you know where to find the key?" They both shook their heads, but neither of them spoke. "He was unique," Beasley pushed the whisky bottle towards Bligh. "Unique," he said it again. "And very useful to Tabula. As an ex-Librarian, Woodman knew all the official side of the House, and later as a political correspondent for the BBC he got to know the journalists' end. *Quite* unique. Unfortunately, he did not know that the switch for the lantern had been moved. It was changed *after* he left the Library staff to join the BBC. I imagine Tom Rendle was on to him and he found him in the Chamber hunting for the light-switch. He had the photo-copy of the Noah Papers in his pocket; and the Mace in his hand..."

The noise Beasley made as he brought his fist down on to the table made Bligh jump. He said nothing, but brushed the cigar-ash from his waistcoat, the green suede one, and waited for the Prime Minister to end his sentence. He waited a long time, but Beasley never ended it. Instead, he pressed a button beside the elaborate leather blotter in front of him, and sat there, saying nothing and waiting.

Malcolm Rawnsley walked briskly to the Cabinet Table without acknowledging Bligh or Lombard and put a red despatch box in front of the Prime Minister. "It's all in there," he said. "All checked and confirmed. Superintendent Macaulay is waiting to see you outside in the vestibule." He turned round and walked briskly back to his private office door at the far end of the room.

Alex Beasley looked as though he was preparing for a Parliamentary performance. He stood up, opened the despatch box and put his hand inside.

"Prime Minister's lucky dip." Austin Lombard was following the performance with great interest.

"Lucky for some," said Beasley. "First prize to Hubert Bligh." Bligh groaned as he put his hand out. "Kevork," he said. The envelope was much the same as the one which had contained the House of Commons deposited paper in Kevork's fantastic office in Yerevan. If anything it had even more seals on it, in the shape of red stars. It was not easy to break open. Bligh had a curious feeling of *déjà vu* as his thumbs worked their way through the battery of seals.

"It's addressed to you, Hubert, as you see, but we had to open it." Beasley had no apology in his voice. "I'm sorry," he said, lying. "We fastened it up again pretty thoroughly."

Bligh extracted Kevork's covering letter. It was not very long. "I'd be glad if you'd read it out to us, Hubert. Your friend the General is quite a wag." Beasley was not smiling. Nor was Lombard.

Hubert Bligh glanced through the letter, looked up at Beasley and nodded. "Sure," he said. "Why not? I always read my letters out to my friends." He sounded slightly cross. He began to read, stumbling occasionally over the manuscript and trying his best not to over-emphasise the infelicities of Kevork's style.

Esteemed Comrade Deputy Bligh. I write to you from my buro in the most ancient city of Yerevan which you recollect very much. I also send to you a photograph (coloured) for the wall of your office in London. The photograph will come to you a little time later from the London Office of the Cultural Attaché, the Embassy of the USSR, W8, when they have, as your Royal Family say, taken out a finger. It is a beautiful picture of the Mountain of Ararat taken from the same place as the picture I have presented once, many years ago, to our old friend and distinguished colleague, Comrade Kim. But now you will notice (as soon as you will have received the photograph) that when it is hung on the wall of your office it will not cause your many friends to think so badly about you. The earthquake which you and I remember so well has occasioned another Little Ararat to grow out of the ground and now there is a Little Ararat at each side of Father Ararat. It is even More beautiful. Your friend, with very warm feelings of respect, George.

Bligh hesitated as he came to the end. He offered no comment.

"And the postscript, Hubert?"

Bligh cleared his throat and began again. *Please to give my very warm regards to Princess Margaret.*

"Not that one, Hubert, the other one please."

Bligh licked his lips and pursed his mouth with a show of embarrassment. He looked up at Beasley, and his face had gone very pale.

"I'll read it out for you, Hubert." The Prime Minister wiggled his fingers irritably until the letter was handed over. "On the principle of the buck stopping here." He began to read in a flat, expressionless voice.

The documents enclosed are sent to you with the felicitations of our organisation SMERSH espionage. The first is the passport of your esteemed Parliamentary Comrade Austin Lombard which was found on the body of (we now assume) Colonel Mustafa Tuna two kilometres east of Horosan.

Beasley looked across the table at Austin Lombard and raised one bushy eyebrow. *It looks like a fat mouse, wriggling.* Bligh felt inclined to smile at his own fancy but thought better of it. Lombard was nodding. "Position spot on," he said. "And it was Tuna. A stupid man, Tuna." As he spoke his eyes were following Beasley's hands as they took his passport out of the inner envelope, the one with only three red star seals. He made to hold his hand out but put it back into his pocket as Beasley placed the passport carefully on the green baize cloth beside the despatch box, out of his reach. Beasley began reading again. His flat expressionless tone was becoming a bit of a bore.

The other is a photograph copy of a message which was discovered on the floor of a truck which was found abandoned with a broken tyre on the road from Trabzon to Lake Cildir in Turkey on 29 November (Note well. Please not to inform Turkish Government that truck was examined). Attached to the message are photo copies of fingerprints found on it.

Alex Beasley sighed a deep sigh as he put Kevork's letter back in the despatch box, laying it flat in the bottom with exaggerated tidiness. "I'll keep this for the time being, Hubert." He glanced quickly at Bligh as he opened the final envelope. "This has been checked," he said. "The fingerprints are confirmed, Woodman's were easy to check—even though the operation was a little distasteful. The other's more difficult. But we managed. We managed. This is the message they found." He began to quote again with his flat, toneless voice.

...Noë tabula kaldec admin armen. Congratulations. Message received and fully understood. House of Commons Noah paper has been despatched by air mail post to Bulvar Palas Hotel Ankara to await collection by you. Causter sends regards. Suggest you feed through Robert Maryon of D. Mail who can be relied upon not to reveal sources. Regards T.W.

Beasley did not hurry as he placed his hand on the buzzer and pressed it three times. "The Lord Chancellor and the Attorney General agree," he said. "Our evidence"—he tapped the paper in his hand—"even with the fingerprints, would not stand up in court. Less still in the House of Commons." He did not look at Superintendent Macaulay as he stepped into the room. "The Superintendent has been asked to see you to your home and then, later tonight, to the airport. I suppose you'll need this." He picked up Lombard's passport and tossed it across the table.

"The alternative?" Austin Lombard put the passport in his pocket and tapped his coat with relief. "Is there one?"

"I suppose there is. You could fight it. Fight *us* I mean." Beasley's face was cold and his voice hard and mean. "The Government, MI5, a majority in the House and, after the way you used Maryon, most of the British Press. If you lose the fight you join Vassall and the others; if you win, you're free. You decide, not me."

Lombard stood up. "What time do we leave?" He was speaking to Macaulay, who was still standing rigidly at attention, it seemed, near the door. No one answered. He walked past Hubert Bligh and tapped him on the shoulder. "Feel like a trip, Hubert? Back to Leros, for example." He chuckled at the expression on Bligh's face. "Never mind, Hubert," he said. "I shall escape the British winter." He bowed ironically to Beasley. "Lucky dip," he said. "Lucky for some."

Author's end-piece

Anyone interested in the naming of one of the more important characters in this book is referred to the Index volume of the Encyclopædia Britannica, 11th edition, Cambridge University Press, 1911.

HOLTZMANN, Wilhelm *see* XYLANDER, Guilielmus.

Wilhelm Holtzmann (in English, WOODMAN) was a German classical scholar of great learning and distinction. He was born in Augsburg in 1532 and he died in Heidelberg in 1576. All his books (he wrote a lot) were written in Latin, and he always preferred the classicized form of his surname, Xylander (in English, HYLAND).

This fact is mentioned to help the author in his relations with the House of Commons and the British Broadcasting Corporation.

S.H.

Blackheath,
January 1969.